DRIFT RACE

Like this? Like this.
Join me on Facebook

www.FACEBOOK.com/DAVIDJUBERMANN

David Jubermann

DRIFT RACE

While every effort is taken to ensure the accuracy of information given in this book, no liability can be accepted by the author or publishers for any loss, damage or injury caused by errors in or omissions from, the information given.

Facebook® and Facebook logos are registered trademarks of Facebook, Inc. App Store ℠ and the App Store logos are registered trademarks of Apple, Inc. Amazon, Kindle, Kindle Fire, the Amazon Kindle logo and the Kindle Fire logo are trademarks of Amazon.com, Inc. or its affiliates. Neither Facebook, Inc. Amzon.com, Inc. or Apple, Inc. were involved in the production of this book and make no endorsement of this product.

www.davidjubermann.com

ISBN 978-0-473-20694-9

Published by Epsum Media Ltd

Understeer is when you hit the wall with the front of the car.
Oversteer is when you hit the wall with the rear of the car.
Horsepower is how fast you hit the wall.
Torque is how far you take the wall with you.

-Unknown Writer

The characters and events in this book are fictional. No attempt should be made to replicate any of the racing activities or sequences described therein.

Please drive according to the speed limit and road conditions at all times.

They were tired – all of them, near the end of their endurance. Breathing heavily, Markus brought the ball up court. Time was running out and he passed it to his teammate from halfway. Sensing an opportunity, his teammate went for it. Dribbling short and low, going in quick before the defence could regroup and establish their zone. Finding a gap, he made it through but his charge lost momentum thanks to a tall defender with long arms. The fade-away jump shot was hurried and it bricked off the rim. The ball changed hands and immediately they were on the defence.

With two attackers running at him, Markus suppressed his frustration and fell back protectively, shielding their basket. "Back on D!" his call rang out urgently. One of his team made a half-hearted effort and ran down the court to offer support but he was well behind. The two adversaries came on quickly with only Markus to challenge them. Sweat trickled into his eyes. He wiped it away distractedly as he watched them. He saw the determined look in their eyes and his teammates behind them, puffed and tired. They had pretty much admitted defeat. He could understand it, he could taste it too, that bitter taste of losing.

Markus glanced up at the scoreboard and scowled. Six points down with just two minutes to go, and this was surely going to be another basket. Suddenly he was angry. They had worked long and hard to get into the final, all that effort and now they would lose anyway. The anger built up swiftly until a cold rage swept through him. It gave him strength. With jaws clenched, he lifted his chin and turned his attention to the attackers who were now upon him.

"Bring it on," he growled, low and aggressive, but loud enough for the player with the ball to hear. Their eyes met and Markus saw a flicker of doubt. As though he had hit quicksand, the player wavered, his body suddenly clumsy and uncoordinated. He had nearly reached Markus when he made a desperate pass to his teammate. Realising the player's intentions, Markus lunged forward, scooped the ball out of the air and before anyone knew what had happened he was dribbling, driving up past halfway, leaving the two confused opponents stranded.

"Markus, open!" No one seemed to exist as he sped up the court. Not the defence, nor his own teammates. Neither did he hear the crowd urge him on.

Markus closed on the three point line and immediately launched into the shot. One of the defenders tried to stop him, jumping high into the block, but the ball left his fingertips unhindered and curled through the air, spinning backwards with orange and black stripes revolving over and over. It flew almost in slow motion and there was no doubt in his mind. He knew it was good. Not bothering to watch the outcome, he was already running back on defence, when he heard the crowd erupt into loud cheers and drum their feet noisily on the floor of the stands, confirming his instincts. He took no part in the celebration nor did he acknowledge the applause.

Reaching the top of the keyhole, Markus swung around, just as the opposition put the ball back into play. They dribbled and passed amongst themselves, draining the clock. It was a cheap tactic and the crowd booed loudly. "Hassle him Andy!" Markus shouted down the court to his teammate, who, bolstered by their recent three-pointer had also tapped into the last of his reserves and hustled the opposition doggedly.

Andy's commitment rubbed off on the others and they put in one last big effort.

"On his left!" Markus yelled. Andy heard him and hounded tenaciously. Feigning right, his opponent dribbled left and Andy dove for it. He got his hand on the ball and made the steal, his reaction so quick that the tall player's left hand continued as though he was still dribbling the ball. Swinging around him, Andy left him standing and pushed up to the undefended basket. His hand curled out in a perfect finger roll. Score! The crowd went nuts. This had been an exciting game for them, with the lead swinging back and forth. There was a lot of noise as some jumped out of their seats and others erupted into more drumming with their feet. Fueling their enthusiasm, the DJ pumped out a quick loop of the chorus: 'We will rock you!' which boomed out of the ceiling-mounted speakers.

The clock froze as the players regrouped and Markus sensed a change in his team. New hope was visible on their faces. He checked the scoreboard again. Just 26 seconds to go now and they were down just one point. Andy and two of the team stayed up front, while Markus and one other fell back on defence. The ball came into play and the clock resumed. Instantly, Andy and his two henchmen went into overdrive, darting back and forth to pressure the ball carrier.

Having learnt from their recent mistake, the opponents now made quick and careful passes amongst themselves. Again they were wasting time. Markus glanced at the clock again. Ten seconds had ticked by. The frustration came back in full flood. The game was nearly up. They were going to lose. The home crowd sensed it also, again they jeered and the opposition heard them. With just 14 seconds remaining, they considered it safe to embark on one last offensive. They passed forward and moved slowly down the court as Andy and his two forwards continued to harass them.

"Ten!" the crowd began to chant the countdown.

"Let them shoot!" Markus' call rang out and Andy responded. Dropping back he allowed the pass to go through.

"Nine!" The pass flew out to the wing, where one of the opponents stood just outside the three-point line, wide and open. It was the player who hadn't missed a shot from there yet. "Eight!"

"Oh no!" Even as the ball was in the air, Markus was running towards him in a desperate attempt to break the shooter's concentration, but he caught the ball easily and went straight into the shot. The ball left his hands and there was nothing Markus could do.

The crowd went silent and Markus' heart was in his mouth as he watched the ball soar over his head. So that was it then, he thought bitterly, it really had been in vain. All eyes in the big stadium were on the ball as it curved for the hoop.

"Short!" Andy's warning sounded in Markus' ears. At the top of the key, Andy could see clearly. And he was right. With a clang, the ball hit the side of the basket and ricocheted, coming back at speed – straight for Markus. Unprepared, he caught it awkwardly.

"Five!" He almost dropped it, but regained control and then he was running, dribbling frantically and taking huge strides, his shoes squeaking on the polished hardwood floors.

"Four!" He flew past Andy and cleared the key. There was one last defender in front of him, running at him with his hands in the air. Markus barely saw him. His eyes were on the distant hoop and his brain worked quickly, calculating the distance. "Three!"

"Shoot! Shoot!" his teammates yelled desperately.

"Two!"

Just short of halfway and still in full stride, Markus jumped and shot with all his concentration and determination. "One!" It left his hand and soared high. The ending buzzer sounded loudly and Markus' eyes flew wide open as the defender ran full tilt into him.

"Oof!" His breath was knocked out of him and, as his foot came down on top of his opponent's, his ankle rolled. He felt something give. He gasped and hit the floor, landing in a heap. His knees struck wood and there was more pain as the skin scraped away. For several seconds he lay there, sprawled and dazed, and he heard the crowd again. Next thing he was lifted up off the court by many hands and people were slapping him on the back, shouting and yelling at him.

"Awesome shot man," Andy grinned at him.

"Can't believe it went in!" His team surrounded him enthusiastically, all talking at once. He struggled and the hands let him go, but when his weight came on his ankle his face contorted and he almost fell. Quickly they grabbed him again. Helping him off the court, they lowered him onto the bench as gently as their excitement allowed and, one after the other, they grabbed his hand and shook it. Markus looked past them and saw the scoreboard; home 84, visitors 82. It had gone in! They had won the championship. It felt unreal. Then his ankle started to throb and he looked down to find that it was already beginning to swell up.

"Hey, could someone get me some ice?"

"What?" Andy's grin slipped. Markus pointed down at his foot in response.

"Oh, no way," Andy stared at it for a second. Then he was gone. He returned moments later, pushing his way through the crowd that had gathered around Markus. Andy laid the big icepacks around his basketball boot and Markus tied it up tightly to control the swelling. "Don't look too good," he spoke honestly.

"It hurts good," Markus admitted with a grimace. "But at least we won."

"Yeah, totally," Andy grinned but then sobered again. "Might pay to get that looked at though, especially if you want to race next week."

"She'll be right." Markus sat a moment longer, but when he tried to stand he yelped and quickly took the weight off.

"Damn," Markus looked at his foot worriedly. He could barely hobble to the changing rooms. Once there, he took his towel and spare clothes from his bag and hopped on one leg to a free shower. He didn't partake in the cheerful banter of his teammates around him. When Markus re-emerged he found Andy standing by the lockers, tying up his shoes.

"How's it?" Andy asked, straightening up.

"Not good," Markus frowned.

"Broken?"

"Bloody hope not."

"Wanna get it checked?"

"Not really," Markus hesitated and looked down at his ankle. "But probably should," he nodded reluctantly.

"I can drive ya," Andy offered.

"Yeah, guess you'll have to," Markus said grudgingly.

Andy helped him hobble out of the changing rooms to the car-park.

"Hey is that him?" Markus stopped suddenly. Across the car-park from them, two guys were putting their gym bags into the back of a navy-blue Subaru. They both looked downcast and disappointed. One of them glanced over and recognition showed clearly on his face. For a moment it looked as though he would approach them, but then he saw Andy's murderous expression and visibly changed his mind.

"Yeah that's him," Andy hissed. "That's the prick that ran into you! Let's go sort him out."

"We should," Markus agreed. "But there's two of them and I doubt I'd be much help…"

"I can take them," Andy was already heading towards them. The two saw him coming. Hastily they jumped into the car and drew the doors closed. Staunchly, Andy broke into a run. The sedan pulled out of its spot just as he reached it. Angrily, he punched the passenger window and the guy behind it reeled back. The driver gunned it and, with a deep burst, the Subaru sped off, leaving Andy gesturing after it.

"Wussies won't fight." Andy came scowling back to Markus, but then he broke into a grin. "Should've seen his face when I hit the window though, priceless."

"Pity it didn't break," Markus smirked.

With Andy's support Markus hobbled to his car, an immaculate white Nissan 180SX, lowered over big three-piece alloys and sporting a full drift-style body kit. He passed Andy the keys and they got in.

The Nissan started with a growl and Andy drove it reverently out of the car-park. Markus winced as Andy graunched the gears, but bit back the sharp words that came to his lips. Soon after, Andy pulled into the hospital car-park and eased the 180 into a vacant space. He gave Markus his shoulder to lean on and together they made their way through the entrance to the reception.

"I'll wait here." Andy went through to the waiting room. Ignoring the others, who were also waiting, he rifled through a stack of dog-eared gossip magazines until he found a car mag. It helped pass the time until Markus reappeared, supporting himself on a pair of aluminium crutches. His injured leg was heavily bandaged, from his foot to just below the knee.

"Damn, you got a cast?" Andy stood up and the others looked over curiously.

"Nah, it's just sprained, but apparently I pulled the ligaments pretty bad."

"Dude, that's about the biggest bandage I've ever seen. How long you gonna be on crutches?"

"About four weeks the Doc said…"

"Jesus, four weeks, so no drifting then?"

"Not next weekend anyway," Markus was sullen. There was no way he could participate in a serious drift competition with his foot like this.

"We should've smashed that guy," Andy said ruefully.

"Yeah, might not have helped," Markus admitted wryly. "But it sure would've made me feel better."

Andy nodded thoughtfully. "We outta here?"

"Let's go," Markus nodded and trailed on crutches as Andy led the way out to the Nissan.

"I could drive for you," Andy suddenly offered shrewdly as he unlocked the driver door.

"Sure, you can drop me home."

"Nah, I mean at the drifting."

"Yeah right, nice try," Markus rounded on him. "Won't have you going out and busting up my car."

"I'll pay for any damage," Andy offered hurriedly.

"That's real decent of ya," Markus scoffed and shook his head. "Forget it."

A cloud slipped in front of the sun and instantly the temperature dropped. Leon fidgeted uncomfortably on the hard, wooden seating. He checked his watch. They had already been here for at least ten minutes. A light breeze whispered across the raceway. It felt cold on Leon's face and bare legs and he shivered, pulling his hoodie closer around him. His elbow accidentally nudged the spectator on his right; a young guy in jeans and a rotary t-shirt with a baseball cap pulled low over his face. Mumbling an apology Leon hurriedly tucked his elbow in. Restlessly, he checked his watch again, it hadn't changed. Why had he let Byron talk him into this?

The cloud passed and the raceway was once more basked in warm sunshine. He had forgotten his sunglasses. With a furrowed brow, he squinted out across the hazy racetrack before him. The smooth bitumen snaked and crisscrossed to provide different routes and allow for different races. Some sections of the course offered a selection of tight, banked turns, while others featured longer straights which looped back upon themselves. Near the middle of the track, on the grass right in front of the longest sweeping bend, a small gazebo had been erected. Leon could see the judges and the, now silent, commentator sitting at a trestle table in the gazebo's shade.

Apart from the St John ambulance that was parked near the judges, the track was devoid of any vehicles. Not a single car in sight. Leon frowned; the track brought back memories, many memories. Fidgeting again, he looked away. Impatiently he leant backwards and the next row of benches in the grandstand dug into his back, reminding him of their presence. He leant forward again. Beside him, his friend slurped his coke noisily through a straw. The noise irritated Leon and added to his mounting agitation. He should have trusted his instincts and not let Byron persuade him to come.

"So where are the cars then?" Leon couldn't contain the irritation from his tone. "What are they waiting for?"

"They're over there I'd say," Byron pointed across the track to a distant concrete wall at the far end, some four hundred metres away. "In the pit lanes."

"I thought it was supposed to be qualifying right now."

"Yeah, not sure," Byron answered distractedly and withdrew a plastic-wrapped sausage roll from his pocket.

"I think there's still a round to go for qualifying," the guy in the rotor t-shirt spoke thoughtfully, having overheard them. "Shouldn't be long – maybe they're having problems."

"Oh okay," Leon nodded and looked around him. The stand was packed with people. He and Byron had arrived late and, in order to get a seat, they had climbed high up in the stand and squeezed themselves into one of the few remaining spots. It was almost claustrophobic. He wished he could leave. He glanced at Byron beside him, who was working his way happily through his sausage roll. Having already paid for entrance and parking, he knew that Byron would resist. Leon sighed and checked his watch again.

"Here they go," A murmur went through the crowd when two cars dispatched without warning from the pit lanes at the other end of the track. One leading the other, they hurtled along the track at speed, in a wide loop that took them first away from the spectators and then back towards them. The sound of their engines grew loud and insistent as they neared.

"They're not drifting," Leon muttered.

"Not yet," Byron interrupted his chewing. "See those cones?" he indicated two, bright orange road cones, that stood on either side of the track not far from the spectator stand.

"Yeah."

"When they reach them, that's where the judging area starts and over there..." Byron swept his hand in an arc, pointing to two more cones, "is where it ends."

"That's not very long," Leon estimated that there was only about 500m of bend-riddled track between the start and ending markers.

"No, they're quick races," Byron agreed.

"So are those the clipping points?" Leon wondered at several more cones, which were placed at specific points along the edges of the judged section. He was beginning to remember some of the terminology.

"That's right, they get points for drifting as close as possible to them, without actually touching." Byron went silent as the commentators introduced the drivers and their rides. Taking the lead was a heavily modified Toyota AE86 Trueno. Built in 1984, it was an old-school machine, but regarded as the car that started the drifting craze and deemed to still be one of the best drift cars of all time. The other was a black C33 Nissan Laurel, nearly ten years younger and initially intended as a comfortable cruiser, the converted sedan now ran a RB25Det Nissan Skyline engine and was stripped of all luxuries, making it a serious drift competitor.

Hurtling in like fighter jets, the two cars tore past the starting cones and slid into action. Streaming an acrid blue cloud of burnt rubber, they engaged in a full drift – parallel to each other with barely a metre separating them. The skill of these drivers was beyond belief as they pushed their machines to the very limits of control, then pulled back just before the point of no return. The crowd around him no longer existed as Leon watched the battle unfold, becoming so involved that he felt the pressure on the drivers, the G-forces of the bends and was deafened by the engine noise. His heart quickened.

The two cars slid out of the second bend with back wheels thrashing to the enormous torque of their turbocharged engines and for one heart-stopping moment they were end-to-end; travelling at high speed with bumpers almost touching. Then they swept into the next bend and peeled out again with their wide rear tyres screaming and tearing at the smooth seal of the track.

With a longer wheelbase and more weight, the Laurel's handling was slower, but thanks to the enormous power of the 2500cc Skyline engine, the deep-dish rear wheels spun effortlessly allowing it to drift at bigger angle than the lighter, nimble Toyota. Although very different, the two vehicles were well-matched as they hurtled through the bends, never straight, always sideways. It was a heated battle, with the Toyota leading and the Laurel tenaciously holding the chase, her big turbo whining rude defiance at the smaller four-cylinder adversary, but then, as Byron had said, it was all over rather suddenly when both cars flew past the end markers.

"The Laurel will take the lead now," Byron explained, but Leon didn't hear him. His eyes were glued to the track and the two competing cars. Pouring the power on, the Nissan caught up with the Toyota and flew past. Together they raced around the track, coming in for the same run, but this time with the Laurel in front. They aimed for the starting markers, and, when they reached them, they did it all over again with both cars launching into big powerslides. In the chase the Toyota was all over the Nissan, pushing it, hounding it, but still maintaining massive angle throughout the drift and billowing plenty of acrid smoke from its churning rear tyres. The crowd buzzed with excitement and Leon was mesmerised. The Nissan fended the Toyota off amiably, preventing any passing, but still it seemed that the blazing red Toyota had the advantage and silently Leon willed it on.

Seconds later they had screamed through the course again, but just as they cleared the final cones, the speeding Toyota suddenly backfired loudly and her engine note lost its intensity, before abruptly cutting out completely. Immediately her brake lights flared as she veered off the track, skidding to a stop. Small with distance, the driver jumped out hurriedly and scrambled to lift the bonnet. All eyes were on him, as he used his fire-extinguisher and a cloud of white erupted around him. The track marshals, wearing bright fluorescent-orange jackets ran in to help. One also carried a fire-extinguisher, but didn't need to use it. The cloud slowly wafted away in the breeze and after a short inspection they helped to push the Toyota slowly down the remainder of the track to the pits.

"What bad luck," Byron spoke up. "He was doing well too." His words roused Leon, who realised he'd been clenching his fists.

"Yeah," Leon agreed, surprising himself with the strength of his disappointment.

"Still bored?" Byron glanced at him shrewdly.

"It's alright," Leon admitted reluctantly and looked around him. Most of the other spectators were getting up and making their way down the stand. "What's happening now?"

"Not sure," Byron also looked about him.

"That was the end of the qualifying," the guy with the rotor t-shirt explained. "They're taking a break until the actual racing starts."

"Oh yeah, so where's everyone going?"

"The pits are open and there's a bikini comp on," the guy grinned. "Dunno about you, but I'm not about to miss that."

"Neither am I," Byron stood up eagerly and hoisted Leon to his feet. "Come on, let's go."

Leon and Byron found the pit lanes densely packed with spectators who had come to get a closer look at the competing cars and drivers, as well as the bikini girls. Many had cameras and were snapping away. Ahead of them the whirring noise of a starter motor cranked an engine over with determination. The engine fired, then coughed, spluttered and died again. With Byron in the lead, they pushed their way through the spectators towards the sound. There were a few grunts of protest, but these were snuffed out quickly when they saw the stature of the big guy that had bumped them.

Having made their way through the crowd, before them stood the same car that had broken down on the track: the red Toyota. Ignoring the onlookers, the driver and another guy in blue overalls were engrossed with their heads under the bonnet. They had removed several parts and were deep in concentration, trying to establish the root of the problem. The mechanic made several adjustments and turned to the driver with little confidence. "Try that." The driver reached his arm through the open window and turned the key, which was already in the ignition. Again the starter motor turned gamely to crank the engine.

The spectators, who had formed a respectful circle around the ailing car held their breath. Abruptly the engine sparked and settled back into a steady beat. Relief played on the driver's face, but instantly turned to dismay when the engine began to splutter again and finally choked off completely. The driver tried once more, but this time the engine didn't even fire. After several unsuccessful revolutions the starter motor began to flag from a draining battery and the driver turned it off. He and the mechanic exchanged a helpless look. A dead engine meant the car was out of action and with it their chances of competing gone.

Leon sensed their disappointment and frustration, as did the crowd around him. They shuffled uncomfortably and began to drift away to view the other, more fortunate cars that were still in the running. Soon it was just Byron, Leon and a handful of others that looked on as the driver and mechanic talked seriously and then the mechanic also strode away, leaving just the driver fussing over the engine bay.

"Come on, let's go and check out that S14," Byron fidgeted and indicated a dark green Nissan Silvia, standing a little way further down the pit lane. The car idled noisily through an enlarged exhaust system, while the driver was busy irrigating the radiator with cold water to ensure it wouldn't overheat. The cars were all being pushed so hard that, in the hot sunshine, it tested their cooling systems to the full. "Looks like the bikini girls are that way too." Already they could hear a chorus of cheering and wolf-whistles.

"I wouldn't mind having a closer look…"

"Sweet, let's go then."

"No, I mean…" Leon nodded towards the broken drift car.

"What, at the Toyota?" Byron looked puzzled.

"Yeah," somehow, Leon felt himself drawn to it.

"But, we'll miss the bikini girls…" Byron protested.

"You go, I'll catch up," Leon turned away and, as he stepped closer, he saw, that unlike some of the other cars, the Toyota carried no number plates and was no longer road-legal. She was now a dedicated drift car. Curiously he looked inside to find that her interior had been largely stripped, including the dashboard and the carpet, down to an almost empty shell. Without the dashboard to hide them, copious electrical cables ran everywhere. Some connected the chunky, aftermarket MoTeC ECU, which was bolted to the floor of the passenger foot-well, while others ran to the hoard of Autometer gauges that had replaced the standard instrument cluster and were set into a custom aluminium panel behind the Momo steering wheel.

The door trims still remained, but the backseat was gone and in its place were the thick, tubular bars of the roll cage. They crisscrossed and ran up and inside the roof of the cabin like a skeleton that encapsulated the occupants within a protective shell. The original front seats had been swapped for two lightweight Bride race seats and red harnesses. At the base of the passenger seat, the small, red fire-extinguisher lay discarded and beside it, the driver had dropped his black helmet. Leon stared down at it. He felt an overwhelming urge to strap himself into the driver seat, put the helmet on and race this car down the track.

If only the car was still running. What a shame, he thought. With an effort he pushed his feelings aside and hesitantly went to the front of the Toyota, stepping up beside the driver. He took in the complicated contents of the engine bay and realised instantly that she wasn't running her stock engine. This one was bigger. He could see where the engine mounts had been re-welded to make it fit. A maze of turbo plumbing surrounded it and more room was lost to a large intercooler and cold air box. No wonder they were having trouble finding the problem.

The driver detected his presence but didn't raise his head from the engine bay. "Man, this sucks, I just can't see what's wrong with this baby," he said grumpily.

"Can I take a look?" Leon asked quietly, almost shyly. The driver turned his head sharply at the unfamiliar voice to find a youth with short black hair beneath a white Nike cap, standing beside him. He had a straight nose and dark eyes, features that hinted at an Asiatic background but at the same time they were still very European. He was dressed lightly in a t-shirt and long shorts. The driver paused and looked at Leon searchingly. There was an oil smear on his cheek and a scowl on his lips. He looked as though he wanted to refuse. But he straightened up and stepped back wearily, wiping his grease-stained hands on a rag.

"Knock yourself out," he shrugged. "I think I'm about ready to give up."

"This isn't the stock engine is it?" Leon thought aloud.

"No, of course not, that's a BEAMS 3S-GE. These things normally run a 4A-GE," the driver replied irritably.

"Right," Leon was not deterred. What could be wrong? Leon's brain worked overtime as his eyes analysed the engine bay, almost in a squint. On the track she had backfired shortly before cutting out and now she was turning over, but not running properly. It was as though there was no spark, or could it be..? Although focused, his thoughts seemed to wander as he searched for the problem. The heat of the engine, the smell of petrol, of hot oil… The image of his dad appeared in his mind. Leon's fingers stilled and he frowned, but for once the image did not incur the mixed feelings, the hurt, that normally followed.

When he was younger and still lived in Osaka, Leon would often go by his dad's massive workshop after school. His dad ran a high profile tuning shop, specialising in street and drift cars. As the boss's son, Leon was allowed to come and go as he pleased and roam relatively freely in the workshop. At first he used to just watch his dad and the other mechanics work, quietly and unobtrusively. One of these times, when he arrived, dressed in his uniform and carrying his schoolbag, his dad was hunched over the engine of one of the cars, working in oil-stained, blue overalls, as he did so often.

Leon had set his bag aside and quietly made his way to his dad's side, while watching him work. There was a gentle and thorough patience about his dad, a patience that was more in character with a doctor or an artist, than a mechanic. His dad had looked up and smiled at him, gesturing for him to step closer. His words played back in Leon's ears: 'Look Leon, here is the culprit – the crankshaft position sensor is broken. That's why it was running poorly and sometimes not starting at all.'

The image of his dad faded, and Leon shook his head to clear it. "The CPS," he said without thinking. The brown-haired driver had been watching him curiously.

"The CPS?" he frowned.

"The crankshaft position sensor," Leon explained.

"I know what it is," the driver snapped. He bumped Leon as he pressed in to peer down to where the small part was located. "But that's bloody obscure. How can you be sure?"

"I just am," Leon shrugged.

The driver straightened and looked at him searchingly, before turning gloomily to the mechanic who had reappeared. "Taz, this joker, thinks the CPS is shot," he indicated Leon. "It's not like we have another with us, eh?"

"Another sensor?" Taz stared darkly down into the engine bay. "Nah man, and we're up again in 15 minutes, they won't reschedule us."

"Yeah, well, I can't get her running, and I don't even know if that is the problem," the driver scowled. Taz looked at him for a full second.

"We can't just forfeit. We've just qualified," Taz bit his lower lip and looked about him broodingly. Around them, the pits were busy as other drifters prepared their cars for the finals and the spectators mingled, looking on in interest. "We could ask one of the others if they have a spare," he suggested.

"A spare sensor? Yeah right, besides, we're the only Toyota here. Everybody else is running Nissans."

"Hey, I might be able to help," Leon heard himself say. The two guys turned back to him.

"Say what? You've got a CPS for a 3S' on ya?" the driver asked sarcastically.

"No, not quite that handy, but I may be able to get one."

"Guess, it's worth a try Cam," Taz turned to the brown-haired guy.

"Maybe, but we only have 15 minutes," Cam was sceptical.

"Try and stall for more time if you can, oh and get that old one out..." Leon was already running, elbowing his way through the spectators and frantically looking for Byron in the crowd. Luckily his big frame stood out and Leon spotted him. "Byron!" Byron turned irritably as Leon pushed his way up to him, but then his face split into a grin.

"Oh, hey man," he immediately turned away again. "Check out these honeys. That dark-haired chick on the left, she is fine as." Leon didn't have time to look.

"Byron, I need the 'Tez key," he blurted.

"What? Why?" Byron wasn't looking at him.

"I left my inhaler in the glove-box."

"Your inhaler?" This time Byron sensed his urgency and turned back to him with quick concern. "You alright?"

"Yeah, but I need that key," Leon pressed.

"Of course," Byron scrabbled in his pocket and hastily produced his keys. "Here... you want me to come with you?" Byron looked visibly torn between helping his friend and giving up the pretty bikini girls.

"No, don't worry, I'll catch you back at the stands." Leon grabbed the keys and took off, leaving Byron staring after him uncertainly.

Leon threaded the Altezza between the other drift cars in the pits and raced up to the stranded Toyota, where Cam and Taz waited impatiently. Stopping quickly, he popped the hood.

"I got it," Taz said hurriedly, spanner in hand. "Screwdriver – flat-tip," the order rang from him a moment later. It was handed to him and he grunted and cursed as he worked with his head in the engine bay.

"We were beginning to wonder if you were actually coming back," Cam greeted Leon when he got out of the Altezza.

"They didn't want to let me into the pits," Leon explained and Cam was about to reply, when a call came over the loud speaker. The next team of racers were advised to get ready.

"That's us – get a move on!"

"It's stuck…" Taz struggled in the Altezza's engine bay.

"Careful, that's not my car," Leon muttered worriedly, he was beginning to regret his decision to help.

"Yeah, alright already…"

"What's the hold-up guys?" Distracted, they hadn't noticed one of the race organisers walk up to them. He wore a fluorescent-yellow vest and held a walkie-talkie in his hand. There was a frown on his face. "The call's gone out, you're up – you should be standing at the line, ready."

"We just need a couple more minutes…" Cam requested.

"You've got two – that's it," the organiser warned and walked to check on their opponent, who sat at the ready, his Nissan 180SX idling throatily and pointing down the pit lane.

"Hear that, we've got less than two minutes. Get a move on," Cam checked his watch.

"Quit breathing down my neck," Taz grunted and concentrated on removing the sensor. "God, come on!" Leon hovered quietly, hopeful and expectant. "Oh, good," Taz breathed a sigh of relief, and withdrew his hands from the engine bay. He ran to the waiting Trueno.

"Alright, finally…"

"Shut up and put your helmet on – be ready to give her a crank," Taz growled as he worked frantically to install the donor sensor.

"Done?" Cam now sat anxiously in his seat, helmet on.

"Wait."

"Hurry up!"

"Try that," Taz jumped back and immediately the engine cranked over, chugging, coughing, but resisting. It didn't want to start. "Come on!" The race organiser was walking back towards them now, shaking his head regretfully.

"Try again," Leon shouted urgently.

"Sorry guys, that's it. Time is up," the organiser called out. Cam swore and hit the steering wheel angrily.

"She's flooded, man. Try it one more time," Leon's words came out like an order. Cam cranked the engine over again. It belched loudly and backfired, blowing a cloud of fuel out of the exhaust. Then it caught with a surge and revved loudly, before idling down again.

"Yeah-ah," Taz shook a fist and laughed happily, but then became serious as he turned to the race organiser. "Reckon we might still be able to run?" The race organiser looked the idling Trueno over thoughtfully.

"Technically no, but..." he turned to their opponent, waiting in the white 180SX. "Andy, it's your call..?" Hidden behind his helmet, the driver of the 180SX shrugged with an air of arrogance.

"You want a whuppin? Come get some."

The race organiser turned back to them with a smile. "You heard him. You're on."

"Smoke him man," Taz lowered the bonnet.

"Yeah, good luck," Leon nodded to the driver.

The Toyota pulled away easily and followed the leading 180SX through the pit lanes at the regulatory 15km/h. Side by side, the two performance cars pulled up at the starting line. Leon gazed after them for a second, with the longing and excitement building up inside him. How good would it feel to once again sit behind the wheel of a high-powered drift car! He shook his head and pushed the thought away.

"I'll be back for that sensor when it's over."

Taz nodded. "Thanks, by the way, and good spotting."

Leon locked the Altezza and jogged out of the pit lanes. Unable to restrain himself, as soon as he was clear, he broke into a sprint. He raced back to the busy stand and immediately saw Byron, who had reserved a seat for him. Breathlessly he clambered up, stepping carefully as he navigated between the seated crowd.

"What took you so long?" Byron called down to him. "Are you okay?"

"Yeah," Leon gasped for breath. He sat down beside Byron and handed him the keys.

"You sure? I never knew you had asthma," Byron looked at him worriedly. "You look messed up."

"I'm okay," Leon nodded and turned quickly to look at the track, but it was empty. The two race cars that he was expecting were nowhere to be seen.

"Oh, good, but hey you fully missed out man."

"What? Have they already raced?" Leon moved agitatedly on the wooden bench.

"Oh, nah, I meant the bikini comp," Byron face creased into a grin. "They were the hottest babes ever."

"Oh that's good," Leon answered distractedly. Where were they? What was the hold-up?

"That chick with dark hair," Byron kept talking dreamily. "Wow..."

"Sounds like I should've been there."

"Yeah, but man if you already had an asthma attack coming on, then seeing this babe would've been like drowning," Byron shook his head and suddenly his eyes narrowed. "Oh hey," he indicated the track. Leon looked out to see two cars leaving the pits and racing out onto the far side of the track. Shielding his eyes against the glaring sun with his hand, he was able to make out the white 180SX whose clean paintwork caught the sunlight and sparkled ethereally through the haze in the distance. The effect was so complete that the Nissan seemed to float gracefully above the ground. But it was not the Nissan that he was interested in. Leading her was the red Trueno. "She's going again," Byron finished in a tone that was filled with anticipation.

Around them, the trickles of conversation stilled and, unconsciously, Leon leant forward as the competitors closed in on the drift zone. In comparison to the sleek 180SX, the boxy Toyota appeared slow and clumsy. The Nissan pushed its prey, keeping right on its tail and maintaining pressure as they raced in. But the Trueno remained unflustered. Keeping her cool, she negotiated the distance to the starting markers with a casual grace. Leon watched with interest, but couldn't suppress a trickle of disappointment at this unenthusiastic display from the leading Toyota. The cars were nearing now and the engine noise of the Trueno became louder. It sounded lively and healthy. So why was the driver holding back?

Twenty metres out from the starting cones the attitude of the Trueno suddenly changed. The 3S-GE engine revved fiercely and in a split-second she went from complacent and docile to a fully enraged monster. With her rear wheels screeching, the lightweight car hurtled into the drift zone. The sudden move caught the trekking Nissan by surprise, but the driver recovered quickly and followed the Toyota with matching abandon. It was an incredible battle that held every spectator in a tense grip, until the two screaming machines shot past the final cones. Leaving the drift zone behind them, they continued to peel out, scrubbing their tyres loudly all the way down the track.

"Man, that was loose," one of the spectators commented.

"Yeah, but not good enough," Leon voiced his opinion. "The 180 had that."

"You think?" Byron queried and Leon nodded his head in silent disappointment. A moment later the commentator announced the judges' score. It came out six-four in the Nissan's favour, as Leon had feared.

"Let's hope the Toyota can lay down another one of its mean chases."

"Yeah," Leon gazed across at the two cars. As he watched, the Nissan caught up with the Trueno and swept past. This time he would take the lead. The two cars curled around the track until they neared the starting cones again. With their approach, the mood of the spectators also changed, once more becoming charged and excited. In unconscious expectancy they leant forward as one.

Andy had been running strong in qualifying and he felt confident, especially now that he had won the first of his two battles, and that was while chasing. This time it was his turn to lead, which he preferred, and the 180SX felt taught and snappy as he peeled her easily through a bend. Furtively, his eyes moved to his rear-view mirror. The Toyota sat close on his back bumper with her engine screaming in a loud frenzy. Savagely she snapped at his heels, challenging him, pressing him, hounding him. Some drifters taped their mirrors up, so as not to be distracted by the pressure from behind, but Andy did not – for him, seeing his opponent so close made the race that much more thrilling.

With adrenaline already racing from the first battle, Andy's speed increased as he flowed through the next series of bends. Quickly he approached the starting cones and flexed his fingers lightly around the steering wheel. He loved this moment. This calm, tranquil moment just before the storm. This moment where you know it is coming and you are committed. The Nissan seemed to sense it too and her engine note altered, becoming more insistent, more urgent. The sound of the SR20Det at the redline was a murderous snarl. Andy stole one last glance at his rear-view. The image of the Toyota filled it, looming red and menacing. Andy smiled recklessly. "Bring it on!"

Working the throttle and hand brake, Andy propelled the Nissan into a perfect power-slide on the first corner. Sweeping through he thundered out, billowing smoke and throwing up dirt and debris as his right back wheel bumped off the track. Immediately he brought her around, dropping the 180SX neatly into the next bend at full opposite lock. Another bend came at him, always he held massive angle and his tyres spewed clouds of smoke. Already he was a good length ahead and he knew that he was winning. Back in high school, when he'd played basketball there had been days when he just wouldn't miss. Shot after shot, he sank ball after ball and his team mates would set him up to become top scorer of the day. Just like that, today was his day. Andy was *on fire* and he knew it.

Andy heel-and-toe down-shifted and spun the wheel, lining himself up for the next bend and the Nissan responded to his confident touch. She seemed to read his mind and smoothly they swept through the course like a tornado, tyres smoking and screaming as Andy instinctively worked the controls. It felt awesome and he loved it. The G-forces pressed him into his seat and the adrenaline flowed through his veins.

"Are you seeing this?!" Byron exclaimed.

"Yeah," Leon replied distractedly. His eyes were glued to the track.

"This is the best race we've seen yet," Byron breathed.

Swift and agile, the Toyota and Nissan battled each other, the red chase car always shadowing, pressuring and trying to surpass, yet unable to quite match the amazing performance of the leading 180SX. Around them, the other spectators couldn't contain themselves.

"That's a whole lot of smoke."

"That guy is insane!"

"Look," Byron exclaimed. "He's doing a reverse entry!"

As he drifted, Andy made every effort to please the judges and maximise on points. He put on a real show, waving his hand out of the window and flashing his lights. In his heightened state he felt invincible but these childish tricks seemed stale and trivial. Anybody with some drifting skill could do them and the judges had seen it all before. He wanted to upstage the rest. As he slipped out of another bend, a short straight lay before him, which led into the sweeper. In this extended arcing curve, right in front of the judging stand, one could hold a drift much longer than anywhere else on the track. A wild idea came to him.

Shoving his foot flat, he thundered down the straight, his car broadside and pouring smoke. At a touch over 110km/h, he lined the Nissan up for the sweeper, working the wheel so that she skidded in with her backend first. He caught her neatly before she could spin and brought her nose back the other way, to point directly at the judges. With the gas pedal to the floor, the rear wheels shrilled overtime and she slid right across the apex.

"Eat that!" Andy yelled and promptly thrust one hand out of the window, upping his already impressive display of skill. Sending a fleeting glance back to his opponent, he grinned. A solid wall of grey-blue smoke completely obscured the track. The Toyota, which must still be chasing was shrouded from view. The end of the sweeper loomed and Andy was about to return his full attention to the track, when a smudge of red flickered through the smoke. Then a gap in the cloud curtain blew open and he saw the Toyota clearly. It was right behind him and coming on fast.

Andy flinched. Still at full lock with his tyres blurring, he yanked his arm back in and spun the wheel. The 180SX wobbled unnervingly at his sudden move. He sensed it instantly. She was about to go.

An astounded murmur went through the crowd and Leon couldn't believe his eyes. The 180SX poured down the straight and then pivoted so that her front end angled back the way she had come and she essentially skidded backwards at over 100km/h, before pivoting back and her front end took the lead again on entry of the sweeper. The manoeuvre had lasted mere seconds, but captivated every onlooker. Still at full power, the 180SX skidded into the sweeper in a broad arcing slide, smoking all the way.

"Reverse entry," Byron repeated and chuckled. "Wow."

"Unreal," Leon uttered. It seemed to defy physics.

"That's a god at the wheel," Byron shook his head, but suddenly tensed when he saw the Toyota close in dangerously fast and the hand protruding from the Nissan disappeared. "Oh oh..." Abruptly the 180SX's nose nudged around and her slip angle increased dangerously.

"Woah," a hum went through the crowd and several spectators came to their feet.

"He's lost it," Byron hissed.

The watchers held their breath as the white car fought to maintain her balance and straighten out again. For a millisecond it seemed she would recover, but then one of her wheels slipped off the track. It was enough to push her past the point of no return and she went into a dead spin. The Trueno had tagged so close that it seemed she couldn't possibly avoid collision, but at the last moment she pirouetted and flew past the spinning car with inches to spare.

Completely out of control, the Nissan spiralled off the tarmac, tyres screaming in defiance. Her rear wheels panned across the grassy soil, biting in deep and throwing up a cloud of loose dirt. The tyre smoke caught up with her and mingled with the dust that billowed thickly around. For a fleeting moment she was lost from view, disappearing behind the smokescreen, but then she spun back into broad daylight again. Her low front bumper scrubbed the ground and was torn off violently.

Finally she lost momentum and came to a stop. Her torn nose pointed at the crowd, over which a hush had fallen. Even the commentator, whose disembodied voice usually boomed through the loudspeakers, had fallen momentarily silent. Through the quiet, the scream of the 3S-GE rattled loudly around the racecourse as the Toyota carried on its run. With a series of wild drifts it rammed its win home and powered out of the drift zone to unquestionable victory.

Antagonised by the sound, the 180SX stirred. Her engine roared into life and her rear wheels churned up a mound of dust and debris. Slewing loosely, she left her front bumper lying on the ground and angled back to intersect the track. Dust turned to tyre smoke as she clawed herself back onto hard, resisting surface. Finding new purchase, she throttled forward, her engine scream unrelenting. The driver was beside himself with fury and he drifted her, first one way then the other, with complete disregard.

Having reached the ending cones, she came about suddenly in a tight turn and doubled back with her tyres squealing brutally as they left thick black lines behind her. Right before the spectator stand the 180SX checked and then rotated on the spot in a number of perfectly executed donuts. The driver ignored the demands of the commentator who was now instructing him to retire. Watching the terrorised machine pushed to the very limit, the onlookers couldn't get enough. The Nissan spun rebelliously on and on until one of the back tyres wore through and blew with a bang, strewing black chunks of rubber across the track.

Even then the driver flogged her on relentlessly, but the sound had changed as she destroyed her barren rim, sanding away the alloy on the abrasive tarmac. Moments later the other back tyre burst and shredded off the rim, scattering more rubber. Her entire back end fishtailed on metal now, accompanied by a shrill, grating whine. Finally, having managed to vent a little and reclaim some distinction, the 180SX shrieked and screeched away back to the pits.

Fuming and scowling angrily, Andy avoided the stares from the other drifters and directed the bruised 180SX back to his spot. Dammit, he was supposed to have won, but instead he had crashed his friend's car, ripped off the front bumper and destroyed the rear mags. How was he going to explain this? Driving sedately now, Andy approached the empty car trailer, which was hooked onto the back of a black '88 Mazda wagon. Where was Markus? Driving past the wagon, he went to pull in beside it and that's when he saw his friend, leaning against the trailer with his hands thrust into the pockets of his navy overalls. He looked far from happy.

His lips pressed in a thin line, Markus watched impassively as Andy pulled in beside him. Andy turned the key off and the engine spluttered into awkward silence. Climbing out, he removed his helmet and walked slowly over to Markus, whose eyes were narrow, focused on the battered front section of his car. Neither of them spoke. Andy stood beside him, his helmet dangling from one hand.

"I kinda spun," Andy fidgeted. "It's not that bad aye..." Markus brow furrowed but his eyes didn't leave the Nissan. "Shouldn't take much to fix..." Andy muttered.

"Where's the bumper?" Markus asked calmly.

"Still out there, the crew will grab it."

"You could've taken this comp out man," Markus spoke quietly, moving his head from side-to-side.

"Yeah... Next time I guess..."

"Next time..?" Markus said disbelievingly. "Man, I can't believe you tried a reversie on that bend! You were ahead as it was. What the hell were you thinking?"

"I wasn't. I was trying to win."

"Dude, next time do some bloody thinking before you bust up my car."

"Chill man – it's hardly as bad as it looks."

"She sure didn't look like that before you went out. I should never have let you drive her."

"Alright, you've made your point," Andy paused. "You know I actually spun because I tried to stop him hitting me... Anyway, sorry." Markus' retort died on his lips. To get an apology out of Andy was a rare thing. His anger receded just as swiftly as it had arisen. "I'll get her fixed up. I'll sort it."

"Just help me get her on the trailer," Markus sighed.

"Okay," Andy gave the keys to Markus, who got into the Nissan and started it up, while Andy went to the trailer and set up the two metal ramps.

"I guess, this way I don't have to worry about the bumper scraping," Markus grinned roguishly out of the window and crept the Nissan forwards, up the ramps. Her tread-less rear wheels clattered on metal and Andy had to run around the back to help push her up. With a bit of straining they got her on. Markus clambered out awkwardly.

"I'll get you some new wheels as well," Andy called up to him. "These ones are stuffed." Markus glanced at the back wheels. Suddenly he grinned and his whole face lit up.

"Must say, even though it was stupid, that reversie was pretty epic and those doughies were all good."

"You saw them?"

"Yeah man, mint while it lasted," Markus' eyes twinkled. Together they dismantled the ramps and closed the back gate.

"So what now?" Andy asked. "Shall we get going?"

"We have to wait for that bumper to show up, so may as well watch the last races."

"Yeah, alright," Andy was less than enthused.

"That was something else," Leon shook his head. He had forgotten his earlier discomfort.

"That guy put on a good show," Byron agreed.

"Yeah Andy is known to go pretty wild," the spectator beside Leon laughed. "Those were some big donuts."

"I'm glad the Toyota won though," Leon nodded. "That means he's in the top eight now, right?"

"Something like that," Byron agreed and looked across the track. "Here come the next two."

The leading car was a bright green S15 Silvia, which hugged the ground on cambered suspension. The chase car, a white RX-7 Batman, decked out in a wide-body kit and running massive 19-inch three-piece drift rims, tagged close behind. Both cars were covered in decals and exuded an air of confidence and ease, as they descended swiftly upon the drift zone. This was their realm. They were the veterans, the top dogs. Leon forgot what he was going to say as their engine bellow thundered out towards him. They cleared the start cones and the show was on.

Effortlessly they swept through the bends, sliding and pouring smoke. Their professionalism emanated so strongly that Leon was instantly taken back to Japan, to the drift circuit where his dad had so frequently competed. Leon used to watch him race from the stands, but when he turned fourteen, for the Grand Prix final, his dad had made him his personal cameraman. That way they were able to analyse the footage and better establish his dad's strengths and weaknesses.

Wearing a fluorescent jacket and sporting a video camera, Leon had been given access to the track's grassy islands and was able to get close to the action. He remembered the final race, his dad's S15 Silvia closing on a bend at phenomenal speed, her meticulous blue paintwork gleaming and sparkling in the sun. Engine roaring, she boldly engaged in a drift and smoke poured from her squealing rear wheels. His dad's opponent, in a heavily modified Nissan 350Z, slid along right beside him. But he was too close. As his dad turned out of the drift to sweep into the next bend his opponent collided with him. Broken fibreglass scattered and the rendering crunch of the two cars connecting at high speed was clearly audible to Leon from where he was filming. Both cars immediately spun out of control. He remembered his dad, flying off course, frantically trying to correct and the people in the stands all coming to their feet.

His dad's Silvia cleared the track, flew across the run-off area and hit a concrete barrier with such force that it sent a tremor through the ground. Leon was running, cold with dread, still clutching the camera, his eyes wide in disbelief, shock and horror. The Silvia, which only seconds before had been so swift and agile, now lay crushed before him. Then it was all shrilling sirens and flashing lights from the emergency teams as they scratched and tore at the wreck, fighting to save the driver, his dad. The security personnel held him back, as the ambulance rushed away with his lifeless dad inside. Leon remembered the judges announcing his dad as the race winner. Only his dad never finished the race, but died in hospital before Leon and his mum were able to get there.

It required an enormous effort for Leon to force the image from his head. His hands were shaking and he gripped the edge of his seat tightly. He took a deep breath, and tried to focus his attention on the track again. The two drift machines had finished their first battle now and were racing around for the second.

"These guys are extreme, eh?" Byron glanced at Leon. "Are you sure you're okay? You look white as."

"Fine," Leon nodded, not meeting Byron's eyes. He took another deep breath.

"Is it the asthma?"

"I'm fine," Leon repeated and deferred his attention to the next battle, this time with the Mazda in the lead.

The RX-7 entered the first series of bends and the bursts of her rotary engine pulsed through the stands. Her tail flared out and her nose nudged fractionally towards the apex, the precursor of drift engagement. She flaunted her talents and effortlessly glided along with such speed and agility that the crowd doubted their own eyes. In a display that bordered on arrogance the driver held off the chase, never pulling too far ahead, but skilfully switching left and right to sweep cleanly through the bends. The sound of tyres and powerful engines blended together. The intensity of the battle was so powerful that it seemed to radiate from them in a visible aura, enticing the crowd so their attention was complete and they sat on the edge of their seats. The white RX-7 flew to victory.

"He'll win this," Leon said quietly as he watched the two cars meander back to the pit lanes.

"Yeah, Simon's a mean driver," Byron replied. "He's pretty much in a league of his own."

Several more races followed and each was as exciting as the previous one. Then it was the red Toyota's turn again. She exploded out onto the track with a vengeance and put on another good show. Both leading and chasing, the driver prevailed against the challenging S14 Silvia and rammed home another victory that saw him into the top four. By now Leon had recovered and he was thrilled by the Toyota's achievement. He couldn't wait to see the outcome of her next run. But when the Trueno came on again she was pitted against a black Cefiro, piloted by a long time D1 driver, and Leon knew she was in trouble. Sitting on the edge of his seat, with his fingernails biting into his palm, he willed the red hatchback to win.

The Toyota fought gamely, but the competition was simply too strong. She couldn't match the Nissan. Throughout the race, the Nissan held bigger angle and swept through the course in an outrageous display of class. The races were over very quickly and for both battles the judges scored in the Nissan's favour. As the two cars rushed back to the pit lanes, Leon had to concede that the Nissan had won fairly.

There were just two races left now and within minutes the Trueno shot out onto the track again. Her final battle was with a black Laurel for third place. The Toyota was chasing and it was obvious that the driver was somewhat shaken by his first loss, but he rallied strongly, applying so much pressure that the Laurel baulked and then made a costly mistake in the tight bend prior to the sweeper. Kicking her tail section out just a little too far, first one of the Laurel's churning rear wheels left the tarseal and then the second followed. Two wheels off the track meant instant loss. Making no mistakes in her second battle, the Trueno retired, having attained a very deserving third place overall. Leon grinned happily.

The final battle was fought between the white RX-7 Batman and the Cefiro. It was a decisive encounter and both drivers gave it their all. High speed, big angle, massive smoke, vicious tyre-scream. It was everything a drift battle should be and the crowd loved it. Although it was close, it was the RX-7 that took the win and thus first place overall.

"You were right," Byron knuckled Leon's shoulder. "Pity they don't have a TAB here, eh?"

"Yeah, but by Murphy's law, if we'd put down money he wouldn't have won."

"Murphy's a prick," Byron agreed with a chuckle.

Leon and Byron chatted animatedly while the top three drivers performed their victory lap – each with a radiant bikini girl waving out of the passenger side window. As the Trueno rolled gently by on the track before the stand, Byron and Leon stopped talking and watched with interest. Her engine burbled easily and the bright sun gleamed on her polished red paintwork. Cam, the driver shook a fist out of the window in a cool salute and Leon smiled to himself – the guy had style.

"That's the chick I was talking about," Byron breathed and for the first time Leon looked at the girl that waved from the red Toyota. Wearing a white tank-top, she sat up on the door sill with her feet on the seat and holding on with one hand while waving with the other. Her satin black hair streamed out behind her and her teeth flashed brightly as she smiled. Even at that distance he could see the healthy tanned lustre of her skin and the excited spark in her eyes. Leon could not take his eyes off her. Right then he wouldn't have thought twice about trading places with Cam – who grinned his success up to the crowd with one amazing girl at his side. After the Trueno had disappeared into the pit lanes again, he was lost in daydreams and Byron had to repeat his question.

"Shall we boost?" he stood up. Some of those around them were also standing up to leave.

"I'd be keen to watch it out," Leon answered him. "Not like we've got anything else to do."

"True," Byron agreed and sat down again. "Alright then."

The girl was there again when the three champs of the day stood on the makeshift podium, clad in their racing overalls. Cam stood on the lowest step but somehow he seemed to have the strongest presence. His achievements were unexpected and remarkable, especially since he was a newcomer to the sport, while the other two had longer drifting histories and actual sponsorship. The black-haired girl handed out the trophies and followed up with a bottle of champagne for each. After they had popped the corks, the three drivers sprayed each other copiously, grinning from ear-to-ear. Still not satisfied, they turned on those around them, which included the event organisers, the commentator and the girl. They scattered, squawking protest like startled chickens. The girl wasn't quick enough and a full blast of spray hit her. Her squeal was audible even to Leon on the stand, but it was filled with humour as she fled. Leon found himself laughing in sympathy.

Beside him, Byron chuckled also. "She should come over here." Leon experienced a flare of resentment at his words, but he remained silent. "Well, that's pretty much it – you alright to get going now?" Byron stood up and smoothed his shirt down. Out on the podium the drifters were walking back to their race cars and the crew were retrieving the cones and dismantling the gazebo. The day was over. It was time for Leon to go back to retrieve the sensor and the Altezza.

"Yeah, alright, I want to go past the pits though before we go back."

"Why? They'll just be packing up," Byron's brow furrowed.

"I kinda–"

"So you're hooked on drifting now?" Byron interrupted with a chuckle and jabbed Leon in the side. "Just can't get enough, eh?"

"Nah, it's just that…" Leon tried again.

"Hey, maybe that bikini girl is still there," Byron interrupted him again and his eyes lit up. "We should totally go, come on."

"Uh, yeah," Leon stood up and they made their way down the stand. A couple of times along the way Leon tried to steer the conversation to the Altezza but then two other guys joined them who were also on their way to the pit lanes. Byron immediately got talking with them. Enthusiastically they discussed the 180SX's spin and the Trueno's unexpected comeback. Although he felt himself getting caught up in their conversation, Leon kept quiet.

Minutes later they reached the pit lanes, which were a hive of activity, as the drivers and crew prepared to leave also. Some were still working on their machines and changing tyres, others were loading their cars onto trailers and still others were simply rumbling their street-legal drift machines out of the pits to join the queue for the exit. Their companions left them and Leon and Byron continued on, working their way through the activity. Almost immediately Byron's trained eye fell on his favourite car type.

"Damn, that's quite a sweet 'Tez."

"Yeah," Leon agreed uncomfortably. He saw the two guys labouring around the Trueno, which stood, with its bonnet up, beside the Altezza.

"It's got the same body kit as mine... Crazy, same wheels too..." Byron read the licence plate and drew to a sudden halt. "What the..? It is mine! What's it doing here?"

"Um," Leon cleared his throat uncertainly. "That's kinda something I've been meaning to tell you," he started out.

"Been meaning to tell me?" Byron rounded on him.

"Here's our saviour." Leon was about to try and explain when Taz straightened up from his task and spotted them. "That sensor worked a treat. Thanks a heap man."

"No problem," Leon indicated Byron beside him. "But you should thank him – it's his Altezza."

"Yeah?" Taz turned to Byron, who nodded hesitantly. "Thanks man. Without you we wouldn't have got our car going again."

"Uh, okay." Byron's brow furrowed.

"Yeah, we're stoked as. I'd shake your hand but..." Taz indicated his oil-covered hands and grinned.

"That's all good," Byron's annoyance turned into a confused smile.

"I've got your CPS right here," Cam held the part carefully in a clean cloth. "I'll put it straight back in, okay?" Leon looked to Byron, who suddenly registered understanding.

"Yeah, thanks," he agreed readily.

"All good, just pop the bonnet." Byron unlocked the Altezza and pulled the bonnet release for him. They looked on as Cam reinstalled the sensor.

"Hey, we're going to a bar later to celebrate," Taz started out. "You two should come, we owe you a beer."

Leon hesitated. "We've actually already got plans."

"Oh, okay. Maybe you could squeeze in just a quick drink?" Taz pressed. "Come on, it's on us – we couldn't have done it without your help today."

"Well," still Leon hesitated, Taz was friendly enough, but Cam barely managed courtesy.

"We'll come," Byron agreed. "Where and what time?" he asked and Taz told them.

"Alright then," Leon nodded. "See ya tonight."

Later that evening, Byron picked Leon up. As they drove it started to drizzle, and by the time they arrived at the bar it was raining in earnest. Once parked, they hopped out and, with heads down and chins buried in their collars they scurried between parked cars towards the pub. As they neared the entrance, they passed by several large, beer-branded umbrellas. Two dark figures huddled beneath them, braving the weather to satisfy their addiction, visible through an orange glow, which momentarily brightened as they puffed on their cigarettes.

Shaking the droplets from their hair, they entered, to find the pub full to the brim and populated by a good mix of young and old. It was loud with everyone trying to make themselves heard over the music that blurted from the ceiling-mounted speakers. Prints and even some real paintings covered the wooden walls and depicted famous sporting heroes. The smell of beer, damp clothing and stale cigarettes was strong and

Leon wrinkled his nose in distaste. Looking around, Byron spotted Taz near the bar. "There they are." With Byron navigating through the press, they made their way across worn carpet.

"Hey guys, cool that you made it," Taz greeted them. "What's your poison?"

"No worries, we'll get ours," Leon declined politely.

"Nah man, you saved the day," Taz insisted. "I'm buying you a drink if you like it or not – for both of you."

"Alright," Leon wavered. "A coke then, thanks."

"Nothing stronger?"

"Coke's good."

"Okay," Taz nodded and turned to Byron. "And you?"

"I'll grab an Amstel," Byron was quick to take up the offer.

"Good choice," Taz approved. They went with him up to the bar, where Cam and a number of others were already standing in a small circle. He acknowledged them with a nod, but made no effort to break off his discussion with a heavy-set, brown-haired guy who had a very pale face and a closely trimmed goatee beard. Leon and Byron stood by idly and watched as Taz vied for the attention of a blonde behind the counter. Finally he had it and she leant close to him to catch his request. Taz turned back while she poured their drinks.

"You've been here before?" he addressed Leon.

"Nah," Leon answered loudly, to make himself heard.

"What do ya think?"

"It's pretty loud…"

"What?" Taz joked with a grin. "But yeah the big match is on tonight, that's why it's so busy… You into boxing?"

"Not really," Leon admitted.

"I don't go out of my way for it either," Taz agreed and assessed Byron. "What about you? You look like you'd be good at it."

"I rule," Byron nodded. "On the Playstation."

"Right on," Taz smiled and gave his attention back to the girl at the bar. He paid her and then handed Leon his coke and Byron his beer.

"Enjoy."

"Cheers." With all the noise it was difficult to talk normally and they turned to the others. Now that everybody had a drink, Cam addressed the small group in a loud voice.

"Thanks for coming – and of course for all the support."

"And to you two for bailing us out," Taz interrupted.

"Indeed," Cam acknowledged Leon and Byron. "From nearly dropping out, to third place," Cam smiled, "Not bad!"

"And that's only after one year in the sport," Taz pointed out. "Officially one year that is. I know you were doing burnouts and doughnuts as soon as you started driving."

"Just getting a little practice in," Cam grinned humbly. "But yeah, in the next comp we'll be going for the title I reckon."

"I'll drink to that," Taz raised his pint of lager and the others followed suit.

"You know, the next one's only three weeks away," the pale-faced guy pointed out.

"Yeah, we've got our work cut out for us," Cam agreed.

"It's back to the track on Saturday," Taz nodded.

"Yup, but right now its kick-back time. I think we've earned it." Cam briefly tipped his stubbie to the ceiling and looked around the circle. "Who's up for a game of pool?"

While the others made their way over to the pool table, Leon and Byron remained standing, clutching their drinks. Neither of them spoke as they sipped them. Leon hopped up on one of the bar stools and put his drink down on the counter in front of him. Byron leant against the bar beside him with his thumb hooked into his jeans pocket and his beer held protectively in his other hand.

"Shall we go over?"

"Probably should," Leon shrugged. "Not that fussed on pool though."

"Yeah, neither," Byron glanced across at the others. "How's the coke?"

"Bit flat... How's the beer?"

"Flat."

"Nice, so you like it here?" Leon asked finally.

"Love it, your friends are real friendly too," Byron muttered. He looked towards the pool table again. Suddenly he froze and drew in his breath. "Dude, she's here."

"Who?"

"The bikini girl, you see her?"

"No." Leon couldn't see above the mass of people.

"I'm gonna talk to her." A determined look came into Byron's eye. In one big gulp he drained the last of his beer, wiped his mouth and put the empty glass down on the counter. "But first, I need to take a leak."

In search for the bathroom, Byron left Leon sitting alone on the bar stool, hunched over the counter with his glass in front of him. The varnished hardwood surface shone with the reflection of the lights behind the counter. Around him the festivities were gaining in volume as the level of the drink sank and then was topped up again. Leon drank his coke and put the glass down again. The ice cubes clinked loudly, in tune with his sudden melancholy.

What was he doing here – in this bar, with these people? He didn't belong. He didn't share their enthusiasm for drinking, rugby nor drifting... Or did he? Leon thought of the day's events at the track, the modified cars, the smell of petrol, oil and tyre smoke. He thought of the crowd and the disembodied sound of the commentators. It had stirred up old memories in him and emotions that he thought he had overcome. He took a deep breath. The noise was beginning to give him a headache. He had to get out of here, but would Byron go with him, now that he was on the prowl? He tried to think of a suitable excuse.

"Are you always this quiet?" Leon shook himself out of his thoughts and looked up at the voice. A girl had stepped up to the bar beside him. She had long dark hair that flowed over her shoulder. Her lips held a gentle smile, but it was her eyes that captivated him, golden with an inner light. It was her, the girl that had driven the victory lap with Cam.

"I have my moments," it took Leon seconds to find his voice. He also smiled but it was self-mocking.

"Don't we all," she nodded seriously. "Now isn't the time though. Taz told me that without you they wouldn't be celebrating. Come on, let me get you another drink." She indicated his glass, in which the ice cubes were melting into a watery brown puddle. Leon hesitated, then shrugged, there was nothing waiting for him at home. "Okay, I'll have another coke then," he accepted and looked around for Byron.

"I'm sure I can handle that," the girl laughed easily and signalled to the bartender. She got his attention immediately. "A coke and another wine thanks."

"Sure, can I see some ID, please?"

"Is this ever going to stop?" She rolled her eyes at Leon. "I guess I should be flattered, at 21 I'm getting pretty old and crusty after all," Smiling ruefully, she handed her driver's licence to the barman.

"Nice photo," the barman smirked and gave it back.

"Thanks," She accepted it humorously and passed it to Leon spontaneously. "Here, while we're at it, why don't you have a laugh too?"

Leon stared at the thumbnail-sized mug-shot image of the girl before him. It depicted a gawky girl wearing glasses and braces, bangs and a long plait that snaked over her shoulder.

"That's you?"

"Pretty bad, huh?"

"So you wear contacts now, Lorna?" he read her name.

"Yup,"

"And I thought mine was bad, here…" Leon gave the card back to her. He took his own wallet from his pocket, flipped it open so the clear licence pocket was showing and handed it to her. She saw an unsmiling youth with closely clipped hair.

"Leon, you look like a criminal. How long did you have that buzz-cut for?" She was studying him. His jet black hair was longer now and fashionably cut. He wore it in an easy, messy style and she had to admit, he was pretty hot.

"Most of high school," Leon admitted.

"I like your hair now – it suits you better…" Her eyes dazzled him. Leon found it difficult not to stare at her. He looked away.

"All thanks to my fabulous conditioner," he spoke into his empty glass.

"So that's the secret," she laughed and Leon revelled in the unaffected and melodious sound. "But enough about hair. What about cars? Do you like them?"

"Not really…"

"You seem to know a bit about them… You fixed Cam's."

"That was just a fluke."

"Come on, from what Cam and Taz told me, you knew what the problem was within half a minute."

"Maybe, but the fact that they were running a 3S', the same engine as in Byron's Altezza was just lucky," Leon shrugged again and watched the bartender fill his coke.

"A 3S'?" Lorna raised an eyebrow. "So you do know your engines?"

"Hey Lorna, talking to our champ?" Leon looked up to find Taz standing behind them. "About cars are we? So what do you drive then?"

"I don't own a car."

"You serious?" Taz stared at him quizzically. And Leon nodded wordlessly.

"Why not – haven't had a chance to steal one?" Cam suddenly appeared at his elbow.

"Uh not exactly…" Leon frowned.

"What's that supposed to mean?" Lorna rounded on Cam.

"Just joking," He defended himself but turned back to Leon. "So have you ever drifted?"

"I've given it a go, I guess," Leon didn't meet his eyes.

"It didn't go so good? Well, hey, it's hardly easy. You should come and watch us practice on Saturday – you might learn a few things." There was a patronising tone to Cam's voice. Leon shrugged uncertainly before he heard Byron's icy voice behind him.

"I don't think he needs you to show him how to drift. I'd say his old man would've taught him some tricks you could only dream of."

"His old man?" Cam asked sceptically.

"Kaito Takahashi," Byron looked him squarely in the eyes.

"For real?" Taz stared at Leon, who still sat hunched over the counter. "You're joking right?" He turned back to Byron.

Byron hesitated. He saw his friend's hunched back and noticed his discomfort. He knew that Leon hated talking about his dad, and regretted his outburst. "Look, forget it," he spoke to Taz and Cam. "We should go, aye Leon?"

"Yeah," Leon agreed and stood up.

"Hey no way – you're the guests of honour," Lorna protested. "And you haven't even had your coke."

"Yeah, come on," Taz nudged him. "It's just started bucketing down outside."

"Thanks, but we'll get going," Leon replied flatly and avoided looking at Lorna; otherwise he would have seen the disappointment in her eyes. He found Cam standing in front of him, staring at him thoughtfully and blocking the way.

"Was your dad really Kaito Takahashi?"

"Does it matter?" Leon asked evenly. Cam stood a moment longer, staring at him with a fathomless expression. Leon couldn't step away from the bar, or at least not without rudely pushing past him.

"I guess it doesn't," Cam lowered his gaze and Leon noticed a sudden change in him. "Pity you're going, but thanks again for your help," he extended his hand. Leon shook it hesitantly.

"Don't worry about it."

"We'll be there from eleven," Cam offered. "In case you decide to come after all."

"Yeah, maybe," Leon answered dubiously and turned away to follow Byron.

"Don't forget your wallet," Lorna called him back. She hopped off her barstool and handed it to him.

"Oh, yeah," Leon had forgotten she still held it. "Thanks," their eyes met for an instant before he turned and made his escape towards the exit. As Leon and Byron stepped outside they were buffeted with cold and wet. It was as though a dam had burst in the sky. Byron hesitated under the awning, which jutted out from the doorway of the pub. "Make a break for it!"

Pulling their hoods up over their heads, they left the shelter of the pub and bolted across the car-park, trying to dodge the dark puddles as they ran. Just before they reached the Altezza, Byron hit the button on his remote and the car blipped and flashed its indicators in welcome. They pulled the doors open and dove inside – hurriedly slamming them shut again.

"Mad," Leon spoke in awe.

"That's rain alright," Byron agreed. For a moment they gazed out at the dark night, towards the fuzzy bar lights, blurry through the downpour. "You know," Byron suddenly rounded on him. "You're a sly little bastard."

"What?" Leon stared at him. "Where did that come from?"

"You know what I'm talking about. The girl – she was mine," Byron accused. "And you were chatting her up."

"I wasn't…" Leon stammered.

"Don't try to deny it," Byron shook his finger. "I saw you."

"Alright, look," Leon spoke adamantly. "I wasn't chatting her up. She came over and starting talking to me. And besides, I'm about the last person who knows how to chat up a girl."

"I suppose you're right there," Byron teased. "You suck with the ladies."

"Exactly," Leon smiled humbly. "So, are we happy now?"

"No. You think she likes you?"

"I doubt it," Leon thought back on those stunning honey-coloured eyes. "But..."

"But?"

"Well, you're right, she's attractive..."

"Attractive?" Byron exclaimed. "That has to be the understatement of the year. Man, even divine doesn't begin to describe her."

"If you say so..."

"So you like her right?"

"I guess so," Leon admitted cautiously.

"Wow, that's about the first time I've heard you confess to liking a girl," Byron grinned broadly. "Alright then, I'll let you have her."

"Thanks, that's real generous," Leon smiled with sarcasm and changed the topic. "So are we just going to sit here in the rain or what?"

"You still want to go out?"

"Not really, not in this weather."

"Let's just head to my place then, fire up the Playstation and grab a feed," Byron suggested and started the car.

"Yeah, okay," Leon agreed.

Byron was renting a two-bedroom townhouse and had it cram-packed with electronic entertainment. When he wasn't working at his cushy music-store job, or sleeping, eating or driving the Altezza, there was a high probability that he was sitting on his couch with his Playstation controller in-hand, gazing intently at his widescreen TV. Unfortunately for Leon, this also meant he was good – very good. They had been playing the same shoot-em-up game for over an hour now and Leon was getting painfully humiliated. It didn't help that he was having trouble concentrating.

"Sorry, I really can't be stuffed with this anymore." Leon laid his controller aside with a sigh. "Got anything else to do?"

"Well," Byron started out. He had rarely seen Leon in such a sombre mood. "I do have some new movies..."

"Any action? I need something to take my mind off..."

"Off what?" Byron prodded.

"Lorna," Leon confessed.

"I was wondering why you've been playing like such a blouse," Byron grinned. "So you've totally fallen for her, huh?! There's only one cure for that."

"And that is?"

"Get hideously drunk..." Byron joked but then became serious when he realised that Leon wasn't smiling. "Alright, look, I've got just the flick for you." He went over to the large shelf that was holding his abundant movie collection. He retrieved the case he was looking for and passed it to Leon. "This is like max-gore-factor-ten and takes every other horror movie I've seen to school. If this doesn't take your mind off her then I don't know what will."

"If you say so," Leon eyeballed the cover dubiously. "Bring it on then."

They put the movie on and sat back comfortably. Byron hadn't lied. For the next hour and a half only horror, blood and guts filled Leon's mind.

"That was full on," Leon breathed when the credits rolled.

"Yeah, told ya," Byron seemed unaffected by what he had just witnessed. He yawned loudly and checked the time. "It's pretty late. Did you still want a ride home?"

"That'd be good," Leon nodded. "Got an early start tomorrow – as always."

"Must say, I so don't envy you," Byron shook his head. "Getting up at six to drive a forklift in a freezer."

"5.30," Leon corrected him with a sigh. "But it's a job."

"A crap job."

"It pays alright," Leon tried to convince himself.

"Yeah, if you do overtime."

"If I do overtime," Leon agreed.

"You should stop procrastinating and find something else."

"Like what? It's not like you're going to get me a job at the music store…"

"They're not hiring anyone at the moment," Byron shook his head. "But there are plenty of other good jobs out there."

"I guess," Leon shrugged and pushed himself out of his armchair. "Cool if we go now?"

Byron hesitated and then nodded. "Yeah, sure," he got up off the couch and grabbed his wallet and keys. Leon followed him through to the internal garage.

"Could catch up on Wednesday maybe," Byron suggested as he pulled up outside Leon's house.

"I'll give you a call," Leon promised.

"Have a good week aye."

"You too," Leon got out and bolted through the rain to the front door. Being careful not to wake his mum and sister, he quietly let himself in and went up the stairs to his room. Tired as he was, sleep didn't come quickly. Lying in bed, his thoughts were in turmoil, filled with speeding drift cars, his dad and Cam's rude behaviour at the pub. What was his problem? Should he meet them at the track on Saturday? Would Lorna be there? Was there any chance that she might actually like him? With his questions unanswered, he eventually fell asleep.

It was past 2am now and the persistent rain thudded onto the roof of the glossy, black Mazda. They drove slowly through empty streets, their dipped headlights illuminating the way and reflecting off wet tarmac. With the cloud covering, it was a dark night, and the rain muffled all sounds so that it was ominously quiet, apart from the gentle purr of the engine and the periodic whirr of the windscreen wipers. A yellow sign indicating a narrow side-street crept towards them.

"This one?" Andy asked.

"One more," Markus answered quietly, trying to sound as relaxed as he could. Normally he would be relishing the excitement, but today he was tense. As they rolled on past the sign and past dark houses, Markus tested his ankle by pressing his foot down against the floor of the car. He grimaced. It still hurt. He shouldn't be doing this. Why had he let Andy convince him to go anyway? They reached the end of the block and Andy drove down a dark, tree-lined street.

"There she is," Andy whispered, interrupting his thoughts. In front of them, parked against the kerb and hugging the ground on super-low suspension and massively wide drift rims, rested a heavily tinted Nissan Laurel. A big-bore exhaust protruded from under her aftermarket rear bumper, which flowed out into a full body kit.

Andy rolled past the Nissan and stopped. He engaged reverse and turned to look over his shoulder. Before backing up, he stole a glimpse at the Nissan. Her nose was illuminated in his reversing lights. A massive intercooler nestled in her front bumper and her hooded headlights made the high-spec drift machine look downright aggressive. To think that she initially came out of the factory as a boring luxury sedan. Now an insane machine, Andy would have dearly loved to take her for a test drive, but that was not what they were here for.

Andy pushed his thoughts aside and backed the Mazda up, against the kerb directly in front of the Laurel. Switching off, he left the key in the ignition. With the engine and lights off, the night was dark and silent with just the continuing thud of rain. Andy's voice sounded unnecessarily loud. "Let's go."

Markus pushed his misgivings aside and opened his door. From there they were all business. They had done this many times before. Only on this night, due to Markus' ankle, the plan had been revised slightly. Armed with his tools, Andy sprinted to the Laurel. Ducking down by the first three-piece 17-inch alloy wheel, he immediately set to work. Carrying a small hydraulic jack and four wooden blocks, Markus knelt down beside him and ran the jack noiselessly under the low body of the car.

"Told ya he left the races with a new set of rubber," Andy hissed, as his fingers busily tried several different locknut keys from a pack at his feet. With eight different keys, they hadn't encountered a locknut they couldn't remove. "She's a three," Andy whispered triumphantly and clicked the wheel brace into the back of the locknut key. He strained for a moment. The wheel brace turned and Andy began on the next nut.

As soon as he had loosened the last nut, Markus cranked the jack frantically and raised the car high enough to push one of the wooden blocks under the car. Meanwhile, Andy ran to the next wheel and began loosening the nuts. Working with haste, Markus undid all five nuts fully, let them drop to clink away on the road, and then lowered the jack so that the car sank onto the waiting block. Leaving the wheel hanging askew, he picked up the jack and moved as quickly as he could to the next mag, which Andy had now loosened.

In this fashion they quickly worked their way around the car. Once Andy had loosened the last nut, he went to the first wheel again, lifted it clear from its hub and ran with it to the waiting Mazda. There he wrenched the rear hatch open and dropped the wheel into the back, before returning for the second wheel. Markus finished loosening the last wheel. He lowered the jack and drew it out from under the car.

Leaving the jack lying on the road, Markus gritted his teeth and pulled the last wheel from its hub before making for the Mazda. Andy was close behind, carrying the third mag, but in his rush, he didn't see the jack. He kicked it and it fell over with a loud clatter. Markus swung around in shock and his full weight came on his ankle. Pain flared and he leaned back awkwardly. Holding the wheel one-handed, he instinctively reached out to steady himself against the body of the Nissan.

"Markus, no!" Andy's warning came too late as the whole car began to move on its wooden blocks, teetering on the verge of balance. Andy held his breath, watching in horror as the car tilted and then the blocks folded beneath it. It seemed to happen in slow motion, but when its empty metal hubs hit the unforgiving tarseal with a resounding clang the night was all lights and shrieking noise. The Laurel's alarm had finally had enough, blaring into the night and flashing indicators.

Andy swore and leapt into action. Heaving his wheel into the Mazda, he ran back and grabbed his friend, who still lugged the last rim, and pushed him forwards. He scooped up the jack, the pack of locknut keys and the wheel brace and ran to deposit it all on top of the wheels. Markus stood waiting and immediately slammed the back hatch closed. The alarm continued to shrill into the night and they could hear a commotion coming from the house now.

Andy ran to the driver's door, yanked it open, leapt into the seat, pulled the door closed, lowered the clutch and turned the key, all in one continuous motion. The engine sparked instantly and revved high as he hit the gas. The moment that Markus was in, Andy dropped the clutch. The front wheels spun freely for a second, encouraged by the wet, before they gripped and the Mazda pulled forwards.

"Look out!" Beside him, Markus pointed frantically ahead into the night. Andy flung the wheel over, away from the kerb to avoid rear-ending another vehicle that was parked in front of them. He steered back to correct and shifted to second gear, pushing the underpowered wagon hard down the dark, sodden street. He still had the lights off, but could just make out the smudgy blurs of parked cars on either side of the street. The window wipers only marginally assisted his visibility. There was a crunch and crash as he came too close to one of the cars. Andy jerked the wheel back. "What was that?"

They suddenly came rocketing out of the darkened street, overshooting the stop sign, straight into a lit-up intersection. Andy reacted instantly, taking first his foot off the gas and braking gently, before nudging the wheel left and then bringing it back into the direction of the slide. The Mazda's tail stepped out, aided by the weight of the wheels in the back, and they slid smoothly across the wet intersection. Once across, Andy heel-and-toe downshifted and let the front-wheel-drive pull them straight.

"Front-wheel drifter," Andy laughed and switched the headlights on. "Wagon-style even."

"Not too shabby," Markus grudgingly acknowledged. "Good thing that the intersection was empty..."

"True," Andy grinned. "Don't want to have to pay for another panel job and re-spray on one of your cars... Must be about time for a brew though, eh?"

"We've earned it," Markus opened the glove-box and pulled out two cans of beer. The first can cracked with a hiss. "Not the coldest," he handed it to Andy and opened the other.

"It'll do." Andy accepted it. "To drinking and drifting."

"Cheers," Markus took a deep draft.

"And here's to not being a clutz on the next job," Andy raised the can again.

"Come on, I gave you an excuse to get sideways. What're you crying about?"

"Dude, I nearly wet myself when that alarm went off."

"You always were bit of a wuss," Markus jibed. "But you're right, that was my bad," he became serious. "Next time, if one of us is crippled, we don't go out."

"Probably shouldn't yeah..." They were approaching another intersection now and out of habit Andy checked his mirrors for other traffic. "Oh, that's what the crash was – we're missing a wing mirror."

"Eh?" Markus leaned over in his seat. There was a moment of silence and then both of them were laughing.

"Four new tyres and a set of deep-dish rims," Andy started, "For a mirror? I think we're still doing okay."

"Yeah, I think we can handle that," Markus chuckled. "I'm guessing the Laurel guy won't be too chuffed though."

"Teach him to park it on the street." Andy had no sympathy. "At least we've got some new tread to play with now." The rate that Markus and Andy went through tyres was unreal. Even a good tyre smoked away quickly when sliding on rough tarmac. It was expensive fun, made even more enjoyable with somebody else paying for it. They didn't mind taking a few extra risks. On the contrary, they relished it. Driving on, they finished their beers and lit up cigarettes.

Sometime later, Andy pulled into his driveway and backed the wagon up to the garage. Quickly they unloaded the wheels in darkness and stacked them at the back of the garage, behind the stranded Cefiro.

"Just as well you keep this garage clean, I would've tripped over something in mine by now," Markus grinned at Andy in the gloom.

"Bloody right," he grumbled. "Finding your tools helps too. Maybe you should try it."

"Uh huh, how long have you been working on this now?" Markus slapped the bonnet of the Cefiro.

"Not that long," Andy dismissed. "And I've been busy…"

"Right," Markus nodded, hiding his smile. He followed Andy outside.

"You off now?"

"I've got work in like four hours – so yeah."

"You're alright to drive?" Andy locked the garage again.

"Of course man, just not drift in a comp is all," Markus' dark shape answered.

"Okay. I might still borrow the Mazda later in the week."

"No probs, just shout out when."

BEEP, BEEP, BEEP… The alarm clock yanked Leon awake. Switching it off, he lay a minute longer, reluctant to relinquish his warm bed, but then he pushed his duvet aside with a sigh and rolled out. He got dressed quickly, pulling on a pair of thermal long-johns and thick woollen socks before he put on jogging pants and a jersey. Still groggy with sleep, he trundled through to the bathroom. He couldn't shower in the mornings, in case his hair didn't dry properly before he got in the freezer. Instead, he splashed some water on his face and towelled it dry. He looked at his reflection in the mirror. His eyes were still half-closed with sleep and his hair stuck out at odd angles. He scowled, but left it. He was only going to work after all.

Taking care not to wake his mum and sister, he hurried downstairs to the kitchen and found the light switch. Inhaling a glass of juice and a piece of toast, he was ready to go. At the front door he pulled on his shoes and stepped outside. It was slowly getting light now, but the morning was cold, overcast and drizzling. He should get his raincoat, but it was upstairs in his room and he had already received two warnings for being late. Reaching a decision, he pulled the door closed behind him and retrieved his bike from the garage. Clipping his helmet on, he set off, peddling fiercely down the street.

Leon reached work several minutes late and raced through the open gates. Ahead of him, the massive cool store warehouse dominated the site. He hated to think how many bitter cold hours of his life he had spent in that building. It contained rows upon rows with racks upon racks of frozen goods, most of them destined for export. Three large transporter trucks were parked outside its entrance and several forklifts were swarming around them, busily offloading large, shrink-wrapped pallets. His colleagues were already at it. Leon slotted his bike into the rack, locked it, and went over to the office to sign in.

"Slept in again?" his boss greeted him grimly as he entered. He was short and heavy-set, with a generous gut and thick black hair that curled around his ears. Leon believed he was in his early forties. What he lacked in height, he made up for in weight.

"Hardly," Leon muttered and scribbled his entry in the roster.

"You know, we can find other people to drive a forklift too," his boss persisted.

"I'll make it up, I always do," Leon sidestepped any confrontation and left the office before his boss could push the issue further. He knew that his boss wouldn't fire him for being a bit late. Leon was the best driver he had; his forklift was an extension of his own body.

In the changing room Leon stepped into his thermal-lined overalls, swapped his shoes for steel-capped boots, and pulled on chunky gloves and a woollen hat. Still not satisfied, he wrapped a long woollen scarf around his neck. Dressed to make an Eskimo jealous, he went out to his forklift. It stood waiting for him where he had parked it on Friday, plugged into the wall. Leon unplugged it and climbed up into the seat, his hands falling naturally on the controls. He thought back to his conversation with Byron. There was no doubt, it was a crap job, but he had to admit, he enjoyed driving his forklift. Perhaps that was what kept him here? His forklift?

"Stop dreaming," his boss's voice spoke beside him. "There's a truck waiting. Here's the pick-list." He handed Leon a notepad. "Now get to work." He strode away.

Leon's breath condensed in a thick vapour cloud around him as he drove into the freezer. At an arctic -22 degrees his nose started to run almost immediately. Initially he had wiped it, but the constant wiping had quickly rubbed it red and raw so now he left it and instead tried to focus on the job. To make up his lost time, he grossly over-stacked his pellets and also spurned the health and safety regulations, staying in the freezer longer than he was supposed to. Two hours later, Leon had picked all the stock he needed, but he was feeling the cold. It was deep in his bones. His hands and toes were almost numb, but his knees were worse. Sitting on his forklift, they were constantly pressed tightly against the material of his overalls and had the thinnest layer of thermal insulation. Shivering, and his teeth chattering, he drove to the exit. The gloomy, raining day outside was a welcoming sight.

He parked his forklift by the *smoko* room and peeled off his hat, gloves and scarf. Inside, he could hear several of his workmates chatting, already enjoying a hot drink. Before he joined them, he wanted to clean himself up. In the bathroom, Leon stared in the mirror. As usual, the snot had frozen on his upper lip and there were tiny icicles around his mouth and eyes. "You are right Byron; screw this for a joke." He turned the hot tap on and the water stung painfully as it ran over his hands, thawing them out, and even more as he washed his face. Feeling somewhat refreshed, Leon went through to the warm *smoko* room. He poured himself a steaming cup of coffee and drank it thankfully while chatting to one of the other workers, but too quickly the break was up and it was time to get to work again.

"Back to Antarctica," his co-worker spoke wryly as he followed the others outside.

Alone in the *smoko* room, Leon sat a bit longer. Sipping his drink, his thoughts wandered. He thought of Lorna. He wondered what she did, where she worked... He thought of the drifters and again remembered the excitement that he had experienced at the race track... Outside, the rumble of a diesel engine interrupted his thoughts. Another truck had arrived. With a sigh, Leon finished his coffee and returned to his forklift. Stalling, he made a show of pulling his hat and gloves back on and checking the battery charge. He still had two hours before he needed to switch to the backup forklift. "Alrighty then..." Lacking any further excuses, Leon clambered on and headed for the freezer.

To take his mind off the polar discomfort he drove like a madman, lifting more weight than the machine could actually handle and, with his back wheels off the ground, he pushed the gigantic metal racks across the concrete floor to get access to the items behind them. His colleagues didn't trust themselves to do it, and made two trips to his one. He got more work done, but also took greater risks. Once again he thought of Lorna and drifting and his driving became even more crazy than usual. As he was going back to fetch his next load, he almost collided with another forklift, but managed to evade at the last minute.

"Leon, you nutcase, watch out!"

"Sorry," Leon waved apologetically as he flew past. Stuff it, everything was insured anyway.

By lunchtime he was numb again and his face covered in more icicles. He couldn't believe how good it was to get out of the chiller and into the warm *smoko* room. But all too soon, the clock signalled his demise and he had to force himself out of the warmth. By now his forklift battery was flat and he had to change to the *Donkey*, a smaller one with less power. Driving the *Donkey* was no fun at all and the rest of the afternoon dragged by slowly. He longed for his next break and when it came, getting back to work afterwards was harder than ever. He knew it was going to be a long week.

On Wednesday Byron called Leon at work and cancelled their plans to meet up, complaining of a sore throat and headache.

He thought it was better to meet up on Friday instead. Disappointed, Leon also stayed home that evening and just blobbed in front of the TV. Trying to find something good, he flicked through the channels and discovered that Top Gear was on. The show had never really captured his interest, but now he couldn't take his eyes off the supercars that graced the screen. The programme ended, leaving him longing for more, but with nothing else on TV to capture his interest, he decided to go to bed, knowing he would have to get up again early.

The next morning Leon was late once again. His boss's disapproval rang loudly in his ears when he made it through the door. As hour after frozen hour crawled by he realised that he actually hated his job and he yearned for the weekend. Then finally it was Friday afternoon and his working week was over. Not sticking around for the usual work-drinks, Leon rode home where he showered and changed. He was in the kitchen, searching the cupboards for a snack when he heard a car horn outside. Byron had arrived punctually as promised. Giving up his search, Leon went outside to meet his friend.

"Hey, how's it?" Leon greeted him.

"All good. How was your week?"

"Average," Leon admitted.

"Hmmm," Byron gave him a long look. "You should really find a new job."

"Yeah," Leon nodded and bit his thumb nail. "Anyway, what're we up to?"

"Not sure," Byron looked up through his sunroof, "It's supposed to rain again."

"Yeah, looks like it could."

"You hungry?" Byron asked, but before Leon could reply he continued. "I know I am. Let's go get some eats."

They made their way to the local Burger King drive-through and joined the queue. Once they had bought their burgers, they drove on, heading to one of the main streets where car enthusiasts frequently gathered to show-off their rides. Byron found an empty park along the street and pulled into it. Switching off the engine and lights, he left the music on low. They chatted while they ate and watched the sweet cars roll slowly by. Although it was still early in the evening, tunes thumped from most of them and the overall mood felt festive. The week had ended, it was time to celebrate.

"Check this beast out," Byron pointed at his rear-view mirror with a chip. A moment later an impressive machine appeared from behind them. Wearing a full Veilside body kit, the surrounding street lights played upon her lush paintwork, glittering gold. Leon caught a quick glimpse of a sullen black vented carbon-fibre bonnet and matching black 19-inch alloys and then she had thudded past.

"That's pretty cool," Leon paused thoughtfully, watching the taillights disappear. "My uncle had one of those…"

"He had a Supra like that?" Byron stopped chewing.

"Yeah, he used to drift it," Leon nodded. "He's actually supposed to be coming to visit on Saturday."

"What, tomorrow?"

"Yeah, wow, it is tomorrow," Leon surprised himself.

"You so have to let me meet him," Byron insisted and continued eating.

"Yeah, if you want," Leon shrugged.

"'Course I want. It's not often you get to meet one of the old-school Japanese drifters," Byron squeezed the last of his burger into his mouth and continued speaking around it. "You know, I still can't believe your dad and uncle used to drift. I wish mine did."

"Yeah, well, I wish they hadn't," Leon's spoke quietly and looked away. "Then at least Dad might still be around…"

Byron went quiet and looked across at his friend speculatively. "You don't know that," he said finally.

"That's why I said: *might*," Leon shot back. "Anyway, I don't really want to talk about it aye…"

Byron nodded and turned away. In silence they watched another car crawl past, this time a Nissan GTR painted a stunning metallic blue and rolling on massive chrome wheels.

"That's pretty tidy, huh," Byron spoke cautiously.

"Yeah…"

"So you're not at all fussed not having your own car?"

"Not when I see your fuel bill…" Leon shrugged but, as he watched yet another modified car cruise past, heading in the opposite direction, he had to admit that driving a car of that calibre would certainly be fun.

"Yeah, it's robbery," Byron ate his last potato chip, before scrunching his rubbish into a ball and dropping it out of his open window. "I doubt it'll get any cheaper though," he grimaced and put his window back up.

Leon frowned with his burger halfway to his mouth. "What did you just do?" he stared at Byron.

"Huh?" Byron looked back at him with bemusement.

"Did you just throw your rubbish out the window?"

"Yeah, so?" Byron frowned.

"The road isn't a rubbish bin," Leon spoke forcefully.

"Yeah, so – everybody else does," Byron shrugged.

"So? If everybody else drove Ladas would you?"

"No, but that's hardly the same thing…"

"Maybe not, but it's not bloody cool, so go pick it up," Leon still hadn't taken another bite from his burger, but now Byron stared at him. Then his eyes narrowed.

"Make me."

Abruptly Leon put his burger on the dash, pushed the door open and got out. He walked around to Byron's side, picked up the pieces of rubbish, which had come apart, and stomped back. He dropped the offending rubbish on the floor of the car and sat down.

"Watch the carpet dude," Byron protested.

"Huh?" Leon picked up his burger again and continued eating.

"You just chucked rubbish on my carpet," Byron stared down at it in dismay. "You're gonna get stains on it, man!"

"Yeah, so?" Leon raised an eyebrow.

"At least put it in a plastic bag," Byron fretted.

"Okay, sure," Leon nodded and picked the bits of the floor, stuffing them into the bag that Byron handed him.

"Sure you didn't get any on the mat?" he asked.

"It's fine."

"Okay, good," Byron was relieved.

They were both still while Leon finished eating. Byron wasn't usually this quiet for so long.

"Look, sorry," Leon broke the silence at last. "That was a pretty rude thing to do..." he paused and then continued in a subdued voice. "I guess talking about my dad still gets to me..."

"It's all good," Byron understood. "You know, you do have a point. I don't like seeing all that trash lying around either."

"It's pretty gross," Leon nodded and yawned suddenly. "So what's the plan now?"

"It's only like 8pm and you're yawning already?"

"Yeah I'm shattered," Leon nodded seriously. "My job's killing me, I'm so over it."

"You know..."

"Don't start," Leon stalled Byron's words.

"Alright, alright, I won't tell you again that I think your job stinks," Byron held up his hands defensively with a smile. "But yeah, I'm still feeling a bit under the weather too, so why don't we just be lame and go to the movies? I heard there's a new action flick that's got some mean stunts in it."

"I could handle that..." Leon agreed.

Leon awoke early the next morning with the sun pouring into his bedroom window. He had forgotten to draw the curtains. He lay there, huddled under his warm duvet, wondering what had woken him, but appreciating the fact that he did not have to get up. A gentle knock sounded on his bedroom door.

"Leon?" his sister's voice asked through the door.

"What?" Leon resented the intrusion.

"Mummy told me to wake you."

"Why? It's Saturday."

"Auntie and Uncle are coming today… You have to clean your room."

"Tidy my room?" Leon's voice came out grumpily.

"And go shopping," his sister said. "Can I come in?"

"Yeah, okay,"

"Are you mad at me?" His sister's eyes were big as she approached his bed timidly.

"No, of course not Tink," Leon used her nickname and smiled at her.

"I'm taller than you!" From where he lay, Tamsin's eyes were barely higher than his own. She must be nearly six soon, Leon thought.

"You sure are," Leon smiled fondly at her. "But not now," he sat up in bed.

"No," she dragged his study chair around to face his bed and hopped up on the seat. "Now I am again!" She exposed the gap in her front teeth as she beamed back at him, a twinkle in her dark eyes. To Leon, they were his dad's eyes.

"True – hey Tink, are you excited about Uncle Daisuke and Auntie Noriko coming?" His sister shrugged uncertainly.

"Are they nice?"

"Definitely," Leon nodded, "They're very nice." He remembered his uncle well. Leon's dad had been very close to his younger brother. They had often raced together and Daisuke always had his car repaired and tuned in their garage. Leon himself had helped work on it once. Daisuke and Auntie

Noriko had often come for dinner. "Yes, I think you'll like them heaps."

"Will they bring presents?" Tamsin asked innocently.

"Ah, that's what you wanted to ask me all along isn't it, about presents?" Leon laughed and jumped out of bed. He picked her up off the chair and lifted her high.

"Put me down, put me down!" she squealed, all the while giggling hysterically. Leon lowered her. "No! Higher, higher!"

"Make up your mind," Leon lifted her higher and flew her around the room, playing aeroplane. He almost tripped on a pile of clothing strewn untidily on the carpeted floor. It sobered him and he lowered her back to the floor. "Off with you, you little devil." She scampered away and Leon was left standing alone in his messy room.

"First a clean room..?" he looked around and groaned. "I may as well get it over and done with..."

"Hi Leon," his mum greeted him absentmindedly, as he traipsed down the steps, dressed in t-shirt, shorts and flip flops, suitable for the warm day.

"Morning." She had her back to him and was busy cleaning the kitchen floor with a broom and dustpan. Her long blonde hair was tied up, out of the way, in a bun. "Getting ready for the relatives?"

"Trying," his mum answered without looking up.

"Let me know if I can help," Leon offered and stepped around her to retrieve a bowl for his cereal from the cupboard.

"That would be good. I still have a lot of housework to do and I also want to bake a cake." His mum seemed stressed. "We're out of gas for the stove, and there are a few ingredients I don't have."

"Sure, no problem," Leon rummaged in the drawer for a spoon. There were none. He tried the dishwasher. "What do you need?"

"I've written a short list, it's on the bench," his mum replied. The dishwasher was full, but the dishes were still dirty. Leon checked the powder tray. It held fresh powder.

"Mum, the dishwasher works a lot better if you turn it on." Leon closed the dishwasher door again and switched it on.

"Oh, I completely forgot," his mum straightened, holding the dustpan in one hand. With the other she smoothed away a loose strand of hair from her forehead. "I must be getting old."

"Never," Leon replied with a wink and coaxed a smile out of her. But it was true, she wasn't even forty yet and apart from some slight creases at the edges of her green eyes, she still looked very youthful. "You shouldn't stress yourself so much though. Uncle Daisuke and Auntie Noriko wouldn't want that."

"You're right," his mum nodded. "I just want the house to be tidy, but the more I clean the more I seem to find that still needs cleaning."

"I'll help," Leon put aside the bowl and took the dustpan from her hand. "I'll finish the kitchen. When do you want those groceries by?"

"Before noon would be good, thanks Leon." His mum handed him her car keys. "You can take the car – for the gas."

"Oh," Leon was surprised. Since his dad's accident and returning to New Zealand, he had rarely been allowed to drive, and never by himself. He'd got his licence by his own initiative, paying for several driving lessons and employing a driving school vehicle for his tests.

"Don't forget to take the list and the empty gas bottle, will you," his mum reminded him and left the kitchen.

Leon drove slowly. He made his way to the nearby supermarket and bought the ingredients his mum had asked for, before heading to the petrol station where he had the gas bottle filled. Having completed his tasks, he sat thoughtfully in his seat. Should he return home already? He still had ample time to spare. His mum didn't need the gas or the cake ingredients for another couple of hours. He remembered Cam's invitation to meet up at the raceway. Cam had mentioned something about 11.00am so they were unlikely to be there yet. But maybe they were out early? Perhaps Lorna would even be there. The thought of seeing her again compelled him, but what about Byron? Leon hesitated. He didn't really have time to pick him up as well. I'll just drive down and check, it's not that far, and if they're not there I'll turn around and go back home, Leon thought to himself and started the car.

The gates to the raceway were open and he drove through, heading down to the pits. He was welcomed by the sound of a screaming engine and squealing tyres. Leon parked outside the pits and got out. From a distance, he saw that there were already a number of people at work in the pits, but he couldn't spot Cam or Taz. He turned to the *brap brap brap* of a rotary engine. A white Batman RX-7 running on heavily lowered suspension and decked out in a full wide-body kit, jolted down the road towards him. It slowed when it reached him. "That's a pretty sick ride you've got there – you planning on drifting that?" The blond-haired driver laughed at Leon out of his open window. It was Simon, the racer that had won the competition the day before. Leon turned and glanced at his family sedan and its embarrassingly high factory stance. He shook his head.

"Just waiting for some others…"

"Okay, but if you change your mind, give me a shout," Simon grinned, "I'd be keen to watch, just for a laugh."

Leon gazed after Simon as he rolled the Batty into the pits, before following on foot. The pits weren't nearly as busy as they had been during the competition. It was easy to make out the individual cars and teams that worked on them. Cam, Taz and the Trueno were nowhere to be seen. He was too early. Looking around, Leon wondered what to do. He didn't know anybody and he felt he didn't fit in. Awkwardly he stood there, fidgeting. Should he wait? It was 10.20am. 40 minutes would be ages. Stuff that.

He wandered back to the Laurel, but rather than getting in, he stopped two metres in front of it and eyed it over critically. It rested way too high on spongy factory springs, that was immediately obvious and the 15-inch factory alloy wheels sported far too much rubber. Yet, it was rear-wheel-drive, and the two-litre engine did have a bit of power. Leon dismissed his thoughts. It was his mum's car – he couldn't take it on the track. Then he frowned. The back tyre had gone flat.

With a sigh, Leon opened the boot and lifted out the spare tyre. He found the jack but the tools were missing. A quick search revealed nothing. Frustrated, he straightened from the boot and looked around. How would he get the wheel off? His gaze went down the road towards the entrance and then turned towards the pits. He had no choice. Quickly he went back to the pits and spotted Simon's RX-7. As he neared, he saw Simon working at the back of the car with another drifter helping him. They had the wide mag wheel off and appeared to be adjusting the suspension.

"Oh, it's you again," Simon glanced up as he approached. "What's up?"

"I've got a flat tyre," Leon said hesitantly. "And was wondering if you had a wheel brace."

Simon looked at him for a second. "Yeah sure. Dan, can you give it to him."

"Here ya go," the other drifter handed it to Leon. "Don't be too long though, we need it for the other side."

"I won't," Leon was already jogging away. He made it back to the Laurel and got to work, first loosening the nuts and then turning the jack furiously. The wheel came off, the spare went on and he lowered the car again. Leon put the flat tyre into the boot and secured it, then replaced the jack. He hurried back to Simon.

"That was quick," Simon straightened up. "Got it sorted?"

"Yeah, thanks," Leon passed the wheel brace to him and hesitated. "Hey, were you serious about me going for a drift?"

"Nah," Simon chuckled. "I was just messing with ya. She wouldn't handle it. The suspension is way too saggy."

"Yeah you're probably right, I've still got forty minutes to kill though, so I thought I could give it a go," Leon tried to sound casual.

"Dude, I'd be worried I'd end up killing myself in that car."

"Don't be, it won't be you in there," Leon forced a laugh.

"You really are serious," Simon looked at Leon dubiously. "Have you even paid?"

"How much is it?" Leon shook his head.

"And I suppose you don't have a helmet or fire extinguisher either?"

"No, do I need those?"

The racer looked at Leon in contemplation, before reaching a decision. "Tell you what, even though I think it's a retarded idea, if you really want to, I'll let you borrow my helmet and extinguisher and take my first run."

"For real?" Leon asked, it seemed too good to be true.

"Yeah, why not, I still have a bit of work to do anyway."

"What about money?"

"I know the guys here – if I tell them you're just taking one run that should be okay..." Simon scratched his chin. "So?"

"I'd be keen as."

"You're crazy," Simon shook his head. "But life's more fun that way... What's your name?"

"Leon."

"Simon," the racer extended his hand.

"I know – I watched you race yesterday," Leon shook it.

"So you really think you can drift that Laurel?" Simon raised an eyebrow.

"I'd take you to school."

"I'd like to see that," Simon laughed and then became serious. "Alright, just don't come back crying to me later."

"Deal."

"Okay, go get it then. I'll speak to the guys now. Cool?"

"Cool," Leon agreed and watched as Simon strode away, before he returned to the Laurel, got in and put his hands on the steering wheel. Many thoughts raced through his head. What are you doing? This is madness! Taking a deep breath, he pushed his sudden doubts aside and started the car. But his misgivings returned in full as he entered the pits again – the realm of modified cars, adjustable suspension, large wide alloy wheels, body kits, intercoolers and turbos running high boost. His car stood out like a donkey in a racing stable. Many of the drivers and crew members stopped their tasks to stare at him with amusement and disbelief. Sitting a little lower in his seat, Leon continued past them to Simon's RX7. He pulled into the space beside it and waited.

"I spoke to them," Simon suddenly appeared at his window. "You've got the green light."

"Uh, cool, when can I go?"

"The next run already," Simon read his expression. "If you still want to..?"

"Of course," Leon answered forcefully.

"Alright, stay put," Simon returned a moment later and opened Leon's door. "Here." He handed Leon a black helmet and helped him put it on and fasten the strap. Then he went around and opened the passenger door. "Hmmm, there's no mount for the extinguisher so I'll wedge it under the passenger seat. Should be tight enough to stop it rattling around – but you can still pull it out if you need to – see," Simon demonstrated.

"Okay," Leon nodded awkwardly. The big, full-face helmet felt heavy on his shoulders. Suddenly he became aware of several others. They had come over and looked on, prodding each other and chuckling.

"Look at this mental!"

"Is this some sort of joke, Si?"

"He's actually gonna try and drift in that?"

"See it's not just me who thinks you're crazy," Simon grinned broadly.

"You only live once," Leon shrugged, trying to ignore the mockery.

"So they say," Simon mused. "But that's all the more reason not to die young…" He cast his eyes around the cabin of the Laurel thoughtfully. "You got anything else in here that might rattle around and distract you?"

"Don't think so," Leon shook his head, but then remembered the items in the boot. "Oh, yeah…" he got out and went to the back of the car. "Can I leave these here?"

"Dude, I can't believe you!" Simon exclaimed when Leon withdrew the gas bottle and groceries from the boot. "I am really starting to think this is not a good idea."

"It'll be fine. I'll just put these here, okay?" Leon left the items in the shade beside Simon's Mazda. He was about to get back into the driver seat when Simon stopped him again.

"Dude, what's that?"

"What?"

"That," Simon pointed at his feet. "You're driving in flip flops??"

"It's all I have with me," Leon nodded.

"What shoe size are you?" Simon demanded and Leon told him. "That's smaller than mine, just a sec," he was about to turn to one of the other racers when Leon stopped him.

"Nah, don't, next you'll get me to borrow another car… Look, I'll be fine."

"Alright," Simon shook his head with a pained expression on his face. "But dude, do me a favour and at least go barefoot – you'll have way more control that way."

"I'll be fine," stubbornly Leon got back into the car.

"I don't know, man," Simon shook his head unhappily.

"Let the looney go Si," one of the racers laughed. "It's not your problem."

"Yeah," another guy in race-overalls chimed in. "Let him kill himself if he really wants."

"Maybe," Simon hesitated. "But I still have a conscience."

"Don't – I already agreed that I wouldn't come crying back to ya," Leon pointed out.

"If you even come back," Simon shook his head again. "Alright just take it easy okay."

"Nah, cut loose," one of the racers called out. "Put on a show."

"Go do it then," Simon nodded reluctantly. "But wait for the signal okay?"

"Okay," Leon agreed. "And Si..?"

"Yeah?"

"Thanks," Leon said and he became serious. "I didn't know it, but I've been wanting to do this for a long time."

"I think I understand," Simon nodded and suddenly his grin was back. "Alright, screw it, go hard man."

"You got it. It's the only way to do it."

"Soft is definitely not the way," Simon laughed and tapped on the roof of the Laurel with his hand. "Off you go, show us how it's done then."

Leon slotted in reverse, backed the Laurel out of her park and then eased her down the pit lane to the starting line where one of the track crew, dressed in a fluorescent orange jacket and armed with a Walkie Talkie, held up a hand for him to stop. Leon slowed to a halt and waited, peering down the track. It was completely wind-still and the day was beginning to get really hot. A dry, stifling heat was bouncing off the tarmac. His thoughts were in turmoil. But then the crew member beckoned him casually and Leon sent his mum's car into motion. The needle of the speedometer climbed steadily and then suddenly he was out of the confines of the pits and in the open. It was an amazing feeling, hurtling down a wide tarsealed expanse with nothing but clear, wide reaching track to pursue. Road rules didn't apply and speed limits didn't exist. There were no police and no oncoming hazards.

The world blurred by and Leon was so lost in the moment, the excitement of speed, that he almost forgot what he was here for. He was here to drift and it required a conscious effort for him to recall what he had been shown, so many years ago. As the track swung around into an easy curve he slowed drastically, steering the uneasy sedan into it, before turning the steering wheel towards the apex and applying the hand brake so that the back wheels produced a pitiful squeak. Scowling, he followed through and straightened out. Mentally he prepared for the next turn.

He made it through his second bend with a bad case of understeer and another sorrowful squeak from his tyres. As he came out onto the straight, the sound of the RB20 chugged hollowly through the factory exhaust system – coming out tinny and nasal. Leon grimaced. The thought that he was being watched by the drifters in the pits made him wince. They were probably having a good laugh at his hopelessly amateur attempts. What if Cam and Taz had already turned up? Were they watching him and laughing also? Was Lorna there? Here he was looking like a complete fool. This was his chance. He couldn't make a meal of it.

Behind the controls, Leon's eyes narrowed and he frowned with new concentration. All that mattered was the track before him and the car. In his mind, he traced out an imaginary line through the next bend and he followed it, downshifting and pushing the Laurel forwards. Nudging the brakes gently on entry, her weight shifted towards the front and her rear wheels kicked free. She wobbled and Leon felt her begin to slide. Then he was straightening out and immediately spinning the wheel in the opposite direction to flow into the next turn.

The hand brake came up and this time the Laurel's back section swung out neatly and he held her there, working the wheel and throttle to keep her stance so that she skimmed through the bend at an angle, with the G-forces pressing him against the edge of his seat. It was an exhilarating rush and without realising, Leon's frown turned into a wide grin. This was far better than riding a rollercoaster, far better than bungy-jumping, far better than... This was it! The grin stayed on his face as he swung out of the turn, countered and lined up its successor.

He was getting a feel for it now as old memories returned, but just as quickly he established the problems with his car. The gutless engine didn't nearly have enough power for him to lose traction at speed. Instead he had to resort to the hand brake to get loose. Even worse was the tremendous body-roll from her saggy suspension and the luggy 15-inch tyres. Simon had also been right about his flimsy footwear – the flip flops didn't help. Quickly he kicked them off before the next bend came at him. Now he was able to get a much better feel for the controls and, as he powered through the bend, he marvelled in awe. How good would this be in a proper drift car?

At each bend he pushed the Laurel that little bit further, until he had the rear-wheels shrilling bitterly and a small cloud of blue smoke tainted his slipstream. The engine note had changed also, becoming loud and aggressive as he floored the accelerator ruthlessly, revving her right to the red-line. The engine rattle heightened his thrill and he felt the adrenaline rush through him. It emboldened him and he thrashed the Laurel down the track with increasing recklessness.

He felt he was getting the hang of it and wondered if Simon and the other racers were still watching, or possibly even

Lorna? Leon's eyes flicked to the dashboard clock. No, it was probably still too early. As he shot down the straight towards the next bend, the imaginary line formed in his mind, but his thoughts stayed on the beautiful girl with the long black hair and those enthralling eyes. He longed to see her again.

Leon's concentration had wavered, but suddenly it snapped back to the track and the oncoming hair-pin. He realised he was going far too fast. Frantically, he crushed the brake pedal into the floor, willing his cumbersome sedan to slow. All four wheels locked up and she screeched across the smooth tarmac of the bend. Gripping the steering wheel with a deathlike hold and with his foot still on the brakes, the Laurel skidded off the track and onto the grass, ploughing up a big cloud of dust and dirt. She floundered there, digging her front wheels in awkwardly as her momentum carried her on towards the concrete barrier at its far side. Her rear wheels lost contact with the ground and Leon thought for a moment that she might roll, but then her front wheels hit something and the whole fore section kicked up like a bucking bull.

Leon's helmet smacked back against the headrest and his vision distorted. Dimly he saw the fence that ran across the top of the barrier fill the windscreen and with a jarring crash, breaking glass and creaking metal the Laurel smashed into the barrier. Leon was flung harshly against his seatbelt and glass scattered around him. Then suddenly, after all the noise, it was deathly silent. Stunned, and confused, Leon straightened in his seat. Petrol, could he smell petrol? Panic seized him and he wrestled with his seatbelt, frantically trying to unbuckle himself. He found the latch and managed to free himself. Shoving his door open, he tumbled out of the car and ran until he was well clear, before he turned and stared back at the wreck in incredulous dismay.

Leaning against the barrier that separated the empty spectator stand from the track, the Nissan stood on its tail with its front end smashed in and pointing towards the sky. He had even dented the wire fence that ran on top of the concrete wall. Leon took his helmet off and stood like that for a long time. Sweat sprouted in tiny beads on his nose and forehead, forming droplets that ran down his face. He didn't notice the itchy discomfort, nor did he notice the burning hot tarmac under his bare feet. His brain was slow from shock and heat. He couldn't believe it. He had crashed his mum's car! How could he explain this? He was supposed to be getting gas for the stove as well as cake ingredients.

Leon turned and looked at the track behind him, back the way he had come – at speed. He squinted and shielded his eyes with his hand against the intense glare of the sun. It was a little shaky. Again, he saw that imaginary line in his mind, the path that he would have needed to take to be able to make it through that last curve at his high speed. How could he have veered from that line? He had seen it clearly on entry. He just didn't have what it took. Maybe that is why he had so readily agreed with his mum to stop driving. Inwardly he had always thought his driving skills were not nearly what his dad and others had made out. The adrenaline from the crash was wearing off now, to be replaced by a sense of despair.

He noticed that he was bleeding from a shallow cut on the back of his hand. Impatiently he wiped it away on his shorts. Some driver you are. He scolded himself. How could you have botched that up? But then her face flickered back into his mind, with the tiniest dimple in her cheek when she smiled. No wonder he couldn't concentrate on driving. He was bewitched. Had she been interested? Leon wondered idly. What could she see in him? He didn't have pots of money or a stylish car. Or any other car, now, he stared gloomily at the wreck and his despair deepened. Irritably he wiped the sweat from his face with the back of his hand.

For no real reason, he rummaged in his pocket and took out his wallet. He opened it and withdrew his licence, looking down at his own image, the image he had shown her, with the buzz-cut hair. His grim face stared back at him from the thumbnail photo. 'You look like a criminal,' she had said and he couldn't deny it. No way would she be interested in him. Scowling, Leon tried to slide his licence back into its slot, but something was in the way. "Damn receipts." Frustrated, he dug out the offending piece of paper, letting it flutter to the ground. He slipped his licence into the slot and put his wallet back into his pocket. Leon turned away from the wreck again. Far across the track, on the other side, he could see the rescue vehicle tearing towards where he stood.

Leon resigned himself to wait. The scalding heat from the tarmac reminded him of his feet. He should move onto the grass, where it wasn't so hot. Bending over, he picked up the helmet from where he had put it down on the track. He was about to straighten when his litter-conscious mind triggered and he picked up the receipt too. Moving onto the cooler grass, Leon's fingers fiddled subconsciously with the receipt. It was folded over on itself. He didn't remember doing that. What was it for anyway? Unfolding it, he scanned his eyes over the text. 'Hey Leon, here's my number. Lorna.' Confused, Leon read over the words again, shaking his head uncomprehendingly and suddenly, through the gloom that darkened his features, a smile grew on his lips.

That's how the rescue team found him, grinning broadly. The makeshift fire engine raced up to the Laurel, and braked loudly. Three firemen raced up to the wreck and sprayed it with a whooshing hiss from their fire extinguishers, to prevent any possibility of fire, while two medics ran towards Leon.

"You alright?" one of the medics asked Leon with concern. He carried a bag containing first-aid equipment. Seeing Leon so relaxed and smiling worried him. Perhaps he had suffered concussion?

"I'm fine," Leon replied.

"You're bleeding," the medic shook his head. Leon touched his cheek. His fingers came away with a smear of blood.

"It must be from my hand, it's nothing." The medics ignored his protests and attempts at dismissal and checked him quickly while he stood. They looked into his eyes and had him move his head. Only then did they step back at his okay.

"That's some bad luck," the first medic, a young man with pale-green eyes and a clean-shaven face commented sadly. He indicated the destroyed Laurel. "You were going pretty good."

"Far too much body roll," the second medic, a middle-aged man with blue eyes and a small web of wrinkles at the corners, commented wistfully. "Why would anyone try and drift a car like that?"

"Sheer stupidity," Leon's smile broadened. He closed his fist over the note tightly, drawing more strength from it.

Looking past the medics, Leon watched as the cloud of gas cleared and the wreck was revealed again. It was a write-off. That was certain. To straighten that chassis, panel-beat out the front, fix the engine, get the vehicle drivable again and finally apply the body filler and re-spray it would be an expensive undertaking. For this old car, it was not worth it.

Somehow Leon was not that worried, he had been working for several years now and, without needing to pay for living costs, he had been able to save a reasonable sum of money. If there were difficulties with the insurance, he would be able to cover the damage by himself.

The tow-truck arrived and backed up to the wreck. Attaching a tow-hook to the tow-clip of the Nissan, the tow-truck driver started the winch. With a grating shriek of bare metal, the Laurel rasped down the concrete barrier and up the ramp until she hunched resignedly on the back of the truck.

"Tough luck, mate," the tow-truck driver approached Leon. "You realise you'll get charged for the tow?" Leon nodded. When there was easy prey, the sharks were quick to close in. "You want me to take the car to your home, or straight to the wreckers?" the truckie joked. He was short and wiry, wearing a black singlet that exposed his muscled biceps and the tattoos on his shoulders. But despite the tough look, the corners of his lips were slightly raised and Leon sensed that he was friendly.

"We'll take her home and I'll grab a ride. Then I can show you the way."

"It's against the company rules," the truckie hesitated and shook his head.

"Come on, my mum would have a heart-attack if you just dropped the car off looking like that," Leon pressed and the truckie wavered.

"Understandably," he nodded reluctantly. "Okay then."

"Cool, oh and can we quickly swing by the pits, I need to return the helmet and pick up a gas bottle."

"I guess so, seeing we have to go out that way anyway," the tow-truck driver grumbled. The medics shouted some last minute advice to Leon as he clambered up into the cab. The tow-truck, laden with its crippled cargo, rumbled back to the pit lanes where Leon received a ribald welcome of hoots, wolf whistles and clapping. Noisily the other drifters made it clear that they had seen it all from the pit lanes. With his cheeks burning red hot from all the attention, Leon had the truckie pull up beside Simon's RX-7. Simon himself stood beside it, his hands on his hips. Awkwardly Leon clambered out of the cab, still barefoot, and handed the borrowed helmet back.

"Thanks," he mumbled.

"Far out," Simon took it from him and looked up at the mangled remains of the Laurel on the back of the tow-truck. "You okay?"

"Yeah, fine," Leon nodded. "And don't worry, I won't cry to you."

"Oh, good," his face suddenly split into a big grin. "You sure put on a show."

"Not quite the show I had in mind."

"I wouldn't have done any better, not in that thing," Simon shook his head. "Next time get yourself a real drift car, you'd do well."

"Yeah, you were doing good," another drifter chimed in. "Should stick at it."

"Maybe, though I doubt there'll be a next time," Leo replied. "My mum will kill me for sure."

"Yeah, that's gonna hurt," Simon was sympathetic. "But don't let it put you off. I don't think there's one of us here who hasn't smashed up a car."

"If you don't crash it just means you're not going hard enough," another drifter agreed with a smirk.

"Yeah, maybe," Leon shrugged and picked up the gas bottle and groceries. He clambered up onto the flatbed and put them on the passenger seat of the Laurel. "Here's your fire extinguisher by the way."

"Ta," Simon reached up and took it. "If you ever want to have another go, give me a shout. I'm down here most open days," Simon offered.

"Yeah, Si basically lives here," the other drifter joked and knuckled Simon's shoulder.

"I'll see," Leon nodded. He turned and climbed back into the cab and the truckie pulled away. As they made their way out of the pits and down towards the gates that led onto the main road, Leon saw a Nissan Terrano approaching. The big four-wheel-drive was pulling a car trailer on which perched a red Trueno behind a rack that held numerous tyres. It took Leon a moment to notice that Cam was driving the Terrano and that Taz sat in the cab beside him. They were engrossed in conversation and hadn't seen him. Lorna wasn't with them.

Without seeming hurried, Leon hunched down behind the dashboard of the tow-truck to inspect his bare feet. Once they were past he straightened up again and directed the truckie to his home.

Leon jumped out of the cab when they reached his home and had the truckie back up the driveway. The reversing beep of the truck sounded so loudly that his Mum came out of the house. Uncertainly, she stood at the front door, staring at the truck and its cargo in disbelief. And then she was running towards Leon. He was worried. "Sorry Mum," he started out when she reached him, but she didn't utter a sound. Instead she folded her arms around him in a big protective hug.

"When racing goes wrong, eh?" the truck driver had stopped his vehicle and also disembarked now. He slouched against the cab and grinned from ear-to-ear. Leon looked away. His mum made no sign of having heard and Leon stood uneasy within her embrace, his arms at his side. Where were the words of discipline and threats of punishment? Finally his mum stepped back and worriedly turned her attention to his injuries. She reached for his chin and turned his face gently as the medics had done.

"You're hurt, there's blood on your cheek."

"I'm alright, the medics already checked me out," Leon replied. Her concern was disconcerting. Where were the harsh words?

"Oh good," his mum still held his chin, "You gave me such a fright," her tone was sad now and Leon thought he detected a trace of disappointment. It was in her eyes. "I couldn't bear to lose you too." Leon hung his head. He felt terrible. His mum had always been good to him and looked out for him. Somehow a scolding would have been easier. Taking charge, his mum turned to the truck driver. "Please leave the car there, in front of the garage." She had not looked at the wreck again. "And wipe that smirk off your face!"

"Sorry," the Truckie sobered instantly and straightened.

"You can send me the invoice."

With a casual dismissal, she guided Leon down the paved path that connected the garage with the house. Tamsin stood on the front door step, silent and even more wide-eyed than usual. She stared across the lawn at the crumpled Laurel, which was slowly being winched off the truck. As Leon approached, steered by his mum, Tamsin looked up at Leon with an awed expression. They shared a look and Leon shook his head almost imperceptibly. His sister lowered her eyes and suppressed the questions that were on her lips.

After the oppressive heat of the day, the house was cool and refreshing. Walking in silence, his mum directed him down the tiled hallway and into the living room. She let him go and walked into the open kitchen. Standing idly before the counter, Leon fidgeted uncomfortably, sensing trouble. Could this be the calm before the storm?

"Did you get the items and the gas?" she asked, almost too casually, and picked up a knife from the counter.

"Yeah, I did, they're in the car," Leon's words caught at her unexpected question.

"Good, thanks," his mum wasn't looking at him as she began dissecting plums. "Please get them once the truck has left."

"Okay," Leon continued to stand silently in front of the counter, unsure of himself. "Aren't you going to tell me off? Or at least ask what happened?" he spoke at last. His mum paused. She laid the knife down again.

"Leon," she sighed, "I heard what that man said... I always knew you would go racing one day." Leon looked down at the floor between his feet. "I also know that you feel bad so no, I'm not going to give you an earful." Leon nodded, and slowly raised his head to meet her eyes. "It was wrong of me to ask you to make a promise that you couldn't possibly keep. Racing is something that you and your dad were always so passionate about." A small tear formed in the corner of her eye. "I shouldn't have tried to suppress that."

"Mum," Leon tried to protest, but she continued.

"Instead, I should have made sure you had someone to teach you to do it safely."

"Mum," again, Leon tried to protest, but again his mum continued.

"Leon, if you want to race then promise me..." she caught herself. "Please just be careful." There was a pleading look in her eye.

"Of course Mum," Leon stood a second longer. "I don't really know what to say," he mumbled. Both of them were silent. "I'll see if the truck has gone now," Leon turned and was about to walk away when his mum spoke again.

"Oh and next time, perhaps you could use your own car."

"But I don't have my own car," Leon turned back.

"Then maybe it's about time you did."

"You mean you're okay with me getting my own car?" Leon asked in wonder. It didn't make any sense. Maybe she was in shock.

"If that's what you really want," his mum replied seriously, but there was a sadness about her. Disappointment? Regret? Leon took it to heart. He knew that the idea of him racing at high speeds was difficult for her to bear. Leon realised that it was affecting her more than she let on. He didn't know how to react. Should he be happy that he would finally have his own car with his mum's consent, while still living at home or should he be distraught as to how it had come about?

"Are you sure?"

"Yes," his mum nodded. "Maybe I could even borrow it, if you get one before I've had a chance to replace mine." She raised a faint smile.

"Of course." The thought of his mum driving his car, which would surely be something far more modified than what you'd expect a mum to drive, made him smile. Leon turned and left the room. His mum stared after him. With a sigh, she picked up the knife again.

Leon walked circles in his room, desperately trying to think what he should say. Finally he picked the phone up for the third time. Dialling her number, he took a deep breath, holding it as the phone began to ring. It rang once, twice… each ring played on his apprehension so that the tension built up inside him.

"Hello?" a girl's voice answered. It didn't sound like her.

"Hi, it's Leon here. I was after Lorna – is she around?" he tried to make it sound casual and unforced.

"Just a sec, I'll get her."

"Thanks," Leon waited impatiently, pressing the phone to his ear. The seconds dragged by.

"Leon, hi!"

"How are you?"

"I'm good. I was hoping you'd call," her voice sounded slightly anxious.

"I only found your note today – that was a cool surprise."

"Oh, I'm glad. I was actually kind of worried…"

"Really? Why?" Leon wanted to know.

"Well, I wasn't sure if you'd think I was weird..?" she said almost inaudibly.

"No, not at all," Leon realised that she was also shy. He found himself grinning into the mouthpiece.

"I didn't want to be too forward," she laughed. "So, it was a good thing Cam distracted you, otherwise I wouldn't have been able to sneak it into your wallet." Her words were like music to his ear.

"You know, suddenly I'm glad for Cam's interruption."

"Me too," Lorna laughed again. "So how are you going?"

"Well," Leon hesitated. "Honestly?"

"Tell me," Lorna invited.

"I had a bit of bad luck this morning…" he became serious.

"What happened?" Lorna was concerned and Leon warmed to her further. He lay back on his bed and began to explain. Except for several noises of disbelief, Lorna listened without interruption. Only when he had finished, ending with his mum's response to the situation, did she speak. "Wow, that is pretty serious."

"Yeah, I feel quite stink," Leon sighed.

"I bet, that really is bad luck," Lorna was sympathetic. "You know, I thought you said you didn't race?"

"I don't," Leon broke off wistfully. "Or at least, I didn't."

"So why did you?" Lorna asked quietly.

"Not sure," Leon thought about it. "I guess, after last night's conversation, and Cam hassling me, I wanted to see if I still had it in me."

"That's not like Cam," Lorna spoke apologetically. "He's usually a real decent guy."

"Maybe," Leon paused. "To me he seemed pretty rude, especially since I helped them with their car."

"I wouldn't lose any sleep over it," Lorna recommended.

"Okay, I'll try not to," Leon smiled.

"Good," Lorna giggled and Leon felt a warm glow in his chest at the sound. She was so easy to talk to. "So do you?" Lorna asked suddenly.

"Sorry?"

"Still have it in you?" Lorna expanded.

"Well, I guess not, I mean I ended up trying to make the car climb a fence," he wanted to make her laugh again. It worked.

"But before you crashed?" she pressed.

"I was ripping, I had big angle and my mum's massive rims were making so much smoke I couldn't see the track anymore," Leon grinned into the phone.

"Right on," Lorna laughed, "And you were playing the harmonica with no hands on the wheel and both feet out the window," she expanded on the joke. "And umm, seriously?"

"Well I guess I was alright. The medic's seemed to like my efforts and some of the other drifters put in a good word," Leon answered thoughtfully.

"You drifted?"

"Yeah, I did get that Laurel somewhat sideways," Leon admitted seriously.

"Awesome, but how come you crashed?" Lorna wanted to change the subject and draw him out again.

"I was distracted..." Leon admitted ruefully.

"By what?"

"Well, by you," Leon grimaced at how tinny he sounded. Awkwardly he waited for her response.

"You were distracted by me? And that's why you crashed?" Lorna breathed.

"I could think of little else today."

"So I guess that means you must be blaming me then?"

"Yeah totally," Leon laughed, "That's why I called."

"Ouch that's not a good start is it?" Lorna's smile carried down the phone line. "How can I possibly make it up to you?"

"You could come out to dinner with me – that'd do for a start," Leon laughed again.

"Well you don't beat around do you?"

"I might be shy, but once I'm on track I go for it."

"Well, since you asked so nicely..." Lorna giggled. "When do you want to go?"

"Have you had lunch?" Leon asked.

"No, not yet, why, you want to go now?"

"Why not?"

"Why not," Lorna agreed. "I guess I'll be driving?"

"Um, yeah, if that's alright?"

"Of course, just give me your address." Leon explained the directions to her. "I'll be there soon," Lorna promised.

After the call, Leon sat a moment longer on his bed. Lorna was picking him up for lunch. He couldn't believe it. She would be here soon. In trepidation he hopped up and ran to the bathroom. He got a fright when he checked the mirror. He looked like he had just crawled out of the gutter. His hair was dishevelled, there was a scrape on his forehead and a smear of grime on the side of his nose.

He didn't have time for a shower, so he quickly washed his face before turning his attention to his springy black hair. She had said she liked his hair, but to Leon his hair was always a problem. Totally uncontrollable, it never did as it was told. Today was no different and it stuck out at odd angles. With the aid of some gel, Leon shaped it into something that was still messy, but less unruly. "Stay," Leon spoke to his own image, but it thwarted him as usual and popped up again. "Arrgh!" Leon scowled fiercely, administered more and managed to stick it down until it held.

"Gelled up real good," Leon made a face in the mirror. A loud giggle suddenly erupted from behind him and Leon spun to find Tamsin in hysterics.

"Do it again," she urged him and Leon did, sending Tamsin into further helpless fits. "Again, again!" Leon smiled indulgently but shook his head.

"Your turn."

With an effort Tamsin recovered her composure. She thought for a second, before grasping her cheeks between the little thumb and forefinger of each hand and pinched them down, while using her even smaller pinky fingers to push her button nose up. She looked like a troll and Leon had to laugh in earnest. "You'd better hope that the wind doesn't change when you do that," he cautioned.

"What does the wind do?" Tamsin lowered her hands.

"Well, if the wind changes when you make a face, then it will stay like that," Leon said secretively. "Forever."

"Forever?" Tamsin's eyes widened and Leon nodded. Tamsin gazed at him thoughtfully, before looking around her. Experimentally she moved her hand in the air. "But there's no wind inside is there?" she said at last.

"No, I guess not," Leon was stunned by her logic. "Not with the windows closed," he agreed.

"So it's okay to make faces?"

"It should be," Leon confirmed and smiled at her. "But just to be safe, you should always do them real quick."

"Like this?" Tamsin repeated her face but this time poked her teeny pink tongue out for effect. Leon laughed at her antics, and she immediately resumed her good-girl expression as though nothing had happened. "Your turn," Tamsin prompted him and once more Leon repeated his face in a flash, so that Tamsin broke into further giggles and her pigtails danced around her head. "More!"

"Sorry Tink, I have to go," Leon shook his head.

"Where do you have to go?" Tamsin didn't bother to hide her disappointment.

"I'm going out for lunch with a girl," Leon answered her and Tamsin was silent as she considered this.

"Is she your girlfriend?" her eyes were big with intrigue.

"No," Leon shook his head, but couldn't quite hide the smile that played across his lips. "She's just a friend."

Tamsin understood, but her eyes didn't leave his face. "Is she pretty?"

"Well, she's not quite as pretty as you," Leon paused as Tamsin preened. "But yes, she is."

"Then she should be your girlfriend," she said promptly with absolute conviction and Leon's smile turned into a grin at her unaffected view of the world.

"I'll see what I can do," Leon chuckled. His humour turned to anticipation as the doorbell rang. "That will be her now."

"So, what're you going to get?" Those honey-coloured eyes mesmerised him. They were sitting alone at a small table for two in the corner of a cafe, overlooking the street. People walked past outside, going about their business, but Leon only had eyes for Lorna. It suddenly occurred to him that he was staring and that he still hadn't answered her question.

"Um..." Leon's thoughts were all muddled. She had tied her long, black hair back in a bun and a wisp had come loose. "You're so gorgeous." Lorna blushed and lowered her eyes self-consciously. For a long moment he didn't realise himself what he'd said. "Sorry," he mumbled, embarrassed. "I didn't want to make you uncomfortable."

"No, no, it's okay. I'm glad you think so." Lorna looked at him again.

"I can't help it," he grinned and her smile shone at him.

"You know, you never did actually answer my question," Lorna said at last.

"Um," it took Leon a moment to recall. "You mean what type of car am I going to buy?" Lorna nodded without taking her eyes off him. "Well a Silvia would be wicked..."

"So the drifting bug has bitten you now too?" she prodded.

"It seems so..."

"Nice. What kind of Silvia? S15?"

"I was actually thinking of one of the older ones, an S13."

"Why?"

"I used to like them as a kid," Leon answered hesitantly.

"It's funny that you say that..." Lorna spoke thoughtfully. "Because my cousin has one."

"Is he selling it?" Leon leaned forward in his seat.

"Actually no," Lorna shook her head. "Not exactly."

"What do you mean by that?"

"Well, it needs to be for sale..." Lorna spoke in riddles.

"I'm listening..." Leon prompted.

"You see, he got busted drink-driving about two weeks ago," Lorna explained. "He's lost his licence for six months and doesn't have the money to pay for his fine – so since he's not allowed to drive anyway, I figure he should really sell it."

"And what does he figure?" Leon asked.

"Doesn't want to, of course," Lorna shook her head sadly. "It's wasted on him. He drives like a lunatic and has no feeling for it. He's already blown two motors in it."

"And you want me to buy it?" Leon raised an eyebrow.

"Yup," Lorna smiled.

"And why exactly?"

"Because you could make it run like a dream," Lorna became serious. Leon found it difficult to breathe when she looked at him like that. Why do you think that? The question ran through his mind, but instead he laughed.

"I guess I'm off the hook, seeing he doesn't want to sell it."

"If you were interested, I could give him a call," Lorna offered. "Maybe he'll think about it?"

Leon hesitated. "I guess it can't hurt to look," he nodded.

"Well that didn't require too much convincing." An intriguing smile played on her lips. Lorna retrieved her cellphone from her handbag.

"No, but then I haven't bought it yet," he grinned back.

Lorna spoke to her cousin briefly and after a bit of convincing he agreed for them to look at his Silvia. They enjoyed the rest of their lunch and then went out to the car.

"Now don't get too excited alright," Lorna recommended as they drove. "Blake has a bad track record with cars."

"You mean he doesn't look after them?" Leon asked.

"Worse than that," Lorna took her eyes off the road to glance at him significantly. "He thrashes them."

"Alright I'll prepare myself for the worst."

When they reached her cousin's home, Lorna parked on the street. "There it is," She pointed to a charcoal S13 which hunched low over mag wheels. "He's painted it..." The car was parked on the lawn and the grass that grew up around her made her look even lower. Leon's tempo quickened. But as he neared her, walking eagerly up the driveway with Lorna trying to keep up, the faults quickly became more apparent. Scarred and battered, her body was in poor shape. The amateur paint job had flaked in places and beneath, Leon could see the original white, un-primed surface.

Leon walked up to it and sagged to a halt. "Ouch." He looked the Nissan over with disappointment. He had tried to prepare himself for a rough car but nothing like this.

"Yeah, woah," Lorna had come up beside him. "Last time I saw the car was about four months ago, just after he bought it. It looked a whole lot better then."

"I'd hope so." Leon walked a circuit around the dark, brooding car. She was covered in numerous scratches. Nearly every panel had a sizable ding. The passenger side mirror hung askew. Leon shook his head regretfully. What a waste. Peering through the tinted windows, Leon could just make out a number of rips in the back seats as well as the smaller pockmarks of cigarette burns. Who could treat a car like this?

Making his way around, Leon paused beside the back wheel. The guards came down so far over the rubber that only half of it was showing. Crouching, he pushed his hand up under the guard and slid it over the tyre. He was surprised to find it covered with plenty of tread. Withdrawing his hand, he stayed crouched down and looked along the length of the car to the front. She rested unbelievably low. There can't have been much more than three inches of clearance, even on tarmac. On impulse, Leon peered up under the guard, this time checking the suspension coil. His doubts were confirmed. The springs were cut. Leon straightened. He turned to Lorna. She had not moved from the spot and continued to look the car over with a mixture of disbelief and disgust.

"You still want me to buy her?" Leon raised an eyebrow.

"No way – I had a feeling it's been wrung around the bend, but," Lorna shook her head and paused. "Not this bad."

The front door of the small, run-down house opened at that moment and a short, stocky figure stepped out. His chin was unshaven and his black hair curled thickly out over his ears. From his rough attire: a torn, black hoodie with worn sleeve-ends and faded black jeans, Leon could quickly see the reason for the state of the S13.

"'Day cuz. Been a while," the man greeted Lorna and puffed on his cigarette. He glanced at Leon. "What's with the Asian?" Leon's dislike was instant, but he pretended not to hear and continued with his inspection of the S13.

"Don't be an prick," Lorna glared. "His name is Leon."

"Is that his real name?" her cousin sniffed. "Or just what he calls himself here?"

"Does it matter? He's here to look at your car."

"Oh yeah, that's good, cause I need the cash now."

"Pity it's taken you this long to realise that. It's looking pretty rough," Lorna grimaced.

"Nah, she's sweet as, what ya talkin' 'bout?" Lorna's cousin was defensive.

Leon put his hand on the passenger side wing-mirror, which hung askew. He rattled it loosely. "Sweet as?"

"If you wanna be fussy…" Lorna's cousin scowled at him.

"Who needs mirrors anyway..?" Leon commented dryly. Moving along, he ran his finger over the deep scratches surrounding the lock on the passenger door. "Thieves?"

"Oh that, nah, accidentally locked my keys in, eh," Lorna's cousin grinned, "Had to use a screwdriver – still locks good tho, so no worries." Lorna's cousin looked proud, like a war hero showing his battle scars.

"Do I like it," Leon made a face.

"Everybody does, she's mint," Lorna's cousin nodded knowingly. "Want me to pop the hood?"

"Don't bother, she's too rough for me," Leon shook his head and stepped back from the car. "She'd need a lot of work before she'd even pass the next warrant," Leon returned to where Lorna stood. "Come on, let's go."

"Okay, sorry, I really didn't know," Lorna apologised quietly to Leon, before she rounded on her cousin. "You really are a wonder Blake! I don't think three hood-rats with baseball bats could've made it look much worse. We'll go and look elsewhere."

"Eh? You're not even gonna come for a spin?" Blake looked confused and baffled.

"Why should he?" Lorna demanded. "What good would it do? Leon's hardly going to buy it looking like that."

"He just told me he liked her," Blake protested.

"Liked her?" Leon turned back in exasperation. "I said she was too rough for me."

"Come on, they're just scratches," Blake smiled evenly. "You're not scared are ya?" he pressed as Leon hesitated.

"Scared? Yeah, I'm scared the bubblegum that's holding her together will fail when I get in," Leon replied coolly as his eyes fell on the ominous machine again. She did look mean. "But alright, I guess there's no real harm in having a go since we're already here."

"Bloody right," Blake's smile faded as Leon put his hand out. "What?"

"Keys."

"Yeah nice try, I'm hardly gonna let you drive."

"Your call," Leon turned to walk down the drive again.

"Of course you'll let him drive," Lorna argued with her cousin. "You don't even have a licence anymore."

"Lorna, you're sounding like my mum," Blake griped. "Okay fine, but you bend, you spend so just take it easy ya hear – she's my baby." He held the keys out reluctantly.

"I can see that," Leon smiled thinly and took the keys.

"Can you open the door for me?" Blake made his way towards the passenger door.

"Sure," Leon inserted the key into the crooked lock and tried to turn it.

"Press the key up then turn," Blake instructed. Leon shook his head slightly, but took his advice and the key turned readily. He hopped into the driver's seat as Blake tapped on the passenger door window. Leon reached across to open the door for him.

"No central?"

"Stopped working," Blake answered evenly.

"I should've guessed."

"I'm coming too," Lorna stepped up and, while Blake held the door for her, she squeezed into the narrow back seat. Once she was in, Blake took the passenger seat. Leon adjusted the driver seat for his slightly taller frame and put the key into the ignition. The engine sparked and caught immediately, thudding eagerly into life. Leon noticed something odd about the sound. He looked over at Blake.

"You changed the engine?"

"Too right, she's running an RB26."

"Oh okay," Leon had never driven a car loaded with the legendary race engine, but he suppressed his intrigue.

"Dude, you don't know what an RB26Dett is?" Blake looked at him aghast.

"Should I?"

"And you call yourself a Jap?" Blake sighed. "It's a Skyline GT-R engine, like one of the best engines out of Japan ever."

"I guess it does sound alright," Leon said wryly and turned to look at Lorna. "Are there any seatbelts back there?"

"Yeah, this one seems to work," Lorna buckled herself in.

"Cool. Good to go then?"

"Yup – all set," Lorna confirmed.

Leon backed out of the driveway and onto the road. He shifted reverse to first and gave the accelerator an extra centimetre to counter their backwards roll before he let the clutch out. The power from the engine jabbed the back wheels as the pressure plates suddenly gripped together. The Silvia responded instantly. With a squeal her rear wheels spun up to a smudge of blue smoke. Playfully she flicked her nose around to point down the street. Startled at her antics, Leon hurriedly eased off the gas again.

"Woah, easy Tiger, I just got new tyres."

"She's got some bite," Leon chuckled.

"As she should man," Blake frowned at him. "She's got 350-kilowatts at the rear wheels."

"Is that all?" Leon asked sarcastically. "I'm pretty sure my Gran's mobility scooter has more than that."

"Now that I'd like to see," Blake laughed. They were jolting down the street between houses and approaching a T-intersection with a main road. Riding on stiff, cut-springs meant that even small imperfections in the road made the Nissan bounce and shudder roughly.

"Damn, rolling down a gravel road inside an oil drum would be more comfortable than this," Leon muttered out of the side of his mouth.

"Watch the speed bump!" Blake exclaimed suddenly and pointed ahead.

"I see it. Take it easy." Leon slowed the car.

"You can't go straight. You gotta go over at an angle!"

"Why?" Leon rolled the ground-hugging Nissan over the raised tarmac. As the front wheels cleared the top and rolled down the other side, the car suddenly bottomed out with a loud clunk that reverberated up from the foot-wells.

"That's why!" Blake shouted at him. "Jesus!"

For a second the car floundered on her belly, but then, with a rasp, she pushed herself forwards until all four wheels were safely on the other side.

"Oops, I'll try to remember next time." Leon braked for the Give Way sign at the intersection and looked both ways. "So where can I test her then?"

"Damn, if you drive like that there's no way you're gonna test her," Blake shook his head. "Just bloody turn around."

"You're kidding, right? How do you expect me to like her without knowing what she can really do?" Leon asked mildly.

"Let him give it a proper run Blake," Lorna instructed from the backseat. "He'll be right."

"I dunno," Blake pinched his lower lip and scowled darkly. "Alright – just watch out for bloody speed-bumps, and don't pile her up or nuthin."

"Don't worry – I already did that to my mum's car this morning," Leon responded.

"Dunno if you're serious," Blake looked pained, "But I wouldn't put it past ya."

"So where do we find a place to test this lemon?" Leon ignored him.

"Lemon?" Blake looked at Leon scornfully.

Idly Leon tried out the climate control switches, but got no response, except a loose rattle from the plastic panelling of the centre console. Next he tested the window switches. The driver's side window seemed to work, but not the passenger's. "Like I said..."

"There's a place not far," Blake spoke wistfully. "Take a left up here."

They were still waiting at the intersection and Leon ensured the way was clear before pulling out. He drove easy and more carefully. If he were to be the next owner then he didn't want to damage it any further and he certainly didn't want to push her until she was warm. But even without boosting high, he could tell the light car had a lot of power.

Initially they drove in silence, but when Leon asked about Blake's engine installation he began to explain, at the same time directing Leon through the streets.

"Bought the engine from a crashed R33 GT-R, along with the loom, computer, radiator, intercooler, fuel pump and some other bits."

"Oh yeah? What about the clutch?"

"Chucked in a new heavy duty one."

"Nothing stronger?" Leon wanted to know.

"Nah, I already cashed out big on the RB," Blake admitted reluctantly. "But a heavy duty clutch is pretty tough aye – so if you don't go completely nuts, it should last a while..." Blake paused for a moment and sniffed. "But then you are Asian."

"You've pointed that out a couple of times now," Leon made an effort to keep the edge out of his voice. "How did you fit the engine in? The mounts are all different right?"

"Just bolted in a Cefiro sub-frame, the 26 goes straight in after that," Blake shrugged.

"But its four-wheel-drive?"

"Yeah, so I got a RB25 gearbox to make her rear-wheel-drive. Easy as."

"I noticed she's got a limited slip diff' too."

"It's just the stock LSD, but I shimmed it up, so it's pretty much locked. Does skids real good."

"I'm sure it does," Leon replied dryly. The controls themselves, steering, throttle response and gearbox felt tight. But the brakes were sloppy and the suspension rough as guts.

"Right, if you take this last left here, you can have a play," Blake interrupted his thoughts. "I guess."

They were in an industrial part of town now, with tall corporate buildings and warehouses on either side. Leon turned into the cul-de-sac that Blake had pointed out. Again, on both sides stood big warehouse buildings and car-parks. As it was Sunday afternoon they stood vacant. Not a person in sight. Leon rolled the car gently down the wide street. It started out straight for about 100 metres before bending in a wide curve to the right and then straightening out again for another fifty metres before coming to a dead end.

"Thought you were gonna test her?" Blake raised an eyebrow as Leon did a casual turn at the street-end and cruised back.

"Just wanted to see what I was in for first," Leon smiled easily. "Looks like someone's been having some fun around here though," Leon indicated the tarmac. It was streaked and crisscrossed with black tyre marks.

"For sure, why do you think I had to get new tyres?" Blake grinned comfortably. "It's not every day we can sort a diesel run, up in the hills."

"I bet you thrash her hard, like you said, she's your pride and joy," Leon said thinly. When he reached the start of the cul-de-sac again, he slowed and came to a stop. "Lorna, I'm gonna give her a whirl… would you rather get out?" Leon turned in his seat.

"No way," Lorna flashed him that brilliant smile of hers. "Impress me."

"I'll do my best," Leon smiled back.

"Impress me?" Blake scoffed. "Yeah right, I'll take her for a spin after and you'll see how it's really done."

"Sounds good," Leon nodded and checked the gauges. The engine was running nice and warm – she was ready to go. Leon nudged the shifter into first gear, pressed the accelerator and eased the clutch out in one fluid motion. As she began rolling he flung the wheel over and trod the accelerator fully into the floor. The engine bellowed and slogged raw power to the rear wheels. They spun with a shrill squeal and the Silvia peeled around in a tight U-turn, pouring rich, blue smoke.

The instant that Leon had the Silvia's nose pointing back down the cul-de-sac, he eased off the throttle and flicked the wheel back to correct her spin. The Nissan fishtailed before straightening, but the moment her rear wheels gripped, he let her go again and she pressed forward, angling down the street. The motor roared as the turbo fed her with cool air and the boost hit with such a vicious pull that they were compressed back into their seats. As Leon pulled second gear the blow-off valve sounded loudly. They boosted again and the warehouse buildings streamed by in a grey blur. With the rev counter hitting 7000rpm, he shifted to third, but the short straight was nearly gone, and the bend hurtled towards them at over 100km/h.

"Woah," Blake protested hoarsely and snatched at the door handle for a hold.

Leon heard Lorna gasp behind him, as he heel-and-toe downshifted and used the accelerator generously. The huge, unstoppable torque from the engine kept the rear wheels flailing at the tarmac with an angry scream. The tyres smoked up large and the S13 slipped into a roaring drift. The front of the car skimmed across the apex of the bend in a tight line. When they were through, he corrected his slide and pulled the Silvia straight again. He brought the brakes into action immediately as the street end loomed, but they were still travelling too fast, and he flung the wheel left, slipped off the brakes and graced the accelerator again. In second gear, the rear wheels spun wildly and he brought her about.

Moments later, they sat at the street end with the engine idling softly and the Nissan's nose pointing back the way that they had come. They were all deathly silent. Even Leon sat in a daze, uncertain as to how he had pulled off that manoeuvre.

"Wow, I'm still alive," Blake spoke up finally, looking down at himself in disbelief. His words broke the spell.

"Right, must be your turn," Leon smiled uneasily.

"Um," Blake hesitated.

"You know, I think that's enough testing," Lorna spoke up behind them. "Why don't we go back?"

"Okay," Leon nodded without looking at her. They drove back to Blake's house in silence. Throughout the drive, Blake seemed rather subdued, but he recovered once Leon had parked the S13 in the driveway.

"You wanna have a look under the hood?" he asked.

"Alright," Leon pulled the bonnet release and handed Blake the keys before he clambered out of the car.

Lorna came to stand beside them as Leon inspected the packed engine bay and Blake pointed out his installation. "It's still got the factory twin-turbos, but no airflow meters. She's also running a couple of blow-off valves and K&N filters…"

Once again Leon experienced a strong sense of deja vu as old memories crowded back while he gazed down at the engine. He wasn't listening to Blake anymore. This was what he had grown up with. This had been his dad's life.

"Well," Leon pushed the memories aside with an effort. "The install is a bit hack, but mechanically she doesn't look too shabby." He straightened up from under the bonnet.

"She's tight as," Blake looked affronted.

"Yeah, as a sieve maybe…" Leon muttered dryly.

"So you gonna make an offer?" Blake demanded. "Or just waste my time?" Leon looked at him and then turned to the car. He took his time to look her over again and analyse his thoughts. The body and interior were in very rough shape. Few of the electrics seemed to work. With cut springs and alloy wheels that had kerb scratches, this car needed a lot of work. But despite these obvious defects, when he had driven her he had felt more alive than ever. Some primal, childhood part of him wanted this car. So what if her body was rough? If he was going to have another go at drifting he was likely to be adding a few dings of his own… And with that engine… Leon couldn't deny his desire but quickly he sought to mask it. Looking back at Blake he shrugged indifferently.

"How much did you say you were after?"

"I didn't, but if I take the price I paid for it and add the price of upgrades then that'd be about good," Blake smiled easily and named a figure.

"I bet it would," Leon muttered dryly, "And no doubt you'll want to add more for the weekend sale and the petrol that's still left?"

"Now that's an idea… Well, seein' I'm a reasonable fella, I'll take a quarter off my upgrades."

"Then how about taking another half off the sale price for all your damages?"

"And then another quarter for the upgrades, since you need to sell it to get the cash for your fines," Lorna chimed in sweetly. Her cousin blinked and his smile dried up.

"Hey, who's side are you on?" he protested again. "A man's gotta eat!"

"Yeah I'm just trying to make it work for both of you," Lorna explained, "See, it's true, Leon did crash his mum's car this morning, so he'll likely have to pay for that too."

Blake looked at Leon and smirked. "Well, it ain't no wonder, drivin' the way you do," he shook his head and turned to stare at the Nissan regretfully. Leon saw Blake's eyes adjust and he wondered if, for a moment, he had seen past his enthusiasm for the car and realised the truly, sorry state she was in, and that he could well have trouble selling her for a better price. "Can't say I'm happy, but if you bring me the cash then yeah," he straightened his head and nodded mournfully. "She's yours." Leon looked over the Silvia again as well. It was a good price, but it was Sunday and the banks were closed, so how could he get Blake the money? He didn't want him to drive it for even one more day. He had to try and get the money now.

"You got internet access here?"

"Course I got the net."

"Cool, well then I could put the money straight into your account with online banking," Leon suggested.

"That'll work. I use it all the time," Blake agreed and led the way inside.

"It probably won't show up in your account until Monday," Leon pointed out.

Blake shrugged indifferently. "Hardly gonna spend it tonight." After making the money transfer, the three of them emerged from the house again. Leon's new purchase stood waiting for him and he felt a sense of pride. While she wasn't in the best condition, she was still one hell of a car and she was his first.

"I'll take the keys now," he reached his hand out and Blake handed them to him.

"No alarm?"

"No alarm," Blake confirmed.

"What about a spare key?" Leon didn't want Blake to get any ideas of taking his car back.

"I lost it down the toilet at a party," Blake explained distastefully. "Wasn't about to fish it back out." Leon smiled and Lorna giggled, but both believed him.

"Alright, well I guess one will do," Leon abruptly put his hand out again and, after only a moment's hesitation, Blake took it.

"Enjoy it," Blake grinned as they shook hands.

"I will," Leon smiled. He turned to Lorna. "So, what're you up to now?"

"Well," Lorna checked her watch. "It's just after four. We could hang out a bit longer maybe?"

"Is it four already?" Leon jolted.

"What?"

"I just remembered that my aunt and uncle are arriving today. I promised Mum I'd be there to meet them," Leon put his palm to his forehead. "But I'm probably already late."

"You should go then," Lorna encouraged him. "You can't disappoint her twice in one day and we can always hang out another time."

"True," Leon hesitated and tried to think of some excuse, but he had none. They stood close to each other, and now that it was time to say goodbye they were both suddenly awkward and self-conscious.

"Well it's been an eventful day," Leon smiled. "Crashed my mum's car, had a great lunch with you, and then bought my first car," he laughed disarmingly to try and lighten the mood.

"Yeah, I guess it didn't start out too good, but I hope it got better." Lorna smiled, but her tone was serious.

"Definitely," Leon also became serious. "There is one thing that would make it even better..." he fidgeted self-consciously.

"Yes?" Lorna asked shyly.

"Knowing that I'll get to see you again soon," the words were out before he could stop them and he scolded himself. He couldn't meet her eyes.

"I'd like that too," Lorna admitted quietly and Leon lifted his eyes from the ground to meet hers.

"That's some of the cheesiest crap I've ever heard," Blake suddenly spoke up behind them, jerking them apart. "I think I'm gonna puke."

"Why are you still standing there? Lorna rounded on him.

"I'll call you," Leon laughed embarrassedly and climbed into the Silvia.

"Come on," Andy spoke to himself, moodily drumming his fingers on the steering wheel. He was waiting at an intersection with an orange Honda Civic beside him. He had borrowed Markus' old Mazda wagon to pick up a new engine for his Nissan Cefiro drift project, which he had started some six months ago, however had made little progress on. By borrowing the Mazda he had made a point of trying to get something done, but it had been a complete waste of his Friday afternoon. The SR20Det engine he had been promised to replace the standard normally aspirated RB20 single-cam waste-of-space had turned out to be in such poor condition that he had refused to take it.

The lights signalled, but not in his favour. Instead the opposing traffic began to cross in front of him. Andy cursed. A loose spring dug into his back and he moved restlessly in the uncomfortable seat. "Change already!" Abruptly the lights flicked to green and he put his foot down. The 1.6L engine revved high and the Mazda pulled herself forward, but the hatchback burst past him with a loud VTEC cackle. Cursing further, he had to brake for the lane merge.

Sometime later Andy pulled up outside his friend's home and was thankful to climb out of the wagon. He made his way up the drive that led to a dark green double garage. To the left of the garage stood a large weatherboard ex-state house, built in typical robust, boxy style with a concrete tile roof and big wooden window frames. The house had been recently repainted in earthy tones and the lawn and hedges that edged the property were neat and tidy. Andy had once mocked Markus for still living with his mum, wondering how he could handle it.

"I can put up with a lot for free rent," Markus' reply had been accompanied by a casual shrug. And as if in afterthought, he had added: "And besides since the old man left, Mum's been way mellow." Andy had to agree, unlike his own mum who stressed out about everything, him in particular, Markus' mum, Tanya, was easygoing. Andy spent almost as much time here as he did at his own place.

Andy headed directly for the garage, guided by the heavy-metal music that was making the aluminium cladding rattle. Reaching the side door, he opened it and went inside. Every time he came here, he couldn't help but look around him distastefully. Markus' garage was a mess. Tools and random junk cluttered the floor and hung from rusty nails and hooks imbedded in the garage's four-by-two framing timber. Unlike Markus, Andy kept his garage spic and span. Every tool had its designated place and was returned there immediately after use. How could Markus get any work done in a sty like this? Andy's focus changed and he saw his friend hunched over the front of his Nissan, his face in fierce concentration.

"Wow," Andy let his breath out in an awed whoosh. He had not seen the 180SX since they had dropped her off at the panelbeater, dented and covered in dirt and grass. But now she had been transformed through paintwork so smooth and glossy that it was almost hypnotic. Andy looked the sleek car over avidly. She rested now on polished deep dish rims, supported by coilover-adjustable suspension set so low that her new low profile tyres nestled well up under the guards. The passenger side of the car was presented to him and on the door and the panel behind the front wheel were artfully placed decals. He was unable to take his gaze away until Markus finally straightened from the engine bay. Carefully he lowered the bonnet with a satisfied half-smile on his face that became almost smug.

"You like?" he chucked his spanner onto the bench behind him. Andy ran his gaze over the entire car once more, from her low nose with the aggressive front spoiler to the side-skirts that pulled her closer to the ground, finally ending on the stylish rear bumper that made her complete. His eyes returned to meet Markus' again and he nodded significantly. He was about to reply when Tanya suddenly popped her head in through the open side door – surprising them.

"Hey you two. Want some burgers?"

"Damn yeah."

"Thanks," Markus took the food off her. His dirty fingers smeared black grease on the paper.

"At least wipe your hands," Tanya rolled her eyes. She left them to it, closing the side door behind her.

"Just adds to the flavour," Markus called after her jokingly.

As they munched on their burgers, Andy and Markus went over the Nissan critically. In particular they scrutinised her front section, where the bumper had been torn off and the guards bent. There was absolutely no evidence of the damage now. The repair job was immaculate. Her white body gleamed with a show-car finish.

"She's mint," Andy breathed.

"Yeah, almost too good to drift," Markus mused.

"Don't drift her then," Andy suggested and Markus glanced at him with a frown.

"What, you crazy? What else will I drift?"

"Could bust out the Mazda," Andy shrugged.

"Stuff it," Markus understood. "She's a lot tidier than before..."

"But she's still a drift car," Andy added.

"And that won't change."

"So you're happy I bent her up then?" Andy's grinned.

"Well, since you're paying for it..." Markus started out but stopped when he saw Andy's expression change. "You want to see the bill?"

"Not now, no," he shook his head glumly.

"You won't like it," Markus admitted. "Next time use a bit of common sense or, better yet, your own car."

"Yeah, whatever..."

"How's that Cefiro coming along anyway?"

"Slow," Andy shrugged and scratched for an elusive french-fry at the bottom of the container. "But steady."

"Reckon you'll actually get to drift her this lifetime?" Markus couldn't refrain. "Or have you forgotten how she goes back together?"

"Good things take time," Andy muttered defensively.

"Maybe if you spent less time arranging your spanners..."

"I'll get there," Andy cut in. "But the SR20 I was meant to be getting today was stuffed. I drove all that way for nothing."

"That sucks, but you should go for something bigger anyway," Markus mused. "Like an RB25 or even a '26."

"Would be nice," Andy was thoughtful. "Pricy though, plus I have to pay off your car now."

"True–" Markus sobered. Andy had not only agreed to pay for all the damage he caused, he had also offered to have the entire 180SX repainted at the same time. "Thanks for that." He knew that, through an early inheritance, Andy had his own two bedroom apartment. And, working a fairly well paying job with no rent to pay, he wasn't exactly strapped for cash. But even so, the offer had been generous. He certainly couldn't fault his friend in that regard.

"I said I would," Andy screwed his empty french-fry container and crumpled serviettes into a ball and threw it at the garbage can in the far corner. It flew wide, hit the wall and landed on the concrete floor.

"Close..."

"Can't win all the time," Andy explained and changed the subject. "So what're we up to tonight anyway?"

"Well, if you're keen to come, take this baby for a spin..." Markus screwed his own food packaging into a compact ball.

"Where to?" Andy asked. Markus did a jump shot and the makeshift ball flew over the Nissan. It hit the rim of the garbage can, bounced up against the wall and rebounded again before dropping into the goal.

"Fluke," Andy commented grumpily.

"Could've swished if I'd wanted to," Markus made a face.

"Where were you thinking?" Andy repeated.

"How about some diesel in the hills?"

"Leon, where've you been?" his mum greeted him with a frown as he entered the lounge. "Didn't I mention that we're having visitors today?" She sat in the lounge with his sister and a Japanese couple, his aunt and uncle.

"Yeah, sorry I'm late," Leon was sincere.

"You're hopeless," his mum shook her head with a half-amused smile. "But now that you're here, surely you remember Uncle Daisuke and Auntie Noriko?"

The couple stood up from the couch and Daisuke extended his hand as Leon approached. "Hello Leon, nice to see you again." His English was very good. He greeted Leon with a warm smile, which was reflected in his dark, twinkling eyes.

"How are you?" Leon bowed his head respectfully as they shook hands. He had not seen them in over six years. At first the conversation was a little hesitant, but with the courtesy of the Japanese culture, Leon soon warmed to them and was laughing easily at Daisuke's open manner. Once again he was amazed at his uncle's grasp of English. But then he remembered that his Japanese grandparents had placed enormous value on it and had endeavoured to ensure that Daisuke and his dad had been raised with excellent English language skills. His auntie's English was also good, but not nearly as good as Daisuke's.

The evening passed swiftly as they caught up with each other. Over dinner, Leon's mum told embarrassing stories of Leon and Tamsin adjusting to New Zealand and later on Leon managed to talk with Daisuke and Noriko about Osaka, which brought back many memories of his childhood. Following dessert, they ventured through to the lounge to relax. The conversation turned to Leon finishing school and getting his first job. Feeling left out, Tamsin couldn't take it any longer.

"Can I have my pressies now," she lisped abruptly.

"Of course," Noriko laughed and handed Tamsin a beautifully wrapped box. Excitedly Tamsin tore into the wrapping, quickly revealing a robotic dog. Even Leon leaned forward curiously. This type of toy was a craze in Japan. Daisuke helped her to unpack the dog, put the batteries in and turn it on. Promptly the little black and white creature began to scratch itself behind the ears and bark with an electronic yelp before it suddenly cocked its leg in true dog fashion.

"It must be a boy," Leon commented and they all laughed.

"It's cute," Tamsin's eyes shone. "Thank you, thank you!"

"Here Leon, we brought you something too," his auntie presented a large shoebox-sized present. With all but Tamsin's eyes on him, Leon unwrapped his present self-consciously.

When he looked through the cellophane window of the box, his face broke into a smile. It contained a radio-controlled car. A black, tricked out Nissan 350Z, complete with body kit, huge chrome wheels and a wing spoiler. "Cool, another car!" He turned the box over in his hands.

"Here use these," his mum handed him a pair of scissors.

"Why's it still scratching?" Tamsin interrupted suddenly. Her dog seemed to have got stuck into an infinite loop of scratching its ears.

"You don't already have one, do you?" his auntie asked with quick concern.

"Oh, no," Leon corrected himself and smiled. "I mean, I bought a real car today, so in a sense this is my second car of the day."

"You bought a car?" his mum was incredulous. "Today?"

"Um, yeah, that's why I was late," Leon nodded, worried by her reaction. "You said it was okay, right?"

"What kind is it?" Daisuke wanted to know. He was trying to find Robodog's reset button.

"A Nissan," Leon replied.

"Nissans are good," his uncle approved. He found the button and the dog's scratching stopped. "Which model?"

"It's a 1989 Silvia." Leon was still checking how to best open the box without destroying it entirely. Daisuke looked up abruptly.

"An S13? Turbo?"

"Yeah," Leon's fingers stopped and he looked up also, surprised at his uncle's reaction.

"Is it outside?"

"Yes."

"Show me," Daisuke instructed and handed the dog back to Tamsin.

"Now?" Leon looked around the lounge and to his mum.

"Go for it," she smiled and nodded to Leon.

"Okay." Leon set his present aside, and hesitantly led the way out of the house.

"You can't be serious!" his mum stared at the discoloured, dented and scratched car sitting on the lawn. She was completely appalled. "You bought this?" Leon remained silent. He should have known. He turned to see his auntie smile encouragingly at him.

"It really is an S13," his uncle walked a slow circuit around the car, before coming back to stand beside Leon. He looked the car over contemplatively. "I think I might have to ask you to let me drive it."

"Uh yeah, sure."

"Oh you boys!" Leon's mum threw her hands up in mock exasperation. "Well, it's going to get dark soon, so we'll be inside." She took Noriko's arm and steered her back to the house. "You've got another ten minutes Missy, and then it's bedtime for you," she spoke to Tamsin who stayed on the lawn. She had brought her new toy dog and was encouraging it to walk across the short grass.

"Alright let's have a look under the bonnet first," Daisuke suggested. "I want to see what I am dealing with here."

"Tell you what," Leon hesitated. "How about you drive her first, that way you can get a feel without expecting anything." Daisuke looked at him thoughtfully.

"I like your thinking," he nodded.

"Here are the keys." Leon handed them to him and stepped up to the passenger door. "Um, the central locking doesn't work so you'll have to open it for me from the inside…"

"No problem," He climbed in and opened the door for Leon. While Leon buckled himself in, he watched his uncle quietly familiarise himself with the cabin. Daisuke remained silent for a while, his dark, slanted eyes scanning the cabin, before he spoke in Japanese.

"It brings back memories?"

"Did I say that in Japanese?" he looked up.

"Yes," Leon smiled.

"It's good to hear you still understand it well... You really should keep practicing." He clicked his racing harness in. "But, yes it brings back many memories."

"Did you own an S13?" Leon asked curiously.

"Of course, we both did – your dad as well, I mean." Daisuke slid his hands around the leather steering wheel. "They're great cars. I am pretty sure that it was also the first car your dad let you drive."

"Really?"

"You sat in his lap and steered. He was very proud," Daisuke nodded with a warm smile. "You would have been barely older than your sister is now." His hands stopped moving on the steering wheel and he gazed through the windscreen, looking to where Tamsin still sat on the lawn in the dimming light. "She's a sweet little girl." His dark eyes were thoughtful. Tamsin was completely engrossed, playing with her new toy, unaware of his gaze. "My brother always spoke about having another child – he wanted a girl."

"Yeah, she's pretty funny," Leon nodded.

"Your dad never knew he was to have a daughter, you know," his uncle shook his head sadly. "The accident happened two days before your mum's appointment for the ultra-sound." Leon sat in silence. Daisuke turned away from his sister and looked at him. "You don't like talking about it, do you?"

Leon stared back at him, and shook his head. "Not really." Daisuke inclined his head in understanding.

"You must still be hurting a lot," he paused and shook his head, "It was difficult for me as well – for all of us." There was sorrow on his face. "But for you it probably feels as though he abandoned you." Leon looked away. "It wasn't like that," Daisuke continued quietly. "Racing was my brother's passion, but he loved you and your mother much, much more than that. He would have given it up if your mother had asked him to." He paused again and took a deep breath. "What happened on that day was a complete accident. It could have happened to anyone, at any time. Nobody is to blame." Leon remained silent. "Your dad died doing something he loved, Leon, if it had to happen, he wouldn't have wanted it any other way." Daisuke was silent for a moment. "Can you understand that?"

"I guess," Leon nodded. "But did it have to?"

"Have to happen?" Daisuke confirmed and Leon nodded. "We all have it in store for us sooner or later, some sooner..." He spoke thoughtfully. "So in that sense, yes, I think it had to happen." Leon nodded silently and his uncle turned his attention back to the controls. "Thank you for letting me drive your car. Like I said, it brings back a lot of good memories."

"Any time," Leon smiled. Somehow he felt a lot better. "I'm interested to know what you think."

"It has been a while since I drove one of these," Daisuke admitted. "Ready?"

"Let's go."

Daisuke turned the key and the Silvia growled. There was a certain magic about that moment when she came to life. Even his sister stopped playing and looked over at the black machine. His uncle cocked his head to one side and looked at Leon with a knowing smile.

"So that's why you didn't want me to look under the bonnet?"

Leon sat stunned, strapped tightly in his race seat. The way Daisuke drove was difficult to comprehend. He weaved the Silvia up the windy road with her powerful engine roaring. The rate of their ascent was astounding. Each corner hurtled at them, briefly illuminated in the headlights before he turned into it, shifted gear and powered through with the back wheels shrilling smoke and the Silvia soaring into a slide. At each bend, he fed the car in smoothly, in such an impressive style that Leon grimaced to himself, comparing his uncle's technique with his own rough and jerky, brute-force approach.

They were travelling fast and his pulse thudded wildly. Yet Leon felt no fear, only excitement, awe and exhilaration. Another bend came at them. Daisuke had the Silvia nestled into it so naturally that her chassis seemed to trill in harmonic accord. She flowed through the turn and came out with a crisp sneeze from the blow-off valve, straightening neatly, ready for the next. Like a purebred racehorse under the trained hands of a jockey, the Silvia responded to his skill, as he coaxed the maximum performance out of her, guiding her, directing, but never forcing or thrashing.

Leon looked over at his uncle as he deftly handled the controls, his hands and feet dancing to the tune of the engine. His manner was calm and controlled. He seemed relaxed, but Leon saw that he was intensely focused. Realising that he was seeing a master at work, Leon felt he needed to make the most of the opportunity, to learn everything he could. Intently, he watched his uncle's every move and Daisuke soon noticed.

"Smooth is fast, Leon," he spoke calmly and his words were barely audible above the bawl of the red-lining engine. "Any good racing driver will tell you that, but more importantly it is controlled and precise – in a competition you get points for that." Leon nodded, understanding, but remained silent and continued to watch closely as they raced on. Another curve flew towards them and the Silvia angled into it, sighting for the apex. Daisuke worked the steering wheel, handbrake and throttle and again her back end loosened. Leon was pressed into his seat and then she was through. Suddenly they had reached the top of the hill, the road levelled out and Daisuke throttled back.

With the headlights on high-beam they could see the tarseal sprawling far ahead, not running straight, but rather undulating and snaking over the hill top in gentle curves. Governed by a steep bank on the left and a slope that dropped away sharply to their right, the road was empty and enticing. It extended into the distance, luring them on.

"You alright?" Daisuke inquired casually.

"That's about the most exciting thing I've ever done," Leon spoke fervently. He meant every word.

"I must admit, I'm beginning to really like New Zealand," his uncle smiled. "This reminds me of the days at Mt Rokkō."

"Really?" Leon had heard the name before.

"Yes, we used to go there for night runs, there'd be five, six, seven cars all drifting up the mountain, and then back down again," Daisuke explained. "You had to react very quickly if somebody happened to be coming the other way…"

"Sounds crazy," Leon shook his head, but grinned broadly with adrenaline thick in his veins.

"We were crazy then…"

"So what does that make you now?"

"Let's find out…" Daisuke grinned with boyish enthusiasm and gassed it. As the revs climbed, the twin-turbos emitted a fierce whine and force-fed air into the combustion chambers. The revs soared all the way to the red-line and the Silvia unleashed upon the road. Involuntarily, Leon pulled the harness tighter around him as the roadside turned into a dark, molten smear. In disbelief, he realised that his uncle had been holding back on the hill-climb. There were no words to describe the intensity of their run.

"Kuso!" his uncle swore as they whipped around a blind corner and were suddenly confronted with a man in the middle of the road, sprinting at them and waving his arms frantically. Daisuke jerked out of his relaxed attitude. In a state of high alert, his brain analysed the situation – their speed, the gesticulating man, the white car taking up the road behind him and, beyond that, the hoard of people and parked vehicles. His eyes narrowed. There was no chance he could slow in time. Gracing the brakes, he downshifted and flicked the steering wheel to the right.

"Woah!" They would hit him, the thought raced through Leon's mind and he sat frozen and wide-eyed, pressing himself further back in his seat. At the very last moment the man dived out of the way. Leon saw him land awkwardly at the roadside and then the Silvia careened past, missing him narrowly. Daisuke's evasive manoeuvre sent the Silvia fully onto the wrong side of the road. Ahead of them, the ghostly white car sat trapped starkly in their headlights. It filled their vision, representing imminent danger. The gap between the road edge and her front seemed far too narrow for them to squeeze through, but Daisuke had no choice. Still running at 90km/h, there was no time to stop.

Leon swore through dry lips and unconsciously held his breath, staring at the car that obstructed their way. Time seemed to slow as they flew in, closing the last few feet. He recognised the car as a Nissan 180SX. He saw that she was in full drift regalia, with big drift style rims. He could even read the decals that adorned her body. Leon braced himself against his seat. They were so close!

"Looks like there are a few dudes already here," Markus commented as they approached the meeting point, a lookout car-park high up in the hills. His headlights fell onto a crowd of youth milling around a number of modified cars. The cars were parked at the edge of the car-park, leaving one side open to the road and the other to a waist-high fence which cordoned off the lookout point from a steep hillside that dropped down sharply to the waters of Lyttleton Harbour far below, now shrouded by darkness. Loud music thumped from one of the vehicles and many had their park-lights on in a festive fashion. It was party time.

"Yeah, look, Tom's already dragging out the diesel," Andy observed, indicating a guy lifting a red fuel container from the back of a parked R32 GTS-T Skyline. "He's getting straight into it."

"I'll have to be quick then," Markus laughed.

"For?" Andy wanted to know.

"Dude, there's way too much tread on the back wheels." Markus downshifted sharply as he closed in on the group and the SR20Det engine growled loud and aggressively through the custom exhaust. Warned by the sound, the people stopped their milling and turned to stare at the fast approaching car, blinking owlishly into its headlights. Lowering his window, Markus shouted at them: "Out the way peeps!" He steered off the road, towards the hoard of punters who scrambled out of his path. Some recognised him then and pushed up around the 180SX when Markus rolled her to a stop in the middle of the car-park.

"Markus, Andy damn, this 180's looking lush," Tom greeted them.

"What's up man," Markus grinned back. "Diesel time?"

"You know it," he laughed wickedly. "So get outta here."

"Nah dude, I think you should get outta here," Markus chuckled and revved the engine once, twice. In an instant the Nissan awoke from timid and docile to raw and aggressive.

"What're you up to man?" Andy pressed. "What about your ankle?"

"I might be a cripple, but I can still paint some Os," Markus replied. "Back up people," he called out and revved the engine again. Tom and the crowd drew back hastily and Andy reached for the door handhold. Markus hit the accelerator, eased up and then revved again so that the SR20Det's revs yo-yo'ed demandingly. At the same time, he locked the steering wheel over and popped the clutch. Power transferred to the rear wheels and they spun up with a shriek, billowing smoke. He flung the Nissan into a tight circle, spinning on the spot. The onlookers rowdily showed their appreciation.

With cheers and whistles still ringing in his ears and the rear tread on his tyres somewhat diminished, Markus rolled away to park up in a vacant spot on the outer rim of the car-park. Grinning widely, he and Andy got out and made their way back to mingle with the others and watch Tom's preparations for the night's sport. The music volume was adjusted and several cars turned and re-parked to point their headlights into the centre of the car-park. With their makeshift stage set and lit, all eyes were on Tom who walked out into the centre of the tarseal wearing bright red gumboots. A chuckle went through the crowd and several wolf-whistles sounded.

"Love the gummies, Tom!"

"Nice touch!"

"I know, they go good with my fuel can, don't they," Tom laughed in the headlights. He held up one hand for silence. This was his show. "From now," he addressed them with an entertainer's flair. "We've got us a smoking ban." Unscrewing the yellow lid, he splashed the diesel generously around him. Quickly it spread out, running out over the sealed car-park in a dark, oily reek that would lubricate and provide much entertainment. Tom dowsed a few last dry spots and, with his container depleted, he returned and eyed his work critically.

"Looks mint, Tom," one of the racers shouted. "That'll work a treat."

"Who'd like to do the honours?" Tom dangled the bait in front of the shadowy faces and got a chorus of response. "What? Nobody? He ignored them laughingly and instead called out loudly. "Alright, in that case, Sam, out you come." Tom came back to where Andy and Markus stood. "You guys are gonna like this," he said knowingly.

An expectant hush fell over the onlookers as an extraordinary Nissan rolled easily into the headlights of the parked cars. Her tyres squelched lightly as she made her way out into the middle of the fresh diesel slick. Sporting an S13 nose cone, the rear end was that of an 180SX, making it a Sil-Eighty. The car was a refined customisation that combined two visually different, but structurally identical machines. The candy-red Nissan crouched low over her enormously wide 18-inch rims that only just tucked within the legal limits of her rolled-out guards. She was graced with a snug-fitting full body kit, comprising clean side-skirts and an assertive front bumper that surrounded a massive intercooler. Hugging the ground and exuding power, she was an awesome drift weapon and everybody gave her the attention she deserved.

"Let's see what you..!" Tom's words vanished as the Sil-Eighty's six-cylinder engine bawled to a high crescendo. Her tyres spun freely, meeting little friction on the well-lubricated diesel spill. *Bah bah bah,* the staccato bursts of power wrung from the RB25Det engine as the tachometer needle hit the rev-limiter, relentlessly trying to push through but always ricocheting back. With her front wheels on hard lock and her rear wheels peeling her around, the Nissan began to revolve on the spot; nose-tail, nose-tail, her yellow fog lights beaming out like a lighthouse, continually pursued by the red of her taillights. Faster and faster she spun, until her lights blended together in an orange streak and smoke nearly enveloped her.

The onlookers, provoked by the intoxicating engine-roar, approved her antics loudly. It was a stunning display and from where he stood, leaning on the bonnet of the 180SX with Markus beside him, Andy grudgingly had to concede that it was performed effortlessly. Continuing to revolve, the driver lowered their window and shook a fist into the air.

"What a poser," Andy muttered under his breath. Markus heard him and chuckled. Only Andy was allowed to be a show-off.

"Don't worry, you'll get your chance to strut your stuff."

"He's hogging it!" Andy scowled.

"He?" Tom turned to him and raised an eyebrow and at that moment a number of wolf whistles sounded. "That's a *she* out there man," Tom smiled as Andy stared at him.

The engine's insistent brawl died down and the Sil-Eighty slowed her crazed dance until she stood still before them. Sure enough, through the open window they could now see that the driver was indeed a young woman. Andy gaped at her. She was striking and had long blonde hair. More whistles and cheers sounded as, almost tenderly, she coaxed her car off the slimy surface and rolled away to park.

"What ya reckon?" Tom smirked. "Not bad huh?"

"Not at all," Markus conceded, but Andy remained silent.

"So how 'bout it gangster, wanna show *him* up?" Tom teased Andy.

"This I gotta see," Markus dug in his pocket and offered the Nissan keys to Andy. "I'll even let you drive my car again."

"Ah, yeah," Andy reached his hand out but froze when a large sedan suddenly pressed rudely through the throng of people, leaving them scurrying out of its path.

"Out of my way!" Ignoring the mass protest, a boxy Holden trundled out onto the pad and claimed the space. With cut springs, the car sat splay-legged and awkward on the slippery surface, only the inner edge of her severely cambered wheels making contact with the road. Her engine thudded a deep, eight-cylinder sound.

"Hey, get off the pad loser," one of the onlookers objected loudly. "Wait your turn!" In response the V8 of the Holden erupted into a colossal growl. Rear wheels churning loosely, the heavy vehicle began to twist and writhe clumsily without real direction. The driver's inexperience showed and she swung indecisively first one way and then the other.

"Boo!" they jeered him.

"Tom, who is this clown?" Andy demanded.

"Never seen him," Tom replied frostily, without taking his gaze from the Holden's antics. "He's gate-crashing."

Undeterred by the hostile reception, the amateur driver flogged the Holden on. Screaming bitterly, the car suddenly kicked out as one of the rear wheels cut through the diesel and bit into the tarseal. With all the power of the V8 behind her, the Holden was propelled forward and she skimmed across the wide slick, angling away from the road and towards the bank. The driver wrestled to bring her back under control, but, with the steering impaired by her sodden tyres, she didn't respond. Too late, he realised the futility and hit the brakes.

The Holden's front tyres cleared the diesel and the last slippery residue smeared away so that they suddenly found grip and she whipped around in a 180-degree turn. Her momentum carried her on and she now skidded backwards on dew-damp grass towards the bank and retaining fence. She hit with a loud bang. The onlookers took a sharp breath and stared in astonishment. For a moment it looked as though the fence might hold her there, but then one of the wooden posts gave with a crack that reverberated around the hills like gunshot. The Holden sagged and her backend dropped. She slipped a metre down the bank and jerked to a sudden halt, coming up short against the galvanised strands of fencing wire, which shrieked against the metal of her body, eating deep scars into her paintwork.

"Woah, man!" Several onlookers rushed towards the snared Holden.

"Just let him drop," Tom grated. "Serves him right."

The Holden's engine had stalled and the music reached a lull. In the quiet, the fence creaked and groaned loudly as it fought to support the weight.

"It won't hold," Markus spoke apprehensively. At his words, the fence shrieked again and sagged further. The Holden trembled dangerously, hanging in its grasp.

"We have to do something," Andy broke into action and took charge. "Someone find me a tow rope!" he shouted at those that surrounded him, then turned to Markus. "Pull the 180 up over there on the other side of the diesel." Markus responded immediately, ripping open the driver's door. He edged the 180SX forward, guiding her around the diesel before backing up into position, on the far side, opposite the distressed Holden.

"Who has a tow rope?" Andy demanded urgently. "Anybody?"

"What about this," a girl ran towards him holding a thick yellow nylon rope with frayed ends. "It's not the longest though." It was the blonde that had driven the Sil-Eighty.

"It's way too short," Tom opined, standing idly nearby.

"We'll never get one long enough," Andy replied without taking his eyes off the girl. "We need to find more and join them."

"Got one more," a guy had gleaned an actual tow rope from one of the surrounding cars.

"Here's another!"

"Good, get them tied together." Andy turned away. "Tom, can you check up the road and stop any traffic coming around the corner?"

"Alright," Tom jogged away, past the 180SX, which stood with her nose just short of the road. Markus still sat at the wheel waiting patiently until the tow rope had been coupled and he received the go.

"How's that rope looking?" Andy asked the girl.

"Nearly there," she was stooped over, frantically tying the ropes together in the gloom. A loud squeak of complaint from the straining fence egged her on. "Done," she straightened up. "Hope it's long enough."

"Give me that end," Andy's fingers touched hers as he snatched it off her. "Tie yours to the 180," he called back over his shoulder and ran towards the Holden, trailing rope. With half its length down the bank, the Holden's headlights angled up helplessly towards the night sky. Beyond them, Andy could just make out the driver, sitting rigid in his seat, too scared to move lest the fence gave, sending him careening down the bank. Pale-faced and wide-eyed, he stared helplessly at the people fussing to prepare his rescue.

The fence groaned again and sagged a little more and the metal wires ate further into the Holden's bodywork. Andy reached it just as the heavy rope came up tight in his hands. It was too short! He turned around to see the girl at the back of the 180SX. Her slim figure was silhouetted against the bright crimson glow of the brake lights. Even in the heat of the moment, Andy reflected on her beauty as she crouched in concentration, connecting the tow rope with her long blonde hair swept back over her shoulders. She was really hot.

"I need another foot!" Andy called out to her.

"Wait, don't yank it!" the girl snapped at him. "I might be able to give it to ya." Having tied her end to the Nissan, she jumped clear. The instant she was out of the way, the 180SX's brake lights extinguished and her reversing lights came on as Markus edged her carefully backwards. "Stop!" the girl raised a hand to reinforce the command when she saw the Nissan's rear wheels creep dangerously close to the slippery black diesel. Silently Andy commended her. He heaved on the tow rope so that it came up tight in his hands. Another bystander ran to his aid and held it while Andy thrust the frayed end through the tow-hook on the front of the Holden. He had just enough length to tie his knot.

"Go!" Andy yelled. Markus heard him. Slowly, he eased the Nissan forward, picking up the slack. The thick nylon rope with its knotted appendages snapped taut with a twang. The Holden responded instantly, her nose moved and was jerked down under the increasing pressure. The fence objected loudly as the Holden's backend was levered up. Creaking and groaning it rasped against her tail, inflicting further damage. It looked like it was going to work, but as the full weight of the big Holden came onto the rope, the 180SX began to falter.

Markus brought on full power and the SR20Det hollered ferociously. The rear wheels squealed and were unable to find enough traction to tow the bulky car up the bank. Thick blue tyre smoke erupted around her as she fishtailed loosely. Back and forth she slid, straining at the rope that ran out dead straight under the tremendous tension. "Get back!" Andy barked at those that stood by too closely, watching with avid fascination. He knew that if the rope gave it could inflict horrible injuries to anybody caught in the whiplash. Hurriedly they drew back.

The 180SX continued to struggle to no avail. Andy recognised the problem. Leaving his position at the front of the Holden, he sprinted around the diesel spill and reached the labouring Nissan. "Get up beside me," he called to the girl and together they hopped up to sit on the back of the 180SX with their legs dangling over the rear bumper. Tyre smoke enveloped them, while their combined weight helped to press the back wheels firmly down into the road. They found traction and staunchly the 180SX shuddered forward with the Holden in tow.

Several others raced in and added their brute strength by pushing on the back of the 180SX and slowly the Holden came up, leaving the distraught fence broken and sagging behind it. Many of the onlookers broke into cheering and clapping when the Holden finally stood straight and level again. Markus buttoned off the accelerator and those pushing straightened up, grinning success from ear-to-ear. Markus left the Nissan temporarily parked in the road with her engine still idling and climbed out to join the celebration. Together, Andy and the girl slipped off the back of the 180SX.

"Good effort," Andy ignored the backslapping around him and turned to her.

"All in a days work," she shrugged easily.

"Wouldn't want to meet up sometime, would ya?"

"Thanks, but I happen to have a boyfriend," she walked away. Her hips swayed faintly, mocking him.

Andy stared after her bitterly. Then he noticed the driver of the Holden. He had got out and was coming towards them hesitantly. His eyes were downcast and he had lost his previous arrogance. Andy turned his frustration on him.

"Well done, you idiot. That stunt could've killed ya!"

"Yeah chump, next time we'll let you dangle and drop," Tom appeared, having relinquished his place on the road. He was quick to add his two cents, moving his hand across his neck to make his point.

"Hey, come on fellas," Markus stepped up beside them. "We were all green at one time." He spoke mildly but his words carried a warning to the young driver of the Holden. "You were pretty lucky. You should have a bit of a play in the wet and on flat ground before you try diesel with us up here."

"You should get that rope untied and beat it..." Andy added, but paused suddenly and cocked his head to one side. There was a faint disturbance in the air, which rapidly grew louder. "There's a car coming!" Andy spun around. "The 180!"

The 180SX stood driverless in the middle of the road, completely exposed and vulnerable. With Markus beside him there was no chance they could get her out of the way in time. By now the disturbance had built up into a loud bawl that reverberated around the hills. Andy launched into a run. He reached the 180SX but ran on, sprinting up the road on collision course with the approaching sound. Tyres squealed and suddenly a pair of headlights appeared around the bend and flew towards him. The full engine howl hit him and frantically Andy brandished his hands above his head, running blindly into the oncoming lights.

"Woah!" Leon exclaimed again as they closed in. Daisuke's left hand dropped to the handbrake. He gave the steering wheel another gentle nudge to the right, and then immediately countered, spinning it left and yanking up the handbrake leaver. The Silvia's weight shifted, her rear wheels locking momentarily and, losing traction, her back section slid out towards the bank. Both rear wheels dropped off the road and thrashed on the narrow strip of gravel as Daisuke brought the RB26 back into snarling action.

In an epic drift they arced around the front of the 180SX. Daisuke had cut it so fine that he managed to avoid a full collision as well as the wrath of the steep bank, but connecting was still inevitable. With a loud rasp the Silvia scraped across the 180SX's front bumper. Then they were past with their headlights sweeping over the gathering of bystanders, shell-shocked and unmoving. The instant they were clear, Daisuke corrected and brought the Silvia back onto the road.

"That was close," Leon ran his hand through his hair. As they rolled away, he spun in his seat to stare at the activity behind them. He saw a commotion as several people milled around the white car. Someone ran out into the road, gesticulating after them. To Leon his intentions were unmistakable. He was furious.

"We should go back," Daisuke began to slow the Silvia, looking uncertainly into his rear-view mirror.

"No way, keep going," Leon was still staring behind them. "They look super pissed off."

"Are you sure?" Daisuke asked, still consulting his rear-view mirror. "I would have to say that it was their fault. You can't just park a car in the middle of the road."

"I agree, but I'm pretty sure they don't see it that way." Leon turned away as they rounded a corner and the scene disappeared from view. "We should get out of here."

"You don't want to have them pay for any damage?"

"I don't think there's much chance of that, at best they might not beat us up," Leon shook his head seriously. "Go for it," he urged.

Daisuke nodded and directed his attention back to the road in front of them. Leon's brooding thoughts of the angry racers receded as Daisuke flung the Silvia on, playing her like a master musician. As each bend flickered at them in the beam of the headlights, Daisuke skillfully eased her into a sweeping slide. He caught her before she overextended and neatly countered her balance, leaning her weight out into the opposite side.

With the ever present danger of the clay bank smudging past to their left and the sinister depths on their right, Leon's excitement was heightened and he revelled in the moment. This was by far the most exhilarating *shotgun* he had ever driven. He watched closely as his uncle raced on, coaxing the full spectrum of performance out of the Silvia, guiding her through each bend with a startling combination of speed, elegance and precision. The car gave him everything she had.

Andy picked himself up off the ground and, massaging his shoulder, ran to the front of the car to inspect the damage. The bumper was cracked and the fresh white paint scraped nearly its entire length. He raised a fist, aggressively shaking it after the black car and its mocking red taillights as it rounded the corner and vanished from sight. He was seething with anger.

"Damn, did you see that guy?" Markus demanded of Andy, running over to where he was standing by the front of the Nissan. "The way he went around the 180 was insane."

"Dude, look, they hit your car," Angrily, Andy pointed to the front of the car.

"Oh, no way, we just fixed that," Markus dropped to one knee. "Look he's cracked the whole bumper and busted an indicator too." Broken fibreglass littered the road in front of the Nissan. Several other racers had stepped up around them, trying to get a look at the damage.

"You can't just let them get away," Tom exclaimed. "They nearly ran you over."

"Let's go after him and kick his ass," Andy agreed vehemently. Not waiting for a response, he ran around to the driver's door of the 180SX. "Tom, get that rope untied. Come on Markus." He jumped in and revved the engine. "Hurry up Tom!" he snarled out the window, egging on the racer who was frantically trying to free them from the tow rope.

"You're in my seat," Markus protested.

"No time, get in," Andy growled and Markus hopped in beside him.

"You won't catch him man, he's got too big a head start," he spoke with absolute certainty. "The way he drove..." Markus shook his head in wonder.

"Rope's off!" Andy immediately threw the 180SX forward. Markus sat quietly, observing Andy's driving as he thrashed the 180SX in staunch pursuit. At one point, when they could see the road curving down below them across the hillside, they saw a dark smudge hurtling along, a pale beam of light cast out ahead of it. The black Silvia was far ahead of them. When they reached the bottom of the hill and the road branched out into expansive suburbs Andy was forced to admit defeat. The Silvia could have gone anywhere.

"We'll see them again," Markus pointed out. "There's not many black Silvia's like that around."

"I'm going to find her," Andy nodded darkly.

For Leon, it was all over far too quickly when Daisuke abruptly reached the bottom of the hill and they were again restricted to the slow 50km/h residential zone. Not long afterwards Daisuke pulled into their driveway and parked. He left the engine rumbling and glanced over at Leon, who sat quietly, reluctant to get out. He was experiencing a mixture of awe and disappointment that it was over. If his dad had been even better than Daisuke, how must he have driven?

"Sorry Leon," Daisuke offered sincerely, misinterpreting Leon's stillness. "I hope it's not bad." He made to get out. "We should take a look."

"Daisuke?" Leon held him back.

"Yes?" his uncle looked at him.

"I need you to teach me to drive like that," Leon said simply. Daisuke looked at him seriously.

"Why?"

Leon reflected on this. "I just need you to," he said simply.

"So I have awakened the speed devil in you?"

"No, I think he was already awake," Leon shook his head earnestly. "But you've made me realise that I've got quite a bit–" Leon corrected himself, "no, heaps to learn."

Daisuke understood and was silent. "What about your mother?" he asked at last.

"She can keep Noriko company while we practise," Leon answered him without any guile.

"I like your thinking," Daisuke grinned wickedly. "When do you want to start?"

"We don't have much time," Leon pointed out. "Especially since I have to work each day."

"Our return flight for Osaka is on Friday," Daisuke agreed. "It's nearly 10pm. Are you tired?"

"Not at all," Leon answered truthfully. He was wide awake. The spine-tingling drive in the hills had charged him with adrenaline. He knew that even if he wanted to, he wouldn't be able to sleep for some time yet.

"Where is a place that is flat and has a bend, where we can throttle it a bit?"

As Leon guided him unerringly out to the industrial area where he had first test-driven the Silvia, Daisuke outlined some of the key drift techniques: the handbrake drift, powerslide, shift-lock, clutch-kick and then the more complicated techniques that used weight transition. Leon listened closely and tried to take it all in, but soon his head was swimming with all the information and unfamiliar terms. They reached their destination and Daisuke rolled along the stretch, pacing it out as Leon had initially done. He nodded. "This will do." Rounding the bend, they reached the end of the cul-de-sac, where he turned around and brought the car to a stop. He switched the engine and lights off. It was dark and silent in the industrial area. With nothing to distract them, Daisuke had Leon's complete attention.

"You asked me to teach you," he turned to Leon seriously. Leon nodded and he continued. "With knowledge comes responsibility. A teacher should always first make their pupil aware of the risks and responsibilities. Alas," he smiled ruefully, "There are many, and we don't have much time, but I do just quickly want to say that a public road isn't a racetrack. We shouldn't have been racing up in the hills like that. We were lucky that we came away with just a scratch. It could've been much worse."

"They were in the middle of the road, it was their fault," Leon began to protest but Daisuke held up one hand.

"What if you hit them and injured or even killed someone?" he asked quietly. "What then? Even if it was their fault?"

Leon was silent. He knew how it felt to lose someone close. He wouldn't want anybody to endure that. "So why did you drive like that then?"

"I guess I wanted to impress you," Daisuke admitted. "To get you excited about drifting, something your dad and I have always been so passionate about," he paused. "But, I got quite carried away. Drifting should be kept to the track," he indicated the dim road before him. "Even this isn't something we should be doing. However, since it is so far from housing I think it is safe enough for now." Leon nodded understanding and with a resolute manner, his uncle began his instruction.

He explained hand and foot placements, the basics of weight transfer, understeer and over-steer, braking and acceleration. Although he was largely self-taught, with his engineering mind he was able to analyse his own techniques and relate them patiently. When he realised that Leon was beginning to nod off with all the theory, he switched to something practical. "Let's begin with a powerslide." Starting the Silvia's engine, he launched her through the single tight bend which made up their course. As he performed the manoeuvre, with the engine and tyres screaming loudly, he again calmly explained his movements to Leon, breaking it into steps. "First accelerate down the straight before the bend, turn the steering wheel into the bend, put the clutch in, floor the accelerator, then let the clutch out fast. When you feel the car sliding, start counter-steering to control the drift and then straighten her out again."

Finally they switched seats, and it was Leon's turn to pilot the black Nissan through the bend, trying to replicate his uncle's finesse. Leon promptly spun, ending up half-in and half-out of the bend pointing back the way he had come. Feeling silly, he drove back to the start and, after listening to his uncle's advice, tried over. Time and again Leon threw the Silvia at the bend, determined to apply each step smoothly and naturally. At first Daisuke urged him to use the handbrake to get the initial loss of traction and then later he showed him how to exploit the RB26's power to perform drift techniques that were difficult or near impossible with a lesser powered car.

They were so absorbed that they didn't realise the time racing by. Leon's skills expanded quickly and, although he didn't say it, Daisuke was impressed with Leon's quick learning. Both of their enthusiasm was insatiable and in the end it was the petrol warning light that drove them to retire for the evening. As they left the industrial area, Leon realised suddenly that he was exhausted. The long time of intense concentration had taken it out of him. When they reached their home and parked again, Leon clambered out with an effort and locked his car. He was ready to stumble across the lawn to the house when Daisuke stopped him.

"There's one other thing, Leon."

"What's that?" Leon turned back tiredly.

"We will need to get some more tyres for tomorrow."

"They'll be fine, they were quite new," Leon opined.

"Well in that case we'll need to get a few sets," he suggested reasonably. "If you want to keep practicing that is."

"Surely not," Leon walked over to check the back tyres. He ran his hand up under the guards. It was smooth under his fingers. He stared dumbly at it in the darkness. The 7mm of new tread was all but gone.

"Still want to be a drifter?" his uncle chuckled.

Leon didn't reply at once. But then he recalled all the fun and excitement. "Yes."

They made their way over to the house. Pausing at the front door, Leon looked back at the dark shape of the Silvia. "What do you think?" he asked quietly. "Of my car – I mean?"

"It's good," Daisuke spoke thoughtfully. "But..."

"But?"

"It needs work – and more grip."

"More grip?" Leon thought he hadn't heard right.

"Yes – more grip, wider tyres and a proper suspension kit," Daisuke turned to him. "Trust me, the more grip you have, the more control you have," he explained. "But then you also need the power to actually lose the grip when you want."

"That does sort of make sense..." Leon spoke cautiously.

"We'll take a good look at your car tomorrow and see what we can do. Right now, I must admit I am very tired and I think I must be a bit jet-lagged."

"Yeah, of course – I totally forgot you only arrived today. Feels like you've been here for ages," Leon admitted. And it was true, having his uncle here felt completely natural.

"I'll take that as a compliment," Daisuke's smile turned into a drawn out yawn.

"So you should," Leon smiled back and also yawned. "And yes, it's definitely time for bed."

"Leon, breakfast in 15 minutes," his mum woke him the next morning. With a habitual frown, Leon instinctively turned over in bed and pulled his blanket higher up. Then he remembered, he and Daisuke were supposed to be working on the Silvia today. With a heave he pushed his blanket aside and sat up. The sun was already shining through the gaps in his curtains. He had slept late.

"Okay Mum. I'll just have a quick shower and then I'll be down," Leon got up quickly and went through to the bathroom. He had only just finished his shower and shrugged into his clothes when the doorbell rang.

"That'll be for you Leon," his mum called up the stairs from the kitchen. "Can you get it?"

"Um, yeah sure," Leon wasn't expecting anybody, but he trundled down the stairs and opened the front door.

"Hey, what's up dude? Where've you been?"

"Oh hey," Leon was surprised to find Byron standing outside. "What's happening?"

"I called you yesterday, but your phone kept going to voicemail," Byron accused.

"Weird..." Leon pulled his mobile out of his pocket. "Oh, woops." He had switched it off when he had met with Lorna and forgotten to turn it on again.

"I also tried calling here but you were out," Byron continued. "Anyway, your mum said I should come over for breakfast." He sniffed the air. "Is that bacon and eggs?"

"Yep," Leon smiled and opened the door wider. "Come in."

"Have you got other visitors?"

"Why? Are you worried there won't be enough food for you?" Leon teased.

"Nah, I was just wondering what that piece of crap is doing here…"

"What do you mean?"

"That black car, parked outside."

"Oh that," Leon inspected his thumbnail. "That'd be mine."

"You can't be serious?" Byron gaped at him.

"Um yeah," Leon was about to close the door but Byron stopped him. He went outside.

"That piece of crap is yours?" Byron stared across the lawn.

"Yeah."

"Damn… Well don't expect me to drive with you," he said finally with an appalled expression on his face. Leon followed him outside and also gazed across the front lawn. Even from where they stood at the front door, the Nissan looked battered and hard done by.

"It does look a little rough, aye?" Leon spoke thoughtfully. He began walking towards it.

"A little rough?!" Byron trailed him. "Try *munted*."

"Well, she does need a bit of work," Leon admitted. Byron turned to glance over at his own pristine Altezza, which he had parked on the street. He turned back again, and scowled at the Silvia.

"Dude, I'd take her straight to the dump."

"Hey, come on man, her chassis is still straight and you know what these machines can do, right?"

"What, drive? Most cars are designed to do that."

"Drift, man," Leon replied exasperatedly.

"Well, yeah, I guess," Byron was dubious. "But this thing just looks like it's been thrashed to hell and back."

"Somewhat yeah, but check this out," Leon unlocked the driver's door. He reached inside, pulled the bonnet release and walked around to the front of the Silvia. "I think you'll like it."

Byron hesitated and then laughed, as he watched Leon scanning the engine bay for the bonnet stay. "Yeah, I do like that... What an awesome car you bought – bonnet stay not included..."

"Come on," Leon's irritation started to show, as he held up the bonnet with his hand. "Take a look." With a show of reluctance, Byron stepped up beside him.

"Eh?" He tilted his head first one way and then the other. "Dude..."

"What?"

"You've got a GT-R engine in here?"

"RB26Dett," Leon confirmed. Byron was silent and continued to peer thoughtfully into the engine bay. He crouched down in front of the car and inspected the intercooler. Finally he stood up.

"Not bad," he shrugged, trying to look indifferent.

"For an RB26 I'll go without a bonnet stay..." Leon laughed and then sobered. "My uncle and I plan to start fixing her up today. Want to help?" Stalling, Byron ran another long look over the dented and scratched body of the Silvia. "Go on, I'll even let ya have a try at drifting her," Leon grinned cheekily.

"What you're drifting now? A couple of days ago you barely drove," Byron scowled.

"True, but my uncle has agreed to teach me..." Leon scratched the back of his head.

"Seriously?"

"He's only here until Friday, but we'll practice each night."

"Wow..." Byron turned envious. Then he nodded. "Bacon and eggs first though."

After breakfast, Leon, Byron and Daisuke went outside to start on the Nissan.

"The suspension and brakes really need fixing, but we'll begin with the engine. Leon, can you open the bonnet?" his uncle immediately took charge.

"Sure," Leon unlocked the car and pulled the bonnet release. "There's no stay though."

"Right, well we need to find something to hold this bonnet up and we also need some tools."

"The toolkit is in the garage. Byron can you get it?" Leon requested. "I'll look for a stick or something."

"Okay," Byron went to the garage door. He pulled it open and stood for a moment. "What the..?" Daisuke and Leon turned at his outburst. Byron had discovered the Laurel, which stood broken in the garage. "Dude, what's this?"

"Um, well, I..." Leon began awkwardly. Even though it had happened less than 24 hours ago, he didn't remember it looking quite that bad.

"You crashed it? When?" Byron asked incredulously. "And your mum didn't lose the plot?" Daisuke left the Silvia and went into the garage. Remaining silent, he walked slowly around the Laurel, inspecting it carefully.

"Yesterday... And no, not really," Leon shook his head uncomfortably and watched his uncle.

"And you didn't hurt yourself either?" Byron also went to inspect the crashed car.

"Just the scratch on my forehead and my neck was a bit sore this morning."

"You must've hit something pretty hard," Byron persisted.

"Can we just concentrate on the Silvia?" Leon asked. They both looked at him and his uncle nodded.

"I thought we might be able to use it for parts," Daisuke explained. "But perhaps not." He waited for Byron to retrieve the toolkit from the shelf and then lowered the garage door behind him.

Leon turned away and searched under the trees that grew along the fence line of the neighbouring property. He found a strong, straight stick and used it to hold the bonnet up securely. Daisuke and Leon immediately began a thorough inspection of the engine bay, running their hands and eyes over the various components. Working with spanner and ratchet they dismantled parts and checked their condition.

"We're going to need a new one of these," Daisuke pointed out. "And this..." Byron stood by, quiet and idle, until Daisuke took pity on him. "Why don't you check the oil? There," he inclined his head towards the dip-stick.

Byron removed it and checked the level. "Seems fine to me." He was about to replace it when Daisuke stopped him and took it out of his hands. He held the tip up to the sunlight and frowned, then sniffed it, before wiping it across his palm. It left a dirty black smear.

"This is no good," Daisuke shook his head slowly and turned to Leon. "Did you not even check the oil when you bought the car?" Leon shrugged helplessly. "New oil and filter," his uncle instructed and with a sigh, Leon noted it down on the growing list. "May as well get an oil catch can while we're at it." He looked around the engine bay thoughtfully. "We need to bolt the battery down properly too. Or ideally, relocate it to the boot," Daisuke twanged the bungee cords to make his point. "The last thing you want is battery acid all over your engine. And to get the best cooling, we should replace the radiator and get some electric fans."

"Right..."

"We need some decent spark plugs and ideally a proper computer..." Daisuke reeled off further items and Leon scribbled frantically to get it all down. "The brakes felt quite worn, so we need new pads... Hmmm, that should be about it... Ah, we also need to get some spacers for the steering rack to get more steering angle. That's very important." Leon stared down at the list in dismay.

"How much is all this going to cost?" he blurted.

"We'll worry about that later," Daisuke shrugged. "You know, in our family we've always had a saying." His uncle switched to Japanese and spoke.

"If you're going to do something, do it properly, or not at all?" Leon translated and Daisuke nodded. "And my dad – did he follow that rule as well?" Leon asked bitterly before he could stop himself. Byron looked down at his shoes. Daisuke's eyes softened.

"Yes. In fact, it was he that would say it to me."

"About drifting?"

"No," Daisuke smiled at a distant memory. "Far from it, it was about doing the dishes."

"Dishes?"

"When we were growing up, your dad and I were responsible for doing the dishes and drying them each night," Daisuke nodded. "I hated it and always cleaned them rather poorly. Your dad used to scold me and tell me this rule, but of course I didn't listen. Then, on my birthday your grandma made Teriyaki chicken, especially for me. It was my favourite you know... but as I was eating it, I suddenly noticed my plate still had dried fish on it from the night before." Daisuke made a face. "I couldn't eat another bite... It really put me off. After that, whenever it was my turn, I cleaned them properly..."

"I hate doing dishes," Byron muttered. "I've got a dishwasher for that."

"So do I – now," Daisuke agreed. "Shall we get the parts?"

"There's a place I know," Byron suggested. "They've been advertising a heap of specials on the radio."

"Let's check them out," Leon agreed.

The three of them hopped into Byron's Altezza and headed to the performance parts store, leaving the partly-dismantled Nissan behind.

"Not a bad ride aye?" As he drove, Byron was keen to get Daisuke's opinion on his prized car.

"Yes, very nice," Daisuke nodded, looking around the immaculate leather interior. "You know, you can drift these too," he spoke thoughtfully. "They slide quite well actually... Have you tried?"

"Nah, haven't," Byron admitted reluctantly.

"We should have a go later, Dai could give us a demo..." Leon suggested from the back seat.

"Uh, that's okay," Byron hastily declined. "I don't want her to start looking like your Silvia."

"It'll be alright," Leon teased. "The 'Tez might even be half as good."

"Dude, she'd put your car to shame," Byron retorted over his shoulder.

"So you're keen then?"

"Hell no. You two psychos stay away from my car," Byron spoke forcefully. "Especially you – after what you did to your mum's car. Anyway, you've already offered for me to have a go in your *Silly*, so I'd rather we just keep wrecking that." Byron drew a breath. "Plus we need to keep the 'Tez driving so there's somebody to tow you back to the shop."

"Good thinking," Leon laughed.

They reached the store and were greeted with numerous large signs that advertised the weekend sale in bright, gaudy colours. Byron pulled into the car-park, which was filled with many modified cars.

"Wow, I didn't realise quite how serious you are about your cars here," Daisuke said as he got out of the Toyota and looked around. He was visibly impressed. "This makes me feel at home."

"Hey, I know that one," Leon pointed at a fierce RX-7.

Byron recognised it also. "That's Simon's machine."

"He won the last drift competition that we went to," Leon explained to his uncle who nodded and eyed the Batman thoughtfully for a moment.

"Let's go inside."

"Check out all this cool stuff," Byron observed when they entered through the glass sliding doors. He turned and saw Daisuke take a long look around the large shop. "Body kits, alloy wheels, tyres, intake manifolds, extractors and exhaust systems, turbos, intercoolers, blow-off valves, fuel systems, suspension kits, steering wheels, gauges, air filters, strut braces... Anything performance, you name it, they have it, or can get it."

"I like it," Daisuke said earnestly. "What's first on the list?"

Leon trailed Byron and his uncle who were like kids in a candy shop. From shelf-to-shelf they went, helping themselves rather than waiting for one of the sales staff. They picked up items, checked brands, scanned descriptions and then accepted or discarded them again.

"What about this?"

"Oh and we should get one of these too..." Rapidly they worked their way through the shopping list, piling the selections high on Leon's outstretched arms.

Once they had the parts they needed, Leon and Byron went to pay, while Daisuke had one last check to ensure they hadn't forgotten anything. As they neared the counter, Leon recognised one of the salespeople to be Simon. He had just finished with another customer.

"Oh hey, how's it going?" Leon greeted him and stood by as Byron unloaded the items from his arms onto the counter.

"It's the drift king," Simon smiled in recognition. "Yeah, all good here. Pretty busy with the sale though… So, crashed any more cars lately?"

"Not yet, but give me another week..." Leon chuckled.

"Why? What're you up to?" Simon picked up one of the boxes that Byron had placed on the counter. "And what do you need this computer for?"

"Um, kinda bought me a car…" Leon scratched his temple.

"Tell me more," Simon invited with a raised an eyebrow. "What type?"

"A Silvia, and a fairly poked one at that," Byron shook his head sadly.

"And you want to put all this into it and then drift it," Simon looked from Byron to Leon.

"With a bit of help…" Leon nodded wistfully.

"And who's this?" Simon asked as Daisuke approached.

"My uncle," Leon replied. "From Japan."

"He drifts, doesn't he?" Simon saw it right away.

"Used to," Leon nodded and turned to his uncle. "Daisuke, this is Simon."

"Hi," Daisuke extended his hand.

"Hey," the two drifters gazed at each other with mutual respect. "Leon tells me you used to drift?"

"A little," Daisuke smiled humbly.

"Did you ever drift Mount Haruna?"

"Occasionally," Daisuke nodded. "But mainly the passes at Mt Rokkō, since it was closer."

"A *touge* drifter. Mean," Simon declared and shook his head before he turned to Leon. "If I were you, I'd get him to teach me everything he can."

"I'm working on it," Leon admitted. "But he's only here till Friday."

"Well, better get onto it then," Simon urged and began scanning the items. Leon watched him apprehensively as he scanned the last one and tallied up on the till. "That comes to..." he named the price and Leon winced. It was much more than he had estimated in his head.

"Can you give us a discount?" Daisuke pressed.

"We already have the sale on, so trade price is about the best I can do," Simon offered.

"Every bit helps. See Leon, if you don't ask, you don't get." And before Leon could, Daisuke had produced his own card.

"You can't pay – I..." but his uncle waved away his protest.

"Leon, think of it as a late birthday present for all those your auntie and I have missed."

"But..." Leon looked at Simon helplessly.

"You want my advice?" Simon grinned. "Take the money and run."

"Bloody right," Byron agreed. "Especially if I was busting my gut working a crappy job."

"Three against one, that's not fair," Leon watched helplessly as his uncle paid.

"You're a lucky man," Simon handed them their bags of goodies. "What sort of work do you do anyway?"

"Warehousing and distribution," Leon smiled ruefully.

"And that involves..?"

"He drives a forklift in a freezer," Byron replied promptly.

"Okay, maybe not so lucky – that sounds bad..."

"Yeah, I'm over it," Leon admitted. "I've been meaning to find something better."

Simon looked at him thoughtfully for a second. "Why not apply here?"

"Are you looking for staff?"

"One of the guys is heading overseas and we haven't found a replacement yet," Simon nodded. "You know much about car parts?"

"Not really," Leon had to admit.

"You know what a turbo is?"

"Yeah of course..."

"What does HKS stand for?"

"Dunno," Leon frowned. "I know they make good parts," he offered.

"That they do," Simon chuckled. "Do you have any retail experience?"

"I worked at Maccas in high school," Leon shrugged.

"Weird, so did I," Simon produced his cell-phone. "You got your number handy?"

"Uh, sure," Leon gave it to him.

"I'll let you know how I get on."

"Cool, but I won't get my hopes up."

"My brother-in-law is the boss, so I'll put in a good word," Simon grinned.

Leon stared at him. "Are you always this helpful?"

"Nah, but I feel a bit bad about you stacking your mum's car," Simon admitted with a smile. "And I figure you might find this better than working in a freezer."

"Thanks," Leon said simply, at a loss for words.

"I'll give you a call," Simon promised. "And Leon, go hard aye – it's not often you get a chance like that," he inclined his head towards Daisuke who was making his way outside.

"I'll try," Leon had to smile. "Catcha later." He turned to follow Byron and his uncle out of the shop.

"Oh, and hey," Simon called after him. "So you'll run in the next comp, yeah?"

"No way," Leon shook his head. "I've only just started."

"You'll be sweet. I'm signing up tonight, so will sign you up too," Simon dismissed his excuse and grinned. "I'll get the shop to pay your entry – we were going to pay for Jason anyway, but since he's leaving..."

"Are you serious?" Leon looked at him speechlessly.

"Yeah sure, and don't worry – I'll warn the crowd to stand well back from the fence," Simon's grin broadened and he gave Leon a cheesy thumbs-up before turning away to serve the next customer.

"Nah, you can't..." Leon's objection petered into silence and he nervously ran his hand through his hair. Simon wasn't listening. Leon stood uncertainly by the sliding door for a long moment, then glanced out and saw that Byron and Daisuke had already reached the car and were looking back towards him. "Dammit," he muttered under his breath and hurried after them. He didn't see Simon look up and smile as he watched Leon leave.

"Si's offered you a job," Byron was waiting by the Altezza. "That's awesome."

"He's going to see about getting me a job," Leon corrected him with a frown.

"Selling parts would be sweet," Byron enthused. "You'll be able to hook me up with all sorts of discounts."

"It would be," Leon had to agree. "But it's not like I'm even remotely qualified for it so I doubt I'll get it." His voice had a bitter edge.

"You will," Byron said with such conviction that Leon was taken aback. He stared at Byron and then turned to Daisuke who had been watching him quietly. He gave Leon an almost imperceptible nod of encouragement.

"We'll see..." Leon shrugged uncertainly. "Simon's crazy. He's also planning to sign me up for the next drifting comp," his voice now held a hint of trepidation.

"What?" Byron frowned.

"I know, he's insane," Leon put his hands on his head. "He even said the shop will pay the entry fee. I tried to tell him I wasn't keen but he wouldn't listen."

"You've only just started learning," Byron exclaimed.

"I know..." Leon muttered. "He probably just wants to see me make a fool of myself again."

"You'll be fine," Daisuke spoke up for the first time. "We've just got a bit of work to do."

"A real competition? In two weeks?" Leon stared at him aghast. "Are you serious?"

"Why not? What have you got to lose?"

"My car maybe? I already smashed Mum's up remember?"

"You'll be fine," his uncle repeated. "You did say you wanted to learn to drift yesterday – this will give you something to aim for."

Leon pinched his lip and stared at the ground broodingly. "So you really think I can do it?" he wanted to know.

"Well, you might not come first, or second or third, but does that really matter? You will certainly get better… And remember – you definitely can't win if you don't even race."

Leon hesitated, but then he nodded. "Stuff it – alright, let's give it a shot…"

"Like I said – you've got my help," Byron nodded.

"And mine," Daisuke agreed.

"Then I'll definitely come first," Leon laughed. He could feel real excitement building up inside him. "Let's get going."

Back at the house, the three of them clambered out of Byron's Altezza and carried the parts up the drive.

"So, you think this car drives good now Leon?" Daisuke put his bags down and rapped his knuckles on the Silvia's bonnet. "Well wait until we have all of this installed," Daisuke spoke seriously and Leon's excitement redlined. He thought of Simon and the competition. Could he really get his car ready and learn to drift properly in time for it? He was definitely going to try.

"Thanks for helping me, and of course for paying," he smiled openly.

"It's my pleasure, Leon," Daisuke smiled. "It makes me feel young again." And for the first time Leon realised that Daisuke was enjoying himself at least as much as he.

Three hours later they were making good progress. They had relocated the battery, changed the brake pads and spark plugs and Daisuke was busy with the more complicated task of replacing the radiator. Meanwhile Leon lay on his back under the raised car and drained the old oil into a pan. Only

Byron scowled fiercely as he worked on installing the new computer. He grumbled loudly and applied himself with half-hearted effort. When he finished doing the oil change, Leon finally noticed his friend's mood and asked him what the problem was.

"I haven't had a bite since breakfast. My stomach is trying to eat itself and I'm slaving away for you."

Leon realised how hungry he was as well. "Let's knock off for lunch now."

"You two go," Daisuke replied without breaking his concentration and looking up. "I'll finish this first."

Leon and Byron went inside to the kitchen and quickly washed their hands. "So what do you feel like?"

"What do you have?" Byron asked. In response, Leon opened the fridge and Byron whistled softly. It was filled with food. "So that's why you live with your mum."

"She must've known you were coming and stocked up," Leon laughed. "Let's make sandwiches. Then we can eat them out by the car."

"Sounds good to me," Byron nodded in agreement.

Once made, they took their stack of sammies outside. Daisuke was just finishing up and his eyes lit up.

"That looks very good, I'll just quickly wash," he disappeared inside and Leon and Byron sat down on the lawn beside the Silvia. Leon decided to wait for Daisuke but Byron immediately attacked his sandwich. Leon smiled as he watched him.

"So have you managed to get over your crush?" Byron teased suddenly without interrupting his chewing.

"Well," Leon scratched the back of his head. "I hung out with her most of yesterday..."

"What? You son-of-a-bitch, so that's why you didn't call?" Byron exclaimed with a full mouth.

"Yeah sorry," Leon quickly looked away. "I figured you'd be alright without my company for a day."

"Some friend you are," Byron muttered darkly and inhaled the last of his sandwich. "Here I am busting my gut for you…"

"Yeah," Leon plucked a handful of grass from the lawn. "But I wouldn't grudge you a date." Byron nodded silent understanding. He wiped his mouth with the back of his hand and looked at his friend earnestly.

"That's real cool, man," Byron mumbled. "I hope it works out," he offered self-consciously and looked down at the plate of sandwiches.

"Thanks," Leon smiled. "And yeah, grab another." He slid the plate closer to Byron. "You know, I was serious about letting you take the Silvia for a spin sometime."

"I'm gonna hold you to that," Byron spoke without interrupting his eating. "I'll show you both how it's done."

"If you drift as well as you eat, then I'm sure you will," Leon grinned. Daisuke reappeared and sat down beside them on the lawn.

"So have you left any for me?" he teased Byron.

"You're lucky you didn't take too long," Byron nodded and offered him the plate of sandwiches. While they ate, Leon and Daisuke discussed their progress. Byron, however, only listened with one ear. Stealthily, he reached for his third sandwich, devoured it and then dabbed longingly at the crumbs on his plate with his finger tip.

"So have we saved your stomach?" Leon asked finally.

"For now…" Byron nodded.

After they had eaten, Byron finished off the computer, while Leon and Daisuke busied themselves fitting the oil catch can and then installing the steering spacers.

"Well, I think we're ready to give her a try…" A couple of hours later, Daisuke put his tools away and wiped his hands on a rag.

"I'll do it," Byron reached his hand out eagerly.

"Cool," Leon passed him the keys.

"Ready?" Byron asked.

"Go for it," Leon grinned and Byron turned the key. With a harsh cough from the starter motor, the Silvia bunny-hopped forwards and nearly knocked Daisuke over.

"Woah!" Byron exclaimed. "Who leaves a car in gear?"

"Um, me I guess," Leon answered apologetically.

"Damn, you almost made me kill your uncle... Alright, let's try that again." The starter motor turned over and coaxed the engine into life. It spluttered reluctantly then suddenly it caught and ran in staccato fits and bursts. "Daisuke, you've killed it. It's worse than when we started." Even tone-deaf Byron knew that no engine should sound like that.

"The timing is out," Daisuke was puzzled. "The only thing that could've done that is the computer..." He got in beside Byron and checked the options on the controller. "I'm not sure..." he said after several minutes of wading through the settings. "I thought these configured themselves. Strange."

"You didn't mess with the settings did you Byron?" Leon asked suddenly, and Byron looked uncomfortable.

"I did have a play," Byron admitted reluctantly. "It looked like it'd be just like Playstation..."

Leon shook his head and sighed. "What do we do now?"

"We have to get a professional tune up," Daisuke replied.

"So no driving today?"

"It wouldn't be a good idea. With the timing out, driving her like this could damage the engine. But it's just as well," he smiled wryly. "Noriko will probably divorce me, if I don't at least have a look around with her..."

"Yeah, that's fair enough," Leon smiled. "I think you'd better go then."

"Yes, but I'll be happy to take her to get tuned tomorrow."

"No, I can do that," Leon said adamantly. "I'll just take a bit of time off work. You should enjoy your holiday."

"That's okay. I want to make sure they do their job properly. I also want to look into getting new tyres."

"If you insist," Leon replied reluctantly.

"Alright, let's put these tools away and then find something to eat – I'm hungry again," Byron locked up the Silvia and passed the keys to Daisuke.

Once they had tidied up, Leon and Byron dropped Daisuke off downtown to join Leon's mum, Noriko and Tamsin who were already there, sightseeing. They then continued on to Byron's to watch a movie. In the middle of it, Leon received a phone call.

"Hey Leon," it was Simon. "Job's yours if you still want it."

"Definitely."

"Cool," Simon continued. "We'll put you on a trial period first, but I'm sure you'll be fine."

"That's wicked. When do I start?"

"Next week ideally."

"Okay, I'll hand in my notice tomorrow." Leon couldn't believe it. "Thanks."

"No drama," Simon dismissed it. "How're you going with those parts?"

"They're all in, just need to get her tuned now."

"You don't mess around," Simon was impressed. "I'll be interested to see how you go in the comp."

"Uh, yeah..." Leon replied. "Byron and my uncle convinced me to go for it."

"Good," Simon laughed. "Trust me, you'll have fun. Anyways, I gotta run. Catch you next Monday."

"See ya," Leon signed off.

"This calls for celebration." Byron had overheard. He went to the kitchen and reappeared carrying two Heineken bottles.

The following day Leon got up early and reluctantly rode his bike to work. He had no motivation at all now and he would have rather called in sick, but he gritted his teeth and pedalled on. When he arrived at work, the first thing he did was hand in his notice – that cheered him up.

"But we've got a huge shipment coming in next week – we need all the staff we can get." His boss was beside himself.

"Sorry," Leon shrugged. I only have to do this five more times, he thought as he signed in, and his mood improved further. Leaving his boss fuming in the office, he went out to his forklift and got to work.

By *smoko* time, everybody knew. When he told his colleagues about his new job they couldn't believe his luck. This helped Leon's mood even further but, nonetheless, his shift seemed to go on and on. He couldn't wait to get home and find out how Daisuke had got on with the Silvia. Lorna also occupied his mind, he wondered how she was. At lunchtime he decided to call her.

"Hi, Leon," she answered. "How are you?"

"Good. Really good actually,"

"Wow – are you enjoying your new car that much?"

"No, I mean it's cool, but I finally got a new job, starting next week."

"Nice. Where and doing what?" Lorna asked and Leon told her. "Serious? That's where Jason works."

"You know Jason?" Leon was surprised. "Apparently I'm replacing him."

"Yeah – he's Taz's flatmate. They've been living together for years."

"Small world," Leon couldn't believe it.

"Tell me about it… I think it's a good job though. I know Jason liked it."

"Can't wait to get out of here that's for sure," Leon agreed.

"I know how you feel," Lorna sighed suddenly. "The course I'm doing at the moment is killing me. I've got an exam for it on Friday. It's going to be near impossible."

"Ouch. I'm so glad I haven't had to do any since school."

"Don't rub it in," Lorna pouted. "But yeah, the more I study, the more I realise how much I still need to study…"

"I'm sure you'll be fine. You strike me as being reasonably intelligent," Leon teased. "But maybe I should stop distracting you then?"

"I'm actually rather liking the excuse, but yeah I definitely still have a lot of cramming to do."

"Okay, well maybe I'll leave you to it… My aunt and uncle are here till Friday morning – but maybe we could hang out that night?"

"That'd be good. I'll be done then and won't be stressing."

"Okay sweet, I'll see ya Friday."

"Yeah," Lorna paused. "Maybe we can go for a drive?"

"Sure – if you want," Leon agreed. "Good luck with your exam – remember to always write something, even if you're not sure…"

"I'll do that," Lorna promised. "Thanks for the tip."

Leon smiled when he hung up the phone. Things were starting to go right again. Crashing his mum's car seemed like a distant memory. But then he looked up at the *smoko* room clock and grimaced. It was time to get back in the freezer.

When Leon arrived home, he saw the Silvia parked on the lawn. As he wheeled his bike up the drive, he couldn't resist walking past her and running his hand over her bonnet. "I won't be long," he whispered quietly and then looked around self-consciously, before continuing on. He left his bike in the garage and went inside the house.

"Hey Daisuke," Leon greeted his uncle enthusiastically.

"Hi," he laid his book aside. "How was your day?"

"Long…" Leon could hardly contain himself. "How did you go with the Silvia?"

"Well," his uncle smiled mysteriously and rose out of the chair. "Why don't I show you?" It seemed to Leon that he had been waiting for him to get home. But just then Leon's mum popped her head through from the kitchen.

"Can you two petrol-heads please stay at least until we've had dinner? It will be ready in 15 minutes."

"That still gives us time to have a quick look," Leon suggested, but his mum hadn't finished.

"I'd appreciate it, if you could set the table, Leon. Since we don't have family visiting often you can use the good china."

"Okay, sure Mum," Leon rolled his eyes at Daisuke and went to set the table. He cheered up visibly when the food was served. Noriko and his mum had really outdone themselves. The dinner was so good that he eagerly worked his way through seconds, as well as a generous helping of dessert. But finally, after showering much praise upon the chefs, they made their escape and went outside.

"Well she's all tuned and ready to go," Daisuke spoke when they neared the Silvia. "I also got some new tyres and a little something else..."

"You didn't," Leon protested.

"Of course I did. Why don't you have a look by the wheels," he teased. Leon kneeled down and gazed at the back wheel. Apart from the new tyres, he couldn't see anything different. They were the same scratched, black painted alloys.

"No, behind them..."

The light was dimming, but as Leon peered in behind the alloy wheels he saw change. The old dirty springs had been replaced with shiny green ones along with the struts. "The suspension," Leon exclaimed.

"Adjustable Tein suspension," Daisuke confirmed. "The real thing Leon. What your dad and I always used, but newer and better."

"Wow..."

"I've adjusted it to what I think best suits your style of driving, but of course once you get the hang of it you can adjust it to however you like."

"Wow," Leon repeated, stunned. "I don't know..." New tyres and adjustable suspension were not cheap.

"Don't worry," Daisuke waved his hand to quiet him. "Come, let's take her for a drive. I think you will find she feels much better now."

Eagerly, Leon opened the driver door, jumped in and reached across to open the door for his uncle. "I don't know how well I'm going to drive…" Leon buckled himself in and patted his belly. "I ate far too much."

"So did I," Daisuke admitted and suddenly burped. "Ah, that's much better." For a moment Leon was surprised, but then followed his example.

"That's helped a lot," Leon chuckled and was about to start the engine when Daisuke stopped him.

"You should wait for that car to go away so that you can really hear the difference."

"Okay." He waited as a blue people-mover puttered past and continued on down the street. When he turned the key, the RB26Dett cranked over and fired instantly. The magic was there again, but threefold. The engine note was more refined, more harmonised. He let her idle easily. There was no up or down movement in her revs anymore – just that constant, throaty hum of pistons.

"You can hear the difference, yes?"

"Totally," Leon was enthralled by that sound.

"Just wait until you drive her. Let's go." Leon let the handbrake off and backed out onto the street. Finding first gear, he put his foot down. Instantly the Silvia's attitude changed and she became discourteous. Her power had been plentiful before, but now it was completely over the top.

"Wow," Leon breathed and immediately eased off the accelerator. "That's so much faster."

"Indeed," Daisuke smiled to himself.

As they made their way out to the industrial area again, Leon became aware of the Silvia's new precision and responsiveness. Everything was enhanced: acceleration, steering, braking, power and grip. The difference was huge.

The handling in the corners was remarkable and the shudder and bounce in the ride had disappeared. The Nissan now clung to the road and Leon found it almost impossible to keep to the speed limit.

When they reached their training ground, Daisuke began his lesson by having Leon perform the techniques that he had taught earlier. With the Silvia's handling vastly altered, it took some time before he got the knack of it again, but when he had it they moved on and tried a more complicated method, which involved thrashing the RB26 to high revs and pushing the car hard through the bend. They swapped seats and Daisuke demonstrated with his typical casual air, making it look as easy as riding a bike with training wheels.

When Leon tried, he misjudged the Silvia's power and his speed was too high. He flew out of the bend, jumped the kerb on the far side and finally came to a stop half-in and half-out of a small shrub. The engine had stalled. Leon sat completely still for a second and stared at the green foliage that hung into his windscreen. His foot was still trying to crush the brake pedal into the floor. "What was that word you used?" he asked evenly.

"What word?" Daisuke blinked.

"The other night, when that guy suddenly appeared ahead of us," Leon prompted. "It sounded like: *kuso* or something."

"I said that?" Daisuke seemed surprised. "I must be losing my nerves." Then he smiled. "But I'm sure you know what it means."

"Yeah, I've used it a few times," Leon grinned.

"This would've been another appropriate moment," Daisuke agreed. "But then, if we continue, I'm sure there'll be a few more," his eyes twinkled and the years between them slipped away until they were partners in crime.

"I'd say you're right," Leon restarted the engine and backed her out of the shrub, bouncing back across the footpath and onto the road. He returned to his starting position and began afresh.

They practised each evening for the rest of that week. Under Daisuke's tuition, Leon made remarkable progress, but quickly became bored of drifting through the same turn time and time again. Whenever Daisuke sensed that Leon's concentration was lapsing and consequently his drifts were becoming sloppy, he immediately had him pull over and brought his attention back by explaining another technique, also stressing that repetition makes perfection.

The week slipped by. Suddenly it was Thursday, Daisuke and Noriko's last day. They would be flying back to Japan the following morning. Leon got up early again and readied himself for work. When he made his way down the stairs, he found his uncle already there, waiting for him.

"Good morning."

"Hi Leon. Are you surprised that I'm here this early?"

"A little," Leon admitted.

"Well, I hoped that you might lend me your car for the day again."

"So you can take her up into the hills for a last thrash?" he joked. Daisuke smiled but shook his head.

"No, I won't race. I promise."

"Do you also promise not to spend any more money on her?" Leon raised an eyebrow.

"No, I won't promise that," Daisuke shook his head again.

"You've spent enough," Leon put his hands on his hips.

"Come on, let an old man have his indulgences," Daisuke insisted.

"Alright, just please don't spend too much more," Leon caved with a sigh and reluctantly gave him the keys.

"I'll try not to."

"You're impossible," Leon shook his head with a smile and checked the time. "Right, I have to go, but I think mum wanted you both here at 6pm – to go out for dinner."

"We'll be here then. Have a good day Leon."

When Leon arrived home from work that evening, the Silvia stood parked at the kerb. He wondered why she was parked there, almost as much as he wondered why his uncle had asked to borrow her again, but he fought his curiosity and went into the house.

"Leon," Tamsin squealed and came to wrap her arms around his leg like a koala.

"Hey Tink," Leon patted the top of her head.

"Hi Leon," his mum's voice came from the lounge. "How was your day?"

"Alright," Leon didn't elaborate.

"Would be good if you could go and get ready – Daisuke and Noriko will be back soon..."

"Okay," Leon dislodged his sister and bounded up the stairs to get changed. He had just dressed and was making his way down the stairs again when the doorbell rang. "I'll get it," Leon offered, but Tamsin beat him to it, ripping the door open and flinging herself at her aunt and uncle.

"Hi," Leon beckoned them in. "What did you do today?"

"We've had a great day," Daisuke replied. "I took your auntie for a day trip."

"It was very nice," Noriko gushed.

"Did you take the Silvia?"

"Oh no, the rental car – it's more comfortable for Noriko."

"Yes, it would be," Leon agreed.

"I see that they have returned her though, like I asked them to. That's good." Leon was puzzled by Daisuke's comment but before he could ask what he meant by it, and why he'd even asked to borrow his car in the first place, his mum appeared.

"I'm hungry," Tamsin tried to recapture some attention.

"Spoken like a true princess," Daisuke chuckled and turned to Leon's mum. "Well, if we're all ready?"

The restaurant had been recommended to them. None of them had been there before, so it was a new experience for them all. It was very classy, with waiters in suits and a leather-bound menu. Leon's mum and auntie shared a bottle of wine, but Daisuke refrained and looked at Leon significantly so that he held back also. The two of them still had work to do. After the meal they returned home and, while the others made their way inside, Leon and Daisuke excused themselves.

"So did you notice anything different with your car?" Daisuke asked Leon as they walked down to the road where the Silvia was lazing under the streetlamp.

"I purposely didn't look," Leon admitted.

"It's not that exciting, but you should take a peek inside."

"Okay," Leon dug in his pocket. "Oh, you have the keys remember?"

"That's right…" his uncle reached his hand up under the left front wheel arch. "Ah good, just like I asked them." He handed the keys to Leon, who eagerly unlocked the car and opened the driver's side door. Immediately he was confronted with tubing that ran along the door frame, up the window pillars and criss-crossed behind the driver's seat into the space where the backseats had been.

"A roll cage!"

"Yes," Daisuke agreed. "I'm sorry about the backseat, but you'll need one for the competition."

"I don't have enough friends to need a backseat," Leon joked. He gripped one of the bars and shook it. It didn't budge. "It's solid as…"

"That's the idea," Daisuke nodded. "It's made from chromoly, which is light and strong." He leant forward and inspected the tubing within the dim interior of the Silvia. "It looks like they have done a professional job."

"I just don't know how to thank you," Leon began.

"Then don't," his uncle stopped him with a big smile and began to walk around to the passenger door. "Let's get going, it is already late."

For the last time they made their way out to the industrial area and went through the different techniques that Daisuke had taught him. Each time Leon pushed the Silvia harder through the same turn they had been practicing on over the past few nights. It now felt intuitive and easy. Confidently, Leon performed the techniques in quick succession, peeling the Silvia around in a tight arc at the end and threading her straight back in for the next. Like a smoking, squealing rollercoaster, the Silvia stormed back and forth through the bend, until, with the sequence completed, Leon brought her to a standstill again. With excitement and exhilaration bubbling through him, he turned expectantly to his uncle.

"Well," Daisuke hesitated with a frown. "A bit more practice will certainly help you get better and smoother," he spoke weightily and Leon looked down into his lap. "No, really," his pretence cracked and he grinned broadly. "You are a natural. You have the car and the talent. If you keep it up, I'm sure you'll do very well."

"You think so?" Leon asked uncertainly.

"Definitely."

"Arigatou," Leon said sombrely. "For everything."

"Daijoubu desu yo," Daisuke waved his gratitude away. "I'd be lying if I said I hadn't enjoyed it. It's been my pleasure." Daisuke paused again, before he became serious. "But from here it's up to you."

"I'll continue practicing," Leon nodded. "And do my best in the comp."

"Good for you," Daisuke enthused. "I look forward to hearing how you get on."

"I'll be in touch," Leon promised. He understood that their time was up. He pulled away from the kerb and they drove back home. He knew he would miss his uncle and auntie.

On Friday, during his lunch break, Leon called Lorna.

"Hey Leon."

"You're sounding cheerful. So the exam went okay then?"

"Yeah, easy as."

"*Easy as* even? Wow and here I remember you saying it was going to be near impossible."

"Oh, that," Lorna laughed. "I guess I just scare myself sometimes. It really was fine in the end. And you'll be happy to know that I wrote something down for every question."

"Good going, now you'll have a good chance at getting 100%," Leon laughed.

"That would be nice, but also extremely unlikely."

"Alright, we'll settle for 99% then... So now that you're done, can we hang out later?"

"Yeah, but actually," Lorna was apologetic. "I've got this family dinner I couldn't pass on..."

"Oh," his quick disappointment sounded hollow in his own ears. "That's okay... maybe tomorrow then?"

"No, I mean, I'd love to hang out today," Lorna replied hastily. "But hopefully you're okay to make it a bit later, after the dinner... maybe about 8pm?"

"Sure," he agreed readily. "I'll come and pick you up."

"Great," she gave him her address.

"See ya," Leon hung up. He went back out to his forklift and started to work again. He had just three hours left in this job and he would be meeting up with Lorna that evening. He hadn't seen her for nearly a week and he couldn't wait. Every few minutes Leon checked his watch. Time seemed to be standing still. He gritted his teeth and plodded on for what felt like an eternity until it was finally time to knock off. With a spring in his step, he headed back to the changing room and hung his thermal clothing up for the last time. After cleaning out his locker, Leon said farewell to his colleagues and left work without a backwards glance.

He arrived home to find the house empty and a note from his mum on the kitchen counter. She had taken Tamsin out grocery shopping. Leon showered and changed, then ate a quick meal. The phone rang.

"'Sup Leon." It was Byron. "How was your lucky last day?"

"Feels good to be done," Leon answered. "No more freezers, no more forklifts."

"Nice. So you're keen to celebrate?"

"Um, I've already made plans to go out with Lorna..."

"You lucky prick," Byron spoke with mock outrage. "How long are you hanging out with her?"

"Not sure – may end up going to a movie or something," Leon sidestepped.

"That sucks, what am I gonna do?"

"Dunno," Leon had to laugh. "Why don't you see what James is up to?" James was another friend of theirs.

"Could do, I guess. He's probably just playing Playstation though. I've been doing that all week," Byron sighed. "Say, how's that Silvia holding up?"

"Real good, and you know what?"

"What?"

"Daisuke got me coilovers and a roll cage," Leon enthused.

"Dude, like I said, you've got all the luck," Byron lamented. "Right, well I'm swinging by tomorrow – it's about time you made good on your promise and let me take her for a spin."

"You do that," Leon agreed. "Have a good night, aye."

"You too," Byron replied gruffly. "But not too good."

At 8pm Leon pulled up outside Lorna's house. She met him at the door wearing casual faded-blue jeans and skate shoes. Her glossy hair was tied back in a loose ponytail and her eyes contrasted vividly against her green sweater. Leon had trouble blinking – he had forgotten how truly gorgeous she was, even wearing something so simple.

"I'm ready if you are," Lorna smiled at him.

"Where are we going?" Leon asked curiously.

"I'll give you directions."

Leon drove slowly. Under Lorna's instructions they made their way high up into the hills, until they were well above the city. They reached a lookout and she asked him to pull over. He manoeuvred the low Silvia off the road and parked on the grassy flat of the lookout, stopping just short of a waist-high fence. Beyond the fence, the hillside dropped away sharply and a panorama of the city opened up.

"We should get out. We'll get a better view." Without waiting for him, she opened the door and got out. "Quick, the sun is about to set." Leon followed her to the front of the Silvia and leant against the bonnet beside her. Close but not touching, they gazed out over the city that sprawled peacefully below them. The sun hung low over the horizon and, as it dipped, its rays flamed red and gold across the sky.

The flock of fluffy clouds basked in the attention and soaked up the rays, so that as the sun sank lower still, and finally slipped beneath the curve of the Earth, they continued to glow, shot through with bands of fiery yellow, orange and red. Leon and Lorna watched and marvelled. The scene lasted mere minutes. With the sun gone, the clouds lost their radiance swiftly and the light dimmed further, making the transition from day to night.

Lorna sighed. It was a contented sound. She leant against him. Their shoulders touched and warmth tingled through Leon. This was a moment that was too good for words. He put his arm around her and drew her closer. They didn't break the silence for a while, each lost to their own thoughts as they continued to gaze out over the city that was their home. Darkness began to settle and the lights sparkled up at them like glittering jewels.

"It's beautiful," Lorna whispered.

"Yeah," he agreed and they were silent again for a long time. "You know, it's crazy to think that there are hundreds of thousands of people down there, all doing their own thing."

"Most of them we'll never meet, let alone get to know."

"Yet somehow we're all linked together," Leon spoke thoughtfully.

"I know what you mean," she agreed. "Look at that light there," she pointed at a flickering pinprick, moving along a distant road. "I wonder who that is and where they're going."

"Maybe they're an old couple, having a big argument," he tried to make a joke, but Lorna didn't laugh. She was quiet and he began to regret his comment.

"Did your parent's fight much when you were growing up?" she asked suddenly.

"No," Leon said slowly, thinking back. "Maybe they hid it from me, but I can't remember ever hearing a single bad word spoken between them. On the contrary actually, I remember how Dad's eyes would light up when he came home and saw Mum..." Leon trailed off. "Do your parents fight?"

"They did," she nodded sadly, "All the time. I hated it, but they're separated now." Leon considered this. He wanted to bring back her good mood.

"Well, maybe it's two young people down there," he indicated the moving speck of light again, "on their first date and they like each other a lot, but are a bit shy..."

"You're right, being shy won't get us anywhere," Lorna spoke quietly and he turned to find her smiling at him. She leant forward, her lips touching his. A warm glow spread through him. They held the kiss for a long time, only drawing apart reluctantly.

"Wow," he opened his eyes.

"Yes, wow," she smiled and shivered suddenly.

"Cold?" he asked. With the increasing darkness the night held a chilly edge.

"A little," she nodded, "But also a little excited." She had a mischievous gleam in her eye now.

"Shall we get back in the car?"

"Soon," Lorna seemed reluctant to tear herself away. She pressed herself against him for warmth and continued to look out. "Do you like living here?" she asked suddenly.

"I do," Leon answered seriously. "It's my home now, and although it's not that big, it has a lot going for it," he paused. "It's comfortable."

"I like it too," she turned to him. "I think that's a good way to describe it." She shivered again. "But it can get a bit cold."

"Very true, let's get back in the car."

"Okay," Lorna nodded. "Can we stay a bit longer though?"

"Sure," Leon replied in anticipation at her continued company. He wasn't yet ready to drive back down either. They got back in the car and sat comfortably, looking out at the city lights.

"So how are you enjoying your new car then?" Lorna wanted to know.

"Heaps," Leon sat back with his hands behind his head.

"You've certainly done a lot to it." She ran her hands along a section of the roll cage. "Looks like you're getting all geared up to go drifting..."

"I'm working on it," he admitted wistfully. "My uncle's been giving me a crash-course."

"Really?" She sat up in her seat.

"Yeah," Leon nodded. "But he was only here for six days. He and my auntie flew back to Japan this morning."

"So he drifts?"

"Yeah, or at least, he used to," Leon inclined his head. "We practiced every night... But, I still have a lot more to learn."

"Is he your dad's brother?"

"Yeah,"

"And your dad used to drift too?" Lorna prompted. It was his turn to sit up and look at her. "Your friend mentioned it, remember?" she explained. "When I first met you."

"My dad used to drift, yes." Leon looked away.

"So it's true," her eyes were filled with understanding. Leon nodded as he looked out of the windscreen at the twinkling lights. "It's okay if you don't want to talk about it," she sensed his mood. Leon hesitated but then began to speak.

"He was one of the best drifters in Japan. He even won one of the early D1 Grand Prix events," Leon's eyes were focused into the distance. "But then it all turned bad," he shook his head slowly. "I was fourteen, but I remember it like it was yesterday. I was right there, filming the race..." Leon let out a quiet, sorrowful sigh. "My dad had lived and breathed car racing. I loved it too. He used to teach me. But when..." Leon drew a breath. "Everything changed when he died... Mum shut out anything to do with racing from our lives..." Leon paused. "She sold the workshop and we moved here. I had to go to a new school, make new friends... It wasn't easy."

Lorna reached across and took his hand. "So, your mum's from here?" she asked hesitantly.

"Yeah, she grew up here."

"But your dad was Japanese?"

"Yes."

"How did they meet?"

Leon turned back from the city lights to look at her. "I'm not sure, I never bothered to ask when I was young, and now I don't really want to ask Mum... I do remember that Uncle Daisuke once mentioned that they met at the racetrack by Osaka. Apparently Mum was completely taken by his driving and stuck around afterwards to get his autograph," Leon explained. "Daisuke was always a bit of a joker though..."

"So maybe your mum was interested in racing as well?" Lorna considered.

"Maybe, but either way, she certainly isn't now."

"Do you speak Japanese then?"

"Yeah," Leon nodded, "But I haven't lived in Japan since dad died... Mum doesn't speak much Japanese, so at home, even in Osaka, we always spoke English and I went to an English school there."

"So that explains why your English is so good."

"I guess," he smiled uncertainly.

"Yeah, no seriously, it's perfect." They were both silent and a little self-conscious. "You know if you wanted to learn more about cars and drifting you could always talk to Cam and Taz. If cars were edible they would have them every day for breakfast, lunch, dinner and dessert," Lorna smiled.

"Yeah, I dunno..."

"Don't know what?"

"I didn't really get the best vibe from Cam..."

"What makes you say that?"

"He was pretty rude when I helped them at the comp and then at the pub he barely talked to either of us."

"I noticed that too, and his comment about stealing cars," Lorna pursed her lips, thinking back. "It's not like him though..." she turned suddenly to look behind her as headlights filled the back window. A vehicle had pulled up behind them. Its engine idled sullenly. They had been so engrossed that neither of them had heard it approaching. "What're they up to?"

"Not sure..." Leon frowned and turned in his seat. He couldn't see past the glare of the headlights, which stood up like rabbit ears.

Abruptly the headlights extinguished. They heard car doors slam and footsteps crunching on gravel. Suddenly somebody tapped on Leon's window and he jerked around. A shadowy figure stood beside his door.

"Wind down your window man," the figure spoke gruffly and gestured to Leon. It was too dark to make out his features.

"I don't know about this," Lorna cautioned.

"Me neither…" Leon hesitated.

"Wind your window down," the figure repeated menacingly and rapped on the window more insistently. "Or I'll smash it for ya."

Leon saw that he meant it and reluctantly lowered his window halfway. "Lost something?"

"That depends…" the figure replied.

"On?"

"If you're the punk that hit us last Sunday night."

"Hit you? What're you talking about?"

"Let me put it in plain English," the figure put his left hand on Leon's open window. "Some nutcase in a black S13, just like this one, hit us last Sunday and scraped all along the front of our 180."

"That sucks," Leon spoke bravely. "Why don't you tell someone that cares?"

"See anything?" the figure ignored him, addressing his question to somebody else.

"I believe so…" a hesitant reply came from beside Lorna's door. "There's definitely a big scratch running along the front guard, but then, the whole car is banged up pretty good…"

"Any white?" the figure at Leon's window pressed.

"Wait…"

"Leon, what's going on?" Lorna asked worriedly, but Leon had turned back to the figure at his window.

"What do you want??"

"It's been mostly wiped away, but I can see some white smears," the other figure straightened up. He went to Lorna's window and nodded. "It's him."

"You heard that?" the figure at Leon's window prodded accusingly. "Still reckon it wasn't you?"

"It wasn't–"

"Year right," the figure sneered. "Our car was just painted and you messed it up."

"It wasn't me," Leon insisted.

"No, it was your old lady that came flying around the corner," the figure laughed ironically. "I think you'll need to cough up some cash, mate."

"What?!" Leon lashed out in frustration. "You were standing in the middle of the bloody road. You're lucky we didn't crash into you."

"Ah, now we're getting somewhere." Instantly the figure pounced on his slip. "So you were there?" He pressed, but Leon remained silent. "I'll take that as a yes," he spoke icily.

"You know, we don't actually care about the money," he paused. "We really just want you to race us – show us the moves you pulled the other night."

"The moves?" Leon flinched. "You're joking right?"

"Race us," it came out menacingly.

"Now?"

"Yup, back down the hill."

Leon hesitated. The last thing he wanted was to have this freak on his case, racing downhill on the windy road. "How about you just leave us alone."

"Race us," the dark-haired guy insisted again.

"No way, not here," Leon shook his head. "If you want to race me then be at the next drift comp."

"You're entering?"

"Yeah," Leon regretted his comment. "Now get lost."

"I don't think so. But, seeing I'm in a good mood, I'll give you a choice. You can race us now or you can get slashed up," the guy's tone was cold. His right hand, which until then had been out of view behind his back, appeared holding a flick-knife. The blade snapped out and gleamed threateningly in the moonlight. Leon gaped at the blade hypnotically before tearing his eyes away. He could make out the guy's taunting half-smile, but his eyes glittered. He wasn't fooling around.

"Better do what they say Leon," Lorna said in a small voice. He turned to her. She looked fearful.

"You sure?" he asked quietly. He had his hands on the steering wheel. Any other time he probably would have been keen to race, but with these guys? Instinct told him that it wasn't a good idea, especially not with Lorna in the car.

"Well, we don't have much choice…" Her eyes were big. "It is just a race after all." Leon looked at her for a full second. That was true. At the end of the day it was only a race. He turned back to the guy at his window.

"Alright, since you insist."

"Good," the guy smiled grimly. "Remember, if you try any tricks and pull out – we'll mess you up." His voice was low, but he continued to smile as he made his threat.

"Sound's scary," Leon retorted. The guy's eyes narrowed.

"You'll start in front. Try to lose me," he grated. "Cause I'll be trying to pass you. Third beep and you go."

"What're we waiting for?" Leon nodded and the guy's eyes narrowed further.

"You're mine." He stalked back to the 180SX, which blocked their way. Wordlessly, his friend followed. The headlights came back on and, with a blast of engine noise and a crunch of gravel, the 180SX reversed back onto the road.

"You sure about this?" Leon asked Lorna.

"No, not at all," she replied heavily, "Did you really run into them?"

"My uncle was driving, and yeah, we may have scratched them," Leon admitted, "But they were just sitting in the middle of the road."

"I doubt they'd believe you if you said it was your uncle," Lorna sighed, "And it probably wouldn't make any difference to them. So I don't think you have much choice. They're blocking the way back up the road, so down is the only way."

"Yeah, it'd be a long way home if we tried to run for it."

"And they'd trash the car if we left it here," Lorna pointed out. They were interrupted by a beep from the 180SX.

"What are you waiting for, wuss?"

"Are you sure you want to come along?" Leon looked at her seriously. "I'm crazy when it comes to racing, you know."

"I know, I've witnessed that first-hand," Lorna suddenly brightened into a smile. "But, hey, I don't really want to wait up here by myself…" A more insistent beep sounded.

"Don't make me come over there!"

"Alright," Leon sighed, "But strap yourself in tight, okay?" He reached for the key and turned the ignition on. The RB26 came awake to an eager rumble. Leon let her idle for a few moments, as he waited for Lorna to adjust her racing harness. He revved the engine experimentally and the 2.6 litre power plant spun up with a growl.

Leon reversed back up onto the road and stopped just a foot in front of the 180SX. He switched on his headlights. A narrow, sealed mountain road curved out ahead of them, with a steep red clay bank on the right-hand side and a grassy slope on the left. It plunged down the mountain side at a steep angle, its depth disappearing swiftly into darkness. Leon shook his head. It was bad enough racing down here alone, but carrying a passenger, with another car chasing and trying to pass? That was just madness.

"Sorry Lorna, I'm not doing this by choice."

"I know, but still, you should whip them."

"What?" Leon looked at her.

"Well, they did ask for it," Lorna pointed out logically. "So you may as well put them in their place."

"You mean you want me to race them – all out?" Leon wasn't sure he had heard right.

"Well yeah, you certainly can't let them pass you." The 180SX's headlights, which flooded the back window, illuminated one side of her face, but the other side was in shadow. Her eyes glittered and Leon realised she was angry. The starting beep resonated from behind them and Leon brought his attention back to the road.

"Alright then," he spoke grimly, "Let's see what this baby can do." The second beep sounded out into the night. Leon sank the clutch and slotted the gear lever into first. The third beep was lost in the bellow of the RB26 as the S13 dropped to her haunches and launched.

Lorna was pushed into her seat and then knocked back as Leon hooked second gear and the S13 kicked out again. The bank to their right was a blur and the first curve was already on them. Leon cut into the apex, downshifted and gassed it. The RB26 rung out viciously, as the back wheels lost traction and churned blue smoke, sliding the Nissan's tail out.

The S13 skidded through the bend, followed closely by the 180SX, which also streamed smoke from her squealing tyres. Like synchronised swimmers, the two vehicles slid through the curve side-by-side, only to disengage again and straighten out fluidly on the exit. One behind the other, they hurtled down the short stretch of straight road that followed, their blow-off valves venting noisily at each shift. The screams of the two engines, mixed with the continuous screech of tyres, echoed out into the dark, moonlit hills.

Another bend came at Leon, this time curving to the left. He raced in with his nerves on edge. They were travelling so fast. Lorna suppressed a gasp and bit her lips. With the engine roaring, Leon downshifted, braked and then clutched into second. Timing the moment precisely, he turned into the curve and flicked up the handbrake. Stepping on the accelerator again, he drifted through the bend. His awareness was heightened by a rush of adrenaline from the speed and the danger of careening into that steep precipice. Straightening out from the curve, he stole a glance at his rear-view mirror and was surprised to find the 180SX right behind him.

Scowling, Leon focused ahead again. Cat's eyes streamed past, glowing brightly as the next bend came at them. His attention was complete now and the vehicle behind him no longer existed, it was just him and the narrow, windy, mountain road. He had to find the quickest route to the bottom. He saw the apex straight away, crisp and clear in the headlight beam. That imaginary line formed in his head, describing a tight trajectory for his path. This time he braked even later and Lorna's muffled squeak reminded him that she was still there, before he punched into the curve and threw the S13's rear end out. The feeling of streaming sideways at such high speed was exhilarating. With engine and tyres screaming, he flew out of the bend and immediately slid into the next.

"Far out, he's pulling away now," Andy grunted and downshifted. He spun the wheel to follow the blazing taillights of the Silvia through the curve. Staying close on the first series of turns had been easy and hardly a challenge for him, but now something had overcome the S13 and her jerky drifts had smoothed out, becoming fluid and graceful. Andy had to use all his skill and concentration just to keep up.

From the passenger seat, Markus glanced across at his friend who sat tense and rigid at the controls. Markus had seen him like this before and was worried. Without the ability to relax into a completely focused state, Andy would never drive to his full potential. It was as though he drove with his head alone. He needed to apply his body fully in order to get a true feeling for the car and its capabilities. As the more experienced driver of the two, Markus decided he would point this out to Andy at the next opportunity. Now was not the time. He turned back to the road. Beyond the pop-up lights that stuck up from the bonnet, the taillights of the Silvia flared crimson briefly and the vehicle presented her driver-side as she slid into the next curve. Blue tyre smoke flew up over their windscreen, whipping away in the slipstream. Andy spun the wheel and followed suit.

The SR20Det screamed under full boost as Andy pushed the 180SX out again and Markus was thrown about roughly in his Recaro seat, first one way and then the other. It was a tight manoeuvre and Markus knew that he himself couldn't have cleared the bend any faster. Silently he applauded his friend. Yet, as Andy came out, they found that the gap from the Silvia had actually widened. They should be catching up on the straights, but the Silvia seemed to ward them off easily despite Andy's efforts, as he continued to punish the 180SX with intense concentration. Markus scowled thoughtfully at their opponent in front. It was the sound that warned him and immediately he cursed himself for not having picked up on it immediately. The deep, staccato bursts of engine noise that rattled back at them from the Silvia was a distinct 6-cylinder sound, not at all like the snappy cackle of the 1.8-litre production S13 power plant.

"Dude, I think he's running an RB," Markus said urgently to Andy. "Sounds like a 25 or even 26."

Andy didn't reply, but instead hissed angrily at the taunting red taillights. He had provoked this race. He had to win – otherwise he would look like a complete fool. Markus glanced across at his friend again. In the subtle illumination of the Silvia's taillights and the glow from the 180SX's instrument panel, he saw Andy's eyes narrow and his expression become set and grim.

They were coming out onto another short straight now and somehow sat some 40 metres behind the hurtling Silvia. How could he have flown through that bend so fast? Andy's next shift was gritty and forceful. With little regard, he slammed the accelerator pedal into the floor. Markus reached for the door handle and flicked a worried glance out of his window, down at the menacing drop that was so close beside him. With the SR' under full throttle, their speed thrust up to 140km/h.

Feeling slightly safer on the straight, Lorna peered quickly over her shoulder. "They're gaining again," she reported to Leon. Her words interrupted his concentration and Leon's eyes flittered to his rear-view. The 180SX was snarling after them and rapidly narrowing the gap.

"That guy's insane, that's way too fast for this bend..." Leon blurted and tore his eyes back to the road. "Oh, no!"

Initially hidden, the dark shadow that covered the smooth tarseal and lured in its unsuspecting victims was suddenly revealed in the beam of their headlights. The bend was wet! Frantically, Leon hit the brakes and steered for the edge of the road to try and cut the right-turning bend with as much room as he could get.

The brake lights from the Silvia glared and her tyres screeched as she struggled to shave off speed. Andy had expected the lights to fade out again almost immediately, but they stayed on. Impulse told Andy to brake too, but he fought the urge, delaying just a fraction longer, which at this speed would gain him precious metres. Still the brake lights stayed on, a blazing warning, and the Silvia veered over to the right side of the road. Alarm bells shrilled in Andy's head and Markus lost his cool. "Brake man!"

Just 15-metres separated the two cars when the brakes engaged and Andy skidded her in. Recklessly, he tried to downshift, but the synchros grated and the shifter popped out again into neutral. They were going too fast, rear-ending the Silvia was unavoidable, unless...

Andy yanked the steering wheel left, aiming for the gap between the Silvia and the roadside, just short of that steep drop. They no longer heard the abrasive scrub of their tyres, the rumble of their engine or the sounds from the Silvia. With adrenaline coursing through their veins, they watched the front of their car veer away in slow motion from the Silvia's back bumper, which loomed before them, big shiny and black. The headlights fell onto the bend and Andy and Markus both saw the wet. They flinched, recognising the danger instantly. With no time to think, Andy reacted instinctively and wrenched the steering wheel back to the right.

The two cars came together with a massive bang. Andy and Markus were thrown harshly against their harness and pain soared through them. The left rear section of the Silvia buckled and caved in. Her taillight exploded, sending shards of red and orange plastic onto the road. The front bumper and fender of the 180SX folded with a clash of metal on metal and the carbon-fibre bonnet warped and cracked.

The strength of the collision shoved the Silvia forwards and pushed her tail around. She angled in towards the red clay embankment, while sending them careening for the drop. Skidding at 70km/h with Andy's right foot locking the brakes, the 180SX seemed to sense the danger and tried to dig her heels in, but then they were on the wet and sliding freely.

Andy swore and Markus gasped. Behind them they heard the screech and crunch of twisting metal before their tyres left the road and cleared the edge. For a moment, Andy saw the city lights shining eerily beneath him and then they dropped with a gut-wrenching swoop. Branches suddenly snapped and cracked around them. They landed with a jarring crunch that slammed them brutally down into their seats. The car lurched and see-sawed awkwardly. Miraculously her engine still idled.

Andy recovered first. He straightened up in pain and the car shuddered and rocked dangerously at his movement. He froze and held his breath until the motion stilled. Carefully, he tilted his head up and peered out over the bonnet. The left headlight still shone brightly, illuminating a confusing scene. There were branches all around. Pine needles? Andy was too dazed to think clearly. Beside him, Markus moved, raising his head with a groan. The 180SX tilted forward slightly. Her chassis creaked and more branches rasped against her body.

"Keep still," Andy hissed. "Take it real slow!" Andy turned to Markus as he straightened cautiously. Blood trickled down his chin. In the poor light it looked gruesome.

"What happened?" Markus croaked, unnaturally loud. His ears were still ringing from the sounds of the crash.

"I think we've landed in a tree," Andy replied shakily.

"A tree? Oh man! I thought you'd killed us." Without thinking, Markus turned in his seat to look around. The car swayed at the sudden shift in weight and began to arc over. They both grabbed for the door holds and pressed themselves back into their seats, gripping so tightly that their knuckles turned white.

Achingly slowly the car's nose dropped until her single headlight lit up the trees further down the incline and its light fell onto the grassy, barren slope below. It was a long way down. Still their angle of tilt increased and, with a mighty groan from the huge tree, the wounded car began to slip slowly off the branch that supported her.

"We're going over! Jump!" Andy's left hand clawed at his harness buckle, which released with a snap. In the same movement, his right hand found the door latch. He heaved at the door, but it was stuck. With a jolt, the 180SX stopped sliding, but pivoted over even further.

Terror seized Andy and he threw his whole weight against the door. It burst open and he tumbled out head first, with hands held out protectively in front of him. Under the force of a nearby branch, the door slammed shut again behind him. Another branch caught Andy in the stomach and then another in the chest, slowing his fall and swinging him around so that he hit the grassy slope feet first. The shock buckled his knees and he fell onto his back. He was winded and in agony. A scream for help echoed in his ears, he looked up fearfully. His eyes flew wide in horror.

The 180SX was still hanging in the tree, high above him. He was blinded by her sole headlight beaming down. With a rasp that rained bark chips and pine needles, the car slid the last few inches down the massive branch that was holding her and her nose tilted fully vertical. She gave a final shudder and another metallic groan and came free. Andy froze in terror. He had no time to get out of the way. His hands flew up protectively above his face and he screamed.

"We're going over! Jump!" Markus was seized by Andy's words and for a moment he hesitated and watched his friend wrestling with his door. Suddenly the car jolted, throwing him forward against his harness and he started to panic. With frantic hands he pushed at his door, scratching at the handle. The door opened readily and relief sparked through him, but then it clanged against wood, barely half a foot open. He yanked it closed and shoved it open again with all his strength, but again it hit wood, jarring his arms. He jerked his head up and realised with terror that the tree trunk was blocking it. His exit was barred. The 180SX was now tilted at an extreme angle and Markus began to slip from his seat, until he was only held by his harness.

"Andy," Markus cried out. "Andy!" He turned back to his friend, but the driver's seat was empty. Andy was gone. "Oh God," Markus' fingers scrabbled at his harness buckle while his feet tried to find a hold in the foot-well. Releasing the clasp, he freed himself and dived across to the driver seat. He lunged for the door handle, but his shoes slipped and the lunge lacked momentum. The gear stick caught his shirt and he fell awkwardly over the seat. "Andy, help!" he cried out again as the car's nose dropped to point straight down.

The car groaned and creaked around him, then grated and lurched. Markus closed his eyes and hung on with all his strength. Suddenly he was weightless again. He heard a scream and wasn't sure if it was him that was screaming. The car hit the ground and the sound of bending metal and breaking glass exploded around him. Losing his hold, he was thrown like a ragdoll. His head slammed into the steering wheel. Concussed and numb, he slipped into the driver's foot-well and lay there in a crumpled heap.

The 180SX's engine had died on impact and it was deathly still in the darkness. For a moment she stood on her crushed nose, her tail pointing helplessly at the sky. Then, with a last despairing groan, she keeled over and went down the slope.

The S13 skidded freely, angling in for the embankment. Lorna squealed and Leon swore, crushing the brake pedal into the floor, but the car had too much momentum. Her nose barely dropped as she shot off the road and jumped the shallow ditch. Although they had braced themselves for the impact, Leon and Lorna were flung violently against their harnesses as the car smashed into the bank, gouging out the soil. The engine stalled instantly and in the sudden quiet, the clunk of falling dirt and clay from the bank rang loudly on the bonnet. "Oh no," Leon looked out in dismay.

The one good headlight lit up the reddish-brown bank in front of them. It seemed close enough to touch. Leon shook his head angrily. "Are you alright?" he turned to Lorna, who winced and wiped a smear of blood from her lower lip. She was pale, but she nodded. "Are you sure?"

"I'm okay," Lorna nodded again.

"Oh good," Leon was relieved. Quickly he turned in his seat and scrutinised the road behind them. Lit up by a gloomy pale-red glow from the Silvia's remaining taillight, the road was empty. Where had the 180 gone? It couldn't have made it far – not after that collision. Leon detected a muffled rumbling in the air, and he strained to listen. Was that an engine idling? It sounded as though it was coming from down the bank.

"I'm gonna check on the others," Leon spoke to Lorna and pushed his door open, clambering out awkwardly. The engine noise was louder outside. He began to walk towards the edge of the bank, but before he got there the noise altered in pitch. A massive crunch and bang followed. Leon ran. Reaching the road side, he stopped in his tracks.

Below, on the grassy slope he saw the 180SX. Ruined, she stood upright on her nose, presenting the underside of her body to him. Her taillights shone at the night sky and the giant pine tree that towered above her. Beside the white car, scrambling away, he could make out the guy that had challenged him. Leon was still searching for the other occupant when the car began to sag over. She came down on her roof. Shattering glass and twisting metal filled the air. Lying upside-down with all four wheels pointed upwards, she slid backwards down the steep slope and suddenly came up on her tail. Her crushed nose rose to meet the sky. The taillights burst under her weight and died. With only the eerie light from the moon illuminating her doom, she went over again and, building momentum, she began to roll. Turning end-over-end, churning up grass and soil, she raged down the slope. Leon stared in disbelief. The din was appalling. Unable to move, he watched the car tear itself to pieces.

Jerking himself out of his trance, he fumbled through his pockets. His cell-phone –where was his phone? He turned and saw Lorna clambering out of the Silvia. "Lorna! We need an ambulance!" he shouted urgently. Before she could reply, he was slipping and sliding down the bank.

The 180SX had finally come to a rest and was lying on her crushed roof. As Leon neared, he saw that all four of her tyres had popped and the rims hung askew. Closing the last metres, the pungent stench of petrol hit him. He heard it trickling freely and falling onto the twisted metal of the car. She must have ruptured her tank. Shutting out the smell, Leon forced himself nearer. "Hello?" he called out, "Anybody in there?" He received no reply and reluctantly closed the last steps, pushing through the reek of petrol. In the gloom of the moonlight, Leon could make out a hand protruding from a tiny compacted opening where the driver side window had been. Black smudges of blood covered it.

"Oh God, he's in there – help me!" Leon cried out, hoping that Lorna or the other guy might hear and come to his aid. Without thinking, he bent down and grabbed the hand. Wet and slippery, it flopped limply in his grasp. Trying to pull him out, he realised with rising dread, that the gap was far too small. He let go of the hand and lunged for the door handle. He heaved with all his strength, but his fingers were smeared with blood and slipped. He fell backwards against the slope.

Spurred on by the continuous drip of escaping fuel, Leon ignored the pain, and bounced back. Was the door locked? He crouched down beside it and, avoiding the gruesome hand, he reached through the broken window and hunted for the door lock. His bare skin grated across jagged glass and blood trickled down his arm.

"Where the hell are you?" Leon gritted his teeth and scowled. Finally his fingers found it. The door wasn't locked, it was jammed. He jerked his hand back out and lunged for the door handle with renewed efforts. He grabbed it in one hand and clasped the window sill with the other. He leaned back with all his weight and strength. The door creaked, but didn't budge. Sharp glass bit into his palm. "Come on!" he hissed, struggling on in desperation. With each gasp, the overpowering stench of petrol fumes scalded his lungs. Leon was beginning to weaken, but still the door resisted him.

"Help me someone!" he cried out breathlessly and suddenly the other guy appeared at his left shoulder. Together they struggled with the twisted door. The car creaked and shuddered and, miraculously, the door gave. It flew open so suddenly that the jagged window sill tore their hands, shredding the skin from their palms. They lost their grip and fell backwards in a heap. The door hit the end of its travel and rebounded violently back against the frame. Electric blue sparks crackled in the night and the petrol combusted with a deep thump.

Lorna heard Leon shout something back at her, but the words were slow to penetrate her brain, which was still muddled from the crash. Watching him disappear over the roadside, she felt alone. "We need an ambulance…" Lorna forced herself into action and, fighting her fear, she clambered back into the Silvia. Finally she found her cell-phone.

"Accident and emergency..?"

"I need an ambulance…" Lorna's voice echoed back at her.

"Where are you?"

"Um…" Lorna looked around her, through the back window of the Silvia, up and down the dark road. She closed her eyes. Where are we..?

"Are you there?" the female operator insisted.

"Um, yes, I think we're at…" Lorna blurted.

"Please state the type of emergency."

"There's been a crash. A car went off the road, I think, down the bank."

"Are you injured?"

"I'm okay."

"Is anybody else injured?"

"I'm not sure, but I think so..."

"Please stay on the line until the emergency vehicles get there," the operator instructed.

"I can't, they may need my help. Hurry – please!" Lorna disconnected before the operator could say another word. She scrambled out of the Silvia again and ran to the edge of the road. Looking down, she could make out the stricken 180SX, lying on her back. She recognised Leon struggling beside the vehicle and another dark shape moving down towards him.

Lorna hesitated, the unreal picture reminded her of a drink-driving advertisement on TV. She shuddered. For a second time, she turned and ran back to the Silvia. Diving through the open driver's door, her fingers fumbled to loosen the small fire extinguisher from its mount in the passenger foot-well. Surprised at how light it was, she ran and jumped over the bank. Her right foot hit a rabbit hole and she twisted her ankle. Sharp pain shot up her leg and with a yelp, she fell, rolling. Still clutching the extinguisher, she managed to get back on her feet and, forcing the pain aside, she carried on, stumbling and sliding down the steep incline.

Markus was stuck. His head spun from its contact with the steering wheel. Clumsily he tried to raise himself, but fell back, panting and injured. The 180SX trembled and whimpered. Anger seized him, driving away his fear. It wasn't supposed to be like this. Grabbing the base of the driver's seat, he pulled himself upwards again and tried to squeeze through the gap between the steering wheel and the seat with renewed effort. "You have to get yourself out of here," he grunted, focusing his energy. Slowly he raised himself and his head came above the level of the seat. Suddenly the car began to move.

His heart skipped a beat and his arms sagged. He dropped back into the foot-well and clamped his eyes shut as they went over. It was terrible. With glass exploding around him, scraping and cutting him, the relentless sound of crumpling metal pounded in his ears. Brutally, he was lifted, dropped and thrown as the car somersaulted down the incline. The roof collapsed and he was crushed further into the foot-well. When the car rose up again, sprinkling glass chips, Markus slid towards the seat. With his right arm still grabbing the seat base, he clung on desperately. She tilted over and then down she came. Markus was tossed harshly against the seat. His wrist got caught in the seat rail and the bone gave with a loud crack. He gasped in agony and let go. He was flung around and his head smacked into something hard. Overcome by darkness, he no longer felt anything.

Markus awoke to a sharp, stabbing pain in his wrist. Something was pulling at his hand. It hurt immensely, but before he could react, the pressure relented and he was able to concentrate on the more immediate pain. His head was droning. He couldn't remember what had happened, but he found himself lying on his back, squashed into a small space. His knees were pressed against his chest and something was cutting painfully into his back. He could barely see and there was a strong odour in the air that made it difficult to breathe. He felt claustrophobic. He had to get out. He tried to move but there was no room. He was trapped. Fear gripped him. Dimly he heard a muffled voice. It was close. He froze to listen.

Something was scratching at the metal by his ear. Markus called for help, but it came out as a weak croak. He was tired and dazed. The scratching continued and he heard a shout. There was a loud clang and suddenly the hard surface against his side flew outwards. Cold, fresh night air flooded in. Relief flowed through him. Help was at hand. He tried again to untangle himself when a low thump resonated in his ears and a sudden intense heat hit him. Flames blazed around him. He tried to shield himself, but the fire engulfed him mercilessly. The pain, oh God! Markus screamed.

Flames shot out from the leaning passenger door and rushed rapidly towards both ends of the car. The fire spread with incredible speed. In seconds the car was engulfed in a blazing inferno. "He's still in there!" Leon tried to press forward, but scalding heat hit him, singeing his hair and eyebrows. It robbed the air of oxygen and made it impossible to breathe. Unable to tolerate the intensity, he was forced back and threw up his bare hands against the scorching blaze. That's when the screams started. Loud and piercing.

"Markus!" the guy beside Leon lost it. Ignoring certain death, he jumped forward at the flames to aid his friend.

"No!" Leon dived after him and managed to grab his ankle. He brought him down on the slope, just short of the blazing Nissan. Sweating heavily, with the flames licking at them, Leon fought to maintain his grip as the guy tried to wrench his foot free. Digging his heels into the soil, Leon dragged him back, choking, coughing, kicking and screaming, away from the insane heat.

Lorna reached them, wide-eyed and frantic. She tried to shut out the screams as she aimed the fire extinguisher and pulled the trigger. Nothing happened. "It's not working!" She tried again. Leon looked up and saw Lorna struggling. He let go of the ankle and grabbed the fire extinguisher from her. He lunged for the safety pin, but there was none. Confused, he shoved the nozzle at the burning Nissan and pulled the trigger. Nothing happened.

A shocking thought went through his mind, but he didn't want to believe it. Again and again he tried, pumping the trigger, but the flames and screams from the Nissan continued. Lorna and the guy were both screaming now. Almost crying, Leon shook the extinguisher in frustration. His worst suspicions were confirmed and he stared at it in utter disbelief. It was empty.

He swore with a rage that he had never experienced and hurled the useless cylinder from him. Abruptly the screams from the Nissan ceased. With a sickening sense of despair Leon stared at the burning vehicle. Lorna stood beside him, small and horrified. The flames were dying down now, but thick black smoke continued to spew up into the night air for a long time.

They huddled together on the dark roadside by the S13. Lorna hugged her knees protectively. Idly she scratched at the dark grass stains on her jeans.

"He didn't deserve that," she whispered fiercely.

"Nobody deserves that..."

Neither of them spoke again. They stared silently and without seeing at the tarmac between their feet, each consumed by their own thoughts. Thoughts that were filled with the horror they had just witnessed. Leon had no idea how much time had passed since that slow, nightmare climb back up the slope, made more difficult by Lorna's sore ankle and him needing to support her. Why why why?! He couldn't believe what had just happened. None of it felt real. That fire extinguisher, that bloody fire extinguisher! Anger consumed him again and he clenched his fists until his fingernails bit into his palms. Where was the ambulance?? Oh what was the use, it was far too late for them anyway... His thoughts were interrupted when he became aware of an engine rumble. That must be them, finally.

Leon rose to his feet as a vehicle rounded the bend at speed. He was blinded by its bright headlights. Holding his hands up against the glare, he frowned. The flashing lights were orange and there was no siren. The vehicle that crunched to a halt before him was a tow-truck. Leon took several uncertain steps towards it. A short figure in overalls and carrying a torch climbed out. "Hey, are you alright?" Worriedly he peered at the two haggard figures, sizing up their dirty and charred clothing, their matted, singed hair and bloodshot eyes.

To Leon, there was something very familiar about him, but the light was in his eyes. "Uh, yeah," it took him a moment to find his voice.

"Oh, good…" the truckie seemed relieved. He shone his torch at Leon. "Hey, I remember you." The revolving orange light from the tow-truck briefly illuminated his face and Leon recognised him also. It was the same tow-truck driver that had driven Leon and the wrecked Laurel home from the racetrack.

"What are you doing here?" Leon snapped at him irritably. "We called for an ambulance, not a tow-truck!"

"They haven't come??" he pointed his torch beyond Leon, to where Lorna sat. "Are you sure you're not hurt?"

"We're fine," Leon replied icily. The truckie nodded.

"You know, they should be here by now," he scowled. "I intercepted their call." A muffled radio crackle came from the tow-truck and the man turned his head to listen. "They're on their way."

"Yeah well, there's not much they can do now," Leon's shoulders slumped.

"Why? What happened?" the truckie shone his torch about him, before turning back to Leon and looking him up and down. "You're absolutely certain you're alright?"

"Mostly," Leon replied solemnly and turned to glance behind him at Lorna, who was very pale.

"Another car crashed into the back of us. It went down the bank and caught fire." It was Lorna who spoke.

"Are you serious?" the truckie looked at her in shock. "Where?" She pointed and he ran to the edge of the road, shining his torch down. "Good grief." He looked as though he wanted to plunge down the slope himself, but he held back. "That's terrible," he shook his head. He walked slowly back to Leon and Lorna. "There's nothing I can do for them, the police will be here soon, you'll need to wait for them."

"That's what we're doing."

"Okay," The truckie nodded and cast his torch around the area again, over the stranded S13. "Is that your car?"

"Yeah," Leon answered cagily.

"I can offer you a tow, if you want?" the truckie offered.

"Guess I need one," Leon sighed.

"What was your address?" Leon gave it to him. "You'll be my best customer soon," the truckie tried to lighten the mood.

Leon didn't smile. He turned away and sat back down beside Lorna, putting his arm around her. With her shoulder against his, they continued to wait for the emergency services.

By the time they arrived, driving in convoy with lights flashing and sirens blaring, the S13 had already been towed away. The leading police car screeched to a halt, followed closely by a fire engine, an ambulance and a second police car. Two policemen hurried towards where they sat. Immediately they fired their questions at them. Were they hurt? Where was the crashed vehicle? Had there been a fire? Leon stood and pointed down the incline. Suddenly the darkness was dispersed by two powerful floodlights from the fire engine, illuminating the gruesome, burnt-out wreckage of the 180SX in a stark, white glare.

Then it was all hustle and bustle. Firemen ran down the slope, dragging hoses that snaked out behind them, and policemen cordoned off the area, putting up beacons to warn other traffic. Two medics appeared. They fussed over Leon and Lorna, examining them for burns, cuts, bruising and whiplash. One applied a cream to the cuts and burns on Leon's bare arms and hands and began to bandage them. Meanwhile a policewoman armed with a pen and notepad, took their names and contact details and tried to extract from them what had happened.

Leon had already prepared what he was going to say and before Lorna could speak, he began to explain: "We were up at the lookout for the sunset and just on our way home when another car suddenly came up behind us – going fast." He paused and Lorna frowned. She was confused, that wasn't quite what had happened. But Leon continued. "I tried to slow down for it and let it pass, but they crashed into the back of us, and the next second we piled into that ditch," Leon paused and pointed to the gouge mark in the bank where they had crashed. He let the policewoman catch up on her notes, before he went on. "I checked on Lorna and she seemed okay, so I asked her to call for help and went to look for the others."

"The others?" the policewoman interrupted.

"The other car," Leon explained. "I heard them. Their engine was still running, down the bank..."

"And then?" the policewoman pressed.

"I... I tried to help, but..." Leon's voice caught.

"But..?"

"But, but just as I got to the car it caught on fire," Leon voice cracked. "And, they... they were screaming..." Leon shook his head as though in a trance. The medic's hands on his arm stilled.

"You didn't put it out?"

"We couldn't, the fire extinguisher was empty," Leon kept shaking his head. "The flames were too hot we couldn't do anything..."

"We?"

"What?" Leon frowned.

"You said: *we* couldn't..." the policewoman pointed out.

"Lorna came down after she called for help, she had the fire extinguisher," Leon said quietly into the shocked and awkward silence. Tears were running down Lorna's face now. The policewoman turned to look at her.

"Sorry, it's my job. I have to get the facts straight..." her tone was apologetic.

"I know," Lorna smiled bravely. But she was confused. She noticed that Leon had said nothing of the dark-haired guy who had threatened them with a knife and later run, wildly into the night. She did not understand why Leon was protecting him.

"So, where's your vehicle now?"

"It's been towed away already."

"Towed away?"

"Yeah, a tow-truck came before you. He said he intercepted the call on the radio."

"I see," the policewoman bristled. She stood with the glare of the police car headlights behind her so Leon couldn't make out her expression. "How are they?" she asked the medics.

"Some whiplash," the medic that worked on Leon answered her. "Due to his cuts and burns, as a precaution I'd recommend that Leon returns to hospital with the ambulance, but Lorna is okay to go home."

"Right," she quelled Leon's objections. "We'll contact your family and let them know that you're alright. Lorna, you'll come back with me."

When the screams of his friend had finally stopped, Andy ran. Terror pursued him. Branches from pine trees and the thorns of blackberry bushes tugged at him, scratching his skin. He hardly noticed. Markus' terrible screams were still filling his head and hounded him down the slope. He ran full tilt into a pine tree. Pain knifed through him and he nearly fell, but managed to grab a branch to steady himself.

Totally disoriented, Andy stood with his chest heaving, gasping for breath. Nausea suddenly overcame him and he braced himself against the trunk of the tree. His vomit splattered loudly on the ground. Soon he was dry-retching, but still the screams continued. Trying to shut them out, he started screaming himself. He bit down on his tongue until the salty taste of his own blood mixed with the acidic burn that scalded the back of his throat. Somehow the pain and the sickly taste helped to steady him.

Breathing easier, Andy began to think more clearly. He knew that the police must be rushing to the scene very soon, and, depending on what the other driver told them, they would be searching for him. He had to get away from here. Forcing down his nausea, Andy wiped his mouth with the back of his hand and pushed on. The going was difficult in the thick vegetation and, with the moonlight only just penetrating through the tree canopy, Andy could barely see. He withdrew his cell-phone, but the feeble light from the display hardly helped, yet it gave him a little comfort as he pressed on impatiently. His friend's screams continued in his head alongside thoughts of the police pursuing him.

An hour later, Andy tripped and suddenly found himself slipping and sliding down a muddy slope. Dropping his phone, he snatched at a branch and managed to catch his fall, mere metres from a steep drop. Shakily, he dragged himself back up the slope. His phone was gone and he carried on, hobbling on his sore ankle and using just the pale light of the moon to navigate. The going was now even slower.

It seemed to have taken him forever, but after several more hours Andy finally reached flat ground and the first houses began. Taking the back streets, he stumbled on. To avoid being seen, he stuck to the shadows thrown by the trees and fences beside the footpath. Occasionally, he had to hide from a passing car by ducking in behind a garden hedge, but mostly the streets were empty and lit only sparsely by streetlights.

Andy made it home just as dawn was breaking. He was hurting and completely exhausted. Like a man in a trance, he unlocked the front door and dragged himself in. He had barely enough energy to close and lock it again before he dropped to the floor in the hallway. Hugging his knees up to his chest, he huddled there, on the cold lino. He thought of Markus. They had spent so much time together. Ever since meeting in high school, they had hung out. They had built cars and raced together. They had so many projects and dreams of getting a placing in the drifting championships. Now none of those would ever be realised.

Again, Andy heard Markus' call for help and his agonised screams. He clamped his hands over his ears and tried to shut them out, but he couldn't and suddenly he was angry. It was his fault. He alone had provoked the hilltop race, there was no denying that, but the driver of the S13 was also to blame. Andy glowered into the gap between his knees. He had been made to look like an amateur. He'd lost the race and worse, caused the accident. The driver of the S13 had literally toyed with him, using techniques that Andy had trouble with. The incredible arrogance of it burnt through him, mixing with Markus' screams until he shook with fury. His frustration turned on the driver of the S13.

He had to get his own back. He had to beat him and prove that they were better. He owed Markus that. The other driver had mentioned that he was entering the next drift competition. A lot of people would be watching. It was the perfect opportunity to put him in his place. But with the 180SX completely shattered and burnt out, he would first need to get the Cefiro ready. "I'll do what it takes Markus... I'll get him for you," Andy spoke his promise. "And afterwards..." he clenched his fists until the knuckles were white. "I'll get him for myself," his voice was calm and his rage receded. He lifted his head from his knees and looked around him.

The morning light had strengthened now and the hallway was filled with a soft glow. Andy stared down at himself. He grimaced. His clothing was torn and had sticky yellow pine sap, grass stains and reddish-brown droplets of blood all over it. He was tired beyond belief, but before he could sleep he would need to clean himself up. With barely any strength left, he forced himself to his feet and hobbled to the bathroom.

A look in the mirror freaked him out. His eyebrows and eyelashes were gone. Even his matted dark hair had been singed in places and his face was black with soot. There were blisters on his cheeks and forehead, his lips were cracked and his eyes bloodshot. He shuddered, tracing the curve of his missing eyebrow with his forefinger. How long would it take to grow back?

Turning away, Andy peeled off his soiled clothing and stepped into the shower. The spray stung painfully on his burns and scratches. He gasped and fought the urge to turn it off. He soaped himself down and watched the grimy water at his feet wash down the drain. Mustering the last of his energy, he tended to his burns and scratches, before he limped to his bedroom. His head had barely hit the pillow before he sank into a deep, deathlike sleep.

Leon lay uncomfortably in his narrow hospital bed. His neck was aching and his cuts were stinging. In vain he sought a better position to lie in, but finally gave up and tried to sleep. Yet, although he was incredibly tired, sleep didn't want to come. He kept seeing the other car roll down the hillside, then the fire and then there were the screams. He wondered how Lorna was coping. He would have liked to be able to talk to her, but he didn't have his cell-phone with him. It must still be in the Silvia. His thoughts turned to his car. How bad was the damage? He didn't want to think about it.

By morning Leon's neck had stiffened up so that he could barely move it. Nurses came and changed his dressings, re-bandaging the cuts and burns. Although he thought this was excessive, he remained quiet while they fussed over him. Finally they drew back and declared him ready to return home. His mum was already on the way to pick him up.

Leon made his way down to the reception area. Outside it was raining. He decided to wait in the foyer, standing alone. It wasn't long before he spotted his mum, striding towards the entrance and dragging Tamsin along by the hand. Both wore raincoats, which were sprinkled with droplets. Tamsin's was entirely red, with matching red gumboots. She had her hood pulled over her head. Leon had to smile. She looked like Little Red Riding Hood. Neither of them had seen him and he watched them for a moment, trying to read his mum's mood. Then he went out to meet them.

"Hi Mum," Leon greeted her awkwardly. "Thanks for coming to get me."

"Leon!" Impulsively, his mum made to hug him, but drew back, realising her soggy raincoat and the bandages on his hands and arms. "I was so worried. Your car... I wanted to come last night, but they wouldn't let me." She held him at arm's length to study him. "How are you? Are you okay?"

"Yeah, my neck is a bit sore though," Leon admitted.

"You'll need to take it easy for a few days," his mum nodded. "Two crashes in one week take their toll." Her tone was concerned, but Leon wondered if she was chiding him.

"I'm not looking to make it a habit."

"I know," his mum spoke softly. "The police called me. They explained what happened and said it wasn't your fault." She saw a haunted shadow pass across Leon's eyes. "Let me know if you want to talk about anything."

Leon nodded and changed the topic. "Did Lorna call?"

His mum shook her head. "She hasn't tried your mobile?"

"I'm not sure. I think it's still in my car. I hope she's okay."

"We should get going," his mum turned. "I borrowed Annette's car, it's just over there." Leon's mum led the way. Tamsin had relinquished her hand and replaced it with Leon's.

"It's okay, Leon."

"I'm sure it will be," Leon agreed earnestly, surprised at how comforting her little hand was. "It just might take time..."

They arrived home to find an Altezza parked on the street, while the black hull of the Silvia stood alone on the lawn, glistening from the recent rain. Even as they approached, Leon could see the damage. A big figure stood near it, wearing a jacket. He turned as they approached. Leon hopped out once his mum had parked and walked slowly over to his friend. His shoes squelched on the lawn.

"Man," Byron gawked at him in consternation. "When I said: 'don't have too good a night', I didn't mean go and trash yourself and your car." His hair was sprinkled with rain drops. Leon turned away from him and all the questions that were obvious in his troubled eyes. He looked upon the Silvia and his stomach filled with dismay. "Yeah," Byron read his expression. "Not cool at all."

The left tail section of the Silvia had sustained the full shock of the initial collision and it showed. It had caved in and was bent and twisted. The taillight was shattered, leaving a jagged hole of translucent red and orange plastic. Leon walked to the front of the car and saw that again it was her left side that had taken the impact. The headlight was smashed and the front bumper pushed in. With dark red soil from the clay bank smeared all over her injuries and gleaming wetly, the Silvia looked as though she was bleeding. Leon felt numb. He reached out to run his hand over her buckled bonnet.

"So dirty," Tamsin stood behind him. She peered out from under her red hood, at the muddy, misshapen front section of the S13, which sat at the same level as her eyes.

"Come along, Tamsin," his mum sensed his mood.

Leon shivered. The rain had abated but he felt cold. Wearily, he turned back to the car and walked further around, finding that her right side seemed to have come off mostly unscathed. The original marks and blemishes of her peeling black paint were suddenly minor and superficial in comparison to the raw wounds he had witnessed so far. He completed his circuit with Byron trailing silently, at a respectful distance. Leon sagged to a stop again in front of the gaping gash in her rump.

"So that's it then…"

"What do you mean?" Byron looked at him quizzically.

"What do you think I mean?" Leon burst out. "I can't do this anymore."

"Do what?"

"Cars and racing. I've already written off Mum's car, and now this…"

"Come on, accidents happen – and this car is definitely not a write-off. The main thing is that you didn't get hurt."

"Well, try telling that to the other guy."

"What other guy?"

"The one that crashed into us and went over the bank."

"What? You got hit?" Byron was incredulous. "What happened to him?"

"His car caught on fire."

Byron eyes opened wide. "He got out though, right?" Leon's anger receded. He looked at the ground and shook his head, tight-lipped. Byron stared at him, aghast. "That's…" he sought to find the right words, but couldn't find them. "Holy…" Byron turned back to Leon and laid his hand on his shoulder. "That's some heavy news, man. I can understand you must feel pretty bad, but you can't go blaming yourself."

"I'm trying not to, but I've had some pretty strong signs now that seem to say racing isn't for me."

"Maybe so, but what about you finding an S13 so quickly and that guy Simon helping you out, and your uncle teaching you to drift?"

"And what about the other driver then? He died man! Is that a positive sign?"

"No," Byron sighed. "Look, I don't know. If you want out, then so be it. But you'll have to make your mind up now."

"Why now?" Leon hesitated and it was Byron's turn to get exasperated.

"Because the competition is this Saturday and it'll take time to get your car fixed."

"Hmmm," Leon pinched his lower lip.

"So what will it be?" Byron asked at last.

"I don't know…I'm tired." Leon rubbed his temples. "I don't want to deal with this right now."

"You start your new job on Monday, right?"

"Yeah,"

"So will you tell them you can't do it anymore because you're over cars and racing?"

Leon cringed at the thought of going back to his old job, his old boss. "No way," he said finally.

"And what about this?" Byron indicated the S13. "You like driving her, right?"

"Yeah, for sure," Leon couldn't deny it.

"And when you went on the track – was that fun?"

"Before I crashed it was."

"And drifting with your uncle – that was cool, right?"

"Yeah," Leon nodded.

"So, you'd want to do it again?"

"Yeah okay, I do," Leon admitted reluctantly.

"Well, let's get your Silvia sorted so you can."

"Okay," Leon nodded carefully. "You know of a place?"

"I've got one in mind."

"Cheap?" Leon asked. "It needs to be cheap."

"They should be reasonable," Byron nodded. "James took his RX-4 to them, and you know what a stinge he is. He had only good things to say."

"Okay then," Leon agreed tiredly. He realised how highly strung he was. He thought of Lorna again. His cell-phone... Was it in the Silvia?

"I'll give the panel-beaters a call now and see when they have time." Byron disappeared into the house and Leon took the opportunity to check his Silvia. At last he found his phone, wedged into a small gap, at the back of the centre console in the driver's foot-well. The display lit up to his fingers, but the Caller ID showed his mum's number as the only caller. Lorna had not called. Byron reappeared.

"They don't have time to start today, but if we drop it off, they'll look at it first thing Monday," Byron suggested. "They close at 1pm though, means we have to go soon. Can you handle that?"

"I'll be okay," Leon took a deep breath.

"Alright, I tow, you roll," Byron said with finality.

Carefully, they towed the Silvia through the sodden streets. Leon turned his hazard lights on to warn other traffic. It felt clumsy being towed and he sensed that the Silvia despised it also. As he shadowed Byron's Altezza, Leon assessed her and was relieved to find that she didn't seem to pull heavily in either direction. It suggested that her chassis might not have suffered much damage.

When they reached the panel and paint shop, Byron towed the Silvia through two tall metal gates, before stopping in front of the workshop. Byron left Leon to untie the tow rope and went to a small office at the side of the workshop. Having retrieved the rope, Leon took a moment to inspect his surroundings.

The yard was densely clustered with other collision casualties. Some of the cars looked to be in substantially worse shape than the Silvia and sat patiently waiting for repair. Others had already received a degree of attention and were covered in grey primer and partly shrouded by tarpaulins to protect them from sporadic rainfall. The rumble of a compressor started from within the workshop and Leon heard the faint hiss of a paint gun.

Byron reappeared with a stocky man in white overalls, whose chin and cheeks were covered in stubble.

"Hi, I'm Paul." He gave Leon a nod and immediately turned his attention to the Silvia. With a thorough, professional eye, he evaluated the reparation involved, while making his way around and ignoring the sodden concrete to inspect her from underneath.

"Structurally she looks okay," he spoke when he was done. "But still, there's a bit of work there."

"How much?" Leon asked cautiously. "If I get the parts."

Paul scratched his chin. Eventually they agreed on a price.

"How soon can you get it done?" Byron pressed.

"We're fairly busy at the moment," Paul looked around the yard significantly. "Thursday would be the earliest."

"Sounds good to me," Byron prodded Leon who nodded. He didn't have much choice. Leon had the quote issued in writing and handed over his car keys. As Byron reversed the Altezza out of the yard, Leon looked back at the Silvia. He took comfort in the knowledge that she was in good hands. They would repair her and he would drive her again soon. Although he was worn out, the thought cheered him slightly.

"What're you up to now?" Byron asked when he dropped Leon back at home.

"I need to call Lorna," Leon answered him. "I want to make sure she's okay."

"Yeah, you do that," Byron nodded cheekily. "Get some rest too – you look like crap."

"I could do with some," Leon confessed. He could always rely on Byron to be straight up.

"I might come by tomorrow and see how you're going."

"Yeah, cool," Leon agreed. He waved Byron off and went inside. Grabbing the cordless phone from the lounge, he went up to his room and dialled Lorna's number.

"Yes?" a grown-up female voice answered.

"Hi, this is Leon. Is Lorna home?"

There was a pause. "She is," the woman replied flatly, almost coldly.

"Can I speak to her?" Leon asked finally, confused at her reaction. He heard her hesitate.

"I'll see if I can find her." There was reluctance in her voice.

"Hello?" Lorna came on at last, she sounded subdued.

"How are you doing?" Leon greeted her cautiously.

"Not good." Her voice was thick and nasal.

"Yeah, I know," Leon understood. He had suppressed his own feelings, shutting the horror from his mind.

"I can't stop crying. I feel like it's my fault," she continued. "You didn't want to race them – I was the one that told you to. If I hadn't then..."

"Lorna–" Leon tried to stop her.

"It's my fault," Lorna gulped, "God, I just feel so awful."

"Lorna..." Leon started out again, but his voice faded. This was not something that could be discussed over the telephone.

"Yes?" she asked miserably.

"Could I maybe come over and see you?" Leon was uncertain. "If that's okay?"

"Um, it's not that it wouldn't be okay," Lorna took a breath. "I barely slept last night and I'm totally exhausted... So I think I'd rather just try and sleep today."

"Are you sure? It's just... I want to make sure you're alright." Leon tried not to let his disappointment show.

"Yeah, I just need some space right now."

"Oh, okay. Let me know when you do want to see me," Leon fidgeted. Did she blame him as well?

"Maybe tomorrow I can come over to you instead?" Lorna asked. Her voice was almost fearful. "I think I will be aching to get out of the house by then... Mum's been relentless."

"Of course," Leon felt relief flow through him. He thought quickly. "You haven't got a car have you? The Silvia is going to be out of action for a while."

"Really? Is it bad?"

"It looks bad," Leon admitted cautiously.

"I'm sorry..." Lorna sensed his mood. "But yeah, I should be able to borrow Mum's. I'll just have to convince her..."

"That would be good," Leon relaxed. "Oh and Lorna?"

"Yes?"

"Bring your swimsuit and a towel."

"Have you looked outside today? It's supposed to be raining tomorrow too."

"Don't forget them," Leon insisted.

"Okay," Lorna agreed. "See you tomorrow then at around nine." Leon heard a hint of that sparkle back in her voice. It made him feel better.

"I'll be ready."

Andy awoke from a deep, exhausted slumber. His head was throbbing and his face and arms hurt intensely. He touched his cheek with one hand, his fingertips brushed over the coarse cotton of his bandages. The events of the night before flashed back into his mind. Markus! It hadn't been just a bad dream. The horror of it flooded him once more. He raised himself on one elbow, wincing at the movement and looked around. His bedroom was dark. What time was it?

Andy looked towards the illuminated display of his bedside radio: 22.13. He had slept for over 15 hours. Awkwardly, he rolled out of bed and, limping on his sore ankle, he went to the bathroom and switched on the light. The mirror stalled him. He stared at the bruised image of himself and was appalled. He looked no better than he had that morning. While bandages swathed the better part of his face, they didn't cover his lips, which were black and swollen. His eyes were bloodshot and big plum-coloured smudges hung beneath them. Quickly, he turned away.

The curtains were drawn in the lounge but a thin beam of light filtered through the narrow gap where they met. Carefully, he peered out into the night. The street was empty and wet in the soft glow of the streetlamps. It was raining. He felt strangely numb. The scene seemed unreal. Dark thoughts consumed him. Why had the police not come? Surely they must know by now.

Andy stayed by the curtain, staring at the dreary day outside. He was confused, uncertain and indecisive. He felt like a caged animal. What should he do? Rousing himself, he pulled the curtains tightly closed and stumbled into the kitchen. He was hungry. After closing the blinds, he rummaged through the cupboards and found a tin of baked beans and half a loaf of white bread. He placed them on the bench-top and looked at the beans darkly. The microwave was broken and he couldn't be bothered waiting for the stove to heat up. He ate them straight from the tin and washed the unappetising mess down with a glass of cold water.

After he had eaten, Andy impulsively unplugged the telephone, before limping back to his bedroom. He slumped down on the bed and stared at the ceiling. Thoughts of Markus and the accident kept swimming in his head but he forced them out. Somehow he was deathly tired. His eyelids felt heavy and slowly they closed.

Andy woke again the next morning. He got up with a groan and made his way to the kitchen. He stood there uncertainly, looking at the bread that he had left sitting on the bench the night before. The open tin of beans stood beside it.

Red marks of tomato sauce were speckled over the bench-top. Andy grimaced. He wasn't hungry. Without thinking, he went through to the lounge and flopped onto the couch. He picked up the remote and turned the TV on. Colourful infomercials greeted him. He turned the TV off again and sat in silence. Should he go to the police?

Several knocks interrupted his thoughts. He tensed but didn't move. The knocks were repeated, coming from the front door. Andy hesitated. The knocks sounded again, this time more insistent. He sighed but stood up and made his way to the front door, mentally preparing himself as he went. He opened it cautiously and froze. Tanya was standing outside. She flinched and stepped back when she saw him, taking in his bandaged face, bruised lips and wild hair.

"So you know then?" She asked quietly. Her eyes were red and puffy. Andy had only opened the door halfway. He nodded, uncertain how to reply. Tanya continued to stare at him. She seemed to have aged since he had last seen her. "You were there, weren't you?" It came out matter-of-factly.

Andy went pale and his heart started to race. Surely she must see the guilt on his ashen features. He could no longer meet her grieving gaze. "Of course, you two were inseparable..." she paused and shook her head with a sigh. "I just can't believe it. It's... It's..." she sought for the right words. "It's just too much..." her voice came out in a whisper.

With his heart beating wildly, Andy remained silent. "How did it happen?" He couldn't look at her, he couldn't reply. "Andy?" Guilt sat like bile in his throat, a burning acid that ate away his words. "Markus always drove too fast, God, I know, I tried to tell him so often to slow down..." Tanya continued quietly, her voice shaking with grief. In her despair, she didn't see Andy's guilt, only his distress. "You couldn't help him?" Still Andy didn't speak. "Andy? You couldn't help my Markus, could you?" Tanya persisted.

"I tried," Andy's voice trembled. "I really tried." This time he looked up and the hurt was genuine in his eyes. "The fire…" Involuntarily, he touched the bandage on his face and shook his head. "I'm so sorry."

Tanya nodded and wiped away the tears that were running down her cheek. "I know you and Markus were good friends."

"The best," Andy replied truthfully. Tanya was about to speak, but her words choked off. Her shoulders slumped. She averted her eyes and looked up at the cloudy sky without seeing. More tears cascaded down her cheeks.

"Sorry," she bit her lip.

"Why don't you come in?" He opened the door fully and led the way to the kitchen, where he offered her some tissues.

"Thank you Andy." She dabbed at her eyes and blew her nose. He stood awkwardly. They were both silent for a long while. "Andy?" Tanya spoke again.

"Yes?" he fidgeted uncomfortably.

"Will you come to the funeral on Monday?" Tanya paused. "I'd really like it if you could be there." Andy stared at her in shock, he had shut his mind to the horrors, but her words pulled him back to reality. His best friend's funeral would be on Monday. Slowly he shook his head.

"No, I…" Andy blurted. "I can't," he kept shaking his head. "Not, not like this."

"Markus would have wanted you to be there," she pleaded, her eyes filled with dismay.

"I… I know, but I'd rather go and visit him alone – in my own time."

"I guess I can understand that," Tanya granted reluctantly. "Your presence will be missed," she admitted. "Please do let me know if you change your mind."

"I will," Andy agreed. He trailed her to the door and watched her climb slowly into her car. Long after she had disappeared from view, he continued to stand in the doorway, staring after her.

True to her word, Lorna arrived punctually in her mum's Mitsubishi Chariot the following morning. Leon stood waiting outside his house with his clothing lightly powdered by rain. As she pulled up, he sensed that she was still very subdued.

"Hey Lorna," he opened the passenger door and got in.

"Hi," she said quietly. Her eyes were puffy from weeping. He felt an overwhelming urge to hug her. There was plenty of room in the big car and he reached over and folded her into his embrace. She clung to him and buried her face against his neck. As they drew apart, Lorna looked past Leon and her expression changed.

"Well, who do we have here?"

Leon turned in his seat to find Tamsin standing on the doorstep of the house. She watched them solemnly with her arms wrapped around her doll. Today she was wearing a pink dress and black lacquered shoes, with her hair in a long plait.

"That's Tamsin, my sister – but I call her Tink."

"You never told me you had a sister," Lorna was intrigued. "Can I meet her?"

"For sure." Leon waved to his sister and she approached them shyly, hugging her doll. "Tink, this is Lorna."

"Hello," she stared at Lorna with big eyes.

"Hi Tink, that's a very pretty doll you have there," Lorna smiled at her. "What's her name?"

"Penelope."

"That's a good name," Lorna nodded approval. "I had a doll once, almost exactly the same as yours."

"You did?"

"Yup, she was called Lucy."

"Do you still have her?"

"You know, I probably do," Lorna was thoughtful. "I'll have a look, and if I find her – you can have her."

"Then they can play together," Tink was enthusiastic.

"Sure can," Lorna laughed. "But I'll have to find her first."

"Off you go now, Tink," Leon shooed her away. "We'll be back later."

"Leon, she's gorgeous," Lorna watched as Tamsin ran up the path and disappeared into the house. "And she has the same eyes as you."

"So people say," Leon smiled at her. "Shall we go?"

She looked at him curiously. "What do you have in mind?" When he unveiled his destination to her, she smiled back at him, agreeing it was a perfect idea.

It felt good leaving the city behind and the weather improved too, the grey clouds clearing to sunny, blue sky. They avoided talking about the accident and instead took turns telling each other stories from their childhood. Soon both of them were laughing and the good mood between them returned. Time passed swiftly and it wasn't long before they reached a small township. Driving slowly, they made their way to the thermal reserve and parked the car. Climbing out, they walked towards the entrance.

"How's your ankle?" Leon noticed her limp.

"Still sore," she admitted.

"The hot pools should do it some good."

"Yeah, but how about your hand?"

"Mum got me a waterproof bandage, so I'll put that on," Leon explained as they approached the counter. "Oh and it's my shout." He dismissed her objections and paid for them both, then led the way between the pools to the changing rooms where they separated. Leon changed quickly into his board-shorts and re-bandaged his hand. Lorna wasn't out yet, so he found himself a vacant locker and stowed his clothing and towel away. He heard footsteps and turned to find her standing behind him on long, shapely legs. He gawked at her.

She wore a white bikini that contrasted beautifully against her tanned skin. With an effort he pulled his eyes away. "Byron was right – I totally missed out on the bikini comp."

"Well, you have me all to yourself now, come on," she took his hand.

They selected one of the smaller pools and sank slowly into it, letting the hot, sulphurous water come up to the level of their chins. They sat back in silence, enjoying the warmth flooding through them, soothing and relieving the tension in their bodies.

"How're you going?" Leon asked much later. There were small beads of perspiration on his nose and forehead.

"Getting a bit cooked," Lorna admitted. At over 40 degrees the temperature was beginning to get to them. Lorna's tanned face had gone an intriguing shade of pink.

"Shall we switch to a cooler pool?" Leon suggested.

"Yeah, that's a good idea."

Trying to avoid other people's feet, they waded carefully through the pool, towards the steps leading out. When she reached them, Lorna climbed the first step and stood up out of the water. Slightly unbalanced, she teetered and then suddenly fell backwards. Unprepared, Leon caught her awkwardly around her waist and she fell back against him.

"Careful," his voice was rough.

"Sorry." Hurriedly, Lorna pushed herself away from him and climbed the steps, this time holding onto the handrail. Confused, Leon stood for a second, before he hurried after her.

When he reached her, she was about to descend the steps into one of the bigger, milder pools. "Sorry if I sounded harsh before, you just gave me a bit of a fright," he spoke softly.

"I gave myself a fright as well," Lorna turned to him and smiled self-consciously. "I just saw stars for a second and nearly blacked out."

Leon realised that she was embarrassed. He slipped his hand into hers and together they walked down the steps and moved to an unoccupied corner of the pool, where they sat comfortably on the underwater bench, with their backs against the wall. Leon picked up the conversation again.

"You know, I get that too sometimes."

"It happens when I switch too quickly from hot to cold," Lorna nodded seriously.

"Yeah, you see this?" Leon turned his head and, with his free hand, parted the black hair above his left temple to reveal a faint scar. "The same thing happened when I was little and stood up out of the bath too fast – Mum wasn't quick enough to catch me and – POW!"

"Ouch," Lorna wasn't sure whether to laugh or not.

"Yeah, but now it's actually quite useful – if I ever forget anything, I can blame it on this. Trust me, it's come in handy." Leon chuckled and was rewarded with a giggle from Lorna.

"I bet, but I must say, I'm still glad you caught me."

"So am I – otherwise we would have both gone sprawling. I wouldn't want to put my head under in that smelly pool."

"No way," Lorna laughed.

"Can I ask you a question?"

"Of course."

"It's a bit off-topic, but do you have any idea why Cam might not like me?"

"Well, I really don't see why he wouldn't..." Beneath the surface of the warm water, she slipped her hand into his and squeezed it. She was silent for a long moment, but then she spoke contemplatively. "You know, maybe he's just scared..."

"Why?"

"Well after..." Lorna's voice trailed off.

"Yes?" Leon pressed gently.

"Well," Lorna tried again. "Cam was best friends with Greg, my ex-boyfriend – they went back a long way... but when Greg and I broke up, Greg began to drift more and more away from the group." To Leon, the other bathers in the pool no longer existed, as he listened to her. "Cam tried to keep the friendship going, but then Greg moved away and we rarely saw him anymore. Not long afterwards, Ollie, another good friend of ours was offered a job in Canada. He took it and then it was just Cam and Taz." Distractedly, Lorna ran her free hand through the water of the hot pool.

"They became real close friends and started a drift project with Cam driving and Taz as engineer," Lorna paused. "So, I think, Cam is afraid he might lose others he cares about…"

"So you think Cam is worried I might take Taz away from him?" Leon asked.

"And me." Lorna didn't look at him. Both of them were quiet for a long time.

"I can understand that," Leon nodded. "I know what it's like to lose friends. I lost a few when we moved here."

"Cam's a great guy," Lorna spoke thoughtfully. "If you don't mind, on the way back I'd like to show you something. It's a bit of a detour though."

"I'm not in a hurry to get back," Leon admitted. They sat together, chatting and enjoying the relaxing warmth of the pool, until both finally agreed that it was time to get out.

"You hungry?" Lorna asked once they had showered, changed and were making their way back to the car.

"I could do with something."

"Are you still alright to take that detour?"

"Of course," Leon confirmed.

"Well the day is getting on…" Lorna looked up at the afternoon sky. "We could just get takeout and eat on the way."

"Fine by me," Leon agreed.

Lorna drove the short distance from the thermal reserve to the takeaway shop and parked outside. "Could you order for me?" Lorna turned to him. "I'd like to duck down the road quickly – I won't be long."

"Sure, what do you want?"

"Just a burger or whatever, same as what you're having," Lorna suddenly grinned wickedly. "Then I'll know if you have good taste."

"You could be getting yourself into trouble here."

Ten minutes later Leon walked out of the takeaway shop to find Lorna already waiting in the car. Balancing the food on one arm, he opened the door and climbed in.

"Smells good," Lorna greeted him.

"And greasy," Leon added humorously. "What are the flowers for?" he noticed a bunch sitting on the backseat.

"I'll show you."

They left the thermal reserve behind them and headed back towards the city. Eventually Lorna turned off the state highway and they began to make their way to the coast.

"You know, this would be a fun road to take the S13 down sometime," Lorna said thoughtfully.

"Are you saying you'd still drive with me then?" Leon asked cautiously.

"No, you drive way too crazy," Lorna's laughed. "I'm saying I want to take your car for a spin."

"You forgot to say please," Leon grinned. "But yes, once she's fixed we'll have to come back here." They relaxed again into an easy silence. The hot springs had taken it out of them and with the soft, spongy suspension of the Mitsubishi cushioning him, Leon felt increasingly drowsy.

They reached the coast and connected back with the highway, heading north. Lorna drove past a small township and not long afterwards, when they were out in the countryside again, she slowed and did a U-turn, driving back slowly the way they had come. To their left, there was a steep incline of red clay while an equally steep grassy bank dropped away on the right. After several hundred metres, Lorna pulled over and parked in a small alcove.

"We'll get out here and walk back – it's not far. Okay?"

"Sure." Together they crossed the highway and walked along the roadside. Lorna carried the flowers. They had not gone far, when she stopped abruptly. Before them stood a small white cross, pegged into the ground, a short distance from the road. It was surrounded by many flowers, most of which were still quite fresh. Lorna knelt down. With careful fingers, she arranged her flowers around the cross and tidied the others. Leon stood quietly, giving her the time and space he sensed she needed. After a while, she straightened up.

"We all lost so much with her." Lorna broke the silence at last. There was no pity in her voice, just sadness. "None of us have ever really gotten over it. Least of all Cam. He comes out here every week..." Leon ran his eyes over the many flowers again – still so fresh. It was not a short drive.

"What happened?" He was affected by Lorna's mood and his voice played tricks on him.

She hesitated for a second. "They had an accident and went off the road. Here." Leon stepped around the white cross and gazed down the bank to a small creek at the bottom. It was a long way down. He stood there, imagining how bad it must have been. Shuddering, he turned back.

Lorna had not moved from her spot in front of the cross. She looked lost and lonely. Thick, silent tears welled in her eyes. Her shoulders were slumped and grief appeared to be weighing her down. Leon gently wrapped his arms around her. Finally, they drew apart and Lorna said her farewells.

"Sorry for getting so emotional," she said in a small voice when they reached the car again.

"Don't be," Leon began, but she hadn't finished.

"I just wanted to show you that Cam is not a bad guy."

"Not many people would go to such lengths for somebody else..." Leon nodded. "Was it his fault?" he asked suddenly.

Lorna hesitated. "You mean the accident?"

"Yeah."

"No," she shook her head.

Both of them remained quiet during the drive home and it was dark when they made it back. Leon yawned when they reached his house.

"You'd better prepare yourself, spending time with me will take it out of you," Lorna smiled mischievously.

"I like the sound of that," he grinned and before she could respond, he leant over in his seat, kissed her and hopped out of the car.

"Bye," standing by the open passenger door, he turned back to her.

"Bye Leon," she laughed.

"You know, we seem to be saying goodbye a lot."

"True, how about: see you later?"

"Better…" he nodded with a smile.

"See you tomorrow?"

"Perfect."

"Good luck with your new job," she called after him.

Andy didn't leave the house for two entire days. Physically and mentally drained, he spent most of that time sleeping, chain smoking and watching TV without really taking it in. He made an effort to treat his burns and his wounds were healing well, but he barely ate. It was the need for cigarettes that finally drove him out on Monday morning, but even then he didn't venture far, paying only a brief visit to the nearby corner store. When he returned, he noticed that his telephone was still unplugged. Not thinking too much about it, he connected it again, lit a smoke and put together some breakfast. Suddenly the phone rang. Andy hesitated but, after the fifth ring, he answered it.

"Hello?"

"Andrew, I've been trying to get hold of you!" an angry man's voice. "You're supposed to be at work and you were supposed to be here on Saturday as well!"

"I'm not feeling well," Andy replied. It was his boss.

"What, you're sick? You could've at least called to let me know. I hope you have a doctor's certificate!"

"I don't."

"Well get one," the voice paused. "Or get yourself to work. Otherwise you won't have a job!" Andy closed his eyes and pinched the bridge of his nose, but remained silent. "Did you hear me?"

"I don't care," he spoke quietly. "I'm not coming."

"I don't think I heard you right?"

"I said: go, take your work and shove it. I quit." Andy slammed the receiver down. He stared at the phone for many seconds. He was out of a job. It felt strange. He couldn't remember the last time he had been unemployed. Andy thought about it. The lack of income didn't matter. He had plenty of savings. Suddenly he smiled. It felt good, as though he had reclaimed some control over his own life again. "I should have done that a long time ago," he said to himself and jumped when the phone abruptly rang again. His face twisted into a scowl and he ripped the receiver up. "What part of piss off don't you understand?!" There was a sharp intake of breath at the other end. A long pause followed.

"Andy, I... I didn't mean..."

"Oh, Tanya! Sorry, I–" Andy blurted, but the phone beeped in his ears. Andy swore quietly and lowered the phone again. He ran his hands over his face. Lighting another cigarette, he drew deeply. Before it was finished, he stabbed it out angrily in the ashtray and picked up the phone again. It rang and rang until he gave up. It was nearly 10.40am. Markus' funeral was in 20 minutes. He could still make it. Should he go? He hesitated. With a sigh, he called a taxi. Quickly he finished his breakfast and went outside.

The taxi dropped him outside the cemetery. He was late. Hesitantly he made his way between the gates. In the distance, across rows of gravestones, he saw a gathering and could make out a few people he recognised. They were all wearing dark suits and he jolted, looking down at his own attire. He wore jeans and a hoodie. His steps slowed. Looking up again, he saw Tanya. Small and hunched over, the enormity of her grief was evident even at that distance. He couldn't go any further. Dumbly he stood there.

Near him was a group of trees. He stepped behind them and watched from afar. There were flowers and speeches, but he couldn't hear over the distance. He stood alone, hidden behind the trees. The bitterness built up inside him as his friend's big black coffin was lowered into the earth and disappeared. His best mate was gone and there was nothing he could do to change it. His thoughts again turned to the driver of the S13 and his fists clenched. He had to get him. The next drift day was on Saturday. He had just five days. Andy fled the cemetery.

Arriving home, he went straight to the garage. Turning on the lights, he stood before his project, positioned squarely in the middle of the garage. Stock-standard and wearing an unappealing coat of faded grey, the Cefiro was tall on factory springs and wheels surrounded by chubby tyres. With four doors, a long bonnet and boot, she was nothing like the sleek, sporty 180SX. She was ugly. Who chose that colour? What were those Nissan designers thinking? She definitely needed some fresh paint. Andy caught himself. He was letting mere cosmetics intrude on his judgement. He knew the potential that was hidden beneath her drab appearance. In deep contemplation, he walked a full circle around her.

The bonnet was still up, where Andy had left it weeks before. The engine bay was filled with a sluggish, normally aspirated DOHC RB20. In Andy's opinion, anything without a big turbo was barely fit to run a lawn mower. The engine desperately needed to go. Along with a new one, he needed a manual gearbox to replace the current automatic transmission.

Andy stepped back from the bonnet and looked over the Cefiro critically again, sizing her up, calculating what had to be done and the parts that he needed. To do it properly, he also required a mechanical LSD, some adjustable suspension and a decent set of alloys, ideally 10-inches wide with low profile tyres. He would have to upgrade the brakes, install a straight-through exhaust, relocate the battery to the boot, get an intercooler and a short-shift kit, and replace both the steering wheel and driver's seat. It would take considerable work and money to turn this ugly duckling into a swan.

He had just five days, he reminded himself and looked at his Japanese cruiser again. Involuntarily, he shook his head, it wouldn't be enough time. There was too much to do, especially going at it alone. With Markus' help maybe... the thought was there before Andy could prevent it. He pushed it away and stared at the car stubbornly. Yes, there was a lot to be done, but he didn't have a job now and he had the whole of each day at his disposal. 'Where there's a will, there's a way.'

His main concern was tracking down the parts in time. Without the parts, there was little he could actually do. He had a number of sources that stole and dismantled cars to order and he knew that if he put the word out, he could have generic parts, like alloys, steering wheels, a race seat within a day, and at a good price. However, a decent engine and gearbox, as well as fitting adjustable suspension, could take longer. Andy pinched his lower lip thoughtfully. There was a lot to do.

He left the garage and went back into the house. Grabbing pen and paper, he jotted down a lengthy list of requirements. The next hour was spent on the phone, checking availability and pricings. First he called four potential suppliers. He knew that they were all extremely unreliable and notoriously bad at delivering on promises to provide items on time. As an incentive, he set them deadlines and offered a 10% cash bonus if his order was delivered as requested. All of them smelt money and were eager to please, but they sobered when they heard the shortness of his time limit and his request for an RB26Dett engine – the top dog of the Nissan food chain, as Markus had recommended. None of them expressed their usual confidence of being able to meet it but all promised to call him back soon and let him know the situation.

Having received no real assurance, Andy felt a growing sense of gloom. In his mind, he again heard the murderous thunder of that black S13 and saw its taunting red taillights. Without a serious engine his Cefiro project would never get off the ground. He *had* to have a '26.

Andy then tried several wreckers, but without luck. One of them referred him to a company that specialised in importing engines. He found new hope when he was told that they could indeed source the power plant, but he winced audibly when he heard the price. It was more than twice the amount he was willing to pay. However, it came with a guarantee and they would be able to deliver within three working days. Andy agreed to get back to them and hung up. They would be his last resort. Idly he wondered if the guarantee covered drift abuse – thrashing your motor constantly at the redline, under the fearsome burden of high boost? Probably not. That small joke cheered him slightly.

Next, He contacted the same small panel and paint shop where Markus had so recently taken the 180SX to be painted. The grizzled owner had done a flawless job, one that had easily met Andy's standard. He didn't need a high-level finish, just something that would cover the dull factory tones and give the Cefiro a lift.

"Stu," a deep voice finally answered after many rings.

"Hey, how much for a full re-spray on a Cefiro?"

"What colour?"

"Pearl-white," Andy replied promptly, although he hadn't actually thought about it. It would be a tribute to Markus and the 180SX.

"Panel work?"

"None, straight painting just the visible areas, nothing fancy," Andy answered him.

"It'll be sanded back and primed. We do it properly here," the voice stated gruffly.

"How much?" Andy insisted. After a moment's hesitation, the deep voice stated a figure in a take-it-or-leave-it manner.

"What's your turn around?" His offer was too good to refuse.

"What's your hurry?"

"I need her to be ready for the competition on Saturday."

There was a long pause. "We'll do it."

"Good," Andy was relieved.

He went back out to the garage and stepped into his dark green overalls. Once he had the stereo thumping, he peeled his sleeves back and moved to the tool rack. The big red metal cabinet and its quality contents had cost him dearly, but to him it was worth every cent. He withdrew the socket set and several spanners. Armed with his ratchet, he attacked the Cefiro. Starting with the engine bay, he began dismantling.

As he freed each piece, Andy quickly assessed its use. If it still had one, he set it carefully aside. If not, which included most items, he tossed it carelessly into a junk-designated corner of the garage. He cursed and grunted as he tore out the Cefiro's vitals with brute force. A rusty radiator hose refused to let go and he flung abuse at it, pulling it from side-to-side and up-and-down. Suddenly it gave and a fountain of fluorescent green coolant gushed out all over the concrete floor. Several drops sprayed up into his face. He blinked in surprise. He had forgotten to drain the radiator! Swearing, he wrestled the hose back on, stemming the tide of cold, slimy liquid. The escaped coolant ran out from beneath the car and formed a pool around his shoes. He had a bucket, but it was in the laundry. He scowled down at the puddle at his feet. Wiping his hands on the seat of his overalls, Andy went back to the house. He grabbed his bucket and was about to return to the garage when his phone rang.

"Yeah?"

"Andy, I can't suss no RB26. Not enough time. Got a '30 block though with a '26 head, work as good or better." It was Flynn, one of the suppliers.

"An RB30 with a RB26 head?" Andy's pulse quickened. He had heard of these bastardised hybrids, which combined the bigger three-litre bottom-end of the older SOHC six-cylinder RB30, with the newer, race-bred DOHC head of the RB26 engine. The final result was a creation of raw power that could output massive low-end torque – ideal for getting that initial loss of traction needed for drifting. Andy was very interested, but didn't show it. "That's only half an RB26," he pointed out.

"The better half," the supplier assured. "Say the word and ya got it at ya door tomorrow."

"Tomorrow?" Andy asked even more dubiously. Was this another one of those grossly exaggerated promises?

"Yup."

"What about the computer and loom?" Without those the engine itself wasn't even useful as a doorstop.

"All there," the supplier stated. "Got a Link ECU."

"That'd work. And a gearbox?" Andy required something strong, which could handle all the power from the RB30.

"Could do one from an R33 GTS-T."

"Synchros still all good?"

"Tight as."

"Alright, what's the damage?"

"We got heaps more, intercoolers, seats, wheels... Can cut ya a deal aye."

"All ears," Andy prompted curtly. All of the parts were hot, stolen from other, probably honest, motorists. Even so, Andy prepared himself to barter. With these people it was important to stand your ground and demand respect, but not to the level where it gave offence. Even for someone like Andy, who was known in these rough circles, it was not wise to get on their bad side.

He ended the call in good spirits. The final price they had settled on sat well in his favour and he had been promised an engine within less than 24 hours. He had to get the normally aspirated RB20 out of the engine bay ready for the new transplant. Bucket in-hand, Andy went back to the garage. While he waited for the remaining radiator coolant to drain, he mopped up the spill with a handful of crumpled newspaper. Once drained, he resumed his task of freeing the engine.

It was late afternoon before he was ready to extract the old block. He positioned his engine hoist securely, connected the lifting chains and worked the hoist until the chains were taught and rigid, supporting the engine's entire weight. Then he removed the last bolts from the engine mounts. The Cefiro shuddered lightly as the engine came free and he could almost hear her utter a sigh of relief. Andy applied himself to the hoist again and slowly, laboriously, he raised the engine. Finally it was high enough for him to swing it clear. With little regard, he dropped it well out of the way in the corner with the other junk items. Andy continued to work over the empty engine bay, picking it clean in preparation of the RB30 transplant. He found himself humming and whistling as he worked. The RB30 promise had done wonders for his mood.

The day turned to evening, but working under the lights in his garage, Andy was so absorbed that he didn't notice. When he was content that the engine bay was clean and ready to embrace its new donor engine, he turned his attention to the underside of the Cefiro and ran his trolley jack under her sills. It was the same jack that Markus had tripped over on one of their tyre stealing missions, causing the car's alarm to sound.

Andy pushed his thoughts aside and cranked the jack. The Cefiro's 14-inch rear wheel swiftly lost contact with the ground. He slipped an axle stand under her to take the weight and lowered the jack again. In quick succession, he repeated his steps on all four corners and soon the Cefiro stood a good half-metre above the floor of the garage, giving him plenty of space in which to work. Andy equipped himself with a series of different-sized sockets and, lying on his back beneath the car, he removed the entire exhaust piping. He would replace it with a 3-inch straight-through mandrel bent unit that allowed easy breathing for the voracious RB30.

When Andy finally emerged from the garage, he was surprised to find it pitch-black outside. Where had all the time gone? Mentally he ticked off his achievements and nodded. He was well on the way. He walked slowly back to the house, tired and aching from the long hours working in cramped and uncomfortable positions. In the kitchen he popped a frozen pizza in the oven, before heading to the shower. When he returned to the kitchen, the pizza was ready. He had forgotten how good hot food was and he ate hungrily, for once having a proper appetite.

Early the next morning, Andy was awoken by sharp knocking on his back door. Swiftly he slipped out of bed and pulled on a pair of jeans and a hoodie. All the while the knocking continued. Hastily he unlocked the back door and pulled it open. Three tough looking characters, wearing black leather boots, dark clothing and black beanies pulled low on their foreheads, were lurking outside in the dark pre-dawn chill. Between them stood a small mound, its contents shrouded by a dirty sheet, while off to one side stood a stack of wheels, in a chest-high tower.

"Got ya stuff," the dark figure in front greeted him gruffly. In the gloom, Andy could see that thick stubble was covering his face. It was Flynn.

"Is it all there?" Andy lit a cigarette, partly because he was still half-asleep and partly to overcome his discomfort at the intimidating company.

"All there," Flynn agreed brusquely. "Where's the bling?"

"Show me," Andy invited, he wasn't about to hand over any money until he knew what he was getting. One of the wheels was lifted from the tower and displayed to him for approval. Andy recognised it at once, a lightweight drift rim, 10-inches wide and already surrounded by fresh rubber. It was exactly what he was after.

"There's spares too." The sheet was pulled from the mound with a flourish, revealing two race seats, an intercooler and steering wheel, as well as several performance items, among them an electronic boost controller and blow-off valve.

"Looks good," Andy commended impatiently, after checking them quickly. "Where's the motor?" At this, one of Flynn's ruffians stepped back and, for the first time, Andy noticed another pile behind them. It was also covered by a grease-smeared sheet, but this time supported by a big wooden pallet. As the sheet was removed from the pallet, Andy flinched. "What the..?"

"The RB you was after," the thug picked a metallic, cup-shaped object from the mound and passed it to Andy. It was a piston ring.

"You didn't say you'd wheelbarrow it here in bits." To Andy's horror the engine was in pieces. Sticking partly out at the bottom of the pyramid, he could make out the six-cylinder engine block itself.

"You didn't ask."

"I don't know about you, but when I order a Big Mac, I don't expect to get it in pieces," Andy was appalled.

"We ain't from Maccas," Flynn growled. "You saying you not paying?" Andy sensed an immediate change in mood. They were more than happy for a fight. He could see it by the gleam in their eyes. He was standing alone at his back door step. They wouldn't hesitate if he gave them any excuse. Staunchly he stood his ground.

"Give us a look," Andy stepped forward and began sorting through the items on the pallet. Aided by the strengthening light from the dawn, he carefully laid the parts out on the concrete slab at his back door. "Bit a space aye," he grated at one of the guys who was in his way. Andy took his time, grouping the parts that he knew must go together. He had helped Markus strip the SR20Det engine of the 180SX several months earlier, so he knew roughly what was what, although not nearly as well as Markus.

"Nearly done?" the men around him were getting restless.

"Nearly," Andy answered distantly, puffing on his smoke. He was crouched down beside the pallet, his fingers grimy and oil smeared.

"Engine ain't hot man," Flynn explained. "Was a mates project, but he's in the can so don't need it now." Andy didn't reply as he continued to assess the items with a serious expression. Fidgeting again, Flynn glanced broodingly at the lighting sky. "Quit messin around."

"Shut up." Andy compared the parts to what he knew made up an engine. It appeared as though the main things were there. Of course, he wouldn't know for sure until he began actually putting it together again. Even if only one piece of the complicated puzzle was missing, the whole lot would be useless to him, as he didn't have time to track down replacements. He grimaced at the thought. If it was true that it really wasn't stolen, it was more likely to be intact. But, either way, he didn't have much choice. If he didn't take it, they would make mincemeat of him.

"Alright," he answered calmly and he saw them relax. "But I sure ain't paying the whole amount."

"Say what?"

"It's gonna take me a day at least to put this back together, if nothing's missing that is," Andy pointed out. "I'll pay normal for the rest, but only three-quarters of what we said for the engine – no more," he said with finality. Flynn looked as though he would argue, but then he glanced at the sky again.

"Make it quick then," he ordered thickly.

"Wait here," Andy went back inside and locked the door. Quickly he wiped his hands clean on his jeans and returned to his bedroom. He withdrew the wad of money from its hiding place and took what he needed, then replaced the rest and returned to the back door.

"Here," Andy handed the cash to Flynn who counted it shrewdly. "If there's anything missing, I'll find you," he said quietly and Flynn looked up. Andy met his gaze and it was Flynn who turned away. The three disappeared around the side of the house. Not long afterwards, Andy heard the unmistakable rumble of a V8 engine start and pull away. He took a moment to appraise his newly acquired purchases before he followed Flynn's example and looked up at the morning sky. Pale blue shot through with orange, but several grey patches were suggesting rain. He needed to get these items under cover.

Over the next two days, Andy worked like a machine. From dawn to dusk, he laboured in his garage with a single-minded obsession, only breaking and returning to the house to quickly force down some food when the hunger became too much. Late each night, he would drag himself back to the house, have a shower and eat a quick meal, before falling into bed.

Initially he had focused on the RB30, reassembling it piece by piece and cleaning any reusable original parts or changing them for the stronger performance replacements provided by Flynn. It was slow going and Andy wished Markus had been there to help him. With his knowledge it would have been straightforward. It wasn't long before Andy hit a snag and was uncertain of how to proceed. He was positive that a part was missing. Angrily he went back to the house to call Flynn. Once in the house, it occurred to him to have a look online, in case anyone had done a write-up on an RB30. Deciding it was worth a try, he switched on his laptop.

Sure enough he found a website specifically dedicated to RB30 tuning. It had many recommendations accompanied by photos and step-by-step explanations. To Andy this was invaluable. Quickly he printed off the applicable pages and made his way back to the garage. With the help of the internet guide, Andy established that he wasn't missing a part after all, but had simply overlooked the obvious. Working more confidently, he patiently coaxed life back into the engine. Once he had put the last bolt in the RB26 head, he stood back to admire his mighty power plant. He had got it together. But would it start?

It was already well past noon, but he was so eager to get his engine in and running that he ignored his growling stomach and slaved on. He spent another 30 minutes bolting in the front-mount intercooler before he turned back to the engine stand. With the help of his hoist, he raised the RB from its stand and swung it over the front of the Cefiro. After aligning it carefully with the engine mounts, he lowered it in. It didn't take long and the RB was bolted in tightly. Now he had to connect everything back up in reverse.

Andy worked fervently. His hands were shaking with excitement as he replaced the radiator plumbing and hooked up the intercooler, while the same question kept nagging at him: would she actually run? It seemed to take ages, but finally Andy connected the last of the sensors and, after patiently replacing the oil and coolant, he straightened up. With a groan he stretched his aching back and gazed down at the freshly packed engine bay. The prodigious hybrid engine had a powerful presence and new excitement ran through him. It was all in place. The moment had arrived.

Buzzing, Andy slipped into the driver's seat and fed the key into the ignition. He went to turn it, but hesitated. There were butterflies in his stomach and the whole garage seemed to tingle with anticipation. "Moment of truth." He turned the key to a hollow click. Nothing happened. "What the..?" For a moment Andy stared at the dead dashboard in dismay. Then it dawned on him and he laughed out loud at his stupidity. He had forgotten to connect the battery. He went to where he had relocated it to the boot and put the connecters back over the terminals. "Take two," Andy grimaced and went back to the driver's door.

This time he didn't hop in, but simply put his hand on the key through the open window. Power was there and the check-lights on his dash flared as he turned the key to ON. "Come on." With a keen whir the starter motor kicked in, trying to spark the engine. Over and over the engine turned but to no avail. The RB showed no sign of life, it didn't catch. Relentlessly Andy kept her cranking over, hoping, wanting her to start. At last the starter motor began to lapse as the battery weakened. Andy surrendered and turned the key off.

For a moment he stood completely still, in total silence, the disappointment tasting like bile in the back of his throat. If he couldn't get it going after all that effort then... A loud curse escaped his lips and his temper flared. In a rush it consumed him, stripping him of self-control. In a blind rage, he punched the side of the driver's door, then, before he could stop himself, he had scooped up a handful of spanners from the floor and hurled them at the garage wall. They clanged loudly against corrugated iron but then rattled harmlessly back to the floor. The lack of damage infuriated him further and, screaming abuse, he lunged at the junk pile, kicking and spraying items in all directions.

Andy raged and cursed until his right foot caught the old RB20 block. Pain blazed up his leg and brought him back to his senses. With an effort he opened his clenched fists and took a deep breath. It calmed him. Ignoring the junk strewn across the garage floor, he limped back to the engine bay and stared at it darkly. "What the hell's your problem?" The answer came back to him immediately and he couldn't believe it. What was wrong with him? He hadn't even screwed in the spark plugs and connected them. For once Andy was glad that Markus wasn't around, he knew he deserved a serious mocking.

"Alright, last try," Andy growled after he had installed the plugs. He put his hand on the key. "If this doesn't work…" his threat was lost as the starter motor turned, pushed by the last reserves of the battery and the RB30 thudded alive. It ran roughly, but the raw, grunty sound pulsed around the garage. The sound charged him with energy. Grinning from ear-to-ear, Andy let out a triumphant whoop.

He stuck his head under the bonnet and when he worked the throttle, the engine spun up to a bellow. Without an exhaust system the din was appalling, but despite it, Andy could hear the turbo spool with a whine. He closed the throttle again and the blow-off valve snickered throatily. Still grinning, he let the RB spin down and pulled his head out from under the bonnet. She needed a proper tune, but she ran! With great reluctance, he switched the engine off again.

His stomach growled loudly, and for the first time that day his thoughts turned to food as he realised how hungry he was. He hadn't eaten anything all day and now it was nearly 5pm. Leaving the garage cluttered with strewn car parts, Andy locked it and made his way back to the house. Searching his cupboards, he realised he had no food and would need to visit the corner store again. He couldn't be bothered so he ordered a pizza and jumped in the shower.

By the time he had dried himself and dressed in clean clothes, he received a knock on his front door. Warned by the tantalizing smell, Andy knew that it was the pizza delivery. He was barely able to contain himself until he had paid and slammed the door behind him, before he tore open the box and fell ravenously upon the pizza. While he ate, he again reflected on his progress. It had been another big day. But there was still a lot to do and now it was just three days until the competition. It suddenly occurred to him that he hadn't even signed up yet. Entries had probably even closed by now. Andy stopped chewing and dropped his piece of pizza back in the box. He ran to the phone.

"Hello?"

"I'm ringing to sign up for the competition on Saturday."

"You're too late, entries closed three days ago." The reply came stiffly.

"Three days ago? You're saying I can't compete anymore?"

"Afraid not," the voice had no sympathy. "Rules are rules."

Andy felt a cold hand squeeze his chest. It couldn't be. All that effort and now he couldn't make good on his promise. His initial dismay was replaced by anger. "Bend them."

"What?"

"Bend the rules," he instructed. "I competed in the last one. I want to compete again now." He kept his voice calm.

"What's your name?" the voice asked dubiously and Andy gave it to him. "Andrew Reed," the organiser reiterated distantly and paused. "You competed in a white 180SX?"

"Yes," Andy confirmed, "But I'm driving a Cefiro now."

"I remember you – you did that reverse entry and then went on to pull that crazy stunt..." the voice mused. Andy didn't answer. "Normally I'd have to say no. But drivers like you keep the crowd entertained. So, okay, I'll make an exception this once."

"Good." Andy provided the answers that the organiser needed to enlist him.

"You've read the new rules, of course?"

"Yep," Andy replied noncommittally.

"So you know you need a fire extinguisher, overalls and a homologated roll cage."

"A homo-what roll cage?"

"A certified roll cage – you can't race without one."

"Why?" Andy exclaimed, "They didn't need them for the last one."

"Well, they're regulation now and that's not something I can bend the rules on," the organiser said flatly. "If you're stuck, you could try…" he gave a recommendation. "They do a good job."

"How long does it take to install?" Andy hesitated.

"Dunno, you have to fill out the paperwork and get it inspected. Could take a few days."

"Man, I don't have that much time."

"Hey don't blame me… look I'll sign you up for now. Give us a call if you need to pull out though."

"Yeah, okay," Andy muttered. Time was running out fast. He had just three days in which to get it all together. He felt like one of the teams from Monster Garage, where he had to meet a strict deadline. Only, he was doing it all alone and his requirements kept changing. He dialled the number he had been given, but this time he was not so fortunate. The company had too much work. A number of other drifters had been caught out by the new regulations and needed roll cages installed before the event. Although he tried, there was no reasoning with the technician. He wouldn't budge.

"Earliest we can do is next week," he offered.

"That's too late," Andy replied. "Is there anybody else you know who might be able to do it?" Andy rang around several other places, but everybody came back with the same answer, until he tried one final number.

"Yeah, we could do one by Saturday."

"How much is it?" he asked, and couldn't believe his ears when he heard the price. "What? That's like more than twice what the other places are asking."

"It's all chromoly and professionally done," the voice responded stiffly.

"I'd want it to be made of titanium at that price," Andy retorted and hung up, scowling. There was no way he was going to let himself get ripped off. But how was he going to sort out a roll cage and get it all certified in the little time he had? He also still needed to get the engine professionally tuned, but it was already 5.30pm. Perhaps somebody was working late and he could still book a time. Reaching for the phonebook, Andy tried a number. It rang and rang, and he was just about to give up when his call was finally answered by an annoyed male voice.

"What?"

"I'm after an engine tune, tomorrow ideally," Andy didn't beat around.

"Fat chance."

"It's important – I need it for the drift comp this weekend."

"Hmmm..." Andy detected a change in the voice. "We could probably squeeze you in tomorrow afternoon, 3pm. Other than that, not till next week."

"I'll take it," Andy agreed. It gave him the morning to get more done.

"Good. What are we tuning?"

"A Nissan Cefiro, with a turboed RB30 hybrid," Andy replied and received a suitably impressed whistle from the other end of the line.

After finishing his phone call, Andy ate the remains of his cooling pizza and decided to slog out another couple of hours in the garage before sleep. During this time he managed to replace all four brake systems with larger vented disks, callipers and new pads. Much later, he returned to the house, washed quickly and crawled into bed. He was already half asleep when it occurred to him that he might be able to buy a roll cage in an online auction. Getting it certified would be the only problem. Tapping into the last of his reserves, Andy climbed out of bed again and booted up his computer.

Browsing through the auctions, he soon found one that sounded promising. Somebody had crashed a Cefiro, the same model as his, and was dismantling it and selling the parts. Among the items listed was a chromoly roll cage. However, the seller was located in a small town, some 230km away.

Couriering something as large as a roll cage, even over such a short distance, would not be cheap. Nonetheless, Andy informed the seller that he was interested and left his contact number, requesting he get in touch as soon as possible. Unable to do much more, he went back to bed and fell asleep almost immediately.

On Wednesday morning, more parts arrived from his various sources. One of these deliveries was of the fibreglass body kit and the precious adjustable suspension. For Andy it marked a milestone. The expensive Cusco shocks were one of the final items necessary to turn the Cefiro into a top drift competitor. With it he could customise her stance and handling with exact precision.

Skipping breakfast, Andy first called the painter and confirmed that the body kit was now ready for pickup. Then he went directly out to the garage and began to install the suspension. It didn't take long. When he was done, he couldn't resist taking it a step further, he wanted to see her on her new rims. With pit crew speed, he bolted the wheels on in quick succession and lowered her down. Once the Nissan was standing on her own four feet, her whole mood changed. She stood lower, stiffer and more surely. Walking several circles around his car, he couldn't stop smiling.

Even without her body kit, she was looking so wicked that Andy felt the adrenaline building up inside of him. He couldn't wait to unleash his new girl on the track. Her power potential far out-did the 180SX, and with her long wheelbase keeping at angle through the drifts would be easier. Yes, Andy thought grimly to himself, with this machine he would take the S13 down... But for now he had to make do with driving to the workshop to get her wheels aligned and her custom exhaust system fitted.

Andy hopped into the driver's seat and turned the ignition. The engine cranked over and settled reluctantly into an unsteady rumble. He let her warm up with the tacho needle yo-yoing like a marionette on steroids, until the temperature gauge pointed mid-way, before reversing the Cefiro out of the cool garage into the warm day. The sun was shining brightly, with only a few white clouds in the blue pre-noon sky, but Andy had eyes for his car alone. He lowered the garage door again with his remote and backed down the drive onto the street. Then, with a casual flick of the hand, he notched the gearshift into first, slipped the clutch and planted his foot.

A tidal wave of noise spewed from the RB30's open downpipe and exploded around the neighbourhood. It was so loud that Andy winced and the Cefiro flew completely off the handle. With a bellow she clawed her rubber into the gritty road surface and raged forwards. Un-tuned and rough as she was, the power from the RB30 was insane. It hit him like a kick to the stomach and he was crushed back into his seat. The street dissolved in front of him and before he knew it, he had to brake to rein her in for the stop sign at the end. Grinning and shaking his head in disbelief, Andy waited for a gap in the traffic, before pulling out.

On her ultra low suspension and wide, sticky tyres, the Nissan sat rock solid on the road and, as he drove, Andy pushed her over the speed limit. He revelled in the incredible rush of seemingly unlimited power. His car was fast and, Andy reflected, completely illegal. She had no Warrant of Fitness or registration. Neither did she have any certification for her recent upgrades, the RB30 and the adjustable suspension. To top it off, the complete lack of an exhaust system meant he well exceeded any noise limit. If the police caught him, they would impound the car without question and send him walking home with a hefty fine. The knowledge of this danger spiced his enjoyment and grinning ironically, he planted his foot further, until the surrounding pedestrians and motorists stared at him in shock.

Much too soon he reached the exhaust shop and reluctantly eased his car off the road and into the small yard. He was greeted by an animated young employee in dirty blue overalls. Leaving the Cefiro in his reverent hands, Andy made his way to the waiting room. Rifling through an unexciting magazine, he looked up through the window as the assistant rumbled the Cefiro onto the large car hoist. It would take at least two hours to get the wheels aligned and the new exhaust system fitted.

He realised that for the first time in many days he had nothing to do. It felt strange. He put the magazine back on the shelf and walked out onto the street. Looking up and down for something interesting, he saw a Burger King sign some distance away. He hadn't had any breakfast so he walked towards it. Taking his time to eat, he returned to find that the Cefiro was still raised high on the hoist, but the assistant was just finishing up. Taking the opportunity, Andy joined him in the workshop and inspected the workmanship himself.

He wanted to be absolutely certain that the job was done properly. He couldn't afford any wasted time. With a trained eye he followed the roomy stainless steel exhaust piping, all the way from the extractors to the muffler. He could see straight away that the job had been done professionally. The weld-beads were neat and tidy, joining the piping cleanly. This was confirmed when the Cefiro was on the ground again. In comparison to her previous engine racket, she was now breathing low and even. Satisfied, Andy paid and rolled the Cefiro out of the yard, in the direction of the tuning shop.

Once there, he stood by quietly, watching the proceedings of the two middle-aged tuners. They set the Cefiro up with her driving rear rims running comfortably on the dyno rollers, before they wheeled out an industrial-sized fan and positioned it to aerate her radiator and intercooler. Their enthusiasm was unfeigned as they raised the bonnet and their eyes fell upon the rare and powerful custom-built engine. With Andy looking on, they fussed over their expensive equipment like wizards and worked their magic, tweaking air-fuel ratios and timing, and correcting the adjustable cam-wheels.

After each adjustment, the RB30 was let scream and the computer plotted a pretty torque and power graph that gave visual evidence of her performance. Guided in this way, they coaxed the very best out of her until the engine no longer bawled its authority, but rather howled it with harmonic perfection. Two hours of concentrated fiddling had flown by, when the two reluctantly admitted that the RB30 was running so good that it was unlikely they could squeeze much more out of her. Andy agreed. As far as he could tell, they had completely ironed out her attitude and he could hardly wait to pay. He wanted to test her on the road.

Before they would let him go, however, they wanted to see how much power she could really concoct. Up until now they had been running her on a conservative boost setting, restricting the pressure from the HKS turbo to 16psi, but to get the final reading they raised it to 22psi using the in-cabin electronic boost controller. They let her fly and the engine spun up in a thunderous crescendo. Andy stared at the performance reading beneath the graph on the monitor. She was pumping out 450-kilowatts at the rear wheels.

When he arrived home, he immediately started his laptop and checked the online auction for a response from the seller of the roll cage. There was none and Andy growled in frustration. His good mood sobered as he realised just how much he still had to do on the Cefiro to get her race-ready and how quickly time was running out. He knew he couldn't depend on winning the roll cage in the auction and without one they wouldn't let him compete. He had no choice, and though he loathed the unfair price, he got on the phone again and made an appointment to get the roll cage installed the following day.

Andy spent the remainder of that evening preparing the Cefiro for the roll cage installation. He removed the front and back seats and pulled up the carpet, then bolted in just the Sparco driver's seat. He fitted the Momo steering wheel and afterwards replaced the standard locking knob in the handbrake with a spin-turn knob, which allowed him to perform handbrake-drift manoeuvres without having to hold the knob down. Again it was dark when he emerged from the garage. Back in the house, he checked the roll cage auction site once more, with little hope. The seller had finally replied, but rather than calling Andy back, he had left his own number for Andy to get in touch with him.

Andy checked the time, it was past 10pm. Stuff it, he thought and dialled the number. It was soon answered and Andy inquired about the roll cage. "Is it homologated?"

"Yeah, it's all certified for the car. I got the log books and everything, but it won't help much. I smashed her up bad. The body's all bent. It's not worth fixing."

"That doesn't matter. See I was thinking of taking your licence plates, the tags and log book as well and swapping them over to my Cefiro. Or have you written her off already?" Andy held his breath and braced himself for the reply, realising what he was proposing was very much illegal.

"I've still got the plates. They're even still rego'd, so yeah, if you want... We'd have to cut the roll cage out though then re-weld it back into your car. You any good at welding?"

"Yeah, I've done a bit."

"Okay, I'll give ya a hand of course."

"That'd be cool." They haggled over the price and soon came to an agreement. It would cost him less than half the price of a new custom one and Andy would get the log book and certification all included. He would drive out to the coast the next morning to meet the seller, who was happy to help and had even offered to rent a TIG welder and organise suitable welding rods and other tools. Andy could hardly believe it and, although he was extremely tired, he couldn't get to sleep. He wanted it to be morning already so that he could get the roll cage. He was also looking forward to testing the Cefiro beyond the borders of the city. Finally his thoughts began to blur and he slept.

It was Leon's third day at his new job and he was swiftly getting the hang of it. He could quote whole lists of suppliers and parts and knew their benefits and shortcomings. The new job and its challenges had also helped take his mind off the fateful events of the weekend, but as he reordered the storage shelves in the back room, his eyes fell on a selection of fire extinguishers and instantly the horrors came rushing back. He forced himself to think of something else, and naturally his mind turned to Lorna.

He had spent Monday evening with her as they had planned and they had enjoyed a fantastic meal at an Italian restaurant. The mood had been good between them. They had joked and laughed. It had been fun. Afterwards they had gone to see a movie. They had made more plans for Tuesday, but Lorna had cancelled at the last minute due to an unfinished assignment and Leon had gone to the gym instead. He had decided to focus on his personal fitness to prepare himself for the upcoming drift day, since his Silvia was out of commission and he couldn't practice his driving. As he hadn't been to the gym in a long time, he took it easy, starting out on the rowing machine, before moving on to weights. Finally, he exerted himself fully on the treadmill until late into the evening. That night he slept solidly.

Lost in thought, Leon finished tidying the shelf and checked the time. Karl, his co-worker, had left him alone in the shop, whilst going out to run an errand. However, it was nearly 5pm and he should be back soon to close up. Leon intended to go to the gym again on his way home to continue his workout, but wasn't much looking forward to it. His body was still aching from the night before. Later Byron would pick him up. Somehow he had managed to convince Leon to come over and play a round of racing on his Playstation.

"Come on, it'll be good practice for ya."

"I'm sure it will," Leon had been dubious.

"'Course– haven't you heard of *hand-eye* coordination? It's like the most important thing in racing."

"No doubt... I guess it might help take my mind off things," Leon had caved.

His daydreams were interrupted by a ding from the bell at the service counter. It made him jump. He hadn't heard anybody come in. Making his way to the counter, he found someone waiting.

"Hi," Leon greeted him in his salesman voice. "Sorry about the wait."

"Oh hey, I didn't know you worked here. Leon, right?"

Leon was surprised when he recognised him. It was Cam. "Yeah, I've only been here since Monday."

"Oh, so you replaced Jason?"

"That's right."

"Good one. Don't mind it?"

"Beats my old job,"

"Cool, hey do you know how much these are?" Cam handed Leon a pack of brake pads. Leon turned to the computer, scanned the barcode and named the price.

"But for you I can do the good-guy discount..."

"Yeah? How good is that?" Cam asked with a faintly sceptical smile.

"Um," Leon tapped several keys and gave the new price.

"That's less than half," Cam blinked.

"Cost price," Leon nodded. "Don't tell anyone."

"Even Jase never gave me a discount like that," Cam handed him the money. Leon took it and worked the till.

"You need a bag?"

"Nah, may as well try something to help the environment," Cam smiled ruefully. "Everything else I do seems to wreck it."

"I know that feeling, but every bit helps," Leon agreed. "Hope the pads go alright."

"Yeah, should do. Hey, by the way, we're having a barbeque tomorrow," Cam corrected himself. "Taz is having it actually, but you should come along, if you're not working."

"Maybe..." Leon nodded dubiously.

"It'll be mint. Taz always goes all out with food and beer."

"I'll see," Leon wasn't convinced.

"Lorna will be there," Cam pointed out.

"Really?" Leon's brow furrowed.

"I called her yesterday..." Cam nodded and paused, but then continued. "She told me about you, and how you've been hanging out." Leon remained silent. "She really likes you."

"You think?"

"Yep," Cam replied with simple certainty.

"Can Byron come?" Leon asked at last.

"The more the merrier," Cam replied with a smile. "No need to bring anything, except maybe some drinks if you don't want to drink beer."

"You sure? He's got a mean eating habit."

"We'll need him then."

"Cool, where is it?" Cam told him.

"I'll see you there," Cam was about to turn away but hesitated. "When I spoke to Lorna she also told me about Friday night... and the crash..." Leon looked down at the counter. "That must have been..." Cam was seeking the right words. "Well... it must've been really bad." He spoke quietly. "I realise we don't really know each other, but if you ever want to talk about it..." Leon looked back up at him and saw that he was sincere.

"Thanks," Leon nodded and Cam was about to turn away again when Leon stopped him. "Lorna also told me about your crash, and... I'm really sorry." A shadow passed across

Cam's eyes. He nodded his thanks and looked away, before he turned and left the shop. Leon watched him go.

Lounging comfortably in his favourite armchair, Byron deftly used the Playstation controller with one hand while he reached for his glass of Coke with the other. Beside him, Leon's attention was complete and he sat on the edge of his seat with his eyes glued to the large flat panel TV in front of him. Both his hands were on the controller, as he tried to guide his race car along the curves of the digitally reconstructed race track, in hot pursuit of Byron. But even when he mustered all his effort, Byron's superior skill still showed and Leon got left in his dust. He tried to make up lost ground by flooring it on a straight, but then a corner suddenly appeared on the display and he couldn't slow in time. He flew off the road and the force-feedback controller leapt violently in his hands.

"Dude what're you doing?" Byron set the glass back down and laughed as he saw Leon floundering in the ditch far behind him. "It works better if you stay on the road," Byron laughed again as he crossed the finish line a moment later. He set his controller aside and got up. "Must be about snack time," he swaggered through to the kitchen and returned with a packet of chips. "Keen?"

"Nah," Leon shook his head.

"Sweet," Byron shrugged, opened the packet and placed it within easy reach.

Byron played the next game entirely one-handed, using the other to stuff potato chips into his mouth. "Dude, the track is that way!" He won again, enjoying the hilarity of Leon's uncoordinated attempts to keep up. But Leon was beginning to get the hang of it, and when they started over he stayed close on Byron's tail, resisting his efforts to shake him. He saw his opportunity and made a lunge, and suddenly he was past him and in front. Byron's jokes turned to curses. He promptly forgot about the chips and took control with both hands again. As they hurtled up to the final bend and closed in on the finish line, locked in intense battle, Byron flicked his tail out in a well-practiced manoeuvre. It gave just a little edge and he came out of the bend beside Leon. Nosing up past him at full-throttle, he flashed across the line a breath in front of him.

"Oh yeah," Leon laughed. "So very almost had ya."

"Dude…" Byron shook his head. "You almost had nothing." Abruptly, he turned and withdrew another game from a waist-high tower rack. "But since you think you're so good, let's give this a whirl." He held it up for Leon's benefit. It was an arena fighting game.

"If you must," Leon rolled his eyes.

They each chose their players from a list of muscle-bound combatants and, when the bell chimed, Byron's brute went berserk and laid into Leon's clumsy meathead with such a murderous combination of kicks and punches that Leon's controller began to shudder in earnest. Although Leon mashed every button and tried various combinations, his player made only the most pitiful effort to defend himself. He took a severe hiding and got completely destroyed in seconds.

"I take you apart," Byron's laughter was back as Leon's player fell over in a heap. "Let's check out the instant replay on that." Leon had to smile as well, when Byron replayed the sequence of his player's demise and they watched him get pummelled once more in slow-motion with computer-generated facial expressions and all.

Each time they played, Leon tried mashing different buttons, but always got hacked to mincemeat – until suddenly he had it. By chance he hit the correct button combination and his timing was spot on. Just when Byron was about to launch into the attack, rendering him open, Leon's player unleashed with a vengeance accumulated over numerous games of ridicule. He didn't hold back. Five astounding seconds of unsuppressed onslaught and Byron's player lay in a puddle of blood. Byron had gone completely quiet. He stared at the TV screen aghast.

"Replay!" Leon pressed the button before Byron could move and he was forced to re-witness his own humiliation.

"Play again?" Leon asked into the long silence.

"Nah," Byron set the controller aside in a subdued manner. "It's getting late…"

"It is," Leon hid his smile. "I get the Silvia back tomorrow. We should take it for a spin and get some real practice."

"Okay, sure. What time?"

"After work I guess… Oh wait," Leon remembered his meeting with Cam. "We're actually invited to a barbeque – but it starts at 2pm."

"I'm only working till noon," Byron's ears pricked up at the sound of food. "Where's it at?"

"Taz is putting it on. Cam invited us."

Byron's expression changed. "And you're going?"

"Yeah, I already checked with my boss. I felt a bit rude asking him for time off so soon, but he was fine with it."

"That's good of him," Byron acknowledged.

"Lorna will be there too."

"Yay for me," Byron was still sceptical.

"Apparently there'll be a lot of food. Cam said you have to come and help eat it."

"He said that?"

"Yup."

"Yeah right."

"Straight up," Leon denied. "Even said he wanted you to meet his sister – apparently she's single and real hot."

"You are such a liar," Byron threw a cushion at him.

"Yeah alright, now I'm kidding," Leon laughed as he caught it. "But I'd bet my Silvia there'll be some girls there."

"Alright then," Byron wavered. "I'll come."

Andy woke early, feeling refreshed and alert. It was time to get his roll cage. He got out of bed and pulled on his jeans and hoodie. In the kitchen he scoffed some toast, washed it down with a cup of coffee and went out to the garage. The Cefiro was waiting for him. Her keen expectancy matched his and eagerly he climbed into the driver's seat. She started on the first attempt and the RB30's six cylinders pulsed forebodingly. Andy took a moment to appreciate the awesome sound and let her warm up, before he eased her out of the garage.

Andy's mood mellowed as he drove. He enjoyed the sense of freedom that went with it. Having largely been stuck inside for the past week, he felt his tension easing and turn to a sense of elation. It seemed to him that there was no stress out here in the open countryside and the tarseal stretched far ahead.

An hour later, as he hurtled up a gentle slope and reached the summit, a spectacular vista opened before him. The road dropped down nearly dead straight to the valley floor, where it panned out and then rose again to curve up gently on the other side, some 4-5km in the distance. With the sun beaming down, and the far side of the valley standing against a stunning backdrop of blue sky, the road sparkled, summoning him. He let her go.

Roaring loudly, the Cefiro threw herself down the hill. She hugged the smooth seal on her low adjustable suspension and wide rims. Andy urged her on with his right foot pressed to the floor. Already at high revs, the mammoth HKS turbo spooled quickly and came on almost instantly, thrusting a gale force wind through the intercooler and into the engine. The Nissan boosted viciously and Andy heard himself laugh. It was such a rush. The pull from the high-torque RB30 bottom-end and RB26 head combination engine was staggering. It had him shoved back in his seat.

The revs ripped up past 7000rpm with the RB crackling hoarsely, before Andy shifted into fourth gear and was thrown back again as the Cefiro kicked out, propelling them on. Their speed surged beyond 170km/h and the fence posts on either side blurred together in a solid stream. The valley floor loomed in his vision and, with a sudden, gut-swooping sensation, the Cefiro screamed out onto flat, level road. Andy hit fifth gear, and egged her on further with both hands on the steering wheel.

Time itself seemed to slow down, as the world hurtled past outside his window, and Andy rode on the waves of his adrenaline. All the despair that he had accumulated over the past weeks, starting with his spinning out at the drift meet, when getting a good placing was so close within his grasp, to him losing the downhill race against the S13 and smashing up the 180SX and of course Markus... all of it seemed to fall away as the needle on the speedometer dropped off the clock, turning well past 180km/h. Andy laughed again, but his laugh cut off as the radar detector on his windscreen shrilled. He flinched and touched the brakes. Involuntarily, his eyes flicked to the speedometer. The needle pointed vertical. He was so, so busted.

Officer Hart sat stiffly in the driver's seat. It had been a quiet morning. Every vehicle that had come past so far had met the speed limit, within the margin of error allowed by his radar. Despite starting very early, so far he had not handed out a single ticket. He had his quota to meet and he was still ten tickets short with the end of the month looming. Just two days to make it up, otherwise there would be no bonus. Hart wanted that bonus. It represented a sizeable addition to his monthly pay. That was why he had come all the way out here. The long, straight road from the top of the valley to the other side was irresistible even to *Sunday* drivers. Normally it was easy pickings. It was still just too early.

A car appeared at the top of the rise in the distance, a splodge of green. It came down the slope, approaching quickly. Hart leant forward in his seat expectantly, but frowned at the digital display of his radar equipment and grunted. "Come on, you can do better than that." The green Subaru neared and the radar display showed its speed dip suddenly. The driver had seen the patrol car and instinctively reduced speed, despite being within the 100km/h limit anyway. The Subaru flashed by and Hart smirked with satisfaction. He enjoyed the respect that his police car commanded. Then he scowled. But why was everybody sticking to the limit? Didn't they want to arrive at their destination quicker? Or maybe they could see him after all?

He turned to look around him. His patrol car was parked four metres off the roadside, under a low, overhanging tree. When he had parked that morning, he had climbed out and scrutinised his lair. He was certain that over the great distance his patrol car couldn't be easily seen through the bushy foliage from either end of the valley. But he, on the other hand, was able to see any traffic from far off. No, it was the perfect spot.

Hart turned back to look out of his windscreen. He knew that a lot of people used radar detectors. He didn't mind, in fact he enjoyed the extra challenge that they presented. He was the hunter. It was up to him to be smart and stealthy to snare his prey without detection. He smiled at the thought. There was nothing more satisfying than writing out a whopping big traffic fine, especially to an obnoxious racer or a pompous SUV driver. The more they tried to reason, the better it felt.

Reaching forward, Hart turned his radar equipment off and settled back again. He had chosen the time and place, now he just needed to wait. He scowled again, he had never been good at waiting. For him it was the worst part. That's why he had joined the police in the first place, in search of excitement and distinction. Little did he know it could be this wearisome. Reclining his seat, he eased back, keeping his eyes on the distant rise. They will come, he told himself. Seven and he would call it a day. That would leave just three for tomorrow. After a moment, he moved again, fidgeting, trying to find a more comfortable position. He folded his arms up behind his head. It felt no better and he adjusted his seat back to being more upright again. Six, he would be happy with six.

A white smear materialised on the rise and wavered there for a second, almost as though it was gathering itself. It glittered as it caught the sun's rays and deflected them to Hart. Then, like a missile, the car dropped, angling in for the valley floor. With incredible swiftness it descended the slope, hurtling in like a javelin. It grew so rapidly in size that Hart was jerked from his thoughts. "Holy smoke!"

For a moment he was slow to react, but then he shook himself out of his trance and lunged for the radar *ON* switch. His equipment came alive. Hart couldn't tear his eyes from the white car. It was on the flat now and smoke suddenly fanned out behind it as it fought to slow. The abrasive squeal of her tyres touched his ears moments later, when the car loomed big in his vision, then the machine thundered past. He blinked and stared at the radar readout with an open mouth. The peak velocity read 233km/h. His mouth twisted into a smirk.

"You are mine." Impatiently, he waited for the computer to locate and verify the offender's registration plate number. It seemed to take longer than usual and Hart jumped when his computer complained with a loud squeak some seconds later. He scowled in outrage. The plate was not listed in the database – it was a fake.

"Oh but I'm going to get you!" He hit the siren, turned the key and the Holden barked into life. With the rear tyres throwing up grass and leaves, he swung the car about and raced after the lawbreaker, who was now a small, pale speck that rapidly ascended the distant slope. The needle on his speedometer soared with surprising ease and swiftly climbed past 150km/h. He grinned at the pull of the V8 engine and the piercing shrill of the siren around him. This was what police work should always be.

By now his quarry had disappeared around the bend at the top of the slope and Hart drove even faster. He couldn't let him get away.

As he flew up the far slope, Andy had his eyes on his rear-view mirror. Far behind him, he saw the police car pull out onto the road in a tight U-turn and there was no doubt in his mind. It was coming after him. To confirm this, the police lights suddenly started flashing, but then Andy hit the peak of the rise and the road curved to the right and the police car was lost from sight. Andy thought furiously. What was he going to do? He couldn't possibly stop. Not now, not after all the work and effort. His car would be impounded instantly if he stopped. He would lose his licence, get a phenomenal fine and most certainly a court hearing, possibly even jail time. The drift competition would be completely out. No, stopping was not an option.

He would have to make a run for it. He knew he had the power to outrun the police car, but what if they had radioed ahead for backup? Would there be another one waiting in ambush ahead? Would his radar detector warn him? Andy glanced into his rear-view mirror again. He couldn't see the police car, but he knew it wasn't far behind. Andy grimaced. The police officer had been waiting, trying to catch somebody speeding and he had fallen into the trap. But why had his detector warned him so late? His good mood, of a moment ago, was gone. "To hell with it, I may as well get some practice in," Andy grated to himself and put his foot down. "Catch me if you can."

Andy felt like a bank heist getaway driver as he shoved the Cefiro at the road, pushing her to the very brink on the windy turns through Arthur's Pass. But she held on and gave him everything she had. All the raw power from the RB30 was at his disposal. He didn't bother checking his rear-view mirror again because he knew that few drivers could match the pace that he set.

Half an hour later, Andy began to relax. He hadn't seen the police car again nor come across anyone waiting ahead. Surely by now the police had given up? Andy continued on, but drove less frantically now. He knew he would have to make a toilet stop soon. Fortunately he saw a rest area sign.

Slowing, he turned off and bumped the Cefiro down to the rest area, which was completely empty. Leaving the RB idling, he went to the nearest tree. Moments later, he became aware of a subtle disturbance in the air – a fluting sound that was just audible above the chirping birds and the gurgling stream nearby. Rapidly the fluting altered in pitch, resonating from the direction that he had come. It became loud and urgent and was accompanied by an insistent engine bawl.

Andy ran back to his car. He had just reached it when the full siren howl hit his ears and up on the main road a white and blue vehicle flashed past. Seconds later there came the harsh squeal of tyres. They had spotted him. Andy dived into the driver's seat and yanked the door shut. Taking no time to buckle himself in, he slammed in first gear and hit the gas. The Cefiro scrambled forwards on the gravel, following the rest area path, which looped back to reconnect with the main road 50 metres on.

After every turn Hart expected to see the back of the white Nissan. But it never happened. Still he raced on, not wanting to give up and admit defeat. He considered radioing ahead to have a road block set up, but this one he didn't want to hand over. This one he wanted all to himself. Broodingly, Officer Hart raced on. The insistent shrill of his siren began to irritate him, piercing his brain and darkening his mood further. He considered turning it off but thought it safer to warn any oncoming traffic. At this speed a head-on collision would mean instant death.

With two hands firmly on the wheel, he glanced down at the speedometer. He was on a short straight and his speed hit 160km/h. Even in the corners it rarely fell below twice the posted bend speed. Where was that Nissan? As he rounded another corner a car suddenly appeared ahead of him in the distance and instantly Hart sat bolt upright in his seat. But then he sat back again and his frustration grew. The car was green. Angrily he planted his right foot to the floor and the Commodore rocketed forwards, he wanted to pass it before the next bend. Why hadn't he caught up with the white car? Surely few drivers could match his police training and the power of his V8. It made no sense and he swore at the green Subaru in front of him before overtaking.

Driving dangerously fast, Hart continued on relentlessly. He navigated another series of bends and poured out onto a straight stretch of road, lined on both sides by forest. A rest area sign flew towards him and suddenly, out of the corner of his eye, he saw a white car and a flicker of movement. Then he was past. The moment had been so fleeting that he couldn't be sure it was the car he pursued, but instinct warned him and he hit the brakes. The Holden skidded with an enraged squeal from all four tyres.

The instant he had slowed sufficiently, Hart threw the wheel over, bringing the Commodore about in a screeching U-turn, and immediately accelerated – aiming for the sign posted rest area a short distance back. But before he reached it, he spotted a blur of white through the trees on his left, moving in the opposite direction. "What's he up to?" Hart frowned and eyeballed his rear-view mirror. Suddenly he realised his mistake and growled in outrage. His mirror showed another rest area sign behind him, indicating a second exit. "Oh no you don't!" Officer Hart was about to throw his car into another U-turn, when the Subaru that he had overtaken earlier suddenly appeared around the corner.

Warned by his loud siren, it had slowed down and he had to wait for it before he could make the turn. Worriedly, he checked his rear-view mirror as the green car passed him and drove on. He just caught a glimpse of the white car, pushing its nose out of the rest stop and slam to a halt, also giving way to the Subaru. Using his handbrake, Hart ripped the Holden around and once again shoved it back the way he had come. The Subaru passed the turnoff and immediately the Nissan pulled out with its back section fishtailing loosely on gravel. "I've got you now," Hart grated to himself as he rapidly closed in on the Nissan.

He flashed his lights, instructing the Nissan to immediately pull over. In response a hand suddenly came out of the driver's side window of the white machine with one finger raised and then the Nissan hunched down and kicked out. It happened so fast that it left Hart stunned. His outrage turned to disbelief as a flame erupted from the large big-bore exhaust that protruded arrogantly from under the Nissan's rear bumper and she exploded into motion. He was reminded of a crouching cat suddenly launching into attack with a speed that cheated the eye.

In an attempt to keep up, Hart forced the accelerator down and the V8 revved loudly, but still the gap between them increased. The hand had been withdrawn and the Nissan was all business as she hurled herself at the next bend, cutting it precisely and thrusting out of it even further ahead. The Subaru appeared before them again and the Nissan sat on its back bumper for a split second before it made its decision and shot out into the oncoming traffic lane in a suicidal overtake that Hart couldn't possibly match. Then the Nissan swung back in, well ahead. Hart stared after it in dismay. How could this be happening? His siren was still blaring and the Subaru tried to pull over for him, but the road was too narrow and only allowed a safe pass 200-metres further on. By then the Nissan was well out of his reach. Hart screamed abuse and smacked his hands angrily against the steering wheel.

For the first time he also realised that the driver of the Nissan was clearly not going to give up and was taking crazy risks. Although he wanted to catch him, he knew that continuing the pursuit would most likely end in an accident. The last thing he needed was to tarnish his record further. Still feeling riled, Hart turned his lights and siren off and slowed the Holden down. He considered radioing ahead and handing the case over, but as he reached for the handset and was about to make the call, his radar blipped loudly. Behind him the same Subaru that he had met on several occasions already, came flying around the corner. The radar reported a speed of 126km/h. Hart smiled at the reading and put the radio handset back on its cradle.

"This time I'll let you go. But I'm sure we'll meet again. And then..." He pulled over and waved the Subaru down. Reluctantly it came to a stop on the roadside behind him. Hart took several seconds to sit and enjoy the moment. He was in no hurry – he liked to let them sit and squirm for a while. This driver had obviously thought the police chase would be well ahead. Taking his time, Hart eased himself out of his seat, straightened his uniform and set his hat at the right angle on his balding head, before swaggering to the Subaru. With an aloof expression that showed his disdain, he indicated to the driver to lower his window.

"In a rush, are we?"

"Oh no, not at all," the driver, an elderly man with white hair answered him quickly.

"Well if you don't consider 126km/h to be in a rush then what would you call it?"

"Surely I wasn't doing that." The driver looked shocked.

"You can't argue with the radar," Officer Hart pointed out.

"I didn't realise," now the driver was apologetic as he noticed the expressionless mask of his captor. "I'm sorry, it won't happen again."

"That's up to you," Hart shrugged. "I'll just give you something to help remind you." He reached for his notepad.

"But…" the driver started out.

"Trust me, I've heard it all before," he silenced the driver. "Now, how about that driver's licence?"

After taking the information, he issued his first speeding ticket for the day.

"Thanks," the driver said thickly as he took it from him.

"My pleasure," Hart smiled.

When the Subaru had disappeared, Officer Hart turned his police car around and made his way back. Keeping his radar on alert, it wasn't long before he found his next offender.

Andy didn't see any further signs of being pursued. It puzzled him and, while he also kept a watchful eye out for any police backup that might be waiting further on, he reached his destination unhindered. The seller, a stocky bloke in his mid-twenties with short hair, answered the door and greeted him with a firm handshake. When they had spoken on the phone, he had agreed to help install the roll cage and after seeing the heavily modified Cefiro, he became genuinely enthusiastic. He was a real Nissan fan and drifter himself. They set to work and started by cutting the roll cage from his wrecked Cefiro and then re-welding it into Andy's. It was slow work, especially since Andy's welds needed to be tidy and professional enough to pass any cursory examination.

Once it was installed and the welds had cooled, they sanded them back and repainted the cage. The seller screwed on the new registration plates while Andy carefully prised all the tags and the low-volume certification plate off the wrecked Cefiro and re-riveted them to his. Satisfied with his handy work, he stepped back and stretched. It had been a long day, and he still had to drive back, but he now had the roll cage and the paperwork to compete in the competition. It was worth it. While they waited for the paint to dry, they filled out the paperwork and went for a late lunch at McDonalds.

It was nearly dark when Andy hit the road again, heading home. He was tired and he took it much easier, driving with his headlights on and his window slightly down. The cold night air and the Cefiro's jolty suspension helped to keep him awake. It seemed to take forever and he was thankful when he eventually reached the outskirts of the city again.

He began to make his way back in the direction of his apartment, when he remembered that there was still something he needed to do. Something he had been putting off. As he slowed and stopped for a red light, he picked up his cell-phone and selected the familiar number with hesitation. Would she still be awake? The phone started ringing, each one sounding unnaturally loud in his ears. He let it ring for a while, but nobody answered. He was almost relieved and went to end the call, but then raised the phone back to his ear.

"Hello?" Her voice sounded nasal, and for a second Andy was reminded again of the day he had last seen her, distraught and in mourning. He was slow to respond. "Hello?"

"Tanya, it's Andy here."

"Andy," her voice caught. "It's good to hear from you..."

"Yeah, I'm sorry about the other day," Andy mumbled. "I thought it was somebody else."

"I know Andy, it's okay." Tanya paused. "How are you?"

"I'm alright." He was about to return the query but stopped himself. "I was hoping I could ask a favour."

"Of course, what is it?"

"Do you still have the Mazda and the car trailer? I was hoping I could borrow them."

"I still have everything that belonged to Markus," Tanya said solemnly. "And yes, of course you can – however long you need."

"That'd be real helpful," Andy was relieved. "I'll come and get them now, okay?"

"Yes, that's fine. It'll be nice to see you."

Andy finished the call and gazed tiredly down at the cellphone, lost in thought. A loud beep startled him and he realised that the light had changed. He drove off hurriedly.

Parking on the street, Andy switched the engine off but did not get out. He stared out of his windscreen. In the light of the street lamps, two long, faded tyre marks ran down the street, right to its end. He and Markus had laid them on the day Markus had bought the 180SX. With a sigh, he got out and made his way slowly up to the house. The exterior light came on automatically as he neared and the front door opened before he could ring the bell. Tanya stood there. She looked even worse. She had lost more weight and the bags beneath her eyes were dark and puffy.

"Hi Andy, please come in," she offered, smiling bravely.

"Oh, that's okay," Andy replied quickly. He couldn't look at her. "I won't stay. I just wanted to get the car and trailer."

"Okay, sure," she covered her disappointment. "It's in the garage – I'll get the keys." She disappeared into the house and Andy remained outside waiting.

"Here Andy," she reappeared and handed him a key ring. He took it and almost flinched when their fingers touched.

"Thanks," hurriedly he walked to the garage. Tanya watched him from the doorway as he backed the wagon out, turned it around and linked the trailer up, then drove out onto the street.

"I'll bring it back on Sunday," Andy called to her after he had driven his Nissan up onto the trailer. Tanya nodded silent acknowledgement. She was still standing in the doorway when Andy pulled away.

Finishing his morning shift, Leon left work at noon on Thursday. He took the bus home and just as he arrived, he saw a black Silvia approach and turn into his driveway. Excitedly he neared his car. She still looked seriously beat up with scratches and dents everywhere and he had to remind himself that he had only paid for the crash damage to be repaired, not to give her a total makeover. The S13 came to a stop and the driver clambered out, dressed in white overalls. Leon recognised him.

"Paul, how'd you go?"

"Yeah good. She straightened up real nice, not like some cars," Leon detected a hint of pride in his tone. "Come see."

Paul led him to the front of the Silvia and lifted the bonnet. With a professional attitude, he pointed out where the repairs had been made. The front section and side panels had been straightened and the radiator and intercooler realigned, while the broken headlight and buckled front bumper had been replaced with those that Leon had tracked down. The bonnet and bumper had also been re-sprayed black to match the rest of the car.

When Leon laid the bonnet flat, it fitted snugly and the natural gaps in the body panels around the lights and between the bumpers were of matching width on both sides. Leon also checked under the car's body – it all looked in order. After completing his careful inspection he had to agree, the workmanship appeared sound. He couldn't find fault, but would she handle properly?

"We put her on the chassis plant three times to make sure she was all in line," Paul read his thoughts. "Each time we took her for a short drive and afterwards we also gave her a wheel alignment."

"That's thorough," Leon acknowledged.

"On the way here, I checked the handling one last time," Paul turned to look at him seriously. "And trust me, she's straight as an arrow."

"Oh good," Leon was relieved. "I plan to drift her."

"I guessed as much," Paul nodded knowingly. "Call me when you need the next lot fixed."

"That will probably be on Sunday already," Leon smiled back. "Since I'm competing on Saturday."

"You drifters are crazy," Paul shook his head. "But I shouldn't complain..."

Leon watched as Paul got into the van that had followed him and drove away. He turned to the Silvia again. Unable to contain himself, he opened the driver door and hopped in. The feeling of sitting back in the moulded race seats was fantastic. He didn't realise how much he had missed it.

His right hand moved up to where Paul had left the keys in the ignition and the car shook herself alive to a deep rumble. The tacho needle climbed its scale, before settling back to an easy idle speed. The boost gauge showed a vacuum and the oil pressure was good. The temperature gauge also rose steadily before coming to a rest at halfway. She was already warm and set to go. Leon had her in reverse gear and was about to let the clutch out before he stopped himself and checked the time. He had just over an hour. If he got changed first, he could take her for a quick drive and go to the BBQ directly afterwards. It made sense. Reluctantly, he switched the Nissan off again and climbed out. Although he grudged the extra time to take a shower, he wanted to be clean and look good for Lorna.

Having finished his two-minute shower, he had just changed his clothes for shorts and a t-shirt and was in his bedroom hurriedly pulling on socks when he heard his mum calling him from downstairs.

"Byron's here."

"Oh," Leon frowned. He had meant to call Byron and tell him to meet him at the BBQ. "Alright, get him to come up," He heard footsteps on the stairs and moments later Byron squeezed his bulk through the door.

"Hey bud."

"Byron!" Tamsin suddenly appeared behind him and flew at the big man.

"Tink, argh," Byron grinned at the little dark-haired creature that stuck to his left leg.

"Hey man, you're early, Cam said the BBQ wouldn't start till like 2pm."

"I thought I could finally take your car for a spin," Byron spoke distractedly, while trying to prise Tamsin off his leg, but his efforts were in vain.

"Um," Leon scratched his temple. "Actually I was planning to take her for a spin myself…"

"Oh real… You've been promising for a while…"

"Yeah, I know but," Leon started out, but then shrugged helplessly when he saw Byron's expression. "Alright, but we'll have to head there straight after." Byron hesitated and Leon realised that he was torn – wanting to use the opportunity to show off his Altezza to those at the BBQ. But the prospect of driving a drift car with one of Japan's very best engines under the bonnet proved irresistible to him.

"I can deal with that," Byron nodded and suddenly grinned like a child with a new toy. "I'm gonna show you some drifting, like you've never seen before."

"I know just the place, let's go." Leon made for the door.

"Cool, um, but what about this little growth on my leg?"

"This works every time," Leon reached down and tickled Tamsin, who promptly broke into a fit of giggles and fell helplessly to the floor. "Let's go before it recovers," Leon smiled and they bolted down the stairs.

The Silvia scrambled at the road, her tyres losing grip, sliding, grabbing and then suddenly biting in so hard that she whipped around and Byron hit the brakes hastily. The tyres squealed and they were thrown rudely at their harnesses as they came to a stop in the middle of the bend, pointing back the way they had come. The engine had stalled and Byron twisted the key in the ignition. In an instant, she thudded back into life.

"You know, you could try–"

"I'm just gonna nail it," Byron snapped and floored it. Backtracking, he brought the Silvia about and again launched her at the bend. Apprehensively, Leon watched Byron's face and bit back his advice. Byron was holding the steering wheel in a fierce grip, his face a determined mask of concentration. This was his fifth attempt at sliding around the bend. Each one had gotten progressively worse as he fought to prove himself.

The turn came at them and Leon knew they had too much speed. The car bucked as Byron downshifted, dumped the clutch and the rear wheels locked up momentarily, before he brought the steering wheel over and flogged her on. With the tacho needle snapping at the redline, her rear wheels broke loose and the Silvia went into a dead-pan slide. Angling straight across the bend, she was aiming for the concrete wall of the warehouse building on the other side.

"Oh oh," Byron saw their predicament and froze. Reacting instinctively, Leon grabbed the steering wheel and heaved at it with all the strength in his left arm, pushing it further over. At the same time he yanked up the handbrake with his right, sending her into a spin to shave speed. The car careened around and made a full 180-degree turn before her rear wheel slammed into the kerb. She bounced back and they were flung roughly in their seats. The engine had stalled again and Leon spoke into silence.

"You alright?"

"Uh, yeah," Byron enounced, looking rather pale. "You?"

"Yeah," Leon nodded and unlatched his harness.

"Man, it's harder than it looks," Byron admitted reluctantly. "Reckon we busted something?"

"Dunno, hope not," Leon opened his door. "I'll take a look." He got out and walked around to inspect the back wheel. Taking a deep breath, Byron climbed out also. He stood back uncomfortably as Leon ran his hands over the battered alloy rim.

"Everything alright?" he asked worriedly.

"Seems okay," Leon straightened with a shrug. "Just another ding to add to the rest," he grinned ruefully and Byron relaxed. "You want to give it another go?"

"Nah, it's not really me," Byron shook his head. "I'll just stick to Playstation – cheaper, more comfortable and I can eat at the same time."

"Fair call..." Leon nodded, hiding his smile. "Speaking of food, we should get to that BBQ."

"Yeah, let's do that."

Leon got into the driver's seat but didn't start the engine. Byron sat down heavily in the passenger seat beside him, looking decidedly green. "Sure you're alright?"

"Better now…" Byron nodded and took a few more deep breaths. "This drifting is a killer – I'm definitely sticking to Playstation and cruising in the 'Tez."

Although he remained silent, this time Leon couldn't help smiling. He started the engine and drove away.

"What a cess-pit," Byron observed when they pulled up outside the address that Cam had given. The house was old and in a bad state of neglect, with peeling paint, an overgrown front lawn and a broken front window. It even looked as though the rusty, corrugated iron roof had sagged slightly.

"It's not what I was expecting," Leon agreed uncertainly. "But I think Taz lives here."

"Yeah?" Byron wasn't convinced. "How could anybody live here – unless they're hobos?"

"It must be it," Leon said. "Check out all the cars."

"That's true," Byron agreed distractedly. "Look, there's even a spot for us," he indicated a gap on the side of the street, before turning his attention to the many vehicles. "Wow."

The street outside the house, and even the overgrown front lawn, was clustered with performance cars. Pretty much all of them had received considerable attention and were modified to a serious level. Nissans were strongly represented: a silver Pulsar GTi-R with low slung body kit and busy 17-inch alloys, a dark green, lowered Silvia S14 on big grungy black rims, a purple 180SX with dark tinted windows and decked out in full body kit, as well as two Skylines that rested stiffly on big mag wheels and boasted huge front-mounted intercoolers. A number of the cars ran rear wheels which didn't match those on the front, signifying that they went through the rear-rubber quickly and hinting at plenty of drift use. Among the other cars was a fully worked Honda S2000 in stylish Veilside trim and a showy Mitsubishi Evolution.

"How good is this," Leon parallel parked behind a venomous Mazda RX-7 Batman, and turned the ignition off. Immediately they heard music thudding out from behind the house. "This must be it. Come on." He opened his door and the music got louder.

"That thing is insane," Byron hoisted his bulk out of the low S13 with difficulty, but despite this, his attention was on the Batman alone. Heavily tinted and resting low over ultra-wide 19-inch deep dish rims, the sparkling black machine had been wide-bodied. A light-weight, vented carbon fibre bonnet had replaced the original and her front bumper was fitted with a monstrous intercooler. Everything had been done, from her streamlined carbon fibre wing mirrors to the subtle decals that adorned her impeccable bodywork. She now sported a twin-pipe exhaust system, four-pot callipers and huge vented disc brakes. There was no denying it, she represented speed and was epically cool.

"This thing has had a mint spent on it."

"I bet," Leon locked the Silvia and came around to admire the Mazda.

"This is like a mini Auto Salon right here," Byron's eyes were wide as he took in the impressive display. "Some of these cars were actually at the show last month."

"Really?" Leon asked, also checking out the cars.

"Yeah totally, this Batty was and so was that *Evo*."

"Hmmm," Leon turned to look at his car, modified though she was, with her marred and puckered panels and kerbed wheels she seemed out of place. "Maybe I should re-park."

"Why? That's a good spot," Byron turned to the house and sniffed the air. "Come on, I smell food." He began walking across the lawn towards the house. Not wanting to turn up alone, Leon was left with little choice but to follow him. Guided by the music, they made their way around the side of the house, along a dark, well-worn path of trampled grass that ran between a head-high wooden fence and the outer house wall. Here the grey paint of the house was in an even worse state of peeling and the timber weatherboards had rotted in places. The air smelled dank and stale. Old car tyres and rusted car parts were piled against the house wall.

"Awesome," Byron muttered. "I might have to ask if they have a spare room."

Rounding the side of the house, the path opened out to a big backyard, which, in contrast to the gloomy path, was basked in sunlight. Again, it was not what they had expected and they stopped in their tracks. The yard was closed off and made private by the same surrounding head-high fence. Unlike the unkempt front lawn, here the grass had been recently cut, probably in preparation for the event. The many trees that speckled the yard, however, had been left untouched and continued to grow wild and bushy. But instead of being unruly, this gave the area a private and natural feel, shielding it from the neighbouring properties to create a small tranquil haven in the middle of densely populated suburbia.

The yard was teeming with people. Like themselves, they looked to be mostly in their late-teens to mid-twenties. They clustered in groups, standing on the lawn, while some lounged in couches and chairs on a large wooden deck at the back of the house. Overall the mood was festive and jovial. People laughed and joked. Many of them were drinking and holding plastic cups, cans or stubbies.

"I think we've found heaven," Byron breathed deeply, inhaling the mouth-watering smell of cooking that wafted towards them from the opposite corner of the yard. He had also noticed the large trestle table near the deck. It was laden to the brink and supporting numerous big bowls filled with food, from chips to colourful salads, breads and dips. Cam had not lied, there was plenty of food.

"Check those guys out," the group of people closest to them had attracted Leon's attention. Closely surrounded by his peers, one of them stood on his hands on top of a large 50-litre keg. He had the keg's hose in his mouth and, while two of them supported his legs, a third worked the keg pump. Red-faced and dripping beer, the drinker was lowered back down onto his feet. Trying to catch his balance, he stepped forward, unsteady and clumsy. With a lopsided grin he wiped his face, using the back of one hand.

"Yup definitely hobos," Byron muttered. Suddenly they were noticed by the drinker.

"Wow, that guy's a giant," he nudged one of his friends and pointed at Byron. "Let's get him up here."

"Definitely," his friend looked over, grinning from ear-to-ear. "Come on man, you're up," he urged Byron.

"Yeah man, your turn," another one of the other drinkers around the keg waved for Byron to join them.

"See, you've already made some friends," Leon smiled, but Byron was still hesitant. "Show them how it's done."

"What're you waiting for boss?" the original drinker insisted. "Come on – live dangerously."

"Yeah, we'll boost you up." Byron's protest was lost in the chorus as the rest joined in. Reluctantly he stepped forward and was welcomed enthusiastically into the group, which opened for him – offering him the keg.

"What? Never had a keg-stand before?"

"We'll teach ya."

Standing alone, Leon looked on with interest as Byron was asked to grip the handles of the large aluminium keg and two of the group grabbed his legs and boosted him up into a handstand. Another pressed the nozzle of the keg's hose firmly into Byron's mouth while a fourth got busy and operated the keg pump vigorously. Copious beer, cold and fizzy, gushed into Byron's mouth. Some of it escaped past his lips and ran down into his hair and he was left with little choice but to gulp frantically. "You're charging. Go hard!" To Leon it all looked very primitive but also rather amusing as he watched Byron swallow frantically and his head turn beetroot from his upside-down position. He was glad it wasn't him.

"You made it," he jumped to find Lorna beside him. "Come, I'd like you to meet a few friends of mine."

"Sure." Seeing that Byron was being looked after, he followed her. She led him over to two girls that stood nearby and introduced them as Katie and Alisa. They smiled at him and offered their hands. Lorna saw immediately that Leon had no idea what to say to these two and quickly whisked him on, having him meet several others until they reached the group concentrated around the three large gas barbeques, which were well stocked with sizzling food. Leon recognised two of the group. Cam was standing by one of the barbeques armed with a big pair of tongs with which he turned the many sausages. Beside him stood Taz dressed in a ridiculous baby-blue chef's apron. He manned another of the barbeques and was in the process of serving a patty to an attractive girl with long brown dreadlocks.

"Here you go babe, your hippy veggie patty is ready." The girl made a face at Taz, but smiled as they approached.

"Lorna, who's your friend?"

"Hey Danica, this is Leon," Lorna introduced him. "And this is Ollie. Ollie, I'd like you to meet Leon."

"Hey ya," Ollie was a tall guy with brown hair. Leon immediately picked up on his accent.

"Ollie came back to visit us all the way from Canada," Lorna explained, squeezing Ollie around the waist. "He's a good friend of ours."

"Oh shucks, you're making me blush," Ollie smiled with very white teeth that stood out starkly against his tanned skin. His handshake was firm and Leon liked his easy manner.

"Taz and Cam you know of course," Lorna pointed out.

"For sure," Cam caught Leon's eye and nodded a friendly greeting. "Good of you to come."

"Heard you're Lorna's new boyfriend?" Taz asked Leon and raised an eyebrow.

"Um," Leon frowned and looked at Lorna.

Lorna rolled her eyes. "Ignore him, he's always like this."

"I'll take that as a compliment," Taz declared smugly. "But if you are, then you're lucky as. I've always dreamed of hooking up with her," Taz smirked and immediately the girls rounded on him.

"Taz!" Lorna punched him in the arm and Danica poured a bit of her beer over his head.

"Oi, children, don't mess with *Chef*," Taz imitated. He shook his head vigorously, spraying beer, and held up his tongs. The girls relented and giggled at his gag. "So how's she going for you then?" Taz addressed Leon again.

"Huh?" Leon stared at him, slightly flustered.

"The S13 – Lorna said you bought it off her cousin," Taz turned to Lorna grinning broadly and prodded her with his forefinger. "I wonder what he thought I was talking about?"

"Taz, give him a break," Cam admonished his friend and Taz sobered. "But yeah, how's that '13?" Cam asked Leon.

"Well, she hasn't broken down yet... So not too bad."

"Heard she's running a Goddy motor," Taz prompted.

Leon nodded and Cam stopped turning his sausages.

"For real?"

"Lorna's cousin, Blake put it in," Leon explained.

"In a light S13 that must be pretty loose," Cam mused.

"I'm all for transplants," Ollie admitted. "Just had a 20B from a Cosmo put into my car. Triple-rotors are all good."

"Did you see his Batman out front?" Lorna asked Leon.

"Yeah I did – very cool," he turned to Ollie. "Are you entering the drifts tomorrow as well?"

"No way," Ollie crinkled his nose. "Spinning up my tyres is fun, but thrashing my car and always breaking stuff... That ain't my idea of a good time."

"Ollie can't handle it. He's a sissy," Taz laughed.

"I'm not the one wearing the blue skirt," Ollie retorted.

"You know, I'd love to see what an RB26 can do sometime – Cam never did take me in his GT-R," Danica spoke up.

"You had a GT-R?" Leon looked at Cam, who nodded slowly. "What happened to it?"

"I kinda busted the gearbox and stuff," Cam turned one of the sausages distractedly.

"It must've been pretty fast though?"

"Yeah, definitely," Cam replied without looking up. "The quickest car I've driven. I sold it though..."

"Pity, I would've liked to see it." Leon hesitated. "But yeah, I've got the S13 parked out front, so I guess we could go for a spin later. There's only one spare seat though..."

"Shotgun," Taz called out instantly and stuck his thumb to his forehead. "Snooze, you lose," he laughed triumphantly as he scored the front seat and Cam and Danica capitulated.

"Lame," Cam smiled ruefully.

"Yeah, what's with that?" Danica pouted. "Leon was offering it to me."

"Too slow," Taz stilled her protests. "But don't worry – I'll tell you all about it," he promised and turned back to Leon. "Hope you're hungry?"

"Um," Leon looked about him.

"Go for it," Lorna urged. "There's plenty."

"It smells good," he agreed.

"Sweet," Cam grabbed a plastic plate and put two sausages on it. "You like onions?"

"Yeah, thanks."

"Taz sort him would ya, some of that steak too," Cam requested, handing him the plate.

"You got it," Taz piled Leon's plate high. "Can't have our driver go hungry..."

"Wow, thanks – that's heaps," Leon took it with two hands.

"All good," Cam smiled and pointed with his tongs to the fold out trestle table. "Cutlery, bread and sauces are over there. Knock yourself out."

"You might even get lucky with some sushi," Taz couldn't resist. "There's no miso soup though."

"Gutted," Leon shook his head in mock disappointment and smiled. "I knew I should've brought some..."

"So Missy, what I can do for you?" Taz addressed Lorna. "A steak maybe?"

Carrying their plates, Leon and Lorna wandered over to the trestle table, where they grabbed slices of pre-buttered bread to go with their sausages and Leon administered tomato sauce to his food. Topping their meal off with salad and a small side of potato chips, they armed themselves with a knife and fork and went to sit down opposite each other on the large deck.

"Cool that you came," Lorna spoke softly, just for him to hear and smiled into his eyes.

"I wasn't sure if I should, even though Cam invited me," Leon admitted quietly. "But I'm glad I did," he added honestly. "Though I'm not sure if Byron will be – tomorrow." Smiling, he pointed out his friend's shoes, which stuck up in the air again, above the heads of those that surrounded him and held him up.

"True, that's going to hurt," Lorna laughed.

"Better him than me," Leon watched Byron's feet snatching at the sky for a moment longer, before taking a bite of his food. "This is good."

"Respects to the chefs," Lorna agreed whole-heartedly and attacked her salad. "Oh, ripped off..."

"What's wrong?"

"I didn't get a single olive."

"You can take mine," Leon offered her the green olive that had come with his salad.

"Are you sure?"

"Of course, I've got another one anyway." Using his knife he moved aside a lettuce leaf, to show her the other olive, hiding beneath it.

"Cool," she leaned over to pick it up off his plate. Her knee pressed against his and suddenly he found himself staring down her top. His heart missed a beat. "I'm such a sucker when it comes to olives," Lorna admitted, straightening up again. She popped it in her mouth and chewed with relish.

"Have the other one too," Leon encouraged her.

"Don't you like them?"

"They're alright, but I'd rather you have them," he tried to sound natural.

"Yum," she began to lean forward but then stopped herself. "Wait," she looked down at her top, which hung slightly open, and then back at him. Leon quickly looked away. "Boys," Lorna shook her head but she couldn't help herself smiling at him. Cheekily, she leaned over even further as she took the olive from his plate. "You know, you only have to ask."

Leon's eyes widened and he almost choked on his hotdog. He stared at her. And then, suddenly they were both laughing. And then he did choke and his eyes began to water, but neither of them could stop laughing, which made it worse.

"Ouch," he knocked his own chest with his fist and finally got his coughing under control. "Ahhh, that seriously went down the wrong way," his eyes were still watering and he wiped the wet away with his thumb.

"I'm sorry," Lorna had stopped laughing too and looked at him seriously. "But you did deserve that."

"I did," Leon agreed. Smiling, they studied each other, before turning their attention to their food again. They finished eating in quiet companionship, while watching everyone else around them. When they had eaten their food, they leaned back in appreciation and continued to relax in the sunshine.

"So are you still going for a drive?" Lorna asked, taking a sip of her wine.

"I think so," Leon nodded. "If Taz still wants to go that is."

"Okay, I'll stay here and let my food digest." She pushed her belly out into a formidable bulge. "I ate way too much."

"That is a mean spare tyre you've got," Leon chuckled.

"Are you calling me fat?" Lorna accused and his smile slipped, but then he saw the gleam in her eye.

"Too right," Taz's voice spoke from above them. "No more sausage for you Lorna, eh boss?" Taz winked down at him.

"Taz, you need help," Lorna threw her plastic fork at him.

"People keep telling me that... Anyway, I'm good to go, whenever you're ready..."

"I'll see ya when you get back, Leon."

"Okay," He followed Taz, who was carrying a Heineken.

"Is that it there?" They had emerged from the side of the house and the Silvia stood before them on the street. With the sun at this angle her many blemishes stood out clearly.

"Yeah," Leon nodded uncomfortably.

"Not bad," Cam had followed them around and stopped beside him. Danica remained silent.

"Pretty rough," Taz frowned and took a gulp of his beer.

"Courtesy of Lorna's cousin."

"Yeah, never met him, but I hear he's rogue as..." Cam was also assessing the black Silvia with a critical eye. "Are these 17s?" Curiously, he moved forward and crouched down by the front wheel of the Silvia.

"Yeah."

"Don't look like it," Taz sniffed. "And you're still on four stud. How budge."

"What's wrong with that?" Leon wanted to know.

"Five stud is stronger and five by 114.3s are a common size. Most drifters run that pattern."

"It seems to work alright," Leon shrugged uncertainly.

"Yeah until your wheel comes off in full drift. Then you've got problems."

"Don't listen to him," Cam chuckled. "He's right about it being more common, in case you need to borrow wheels with fresh tread…" He ran his hand over the worn front tyre. "But I've never heard of drifters going out and actually snapping their wheel studs..." Cam broke off and became serious. "Taz come look at this."

"Huh?" Taz hesitated, before he went over to Cam.

"See what I see?" Cam pointed in behind the front wheel.

"What is it?" Danica wanted to know.

"Fully adjustable Tein suspension," Cam said simply.

"Eh," Taz crouched down beside his friend.

"And look at how much camber he's running," Cam mused and Taz pinched his lower lip.

"This wouldn't have been on the car when you bought it," Taz turned back to Leon questioningly.

"My uncle got it for me…" Leon agreed.

"Did he install and adjust it?" Cam wanted to know.

"Not sure," Leon shrugged. "I assume so."

"Pop the bonnet, would ya?" Cam straightened up.

"Sure," Leon stepped around to the driver's side, unlocked it and pulled the bonnet release. Taz and Cam raised it and Danica squeezed between them for a better look.

"Well, you weren't lying," Taz eyed the large straight-six pressed into the engine bay. "It really is an RB26…"

"Straight up," Cam nodded and turned his attention to the camber plates on the strut towers. "That's interesting…"

"Should give her a crank," Taz requested with his head well buried in the engine bay. Leon fed the ignition and turned the key. The engine came to life. "Sounds good," Taz emerged again.

Although he was pleased that the previous mockery seemed to have dried up, Leon didn't know what to make of their inspection. Cam was silent and thoughtful, while Taz was looking glum, as though his favourite cat had just been run over.

"So did you still want to go?" Leon addressed Taz.

"Wouldn't have it any other way," Cam lowered the bonnet and reached for the passenger door handle.

"Dream on, I called it remember," Taz stepped forward. Cam looked into the interior and saw the roll cage and the missing backseat.

"True, you did," he acknowledged and stepped back. Before he got in, Taz tipped his bottle to the sky and sculled the remaining beer, then tossed it into one of the overgrown shrubs that lined the boundary of their section. Burping loudly, he climbed into the passenger seat and harnessed himself in.

"Sorry guys," Leon was apologetic.

"You'll just have to take me another time," Danica smiled.

"Will do," Leon promised and hopped in.

"Damn, it's hot in here," Taz wiped his arm across his face.

"Yeah sorry, the air con is gone."

"Glad to hear it, it sucks like half your horsepower," Taz exaggerated. "Fortunately I've got some reinforcements to keep me cool." He pulled another Heineken from his pocket.

"Where do you want to go?" Leon had to laugh.

"Turn around, I'll show ya," Taz pointed behind him. "Let's get this show on the road."

They drove in silence, except for the occasional word or slurp from Taz as he enjoyed his cold beer or gave directions. Quickly they made their way out of the suburbs heading out to the more rural farms and lifestyle blocks.

"Well here we are," Taz said some time later as they turned onto a long, narrow country road, framed by a shelter belt of willow trees that gave way to paddocks of lush green grass and grazing sheep. "You can cut loose now."

"You sure? What if there are animals on the road," Leon gazed ahead of him apprehensively and continued to drive at an easy 60km/h.

"I'd only be worried if it's a pig," Taz guffawed at his own joke. "Come on – you're putting me to sleep." He tipped his bottle up to take another swig.

"If you insist," Leon said wryly. The road looked empty enough. With an easy flick of his wrist he downshifted to second gear and stepped on the accelerator. The engine responded instantly and the turbo spooled with a fierce whine. Torque socked the back wheels and they immediately broke free. The Silvia squirmed momentarily on her churning rear tyres, but when Leon eased back on the gas, they gripped again and the car lunged forwards. In the middle of his sip, Taz snatched for the handhold, but wasn't quick enough to prevent some beer spilling on his face. It trickled down his chin and dripped onto his t-shirt.

"What're you trying to...?" His words were lost in the roar as Leon let her go and the S13 accelerated in earnest. The needle on the speedometer soared upwards, within seconds approaching 100km/h. Leon flicked to third gear and boosted again. The needle hit 140km/h, before the straight ceased and a turn was upon them. Able to see through the turn, Leon braked and spun the steering wheel towards the apex, downshifting at the same time. The S13 settled staunchly into the drift and swept through the bend with style.

Another straight followed and Leon levelled out and had her flying past 160km/h before he reigned her in for a series of three successive bends. With an easy grace he steered his Nissan into the first one, sliding out cleanly with a squeal of rubber on coarse tarmac, then spun the steering wheel to opposite lock, slipping into the second, still at high speed. As he pushed his ride harder and faster, Leon was so immersed that he completely forgot about his passenger.

With adrenaline pulsing, he hit the third corner at full tilt, but suddenly realised that the turn was much tighter than he had anticipated. Reacting quickly, he braked viciously into the corner, brought the speed down and turned in hard. Momentarily unbalanced by the sudden oversteer, the Nissan wobbled unnervingly and, as Leon accelerated again, her weight shifted and her tail swung out. He was losing it. She was going to spin!

Tense and worried, Leon reacted instinctively and counter-steered. Frantically he flung the wheel over into the slide. The balance of the car shifted again, but his quick reaction had pulled her out of the spiral so that she now skidded broadside across the curve, gushing smoke from her back tyres. Her screech cut off abruptly as her back wheels slid off the road, ploughing up sand and gravel. Clinging desperately onto control, Leon managed to coax her back onto firm seal and, as both rear wheels found good purchase, he throttled forwards, hurtling out of the third bend and down the next straight.

"Stop the car, stop the car," Taz blurted urgently and Leon flinched and hit the brakes. "Pull over!"

"Are you alright?" Leon looked across at Taz anxiously, but he didn't answer. He looked as though he was in pain. Leon slowed down and pulled over on the grassy roadside. Not waiting for the car to come to a complete stop, Taz set his stubbie down, found the door handle and leapt out. With two quick bounds he cleared the roadside and stepped up to the five-wire fence. Standing with his legs apart and his back to Leon, he tilted his head to the sky. Leon understood then. He averted his gaze but couldn't help smiling. Finally Taz came back. He sat down in the passenger seat and pulled the door closed in a relaxed manner.

"That's a lot better."

"Sorry if I scared you," Leon offered soberly.

"Scared me? You wish. That was just the beer," Taz picked up his bottle again and took another drink. "What're you waiting for? Are we were going for a fang or not?"

"Uh huh," Leon nodded grimly. This time he planted his right foot and thrust the Nissan back onto the road from standstill with her rear fishtailing freely. Straightening her out, he up-shifted to second. He felt her gain traction and was just about to let her go properly when a Holden slid out from a side road ahead of them and came to a rest at the stop sign. Tell-tale blue and yellow stripes adorned the sedan's body and patrol lights garnished her roof.

"Woah," Taz warned urgently and sat bolt upright in his seat. Leon hastily applied the brakes and the Silvia slipped back to the speed limit. They drove on, both of them sitting in silence, watching the patrol car out of the corner of their eyes.

"What's he doing out here?" Taz wanted to know.

"No idea..." Leon replied worriedly.

"Were you over?"

"Slightly, yeah."

"Reckon he noticed?"

"Dunno... Hope not."

"He's just sitting there..." Taz glowered. They could feel the eyes of the police officer boring into them, scrutinising them like bugs under a microscope, and then they were past, moving at a very controlled speed.

"Is he following?" Taz asked a moment later, not wanting to turn around and attract attention.

"No," Leon eyeballed his rear-view mirror. "Hasn't moved." The patrol car still stood at the stop sign, now some 40 metres behind them. "Maybe he'll leave us alone."

"That'd be a–" The shrill of a police siren interrupted Taz. Leon flinched. The police car had pulled out and was after them, its lights flashing red and blue.

"Oh man." Leon had no choice. Slowing down, he pulled over. "Put that beer away," he hissed at Taz, who tucked it behind his seat. They sat quietly as the police car stopped close behind them. Nothing happened for nearly a minute and then the police officer got out and marched up to them. Leon lowered his window.

"Going for a wee spin, are we?" his brittle voice was thick with malevolence.

Leon looked up at the burly policeman. He had his peaked cap on and dark eyes sat above a hooked nose and bushy moustache. Unsure of how to respond, Leon remained silent. "What, you don't speak English?" The policeman demanded. He placed two big hands over the window sill and bent down to peer into the interior of the Silvia. He sniffed the air and his eyes narrowed. He straightened up again. "Licence." It came out like an order and Leon fished out his wallet, withdrew his licence card and handed it over to him.

The policeman scrutinised it, before taking out a notepad and pen from his breast pocket. Quickly he scribbled some notes then shoved it back at Leon.

"Been drinking?" he produced an electronic breathalyser.

"Just coke," Leon replied.

"Smells like beer to me," he stuck the breathalyser in front of Leon's mouth. "Name and address, speak slowly and clearly." Leon spoke as normal as his agitation allowed. The policeman checked the display and, watching his face, Leon detected disappointment.

"Did I pass?" Leon wanted to know, but the policeman began checking over the Silvia. Ignoring Taz who watched him with obvious dislike, he first confirmed that the WOF and registration were up to date. Finding no fault there, he assessed all tyres and finally got down on one knee and examined up behind the wheels. Straightening, he came back to Leon's window.

"You got certification for the adjustable suspension?" he asked gruffly.

"Um," Leon swallowed worriedly.

"We do," Taz grated. "Want us to pop the bonnet? I can show you."

The policeman hesitated and then shook his head. "Just stay out of trouble." He strode away and Leon watched him get back into his car.

"Does that mean I can go?"

"Yeah, come on let's get out of here."

"I really thought he was going bust me for something," Leon started the engine and drove away.

"He wanted to," Taz scowled. They were silent, each lost to their own thoughts, until Taz randomly sniffed the air in an exaggerated re-enactment of the policeman, which made them crack up.

"Shall we just head back?" Leon asked.

"Yeah, Officer Killjoy has spoiled it for me too."

Sometime later, Leon parked the Silvia back in its niche outside Taz's flat and the two made their way around the side of the house. Leon immediately saw Byron, still drinking and talking to one of his new friends. He was looking a lot worse for wear. Leon was about to make his way over to him, but then Cam appeared, closely followed by Danica and Lorna.

"How'd it go?"

"Taz almost wet himself," Leon joked.

"He always was a wuss," Danica teased her boyfriend.

"Hardly," Taz shrugged easily. "Beer got the better of me, that's all."

"So she goes good?" Cam prodded.

"That she does," Taz looked at him significantly and nodded. "Trumps the Trueno for sure... Power, handling... In every way."

"I expected as much. And how'd he drive?"

"What is this, some kind of *Leon-analysis*?" Leon protested.

"We gotta suss out the competition," Cam shrugged easily.

"Competition?" Leon raised an eyebrow. "I'll hardly be racing against you. I'll be happy if I just make it through the qualifying rounds."

"You'll have no trouble doing that," Taz dismissed and turned to Cam. "He's got it down good. Lots of speed and angle. But yeah, in the end you're still a better driver..." Taz suddenly laughed. "You know, he almost stacked it on that third corner and then nearly got a ticket."

"You got pulled over?" Danica demanded.

"Yeah, one of them was hanging around our fun park like a bad smell," Taz replied.

"What happened?"

"Tried to bust us – checked over everything. Fortunately he was gullible and bought my bluff."

"What do you mean?" Leon looked at Taz quizzically.

"Well, if he'd wanted to see the cert' for the suspension then we would've had us a problem."

"Why?"

"Because there's no cert'."

Leon stared at him. "Are you serious?"

"Yeah, Cam and I checked. It's not certified for anything – not the new engine, the adjustable suspension, the roll cage..."

"The font window tint is also too dark," Cam nodded.

"Your car's not legal – he could've taken it."

"Oh," Leon swallowed. "I had no idea."

"We've had our fun with the law... so we tend to keep our cars legit now, or just don't drive them on the road," Cam pointed out. "Like the Toyota, that's purely a track car – there it doesn't matter so much."

"Might be worth looking into getting it certified," Lorna suggested quietly and squeezed Leon's arm.

"The last thing you want is to lose your car."

"Yeah definitely," Leon acknowledged thoughtfully. "I totally didn't realise, but thanks for bailing me out."

"All good," Taz grinned. "It's not every day I get away with lying to a cop."

"Mmmm, I'm kinda worried about driving her home now," Leon admitted.

"You'll be right, but best rent a trailer for Saturday," Cam suggested. "There's often police checking cars near the track."

"I noticed that," Leon remembered seeing them pulling people over when he and Byron had gone to the drift day.

"Trailers aren't that expensive."

"Good idea. I think Byron's dad has a Hilux. Maybe I can use that to tow it…" Leon mused and looked over to his friend again. Byron now had his arms around the shoulders of two drinking buddies. His hand clutched a vessel of beer while the three of them swayed together and sang loudly to the Johnny Cash song, which sounded dated after the previous techno music. "He's a mess." Leon was appalled. "Sorry guys, but I think I better get this guy home."

"He's fine," Taz grinned. "Just having fun."

"He's not a big drinker," Leon shook his head. "I wouldn't want him to make an ass of himself."

"No worries," Taz nodded. "Be seeing ya on Saturday then."

Leon shook hands with Taz and Cam, but failed to hide his discomfort when first Danica and then Lorna gave him a hug.

"Bye Leon," Lorna held him at arm's length and smiled, yet she couldn't keep the disappointment out of her eyes. "You should call me tomorrow."

"Will do," he promised. He left the group and made his way over to the drinkers. But held back as Byron suddenly left his mates and approached a pretty blonde who stood alone.

"Hey, I don't really know my way around here and was wondering if you could help me out with some directions?" Leon overheard him say each word with careful deliberation.

"Sure," the girl nodded politely. "If you're after the toilet – it's inside."

"That's good to know," Byron replied. "But I was actually wondering what the quickest way was to get into your pants." For a moment there was dead silence and even Leon thought he hadn't heard correctly. With a movement that cheated the eye, the girl suddenly lashed out. There was a loud slap and Byron stumbled backwards, holding his cheek. The girl turned on her heel and stalked away. Byron's drinking buddies, who had been listening, burst out into loud guffaws and came to clap him on the shoulder.

"That was so awesome."

"Solid gold!"

"Better luck next time," Byron grinned stupidly and massaged his cheek.

"Hey Byron," Leon approached them hesitantly.

"Leon, come have a drink with us."

"I think it's time to go, eh?"

"Don't be a sad sack," Byron slurred. "Just one won't hurt."

"I'm good," Leon shook his head and thought quickly. "We could go play some Playstation."

"Playstation?" Byron's brow furrowed and he wavered. "That might be cool…"

"Don't listen to this flake, there's still like half a keg to get through," one of the drinkers spoke up. "And afterwards we'll hit the clubs."

"I'll stay," Byron took the bait eagerly.

"Okay, I'll see you tomorrow," Leon knew he wouldn't change his mind. "Oh, do you think we can borrow your dad's car on Saturday? I want to put the Silvia on a trailer."

"The Hilux?" Byron closed his eyes and scratched his head. "Should be okay I guess… I'll ask him."

"Thanks. See you then." Leon made his way down the side of the house to the Silvia. He was just about to get in when he heard a call behind him.

"Leon." She stood in the shadow, between the fence and the house wall.

"Hey," His heart skipped a beat.

"I saw you leaving..." she started out. "Alone..."

"Yeah," Leon gazed across the top of his car into her eyes. "Byron wanted to stay."

"I'm glad."

"Why's that?"

"You've got a spare seat now," Lorna replied. "And I can come with you."

Leon woke with smile on his face, but instead of getting up, he continued to lie, marvelling at the girl curled up beside him. Her peaceful face enthralled him, and he continued to watch her, unable to tear himself away. Finally, realising he would otherwise be late, he slipped out of bed and tip-toed to the bathroom. After a quick shower he changed into his work shirt and a clean pair of pants and went back to find her still asleep.

"Lorna," he spoke gently and nuzzled her ear. "Wake up..." Her eyes opened and Leon watched as they came into focus, meeting his.

"Morning handsome, are you off already?"

"Yeah, I have to go to work," Leon tried to hide his disappointment as well. "Don't you need to get up too?"

"What for?"

"I dunno," Leon shrugged. "Whatever it is you do... Being a student..."

She smiled at him, and nodded her head. "Exactly, I'm a student: this is what I do. I only have one lecture today and it's not until one o'clock."

"Wow, you've got it good," Leon gazed down at her stunned. "To think Mum actually wanted me to go to Uni... Maybe I should have, then I'd be able to sleep in with you."

"That'd be nice," Lorna admitted. "But not all courses are as cruisy as mine." She laughed. "I'm just doing B.A."

"A Bachelor of Arts?"

"Bugger-All," Lorna corrected.

"I see," Leon teased. "Well if I'll be the one earning the money, then I'll expect you to be the one in the kitchen."

"You wish," Lorna suddenly threw her pillow at him. He jumped back, but wasn't fast enough and it hit him in the face. Quick for retribution he picked up the pillow and was about to fling it back when he saw Lorna yank the blanket over her head and go into hiding, cocooning herself into it. He cracked up and had to laugh more when he saw the rolled blanket shaking with her laughter, but then he sobered as he remembered the time.

"Dammit, I need to go," he threw the pillow aside.

"Okay," came her muffled reply as she unrolled herself and reappeared. "I'll catch you later though?"

"Yes." He leant down and kissed her.

"I know that look," Simon, whose shift coincided with his for once, picked up on it immediately.

"What?" Leon asked.

"Dude, I can see love hearts coming out of your head."

"Yeah right…"

"Don't even try to deny it," Simon was all teeth. "So who's the lucky lady?"

"That's for me to know," Leon replied defensively. "And you *not* to find out."

"Oh, tell all."

"Maybe I'll let you meet her one day," Leon sidestepped. "But right now, I need to sort some more tyres for tomorrow…"

When the topic was cars, Simon was all business and he immediately became serious. "What do you need?"

"Maybe three sets of spares, on rims."

"Not more? I'd hate to run out of tyres in the comp... You can always use them later you know..."

Leon shook his head. "I can barely afford three as it is."

"You'll regret that," Simon voiced his opinion. "But, I'll sort it," he picked up the phone and spoke with the tyre dealer as though they were old friends.

"They've only got six rims left for your stud pattern anyway," he turned back to Leon. "They're kerbed so he'll let you have them cheap."

"Mint, now how about a car trailer?" Leon asked when Simon finished the call.

"Yeah, I know a place. Want me to check for ya?"

"That's okay," Leon shook his head. "Just give me the number. I need to get hold of my mate first anyway." Leon picked up the phone and dialled Byron's number. He let it ring, but received no answer. He kept trying throughout the morning and finally, in his lunch break, he received a disgruntled:

"What?"

"Byron, hey, I've been trying to get hold of you..." Leon paused when he heard a groan. "You alright?"

"Not really."

"You at work?"

"No."

"Where then?"

"In bed."

"Still?" Leon exclaimed. "It's past noon."

"Real? Oh argh..!"

"Sounds like you're dying?"

"Feels like it."

"Hungover, huh?"

"You could say that..."

"So you made it into town then?"

"I think so – yeah."

"Was it good?"

"Maybe, I don't really remember…"

"Must've been," Leon had to smile. "So, is your dad okay about the Hilux?"

"What do you mean?"

"I asked you yesterday, I need it to tow the Silvia…"

"You did?" Byron's voice was vague. "I'll call you back."

"Thanks." Leon hung up. He wondered what to do next, but true to his word, Byron called back quickly and confirmed the Hilux, even for that evening.

"I can get you after work. I just need a bit more sleep first."

"Cool," Leon laughed and ended the call. From there it all fell into place. He arranged a trailer and bought a new fire extinguisher and helmet from his work. With the main necessities out of the way, he tried to cater for any unplanned eventualities and, at Simon's recommendation, bought a selection of spare parts that might allow him to keep his car in the running. This included the basics, a fuel can, more engine oil, spark plugs, brake pads and of course, the ever-useful cable ties. With his credit card wincing, but his enthusiasm unabated, he was finally ready for his big drift day.

The rest of the afternoon went quickly and, as promised, Byron picked him up from work.

"See ya tomorrow Si." Dragging his purchases out to the Toyota, Leon gaped when he saw Byron. His usually big, jovial friend seemed to have shrunk. There were dark rings under his eyes and his skin was pale.

"You look like crap," Leon greeted him and smiled at the irony, it was his turn to be honest.

"I feel like it too," Byron forced a grin. "But don't worry, I'll be there tomorrow."

"Cool." Leon let Byron sit in silence while they drove and he did all the talking. He explained the next day and how

Byron would be able to help with changing tyres and anything else that might come up, particularly any mechanical problems. Byron readily agreed. They picked up the rented trailer and spare rims and drove to Leon's. Byron backed the trailer up the driveway alongside the Silvia and together they unhitched it. However, when Leon invited him in, Byron declined and excused himself from anymore socialising.

"Sorry, I need to recuperate for tomorrow."

"No probs," Leon understood. "See you in the morning."

"You got it," Byron waved and drove away.

Inside, Leon found his mum standing in the hallway. It seemed that she was waiting for him and he had a feeling he knew why.

"Hi Mum, how was your day?" he greeted her awkwardly.

"Good," his mum replied. "I must say I got quite a surprise this morning though."

"Oh yeah…" Leon mumbled and made a show of untying his shoes and putting them on the rack.

"She seems very nice," his mum continued. "Pretty too..."

"She is," Leon nodded, not looking at her.

"I hope you don't mind, but I invited her over for dinner."

"When?" Leon looked up and saw her smiling at him.

"At seven."

"That's in five minutes," Leon blurted.

"I know, you'd better get cleaned up," his mum suggested and Leon looked down at his work clothes. It had been a hot day and he desperately needed a shower.

"You might have to keep her company until I'm done," he ran past his mum and shot up the stairs to the bathroom.

When Leon came back down the stairs, clean and in fresh clothes, he found Lorna and his mum chatting in the kitchen. Tamsin couldn't even get a word in and was busily tugging at her mum's skirt to get their attention.

"Hey Leon," Lorna interrupted her conversation and turned when she saw him.

"Hey." He was awkward in front of his mum and gave her a quick peck on the cheek. To make matters worse Tamsin giggled at him.

"Eww Leon!"

"I've got one for you too, Tink," to hide his embarrassment, he bent down hurriedly and picked her up, lifting her to his eye level, and planted a kiss on her cheek.

"Yuck," she giggled and frantically wiped it away with little hands.

"I just can't get over how cute your sister is," Lorna said as Leon set Tamsin back down. "Oh, I almost forgot." She produced a doll with blonde hair and a blue dress from her handbag. "Tamsin, I want you to meet Lucy."

"Hello Lucy," Tamsin fell in love immediately and eagerly folded the doll into her arms.

"Can I keep her?"

"She's all yours now."

"That's really nice of you Lorna," Leon's mum spoke.

"No problem, it's nice to find her a new home."

"Well," Leon cleared his throat. "Dolls are great and all, but how about that food? I'm starving."

"Oh you..." his Mum chided. "But yes, it's almost ready."

They laughed a lot during dinner and Leon relaxed as he saw that his mum and Tamsin got on well with Lorna. After dinner they all cleaned up together and, against all protests, Lorna got busy scrubbing the pots.

"Don't get too used to this," she warned Leon when she caught him looking at her thoughtfully. She waved the brush threateningly, dripping suds. He put the dishes down, which he had carried in from the dining table, and backed away.

"I'll just enjoy it while it lasts."

Afterwards, Leon and Lorna said good night and went up to his room to watch a movie.

"What movie did you have in mind?" Lorna wanted to know once they were in his room.

"None. I just wanted you to myself."

"Really," Lorna raised an eyebrow. "And why would you want that?"

"I'll show you."

Leon woke early. They had left the curtains open and golden light already flooded his bedroom. Today was the big day. He sat up so abruptly that the bed shook and he woke Lorna too.

"Morning," he gazed down at her. "How did you sleep?"

"Good," she yawned. "But a bit more would be better."

"Oh come on, it's time to go racing," Leon bounced excitedly on the bed.

"Alright," she sat up, rubbing her eyes. "Let's go then."

"That's my girl," he hugged her spontaneously and sprang out of bed.

They took turns to shower quickly and then went down to breakfast. Just when they had finished eating, Leon became aware of a diesel engine rumble approaching outside. Opening the door, he stepped out and was surprised by how warm it was already. He looked across to the driveway and saw that Byron had arrived. Leon went over to his friend as he climbed out of the cab, still looking a bit on the pale side.

"Hey man, not late am I?"

Leon shook his head. "Feeling better?"

"Much," Byron nodded. "And how's our drifter?"

"Good," Leon dismissed the question. "I'm keen to get going though."

"Yup, cool." Together they dragged the car trailer over to the back of the Hilux. Hitching it on, they lowered the ramp in preparation for its cargo. "Damn," Byron grunted and ran his arm across his brow. "I'm sweating already."

"It's supposed to get real hot today," Leon agreed and moved over to the Silvia. He slipped into the driver's seat and a sudden wave of excitement hit him. When he turned the key, she pulsed eagerly to life, idling high before settling back into an easy burble. Taking a deep breath, he slotted in first gear and carefully eased her onto the trailer. Once she was on, Leon switched her off again and quickly fitted the new fire extinguisher while Byron lifted the trailer ramps and tightened the straps holding the car in place. Next they turned their attention to all the spare parts, the toolkit and the fuel container, making sure that everything was there. Finally, Leon retrieved his bag, which contained his shoes, race-overalls and helmet and chucked it on the back of the Toyota.

"Can you think of anything else?" Byron asked.

Leon didn't reply right away, but looked over the trailer and the items on the back of the Hilux thoughtfully. Finally he shook his head. "Pretty sure that's it."

"So we're good to go?"

"Nearly," Leon turned back to the house. He was just about to go towards it, when Lorna appeared, lugging a blue cooler. "Ah, here she is."

"Oh, you lucky..." Byron breathed from behind him. Leon was unable to suppress his smile. He didn't turn around.

"Dude, I can't believe it," Byron hissed. "And she's even carrying food." This time Leon had to laugh.

"What's so funny?" Lorna eyed them suspiciously.

"Nothing," Leon sobered.

"Is that for me?" Byron also sidestepped neatly.

"Um, yup," Lorna smiled. "Some of it."

"Nice," Byron reached out and took the cooler off her, placing it carefully with the rest of the items on the back of the Hilux. "So are you doing another bikini comp today?"

"They're not having one this time," Lorna shook her head.

"But that's the only reason I'm going..."

"I thought you were helping with the car?" Lorna laughed.

"Hardly," Byron shook his head and indicated the Silvia on the trailer. "He doesn't need me – that thing's unstoppable... So will your friends be there?"

"Katie and Alisa said they'd go," Lorna nodded. "And Danica of course."

"Are they single?" Byron pressed.

"Katie and Alisa are," Lorna smiled.

"Alright," Byron rubbed his hands together, but then his expression changed. "Did one of them happen to slap me on Thursday?"

"Alisa told me about that," Lorna giggled. "She said she landed you a good one."

"Oh okay," Byron scratched his cheek awkwardly.

"She also wanted me to tell you that she was sorry, and if you were still interested in knowing the answer, then I should give you her number."

"Are you kidding?" Byron burst out, but then his brow furrowed. "I don't remember what I asked though..."

"She didn't say, but it must've been good."

"You should call her," Leon kept a straight face.

"Or just talk to her at the track," Lorna suggested.

"You can tell her you're sorry as well," Leon nodded, but had to look away.

"Maybe I should... Anyway, we should go."

They clambered into the Hilux, with Lorna squeezing into the narrow back seat. Byron was just about to pull away when Lorna stopped him.

"Leon, there's your mum, I think she wants something."

"Dammit, she'll probably try and stop me from going," he sighed as his mum hurried over to them. He wound down his window. "Hey, what's up?"

"Leon," she stepped up to his open window and held out a folded piece of clothing. "I've kept this for years," she paused. "I was hoping you might wear it today."

"Uh, okay..."

"It's your dad's," his mum noticed his expression and unfolded it. It was a singlet. "He wore it to every race… He used to say it was his good luck charm," She bit her lip and looked down at it. Leon noticed that her hands shook. "But not on that day…"

"Why not?" Leon swallowed.

"I washed it but forgot to put it in the dryer…" His mum couldn't meet his eyes. A tear slid down her cheek and she wiped it away quickly. "He couldn't wear it because it was still wet," she ended simply and Leon stared at her. Byron and Lorna listened to their exchange in silence.

"I'll wear it," Leon's voice was quiet but purposeful. He reached out and took it from her. "Thanks Mum."

"Please be careful," she forced a smile.

"I will," he promised. "I'll see you later." His mum was standing on the lawn, watching them go, as Byron rolled the Toyota out onto the street with the trailer and Silvia in tow. Making their way to the raceway, they remained silent for a long time. Leon gazed down at the white singlet. In the centre of the chest was a red Nismo logo and beneath it, written in black marker pen, was a faded signature. "Who do you think signed it?" he asked quietly and Byron glanced across, while Lorna peered over his shoulder.

"Not sure," Byron shook his head. "Definitely a Japanese name though." He turned back to the road.

"Whoever it was must've meant something to my dad, so it's going on…" Leon took his t-shirt off and slipped into the singlet. It fit him well and the light cotton felt good against his skin. "I think I'm ready now," he was only half-joking. Lorna reached over and put her hand on his shoulder.

They reached the raceway and Byron drove the Hilux in between the gates. They were waved on towards the pits and found that many other competing racers had also made an effort to get in early. The pit lanes were buzzing. Byron drove between the clutter of cars, wheels, tools and crew, looking for a vacant position that they could claim for themselves, but the pits were crowded to overflowing and none of them could see a spot to make their base.

Rolling along slowly, they gazed around at all the activity. Drifting had certainly taken a firm hold now as a legitimate motorsport. The competition was abundant and the cars were outright mean. Many of them sported deep-dish rims, big body kits, lowered suspension and were lavishly decorated and decaled with the logos of their sponsors.

Silvias and Skylines were by far the majority. Other vehicles that speckled the lanes included Cefiros, Laurels and several 180SXs. There was no doubt that Nissans were dominating the drifting world and it was refreshing to see something different when they laid eyes on Simon's RX-7, which was standing at an angle, with the bonnet raised and both back wheels off the ground. She had been re-sprayed for the occasion and the straw-blonde drifter was busy beside it, working solidly. He looked up as they coasted past and caught Leon's eye.

"Slept in, did ya?"

"Nah," Leon laughed and Byron brought the Hilux to a halt. "Hardly slept at all."

"I wouldn't be able to either," Simon chuckled. "Not with her around," he nodded at Lorna.

"Uh, um… That's not what I meant."

"I know," Simon grinned. "But it's fun hassling you." He left his task and stepped up beside Leon's passenger door. Reaching through the window, he extended his hand to Lorna in the back. "Since Leon is so bad with introductions… I'm Si."

"I know," Lorna smiled warmly.

"Wow, you wouldn't happen to have any sisters?"

"None your age," Lorna laughed.

"What about single friends?"

"I've already baggsed them," Byron spoke up defensively. "And I'm not sharing."

"I'm always too late," Simon shook his head regretfully.

"Not when it comes to drifting though, eh?" Leon tried to steer the conversation back. "So you all set for it?"

Simon didn't reply at once and his expression changed. He turned and looked over his Batman. "You want some more advice?" he paused and shook his head in mock exasperation. "Stick to pistons. I mean, rotors haul when they haul, but they really like to make problems – the sort of problems you don't want just before the race."

"Why, what's the issue?"

"Only had her rebuilt recently, but I think the Apex seals are going again already cause she's drinking oil and fouling up the plugs."

"Sure hope she holds up," Leon sympathised.

"No, you don't," Simon chuckled and shook his head, "We're competing against each other."

"Not this again," Leon rolled his eyes. "Cam and Taz were saying that yesterday... Dude, I'll be happy if I win a battle."

"We'll see," Simon smiled knowingly. "But, you should get ready. They're starting to check each car now."

"Right, we'll catch you later," Leon replied and Byron threaded the Hilux on. A little way further they found what they were looking for, an unused niche, between two other drift teams. It was large enough to accommodate the Hilux and trailer, with room left over for the Silvia. Byron slid into the gap and switched the Hilux off. The three of them clambered out.

"Good luck," Lorna turned to Leon. "We'll be yelling our heads off for you."

"I'll try not to climb any more fences," Leon grinned and gave her a hug.

"You'll be fine – just have fun."

As Lorna left to find her friends, Leon and Byron immediately got busy. The Silvia was rolled off the trailer and they set up camp around it, placing the trolley jacks and their tools within easy reach. Working quickly, they launched into the task of readying the Silvia. All the while they were egged on by the roar of engines and shrill of tyres, which provided a carpet of noise as other drifters, who had been checked and cleared, began their practice rounds.

The track official arrived and Leon and Byron stood back and watched nervously while he inspected the Silvia. It didn't take long and they relaxed when he approved them and moved on to check the next competitor. They were giving her one last look-over when a Nissan Terrano stopped beside them. Leon recognised the occupants and the red car it towed.

"Wazup!" Taz called out.

"Hey guys," Leon went over to the vehicle.

"She's all good?"

"Yeah, she should run alright," Leon gazed at his car. Hugging her broad wheels on short, cambered suspension, the bruised and battered machine was still holding her own and instilled excitement in him.

"She went fine when you took me for a spin..." Taz opined.

"Yeah, if you have any trouble though, make sure you come find us," Cam spoke up. "We might be able to help."

"Even though we're competing?" Leon raised an eyebrow.

"'Course," Cam laughed. "Besides, we still owe you one." His eyes narrowed suddenly. "Where'd you get that?"

"What?"

"Your top," Cam pointed at his chest.

"It was my dad's, why?"

"It's signed by Keiichi Tsuchiya."

"Keiichi Tsuchiya?" Leon looked down at the signature in the middle of his chest. "Who's he?"

"He basically invented drifting," Cam and Taz both stared at him.

"That explains why it was my dad's good luck charm," Leon said wistfully. "Apparently he wore it when he raced."

"I would too," Taz was envious. "I'd even sleep in it."

"You have to look after it," Cam agreed. "Especially if it was your dad's." Leon nodded uneasily, but didn't reply. "Well we'd best get moving." Cam changed the topic.

"Okay," Leon watched them rolling away.

"The inventor of drifting?" Byron interrupted his thoughts and Leon turned to him.

"That's what they said," he shrugged uncertainly.

"Well if Cam's right," Byron mused. "Then make sure you wear it under these," Byron handed him his overalls.

"Alright," Leon accepted them. "Can you start the car and get her warmed up?"

"Sure," Byron agreed readily and went to the S13. Turning the key, he left her idling and came back to Leon, who had shrugged into his tight-fitting, fireproof race-overalls and was pulling on the slim driving shoes.

"Looking nice," Byron teased. "You just need a cape now."

"Very funny," Leon made a face. "Some board-shorts would be good though. It's way too hot for this."

"I have to agree with you there," Byron nodded and Leon noticed there were beads of sweat on his nose.

"You can start your practice laps now," one of the race officials appeared.

"Okay, thanks..." Leon finished tying up his laces. Eagerly he went to the S13. Byron stood by his open window and watched as Leon strapped himself in and pulled the black helmet over his head.

"Ready?"

"Yeah, think so," Leon revved the engine experimentally and the RB26 wound up with a deafening growl.

"She is," Byron grinned. "Go show them who is boss."

"You got it," Leon held out his hand and they high-fived.

Andy stood waiting at his front door step. Restlessly he looked up and down the street and then checked the time again. It was nearly 8am. The guy was late. Fuming and fidgeting, Andy considered going back inside and phoning him. He was just about to, when he saw the van turn into his street.

"Finally!" Andy stormed down to the footpath. As the van neared, his eyes were drawn to its trailer with gleaming cargo. The Cefiro perched gracefully up on the trailer, flaunting her magnificent new pearl-white paint. The van slowed and pulled up beside him. Stu stepped out.

"Sorry I'm late," he offered reluctantly.

"No problem," Andy replied distractedly and went to his car. Lounging low over her lightweight racing alloys, adorned in her aggressive body kit and sparkling white perfection, she was a far cry from the gawky family sedan that she had been. Andy reached out and ran his hand over her smooth front fender. I wish you could see this, he thought of Markus.

"Well, the whole workshop worked on her and she's all done, the paint even seems pretty dry..." Stu intruded on his thoughts and with an effort Andy tore himself away. "Normally we don't recommend such short drying times."

"I didn't have any more," Andy nodded and checked his watch. "I need to go as it is."

"Right, I'll roll her off."

"Sounds good, she's going straight on the other trailer," Andy indicated the Mazda and the car trailer sitting ready with its ramp down. The six spare sets of wheels, each wrapped in brand new rubber, already occupied the racks at the front.

"You going racing?" Stu asked gruffly and went to the back of the trailer to lower the ramps.

"Yeah," Andy helped him.

"Sounds like our work won't last too long." Stu looked at the spotless Cefiro mournfully.

"I'll try and look after her."

"Right you will," Stu muttered. He climbed up onto the trailer, opened the driver's door and squeezed himself in. The Cefiro sprang to life and Andy smiled at the awesome sound.

The raceway was already bustling with activity when Andy arrived. Most of the places in the pits had been taken, and he got many mixed looks as he drove the wagon through, trying to find a place to set up. Some of them had known Markus and knew that the Mazda had belonged to him. Andy ignored them and slowly drove on, scanning the competition and searching for a vacant spot. He was looking for the tell-tale RX-7 Batman, the red Trueno and of course, the black S13. He wanted to be close to his main rivals, but when he saw the RX-7, it was surrounded by other drifters. He had arrived too late. The red Trueno, standing at an angle with her rear end propped up, was also hemmed in.

Two cars on from it, Andy found a spot large enough. It would have to do. Aware of the scrutiny, he was careful to avoid jack-knifing and backed in cleanly. Continuing to ignore those around him, he got out and went to the trailer. As he loosened the left ramp, he heard footsteps behind him.

"That's a wicked ride."

Andy turned to find another drifter approaching. Like himself, he was dressed in tight-fitting race-overalls. It was Tom, the guy that had hosted the diesel run up in the hills.

"Just got her finished," Andy offered remotely, making no effort at pleasantry.

"What're you running under there?"

"RB30."

"Nice. Lots of torque huh?"

"Yeah," Andy agreed. He looked past Tom and suddenly his expression changed. A black Silvia had pulled out and was moving away from him, towards the start line. The pock-marked paintwork and dark window tint... Andy checked the registration plate and his jaw clenched. There was no doubt. It was the same S13 that he had battled on that fateful night. The driver was here, just like he had said. His eyes followed the Nissan as she prowled down the pit lane and joined the queue of cars at the start line.

"Andy, I'm sorry about Markus, eh," Tom paused and fidgeted. "We all are."

"Yeah," Andy nodded curtly before turning back to the car trailer, leaving Tom standing awkwardly behind him. Grimly he lowered the ramps and then got up to roll the Cefiro down onto the smooth seal. There was drifting to be done and it was time he made good on his promise.

Leon had never driven in complete race gear and the full-face helmet was heavy and restrictive around his head, while the tight race-overalls were almost claustrophobic. But despite his discomfort he was charged with anticipation as he stood in the queue behind two other race cars. This was merely practice, but already he could sense the adrenaline building up inside him. He could hardly sit still as he took in the cars he was competing with – a feral-looking Nissan R32 Skyline GTS-T with dented panels and a cracked fibreglass body kit ahead of him and the pristine S14 Silvia that lurked beside it.

Bright orange and dressed in a wide-body kit, the decaled S14 was decked in carbon fibre, from the vented aftermarket bonnet and side mirrors to the huge oversized spoiler. While, compared to her bruised rival, this machine was sublime, Leon knew that neither of them should to be underestimated. He had seen them perform in the earlier competition and knew well that they meant business. He would need to fight hard to keep up, let alone stand out to the judges.

Leon looked over as a fourth competitor nudged in beside him, a navy-blue Series 5 Mazda RX-7 who spurned the Nissan trend, but was modified to a similar degree and squatted low on cambered suspension with tyres stretched tightly over black rims. The staccato bursts of her rotary engine, exhaling through a big-bore exhaust, broke the blended rumbling of the three idling Nissans and reverberated around them. All of them quivered with barely suppressed excitement as they awaited the signal of the race official.

Abruptly the signal came. The lead Skyline driver revved his engine and the rest followed suit. Together they unleashed upon the track. Breaking their pair-formation into single-file, the four cars thundered down the smooth expanse of tarseal and Leon was among them. Tightly harnessed into his race seat, he was in another world. He couldn't believe it. How could I have denied myself this? He shook his head. This intense thrill of the race-prepped S13 propelling him down the open track with the other competitors racing ahead and hounding him from behind. The speed, the freedom, the rush – this was it!

As he came around, on the approach path for the starting drift markers, he glanced over to the embankment where the spectators were. His eyes widened in surprise. It was crawling with people. It seemed that half the city had come to watch this long-awaited competition. Spotting Lorna would be an impossible task. Leon turned his head away and took a deep breath. It required an enormous effort to summon his concentration and focus on the job at hand.

Pretending it was a real race, he chased like a maniac, shadowing and coveting the two cars ahead of him, and brought the Silvia angling in on the drift markers right behind the orange S14. They entered the drift zone and immediately the two lead cars stepped out in arcing slides that sent smoke spewing back at him. Gritting his teeth, Leon followed their example and also swept sideways with blurring tyres. Spinning the wheel, he downshifted and straightened out to exit the bend at speed, right behind the S14.

The next bend was instantly upon them and the orange coupe's tail thrust out again at a huge angle. Leon followed suit. He tried to close the gap further, but this time the smoke was so thick he could taste it – the acrid tinge on the back of his throat as it flooded through his open window, stinging his eyes and nostrils. In an instant it filled the cabin of the S13 and suddenly he couldn't see. Driving blind, with fear gnawing at him, his eyes strained to make out the track. Then, just as quickly, the smoke dispersed as the slipstream sucked it from the cabin like a giant vacuum cleaner. His vision cleared but what he saw sent waves of shock ripping through him.

Directly ahead, the Skyline had spun. It sat in the middle of the track – facing back towards him. Reacting frantically, Leon braked and flung the steering wheel over. The sudden transfer in weight threw his car off-balance. She teetered on the edge, threatening to lose control and spin herself, but miraculously she clung on and began to slide again. Continuing to brake, his tyres scrubbed away to a fierce shriek and they skidded past the stranded Nissan with millimetres to spare.

Leon corrected his mad slide to prevent flying off the track and managed to keep three wheels on the seal. With his hands trembling, he tried to focus on the next bend, the sweeper, but his speed was way down. Still he coaxed the Silvia forward, yet only managed to press her backend out in a furtive slide as he continued through. He knew it was poor. Angry at himself, he shoved his foot down. The ending cones flew past and he shot out of the drift zone. The S14 was well ahead and already entering the pits. Leon trailed her in.

When he neared their spot in the pits he saw Byron running over from where he had been watching on the concrete parapet that separated the pits from the track. "That was so close! Are you alright?"

"Yeah," Leon nodded and parked the Silvia.

"Good dodge," Byron was relieved. "The RX-7 slammed right into the Skyline."

"Are you serious?" Leon demanded, his own shock momentarily forgotten.

"Yeah, it was intense. He wasn't as quick as you," Byron nodded vigorously. "Come see." He was already running back towards the parapet. Many of the other drifters and pit crew were hurrying towards it also and climbing up the steps. Leaving the engine idling, Leon clambered out. He ran after Byron and squeezed up beside him. The others were all talking at once, but Leon ignored them and gazed out across the track, to where the Skyline and the RX-7 lay. Surrounded by body kit remnants and shattered glass, they made a tragic sight. The safety crew fussed around them. Eventually the drivers were led away and Leon was relieved to see that they didn't seem hurt.

"Well, they won't be racing anymore today," Byron mused.

"Not in those cars anyway," Leon bit his lip. How much effort had it taken them to prepare for this day? And now it had ended for them during their practice run, before the qualifying had even begun. They continued to watch as the crew worked quickly, towing away the two wrecks and sweeping the track clean. Slowly the other onlookers began to disappear back to their cars and Leon and Byron returned to the Silvia. As they approached they could hear her cooling fans working overtime to dispel the high temperature from the engine bay. Byron eyed her over critically. "You know, rough though she is, I still don't want to see her being towed back."

"Neither," Leon nodded, but didn't smile and Byron looked at him closely.

"You okay?"

"Yeah," Leon answered hurriedly. "Come help me check her over again."

As the sound of punished engines and tyres resumed on the race track, they made a quick circuit around the S13. They found the tyres already well-worn, just from that one run, although there was still enough tread on them. The suspension also looked fine and Leon straightened to lift the bonnet, but hurriedly dropped it again.

"That's hot!"

"Wait a sec," Byron went to the Hilux and came back. "Here use this," he handed Leon an oil-stained rag. "And this," grinning broadly, he produced a stick.

"You brought it?" Leon stared at the stick.

"Thought it might come in handy."

"Give me that," Leon took it and, lifting the bonnet gingerly, tilted his face away when the heat of the engine hit him. He quickly pinned the bonnet up and backed away again to give the heat time to escape. Once it was safe to return, he ran a quick eye over the engine. Everything seemed in order, but then it should be, it was built to be abused. Looking down at the impressive engine, Leon was recharged. His misgivings faded and were once again replaced by excitement.

"Looks fine," he lowered the bonnet again and wiped the sweat from his forehead.

"Good," Byron nodded. "Cause, you should get some more practice in."

"You're right."

"Just maybe hold back a bit for now."

"Yes Mum," Leon lifted the helmet back over his head.

This time there were no other cars waiting and he was first in the queue. Glancing in his rear-view he saw a familiar competitor coming up to join him, and moments later the sleek car slid in to his right. The driver lowered his window and his white teeth showed in the gap of his open visor.

"Leon, what's happening?"

"Not much," he grinned back. "I'll just drift all over you."

"Dreams are free," Simon laughed. "My awesomeness is way out of your reach!"

"Yeah, but what about your car?" Leon chuckled. "Rotaries blow remember."

"She'll hold up. She hasn't let me down yet."

"First time for everything."

"First time you saw this?" Simon raised his middle finger.

"Nah, I've seen a few idiots in my time."

"No doubt whenever you look in the mirror, but hey, time to go," Simon pointed forwards. "See ya on the other side."

With these words the Batman throttled off the line like a missile leaving Leon stunned in his seat, but he reacted quickly, and shot forward in hot pursuit. Bawling down the track with Simon leading the way, the other cars followed closely. As they hurled in on the drift markers, he noticed Simon slowing down and the gap between them shrunk until Leon was right up on his case. The Batman's backend whipped out and she presented her flank to him, almost at full broadside. Simon poured the power on and the 13B crackled and hissed, spitting fire from her twin exhausts. Wheels spinning loosely, the RX-7 trailed smoke as she slipped out of the first bend and entered the next at maximum angle.

Simon's style and talent was immense, and Leon realised his own slides were amateur in comparison, but he caught on immediately and, imitating Simon's technique, he began to use the power of his engine more to maintain the drift, rather than relying on his inertia. It felt awesome and, ignoring Byron's words, he flowed through the course in what felt like one continuous slide, keeping right behind Simon. The sweeper loomed before him and Leon let the S13 go, giving everything she had. He poured through it in an epic drift that had him parallel to Simon with just a foot of separation, tyres smoking and squealing all the way. Coming out of the sweeper, they straightened together in sync and the two cars hurtled past the ending markers at full tilt.

The sound of their engines echoed loudly around the raceway, but not loud enough to drown out the crowd. Simon shook a fist out of his window and the crowd hollered even louder. Suddenly Leon realised that the gesture was more directed at him and couldn't help but grin as he followed his friend in.

Rolling easily down the pit lane, Simon came to a halt just after Leon's base and hopped out. He waited for Leon to park, before stepping up to his window.

"See I knew you had it in ya. That was wicked."

"Yeah?" Leon wrestled his helmet off. "Your awesomeness didn't make me look like a noob?"

"Well, sure I still smoked you," Simon grinned. "But if you drive like that in the qualifying you'll get through for sure."

"That'd be good."

"Yeah, then I can shut you down in a real battle," Simon's grin broadened.

"We'll see, but you should be more worried about Kyle."

"Yeah, I am a bit. He's been driving solid," Simon became serious. "But I'm more worried about the Batty overheating..."

"Supposed to get hotter too..."

"Yeah, not good," Simon roused himself. "I better go."

Simon went back to the Mazda and Leon started on his own round of checks again. Crouching down at the rear wheel, he ran his hands over the worn back tyre with a frown. They were wearing much faster than he had expected.

"Hey," Byron appeared. "I was just at the embankment."

"Uh huh," Leon spoke distractedly.

"I saw Lorna – she had some hot friends with her."

Leon's fingers stilled and he looked up at his friend. "Did she see me drive?"

"'Course she did."

"And?"

"And what?" Byron teased.

"What did she think?"

"She loved it – she wouldn't shut up," Byron smiled and Leon suddenly grinned from ear-to-ear. "You and Si fully hauled," Byron continued. "You should've heard the rest of the crowd, and the commentator."

"Cool."

"Yeah, you just keep doing what you're doing," Byron was adamant.

"Okay," Leon agreed and stood up.

Leon drove several more practice laps and his confidence grew with each one. Concentrating on fine-tuning the techniques he had gleaned from his run with Simon, he maintained good speed and kept it smooth and fluid. Under his guidance, the S13 had hummed right through the chicane, rear wheels milling flat-out. He had tackled the sweeper on a near-perfect line of attack each time, holding his drift all the way through and hitting each clipping point cleanly to come pouring out onto the straight at high speed. The noise of the crowd followed him back to the pits.

Leon and Byron worked quickly to replace the, now bald, rear wheels with fresh ones that sported a good 8mm of tread and checked over the car yet again. Mechanical issues, accentuated by the sheer heat of the day and the pressure of the race track, meant cars were already dropping out of the competition like flies. Leon did not want to suffer the same fate so he scrutinised the S13 over thoroughly after each run, before quickly sculling water, towelling the sweat from his face and heading out again.

Leon went into the first qualifying run feeling very confident. Artfully he flowed through the entire course, smoking, sliding and putting on a real show to gain style points. He flashed his lights at the judges, waved a hand out of the window at full lock and put on a dominant performance. Four times he slid through the course and each time felt better than before.

Finishing his last qualifying run, he returned to the pits and parked. Leaving the car with Byron, he joined the other drivers, who stood in a huddled group. Jokes and laughter belied the tension as they waited for the verdict of the judges.

"The judges have decided..." the commentator's voice finally crackled over the loud speakers. "Those drivers making the top sixteen are...." He left them hanging for a moment before calling out the first name.

"Simon Anders..."

More names were announced and Leon smiled when he heard Cam's come up. Then his heart nearly missed a beat when his own name echoed eerily out around the racecourse.

"Told ya you'd get there," Simon was suddenly beside him and knuckled his arm. "Good moves man."

"Good moves yourself." Leon's face cracked. He punched him back, but Simon dodged.

"Hardly, I always knew I'd make the cut."

"Yeah? Been giving favours to the judges again?"

"Whatever it takes," Simon's eyes twinkled.

"Each to their own," Leon made a face, but couldn't contain his smile. The rest of the names were announced but Leon was no longer listening. He didn't care. All that mattered was that he'd made it through. He'd been given the chance to put his talent to the test in the battles. He was still day-dreaming when the drivers around him suddenly began to disperse and hurry back to their cars.

"What's happening now?" he called after Simon.

"Weren't listening, huh?" Simon accused and Leon shook his head. "We've only got five minutes till the briefing and then another fifteen before the battles start... I still need to suss something on the Batty."

"Oh, okay," Leon nodded and returned to the S13. Byron saw him coming, and, his dignity momentarily forgotten, ran to meet him. "Dude!" he cried out. A huge grin covered his face and for a moment Leon thought his friend was going to pick him up. But then Byron stopped in front of him and grabbed his hand, shaking it so vigorously it felt like his arm would pop out of its socket. "You made it, you fully made it!"

"Thanks," Leon hurriedly dislodged his hand out of Byron's paw. "I'm stoked. Your help's been awesome too."

"Don't mention it," Byron led the last metres back to the Silvia. "So what's happening? When are the battles starting?"

"I've only got a few minutes now…" Leon explained.

"I'll check her over some more while you're at the briefing," he offered.

"Cool," Leon accepted gratefully. "Can you have a look at the back struts? Something felt loose there."

"Will do," Byron nodded. "Oh look," he indicated with his chin. "Someone's here to see you."

"Leon," he turned at the familiar voice when two arms were suddenly thrown around him and he was hugged tightly. Leon stood for a moment, unmoving. But then he closed Lorna into his arms, and, ignoring the looks from some of the others in the pits, he hugged her back.

"I thought the pits were closed to spectators?"

"I know," Lorna looked up into his face. "But I had to see you and wish you more good luck."

"Thanks," he replied seriously. "It means a lot." Leon let her go reluctantly when he became aware of the other drivers making their way to the meeting. "I think I have to run now."

"Okay, just one more thing…" And before he could reply, she kissed him. "That's for drifting so well," she drew back.

"You're amazing." Leon smiled stupidly.

"I could say the same thing about you," Lorna chuckled.

Smiling, Leon watched her leave and then turned back to Byron, suddenly realising that he was still standing right behind him.

"I'll be back in about ten," he said quietly, not meeting his friend's eyes.

"Sure thing," Byron acknowledged. "And Leon?"

"Yeah?" he braced himself for ridicule.

"You're right: she *is* amazing," Byron met his eyes squarely. "You're real lucky."

Leon nodded dumbly. He turned away and began to follow the other drifters when he heard a call behind him.

"Wait up." Swinging around, he saw Cam and Taz coming towards him. He stopped to let them catch up. "Wicked that you got in."

"Yeah, thanks. How's the Trueno?"

"Good," Cam replied. "Apart from changing tyres, nothing needs doing, so Taz thought he'd come along as well."

The three of them reached the other drifters who were standing quietly in a semi circle, with two race coordinators waiting for the last ones to arrive.

It was just past noon now and the sun stood at its zenith, beaming down in full force. Hunching at the worn back wheel of his Cefiro, Andy cranked the trolley jack doggedly to raise the tail section from the ground. As he worked, sweating heavily, he scowled at the other drifters around him. They were here to battle against each other, yet many of them chatted and joked as they prepared their cars for each race. Andy himself took no part in the conversations. He wasn't here to make friends – he was here to win. So far the Cefiro had held up well – very well. The brutal, high-torque power from the RB30 was unstoppable and with her new suspension and wide wheels she was a natural slider. He had qualified comfortably among the top sixteen drivers and barely had to exert himself.

Brooding, Andy removed the remaining nuts and lifted the wheel off the hub. Yes, she was running strong, but now that the novices had been purged, he wanted to put her to the test against the other drivers, especially the black Silvia. He had seen her faultless performance in the qualifying rounds. He had seen her slide smoothly through the course, smoking and showing off. He had heard the crowd cheer and whistle. His jaw clenched tightly as hatred consumed him. With an effort he brought his emotions back under control. He desperately wanted to put that arrogant driver in his place, but to do so he first needed to make his odds more favourable against the other competitors. Impulsively he glowered across at the red lift-back, which was parked nearby. The old Toyota represented strong competition, but the RX-7 Batman was an even bigger rival. Could he get to it?

Plotting darkly, Andy lifted a new wheel onto the naked hub and replaced the nuts. He was in the process of lowering the jack again, when the loudspeakers boomed around the pit lanes, instructing all qualifiers to attend the battle briefing. It was the call that he had been waiting for. Quickly he tightened the last nut, before standing up and reaching into the open window of the Cefiro. He withdrew a small bottle and tucked it into the pocket of his overalls.

By now the other drifters were making their way out of the pit lanes, but Andy took his time and walked slowly, trailing them at a distance. When he approached the red Trueno, he saw that no one was near it. Quickly he bent down and pretended to tie his shoelaces while he waited for the last of the drivers to leave.

Glancing around him, Andy made sure that not even the handful of crew members that stood chatting idly, a few cars away, paid him any heed, before he slipped across and hunkered down beside the Toyota. Fortunately the driver had left the bonnet up to aid the engine cooling. This made Andy's task all the easier. Deftly he reached up and unscrewed the oil cap on top of the engine, then withdrew the bottle from his pocket. His fingers shaky with haste, he pulled the lid off and shoved the tip of the bottle into the oil-fill opening. With the contents of the bottle half empty, he withdrew it and quickly replaced the oil cap. Peering around again, he confirmed that he was still not being observed, before he stood up.

Walking on, he reached the Silvia and, unable to believe his luck, he found it unattended. Once again, he glanced around him, before moving purposefully over to the black machine.

"Leon? You back already?" suddenly a muffled voice came from under the car and Andy jolted. In his haste, he had nearly tripped over the pair of legs that stuck out from beneath the back of the car. He recoiled and scurried away. Several cars further on, he saw the Batman RX-7 waiting for him, standing alone with her bonnet up.

"Hey you," a shout made him jump. He considered ignoring it, pretending he hadn't heard, when the call was repeated. It was clearly directed at him. Hesitantly, he turned around. Back near the Silvia, a big guy with messy hair was gesturing to get his attention. "What're you doing?"

"Uh."

"You're competing right?"

"Yeah..."

"You're supposed be at the briefing."

"Oh, right," Andy acknowledged and hastily turned away. His gaze swept mournfully over the Batman RX-7, just a few feet in front of him. He still had half the contents of his bottle and this car represented his main competition, even more so than the Toyota. But now that he was being watched, it may as well have been behind a prison fence. He couldn't get near it undetected. Scowling, Andy hurried to the meeting.

After the briefing, Leon found himself at the start line again. This time, however, it was the real thing and his first challenger was a very capable-looking, silver Nissan 180SX. Fitted with a full Vertex body kit and dumped out low on 17-inch rims, she oozed performance. Leon knew she would be a formidable opponent, but he found it difficult to concentrate on the race ahead. High in the blue, cloudless sky, the sun blazed down relentlessly and the heat was stifling. Sitting at rest and without air-conditioning, the black Silvia was quickly turning into an oven. Leon struggled to breathe. Sweating heavily, he peered out through the narrow view afforded by his open visor and waited for the signal. To make matters worse, he had left his sunglasses back in the pits and before him the track was glaring bright and painful.

"Let's get going already," Leon muttered. Once he got moving and the cold air swept past his open window it might just be bearable. Leon took a deep breath and blew it out noisily, directing it up over his face. While this gave him a brief moment of respite, it also dislodged a droplet of sweat from his brow. The drop trickled down, thick and salty and ran into his eye. It stung. With a lethargic movement, he took his right hand from the steering wheel and ran his fingers across his brow inside his helmet. It came away wet with sweat and he stared at it in disbelief, before wiping it dry on the leg of his overalls.

"It's out of control, eh?" his opponent called over to him out of his window.

"Yeah, I'm melting in here," Leon shook his head.

"I reckon if he doesn't let us go soon, I might have to bail on this and make a run for the beach," the other driver joked.

"I might have to join you," Leon chuckled and without thinking, he put his arm out of the window. His hand came in contact with the body of the car and he almost heard the searing hiss of vaporising sweat. With a yelp he jerked his hand back inside.

"Dude, I heard that from here," his opponent laughed.

"I could cook eggs in here," Leon took a deep breath.

The sudden fright and sharp pain woke him up and when moments later the signal was given, he responded quickly and with confidence. With deft fingers he brought the Silvia rearing off the start and thundering down the smooth seal.

The 180SX fell in behind. Accompanied by a murderous howl, the two cars blew out onto the track and closed in on the drift markers at 170km/h. The first bend shot at them and Leon feinted into it, then flicked the wheel back the right way and hammered the accelerator, causing her backend to slide out. Both rear wheels lit up and she screeched loudly as she went into the slide. Buttoning off, he counter-steered and feathered the throttle to hold her at big angle all the way through.

With the RB26 popping and crackling on the rev-limiter, he had the S13 raging out of the first stage of the S-bend and immediately swung the wheel into oversteer for the next, flinging her the other way. The Silvia's chassis groaned under the strain, and her roll cage and strut braces worked to hold her rigid. Ignoring her protest, Leon nipped at the handbrake and neatly countered. Catching her slide on opposite lock, he guided her through, gushing smoke and spitting noise.

Pouring out of the S-bend, the Silvia's weight transferred to the back again and for a split-second Leon eased the power, letting the rear wheels grip once more. The instant she began to straighten, he hit the accelerator to slingshot into the sweeper at full tilt. With his left hand on the handbrake, his right fought to hold the steering wheel. Her back end swung outwards as her rear wheels broke loose. He held her there in perfect equilibrium, gliding around the sweeping bend in a majestic arc. Then he was past the ending markers and it was time for his opponent to lead the way.

The silver 180SX also put on an impressive performance, but Leon hounded fiercely, all the way around the track. When he flowed out between the ending markers, right behind it, the judges announced their score and Leon exulted. He had won!

Back in the pits, Byron's enthusiasm was overflowing as he commended Leon on his driving. Unfailingly, he checked over the S13 while Leon got out. Unzipping his overalls to the waist, Leon fanned his singlet against the oppressive heat and drank deeply from his water bottle. But before long he was called up again. Taking another quick gulp of water, he zipped his overalls up, clambered back into his black oven, and returned to the start line.

His next challenger was a Nissan Laurel. Again Leon led the way and put down another formidable run. Then it was the Laurel's turn to lead, but the race ended abruptly when the driver overcooked it on the S-bend and spun out.

Andy had driven his first race with single-minded passion. He had learnt from his past mistakes and toned down his reckless and flamboyant style, but nonetheless he had driven his Cefiro hard, keeping the RB30 hollering murderously at the redline through the entirety of the course. Finishing victorious, he had returned to his place in the pits, his performance applauded by the judges and commentators.

In the pits, Andy maintained his resolute concentration and focused his attention on his car. The Cefiro was running flawlessly and he knew he had one of the best vehicles on the track. This knowledge increased his determination – he had to beat the black S13.

As the other drivers battled, Andy kept a watchful eye out and observed that the black coupe had also progressed to the top eight. When he was called forward again, he grimly hoped to find himself pitted against it, but instead it was the red Toyota that challenged him.

Leon was in the top four now, but despite his achievement, he and Byron were sitting glumly in the pit lanes, cowering down in the small strip of shade cast by the Silvia's body. The heat was now so intense that Leon had taken off his helmet at the first opportunity and stripped his overalls down to the waist. Byron was also troubled and they barely spoke. Every so often they took a sip of lukewarm water, but it seemed that it was sweating from them faster than they could drink.

Many of the other drivers were suffering car problems now. Overheating was the main concern, and the few drivers that were still in the competition were irrigating their radiators with cold water hoses or had switched the engine off, but left the ignition on, allowing the electric fans to continue their work unhindered. One unfortunate Skyline driver had stripped second and third gear in his transmission and another driver had burnt out his clutch. For them the competition was over. The S13, however, seemed immune to Leon's punishment. Calm and unaffected, she just kept on going. But they did have another problem and Leon was worried. A shadow suddenly loomed over them.

"Si, what's up?"

"Hey champ, bit warm, huh?"

"It's a killer," Leon agreed. Like himself Simon had stripped off the upper part of his overalls, even so he noticed that Simon was red-faced and sweating heavily.

"I'm dying," Byron groaned darkly and wiped his arm across his forehead.

"It's not stopping you though, huh?"

"Yeah, you're pulling some big moves out there," Byron looked up at Simon. "You'll take this comp out for sure."

"That's the idea," Simon smiled. "Unless this guy keeps it up. Then I'll be in trouble." He turned to Leon. "For a noob your driving is off the hook."

Leon had to smile. "I'm trying…"

"You'd better be, otherwise I'd be real worried," he glanced at the S13. "Is she handling the heat okay?"

"She's chewing through tyres like there's no tomorrow."

"I'm not surprised," Simon put his hand on the Silvia, but withdrew it again hurriedly. "She's the mean smoke machine. The crowd's loving it."

"Yeah, but we're on our last set now," Leon scratched his cheek. "And they're nearly worn through. They won't last another race."

"Are you serious?" Simon confronted him. "I told you you'd need more."

"Yeah, you did," Leon sighed. "But I didn't listen, did I."

"I've got another set, but I'll need them myself."

"They're the wrong stud pattern anyway..."

"Yeah true," Simon shook his head. "Maybe one of the others who've been knocked out has some spare wheels left." He looked around the other cars. "I'd be surprised if anybody's on four-stud though..."

"It's all good," Leon forced a smile. "I'm pretty happy getting this far... from here I'd pretty much be racing against you or Cam anyway and I don't really want to compete against my mates..."

"We're not your mates," Simon smiled. "I'll go ask."

"Thanks," Leon accepted hesitantly. "Don't worry too much though."

"I'll see," Simon promised and left.

"Speaking of Cam," Byron spoke up after a moment of silence. "I think he's actually racing right now." He indicated the parapet with his chin. "Want to go watch?"

"May as well," Leon pushed himself to his feet.

It was his turn to chase and he pursued the white Cefiro closely as they were powering into the drift zone. He had heard the commentators announce the first run of the battle in his favour at six-four, but although he was holding the advantage Cam was worried. Something wasn't right with his engine, the usually fiery 3S-GE roar held a distinctly odd pitch. Yet he had no time to dwell on it as the Cefiro shot between the starting cones and the game was on.

The Nissan immediately slipped into a tight drift and Cam shadowed her, sticking to her like glue with his steering wheel locked over and the Trueno sliding broadside. Ahead of him, the Nissan powered into the sweeper, right in front of the judging stand. With his engine blaring hoarsely at the rev-limiter, Cam chased her aggressively. Bumper to bumper, he hit the apex and swept out, using the whole of the track.

The Cefiro's power sounded defiantly from her oversized exhaust and Cam was right on her tail as tyre smoke enveloped him. Pouring into his open window, it filled the Trueno's cabin and he could barely see. The taste of it on his tongue and the burnt-sweet smell in his nostrils acted like a catalyst to his recklessness. He flung her into the opposite lock and knew that he was holding a better line. He would take this out, but the pitch of his engine suddenly rose to alarming levels. Almost instantly the noise mutated and turned into a high-pitched shriek. Harsh and abrasive it clawed at his nerve endings, making the hair on the back of his neck stand up.

The Toyota lost power and straight-lined, unable to deliver the torque to the rear wheels and hold the drift. Something was very wrong. Grimacing at the terrible, agonised sound coming from his engine, Cam swore and glanced in his rear-view mirror to see tarry-black smoke spewing out behind him. She was burning oil. Ahead of him, the Cefiro was pulling away effortlessly and Cam could taste bitter defeat. In anger, he forced the throttle into the floor.

With a last mournful effort the 3S-GE gathered her reserves and gave him her all. She blurred into high revs and the tacho needle hit the redline. The turbo came on strong and the Trueno responded instantly. Savagely she tore after the Nissan, but a large gap separated them now and Cam knew it was to no avail. While his Toyota pointed down the track straight as a nail, the Cefiro still made big angle and more smoke than a forest fire. Cam swore again, this time with resignation and his car heard him. It was over. She gave up. The mortally wounded 3S-GE threw her internals with a brutal bang and flames flared out from beneath the bonnet. Dazed from the din of the detonation, Cam slammed on the brakes and skidded his car off the track.

Summoned by the explosion, the safety crew sprinted towards him, but Cam didn't wait for them. He feared for his Trueno, like a mother for her child and, with frantic strength, tore the fire extinguisher from its mount. He ran to the front of his stricken machine and, ignoring the flames, ripped the pins out, threw the bonnet up and unleashed with the extinguisher. He took no chances and held the trigger down until it was empty. By then the safety team had arrived and were letting loose with their own extinguishers. Finally they relented and stood back while the gas blew away in the breeze.

Cam looked over the blistered contents of his engine bay with drooped shoulders and heavy disappointment. The fire had made its mark. The result was heart wrenching. Echoing across from the distant loudspeakers, he heard the commentator's words, reiterating the drama to the spectators and almost apologetically announcing his loss. Turning away, Cam looked across and saw the tow-truck, making its way towards him. The Cefiro was nowhere to be seen. It had long finished the race and disappeared back to the pits.

The tow-truck brought Cam and the Toyota back to the pit lanes. Leon and Byron were there to offer support.

"Real sorry," Leon was sincere.

"Yeah, thanks," Cam nodded and smiled ruefully. "Guess it's my turn to get towed home."

"You saw that?"

"No not really," Cam admitted. "But of course we heard about it – I sort of wish this was mum's car now, then it'd be her problem."

"Yeah," Leon chuckled. "But mums have a way of making their problems, your problem."

"I've noticed that."

"Well it's up to you now," Taz pointed out. "I'd hate to see that Cefiro come in the top three."

"Yeah," Leon nodded. "But I'm pretty much out as well."

"I thought you won your last race. You got car issues?"

"The car's okay, but we've got no more tyres," Leon was glum. "The tread I've got left won't last. I'll be lucky to make it through the first round."

"Just grab our spares. We've still got four with full tread," Cam offered immediately.

Leon shook his head. "I'm on 4x114.5 remember?"

"So are we," Cam replied. "Well, sort of."

"What? No, you're not," Leon turned to Taz questioningly.

"We are…" Taz admitted sheepishly.

"See for yourself," Cam indicated the Toyota.

"So what was all that about five stud being better?"

"It is better," Taz answered cautiously and suddenly broke into a grin. "But I was really just thinking of you."

"Well, damn me," Leon grinned back at him and new excitement flowed through him. "So you're really on 4x114.5?"

"No, we're on 4x100, but our spare set is multi stud," Cam replied. "We don't really trust them and always run them as a last resort, but they'll fit."

"Far out, that would be mint. I'll obviously pay for them."

"No worries," Cam shrugged. "Just try and beat that Cefiro." He and Taz pulled the wheels from the rack on their trailer and handed them down to Leon and Byron who accepted them gratefully and hurried away. "Well, that's us then," Cam sighed. They stood idle and uncertain, while around them, the bustle and excitement of the remaining contenders continued. Cam looked over to Taz who leant dejectedly against their broken car, also unsure of what to do next. It was a strange feeling and somehow it seemed unreal – a huge anticlimax.

"Shall we bail?" Taz asked broodingly.

"Dunno," Cam hesitated and gazed around at the other drift cars. There were only five still in the running. Two of them, a Holden Monaro V8 and Simon's RX7, were rolling out of their parked positions to run the next race. His gaze continued around and suddenly his eyes met those of the drifter he had just raced. He was hunched by his white Cefiro, working on the back wheel and watching him covertly. The instant that their eyes met the other drifter hurriedly looked away and busied himself with his task. Cam thought he detected a slight flicker in his expression – guilt maybe? Perhaps he had imagined it. He grimaced and turned back to Taz. "Stuff it. Let's see how Leon goes."

"Okay," Taz agreed and together they made their way over to the parapet.

Leon and Byron ran back to the waiting S13 with the fresh tyres. Within minutes they had the new set of wheels on and, while Leon tightened the wheel nuts, he sent Byron to tell the race officials that they were back in business. Byron came hurrying back almost immediately.

"You can go," he called out, still some metres away. "But you're up against Kyle."

"Ouch, okay."

"Here, I'll finish that." Byron yanked the wheel brace out of Leon's hands. Once more Leon donned his helmet and struck out apprehensively for his biggest contest yet.

He arrived at the starting line, and found Kyle's S15 Silvia already waiting. It dawned on Leon that he was running with the professionals now and his resolve began to weaken. His hands shook slightly and his grip on the steering wheel was tense. It's only a race, he told himself, wishing now that he had asked Daisuke for advice on how to deal with the pressure, but before he could think any more about it, the signal came and the S15 burst into motion – leading the way.

Leon battled fiercely, giving it his best shot, but his skill fell short. This competitor was simply too strong. With his pumped-up S15, Kyle trumped Leon's effort in almost every way, putting out bigger angle, more smoke, more show and higher speed. He also made better use of the track, nailing each clipping point perfectly and overall he set a higher standard. Leon summoned his last reserves but it wasn't enough. His first battle played out six to four and then in his effort to make it up on the second run, and match the broad slip angle of his opponent, he came into the sweeper way too hot and almost botched it. So very close to spinning, he trod on the brakes to save himself and the S13 immediately straight-lined painfully.

With insufficient speed to perform his now-signature broad slide through the sweeper, Leon had no chance of recovering from his costly mistake and making it through to the final. Coming out of the drift zone, his speed crept up again and the wind whistled through his open window offering some respite from the heat. The immaculate S15 trailed closely behind him and his disappointment slipped away. He still had a chance at coming third.

"Don't worry about it – you did primo, man," Byron misread his expression when Leon returned. Cam and Taz were with him.

"Yeah," Leon replied, but when he tried to get out, Byron restrained him gently. "We'll sort this." Cam and Taz nodded agreement. Professional and fast as a formula one team, they got busy around him, checking the S13 for problems. She had been pushed hard and the signs of her strain were beginning to show. Her temperature was up, with the water boiling in the radiator and gingerly Cam topped up the overflow, while Taz and Byron inspected her suspension and undercarriage. Finding no problems, they nodded.

"Go get him."

Leon acknowledged with a wave and rolled out again. He pulled up at the starting line but found it empty. Ahead of him, the track official was chatting idly with another crew member. Leon pushed his visor up, lowered his window and settled back to wait. He was contesting for third place. He could hardly believe it. What would Daisuke think when he told him? He smiled at the thought and squeezed the steering wheel slightly.

Out of the corner of his eye, he saw the white Cefiro pull up beside him. He turned to acknowledge the driver and was surprised to see his features scowling and unfriendly. "Hey you, yeah you! You're going down!" Leon flinched at the voice, more so than the words. His smile slipped and he stared at the driver. He had never seen his face properly, for it had been in the shadow of darkness on that fateful evening, but there was no doubt in his mind – it was the driver of the 180SX, the one who had held the knife. His voice was still etched into his memory and in an instant the crash replayed in his mind.

"I gave you a chance then – but not this time." The words were filled with barely suppressed violence and his eyes blazed. Leon couldn't meet his fierce gaze. Instinctively he began to turn away, but then he saw the flames again and heard the screams, the screams of excruciating pain and those echoed in desperate frustration by this man who had forced them to race. His own anger began to seep into his blood and then increased ten-fold as the image turned to his dad.

"I'm all for second chances," his voice came out sharp and brittle. "Why do you think you're not in jail right now?!" He met the other driver's eyes and it was his turn to flinch. "I think it's you who's had his chance," Leon added coldly and turned back to see the race official signalling. He took a quick, deep breath and threw the Silvia into motion, launching her forward. In his rear-view mirror, he saw the Cefiro start slower and hop unsteadily off the line, but then in one heart-stopping instant she exploded after him, blowing his lead to smithereens and hounding him all the way down the track.

Leon shot between the orange marker cones and got down to business, smoking away Cam's fresh tyres with sadistic relish. Sweeping through the S-bend in a tight line, he continued on fluidly into the next. But always the Cefiro covered him and anticipated his every move, sticking like glue and pressing him on, while dominating at huge angle. Despite trying to concentrate entirely on his driving, Leon was acutely aware of it behind him, ever sideways and billowing smoke. He tried his utmost, but couldn't shake him and suddenly it hit him that he was losing.

Biting his lower lip in frustration, he reapplied himself and burst into the sweeper at full tilt. Clutch kicking on the way in, he punched her rear end out and sent her gliding through the banked horse-shoe bend. Thrusting his left knee up against the steering wheel, he held her at full lock, shaking both fists out of his window, before yanking them back in as the end of the sweeper loomed. His hands back on the wheel and his right foot planted flat, he came rocketing out onto the straight.

He flew out of the drift zone with the Cefiro filling his rear-view mirror and knew it was good – but was it good enough? He continued his run along the looping track, swinging back around for the second battle, but kept his engine note low and listened intently for the commentator's announcement. Moments later it came, only just audible above the engine.

"Andrew Reed leads six to four."

Leon scowled. At that moment a thunderous snarl erupted behind him and the Cefiro nosed arrogantly up on his left. Leon couldn't help but glance over as the other driver pointed at him threateningly and then extended his middle finger. A loathing smirk covered his face, but before Leon could react the Cefiro thundered past to take the lead.

They were travelling at 140km/h and Leon was amazed at the ease with which the white sedan had overtaken him. They were still flying along the straight, with a hundred metres to go before it curved back around to the starting markers, when suddenly the Cefiro's taillights flared brightly and Leon had to stomp the brakes to avoid collision.

"What the..?!" he exclaimed at the erratic manoeuvre. There had been absolutely no reason for it. Then it occurred to him. The other driver was toying with him, bullying him and rubbing the loss in his face. His self control suddenly snapped. Angrily, he smashed his hand into the steering wheel. He couldn't lose. Not to him. Not now. He remembered Daisuke's words: "If you're going to do something, do it properly." His eyes narrowed and he pushed the throttle open.

The gap between them had widened, but Leon didn't relent. He shoved his foot down and the S13 went ballistic, closing in so quickly that within seconds, she was on the Cefiro's back bumper, tagging so dangerously close that mere inches separated the two cars. Power emanated from them as they angled in once more for the two orange starting cones. Black against white, their determination filled the racecourse, drawing in and captivating each spectator. Everybody could sense it. This was not a normal race. This was different. This was war.

The two cars flashed through the cones and immediately both swept into big arcing slides with engines and tyres screaming murder. The commentator's words dried up as even he was lost in the moment, awed by the display of the two drifters, who were pushing their cars and skills to the very limit. Ever so aware of each other, they blocked and parried aggressively, fighting to get the upper-hand.

"Go Leon, make this one count!" Lorna hammered both fists onto her thighs as she sat cross-legged on the grass.

"He can't hear you, you know," Byron grunted. He had gone to the embankment for a better view, but his own eyes never left the two cars out on the track and his sandwich lay forgotten on his lap as he silently willed his friend on.

Flying out of the S-bend, the Cefiro had set a manic pace and was leading with strong determination. In her previous performance she had exuded utter dominance for the entirety of the race, but now she was suddenly shifty in her response and almost defensive, like the top dog protecting her reign from the new alpha. Always the Silvia was right on her case, hunting her ruthlessly as Leon savaged across the tarmac with his rear wheels spitting and hissing smoke. Flowing through another bend, the coupe continued on her rant and the acrid cloud of grey fanned out behind, following her through.

For an instant they were both lost from view and Byron craned forward searching for a glimpse, the moment they would reappear. When they did, the Cefiro was streaming into the sweeper and the S13 breathtakingly close behind. Making huge angle, the aggressive coupe cut in so tightly that her right front wheel dropped off the track. Recklessly she pushed on, sliding across the apex, her RB26 screaming at the redline. Then she was right on the inside of the Cefiro, locked neck and neck in battle.

"Go Leon!" Lorna screamed again and jumped up, caught by the intensity of the moment.

"Out the way!" Byron yelled as other spectators came to their feet, blocking his view. He too pushed himself upright. His sandwich fell to the ground, but he didn't notice as Danica and the other girls around him all started screaming, egging on the black car out on the track, which was fighting madly to make the pass. It was so close. Leon was going to do it! Byron couldn't contain himself. His dignity forgotten he joined in, yelling wildly at his friend.

Sliding through the sweeper, Leon suddenly found himself on the inside of the Cefiro. The exit loomed and beyond that the ending markers were gleaming bright orange. Leon saw his opportunity. He ripped the gear lever back into second, and viciously forced the gas pedal to the floor. The Silvia went berserk. Still at full lock, she skidded forwards, nosing up past the white Nissan and pushing ahead.

His opponent reacted quickly in an attempt to catch him and in a brute display of her power he too stabbed his car forwards. Full of defiance, Leon kept his foot on the accelerator and had the RB26 mincing its pistons above 8000rpm before he flicked the steering wheel and switched his slide, boxing the Cefiro out. His cabin was filled with noise and energy as he drifted down the straight and burst out between the ending markers.

His heart pounding, he reined the S13 in to slow her crazed run and watched his opponent shoot past him, continuing to terrorise the track. Tyres smoking and shrilling, he vented his frustration and anger for all to see. Being passed in a drift battle could only mean one thing, and expectantly Leon waited for the announcement.

The whole racecourse was hushed silence while everyone was waiting for the judges' decision. Only the white Cefiro scorned them and carried on, its fury unabated. It felt like an age, but was in fact mere seconds before the verdict was revealed.

"Leon Takahashi, ten to zero." Immediately the silence was shattered by applause, whistling and cheering.

"He's won," Byron punched the air. "You did it!" he whooped loudly, but realised suddenly that Lorna and the other girls were watching him with a smile.

"You know he can't hear you right," Lorna inquired sweetly and her eyes gleamed.

"Uh, yeah, course," Byron looked away sheepishly, and saw the Silvia heading back to the pit lanes. "I'd better get back," he drew himself straight.

"Don't want your sandwich?" Lorna asked quickly, indicating towards the ground.

"Oh yeah," Byron looked down and his expression changed to dismay. "Errr..." His sandwich was in a sorry state, squashed and covered in dirt. In his excitement he had trodden on it. "Actually, I'll leave it with you – you look like you could use it more than I."

"That's real thoughtful of ya," Lorna laughed and pitched her voice low so that only he could hear. "By the way, you just missed Alisa – she went to catch up with another friend of hers, but I'll try and get her to come down to the pits later."

"Okay, cool," Byron nodded cheerfully and hurried away.

Leon drove back to the pit lanes on a huge high. Not only had he beaten the Cefiro, he had made third place. He couldn't wait to tell Daisuke. He rolled the S13 back into his slot, where Cam, Taz and Byron were already waiting for him. They all wore impressed grins and Leon became aware that he too had a huge smile on his face. The instant he had come to a standstill, they surrounded his car.

"Good stuff."

"Mean effort!"

"Thanks," Leon got out and pulled his helmet off. "But we should go watch the final."

"Yeah, it's about to start."

"First I got to take these off though," Leon unzipped his race-overalls and quickly peeled the upper part off. Underneath, his shirt was damp with sweat. "Wow, that's so much better." He undid his shoes and without hesitation proceeded to pull his pants off, until he stood beside his S13 in only his shirt, socks and boxers.

"Dude, you got heatstroke or something?" Byron asked.

"I do feel a bit funny," Leon laughed and went to the Hilux, where he found his shorts. Cam shook his head as Leon pulled them on and stepped into his shoes again.

"Right, let's go." They ran over to the concrete parapet to join the other drifters. All of the others had been knocked out now and it was just Simon and Kyle fighting for first place.

"Nice driving, Leon," the other drivers made room for them as they squeezed up.

"Well here they go now!" The commentator announced and all eyes were on the two cars – the Batman and the S15 as they exploded out on to the track, accompanied by the murderous crackle of their engines. It was beautiful to watch, for although they drove at the limit, pushing each other and flogging their cars, there was an underlying calm about them and a real sense of control. They were professionals who knew their craft. Once again the entire crowd was absorbed, watching two masters fight it out.

Go Si! Leon was silently clenching his fist without realising.

"Far out they're loose!" One of the drivers beside him exclaimed. The Batman and S15 slipped through the sweeper in a tight parabola, before flying out of the zone. To Leon it seemed like neither had gained the upper-hand in that first battle and his hunch was confirmed when the commentator announced a five to five tie.

"Come on Si, put your foot down," Byron muttered, voicing Leon's own thoughts.

The two top drivers blurted down the track at full tilt and came back around for their second battle. The S15 had taken the lead and Simon was hunting him, right behind. He chased like the devil, in a wild frenzy – the cat after the mouse. He blitzed through the course and the judges awarded him a six to four win. Leon and the crowd hollered their approval. As Simon came rolling back into the pits, the other drivers swamped his car and applauded him rowdily. Finally they moved aside to let him continue on down the lane, grinning broadly through his open visor with Kyle closely behind.

One of the race coordinators appeared and waved them forward. His eyes searched the other drivers and found Leon. "Hey, you're up for the victory lap," he called out and Leon nodded. Somehow it all felt a bit unreal as he went back to his Silvia and hopped in. This time he didn't bother with his helmet and just drove in shorts. Together they headed out on the track again with Simon in the lead, driving at an easy 50km/h, closely followed by Kyle and Leon bringing up the rear in third.

They made their way around, waving to the spectators. Simon came to a stop in front of the embankment, where the track crew had erected the small podium. Leon and the S15 slid in beside him. The three top drivers got out and approached the podium. Clowning around, Kyle pushed past

Simon and bounced up to the highest step. He grinned down at Simon and performed a quick jig for the crowd.

"You poser," Simon protested humorously. "That's my spot," he pushed him off, then stepped up and took his rightful place, holding up both fists in triumph. Leon laughed at their antics and settled for the third step as the commentator arrived, closely followed by one of the track crew who carried the trophies. The commentator read out their names and placing, before handing out the trophies.

Leon received his first and accepted it reverently. It was the first trophy he had ever won. The commentator then thrust a bottle of bubbly into his free hand and moved on to Kyle, who took his trophy and immediately began opening his bottle. This time there were no bikini girls to spray and Leon quickly realised his intentions. Setting his trophy down, he worked on his own bottle. Meanwhile Simon was given his monster trophy and went on to wave it vigorously above his head for the crowd, while staging a little victory dance of his own.

"Si, stop showing off," Leon reprimanded him as his champagne cork popped. Holding the bottle in both hands, he plugged his thumb over the opening and shook it. "You look like you could do with a shower." Aiming it at Simon, he released his thumb. Foamy, pressurised champagne exploded outwards in a mass of spray that hit Simon squarely, instantly soaking his hair and the fabric of his overalls.

"Oh, you..!" Simon was so surprised that he nearly fell off his step, stumbling, he clung to balance with the frothy liquid streaming down the side of his face. Leon grinned widely but then his expression changed as Kyle unleashed and the next instant his own shirt was sodden and his face ran wet. Retaliating, he fired a blast back and managed to get him good, but by then Simon had tossed his trophy back to the commentator and ripped the cork off his own bottle. Spray flew in all directions until all of them including the commentator were drenched and reeking. Leon dribbled the last of his champagne into his own mouth and the other two followed his example. It tasted really good.

They left their empty bottles with the track crew, who were already beginning to pack up, and ran back to their cars. First the S15, then the S13 and finally the RX-7 Batman started in a thunderous roar. Building revs, the three engines blurred in a harmonic concerto, getting ever faster and then all three dropped the clutch and began revolving on the spot in unison. Tyres shrilling and erupting smoke, they painted big, black circles on the track. Thinking the entertainment finished, some members of the crowd were already beginning to wander away, but came running back, beckoned by the brawl of high performance engines burning rubber. Around and around they went until they were entirely enveloped in their own smog. Eventually they stopped, one at a time, and slinked away. The spectators watched them go and then they also began to disperse. It had been a good day.

Back in the pit lanes everybody was packing up to go home. Byron laughed when Leon parked and emerged still wet and sticky.

"Champagne shower?"

"Yeah, wouldn't recommend it," Leon shook his head and made a face. He peeled off the shirt and put it carefully away, then dried himself with a towel and took another shirt from the Hilux.

"I suppose that's it then?" Byron wanted to know. "We're clearing out too?"

"Yep – once we've tidied up."

"Okay," Byron nodded and got to work. They manoeuvred the Silvia onto the trailer and began stacking the used wheels onto the rack when Cam and Taz pulled up beside them.

"Hey champ. Bit wet?" Cam laughed.

"Mostly dry now," Leon smiled down at them from where he stood on the trailer. "But I can't wait for a shower."

"Yeah, me too – today's been hard work."

"Thanks again for those wheels. I couldn't have done it without them."

"You put them to good use," Cam approved.

"What're you guys up to later?"

"Dunno," Cam shrugged and indicated the broken Toyota behind him, hunching on her trailer. "Not much to celebrate, that's for sure."

Leon nodded. "Do you know what happened?"

"Not yet," Cam shook his head gloomily. "I'll take her apart when I get home and have a look."

"Why not leave it for tomorrow and come for a drink instead?" Leon suggested and Cam hesitated. "Come on, this time I owe you one, so it's my shout." Cam's expression changed and he smiled again.

"Okay then – why not."

"Sweet, we'll catch you later – same place."

"Sounds good," Cam agreed. He drove away, towing his trailer with its broken cargo. Leon and Byron finished up quickly, stacking the last of the tyres onto their trailer and tidying away their tools. Soon they were ready to go.

"I wonder where Lorna is," Leon spoke aloud.

"Right behind you," Byron smiled and Leon spun around.

"That was wicked." She stood before him.

"Thanks," Leon grinned at her. "You know, I really like it how you keep sneaking up on me."

"Good," Lorna laughed and turned to Byron, who was staring at the attractive blonde that accompanied her. "Byron, you remember Alisa right?"

"How could I forget," Byron mumbled and held out his hand. The girl took it. "Sorry for being an idiot at the BBQ."

"You can make up for it," Alisa flashed even white teeth. "I'm sorry too though – for hitting you."

"I'm sure I deserved it," Byron admitted. "So are you coming out tonight?"

"What're you up to?"

"Just going for a drink to celebrate this man coming third," Byron prodded Leon. "Apparently he's buying."

"In that case, how could I say no?" the girl laughed and her blue eyes twinkled.

"Nice. If you need a lift later, I can come and get you," Byron offered.

"Cool," the girl accepted. "In fact I was kinda hoping I could hitch a ride with you guys now... My friend has already left and Lorna thought it would be okay..."

"No probs."

The four of them piled into the Hilux and Byron threaded it along the pit lane with the Silvia in tow. They waved to some of the other drivers as they went and Leon had him stop when they reached Simon, who was just finishing up and getting ready to leave also.

"Hey champ," Leon called out to him. "You're coming tonight, right?"

"What's the plan?" Simon asked and came over. Leon told him, but Simon didn't seem to be listening. His eyes were on the two girls in the back of the Hilux.

"How do you two get to be so lucky..." he hissed so that only Leon and Byron could hear.

"What're you grumbling about – you just won the comp," Leon suppressed his laugh.

"Yeah, well my trophy won't keep me warm will it?" Simon pointed out.

"So you'll come?"

"Only if they bring a friend," Simon spoke up.

"A friend?" Lorna raised an eyebrow at Alisa.

"We don't have friends," Alisa shook her head with a laugh. "That's why we hang out with these two."

"But we'll try to find one," Lorna smiled. "Just for you."

"Don't let me down now," Simon pointed a finger at them, trying to maintain a straight face.

"So that's a yes?" Leon raised an eyebrow.

"You'd have to pay me not to go," Simon nodded and his grin was back.

It had been a busy morning for Officer Hart. Stopping and checking cars destined for the drifting competition had proved to be lucrative for him and his two colleagues. They had already found several vehicles to be non-compliant, without an up-to-date Warrant of Fitness and registration. They had also fined several other drivers who were breaking the law by blatantly speeding down the long stretch of road leading to the racecourse. Hart had no sympathy as he issued yet another ticket. The young driver took it defiantly and drove on and Hart gestured to the next car to pull over. This one was a rusty, old Toyota with a loud exhaust and filled with teenagers. Hart smirked when he saw the dismay on the driver's face. This was going to be fun.

While he enforced the law, Officer Hart kept an eye out for one car in particular. Instinct told him it would be here, but as the morning progressed and his hand became sore from writing out fines, he still had not seen the white Nissan. Towards noon the traffic to the raceway slowed and only the odd late comer continued to trickle through. Officer Hart and his colleagues returned to their unmarked patrol car to escape the stifling heat. With windows up and air-con on the highest setting, they settled back to wait. In the distance they could hear the sounds of the battles, but they ignored them and chatted to pass the time.

A couple of hours later, Hart abruptly stopped mid-sentence and straightened in his seat. A black Mazda had left the raceway and was making its way down the road towards him in a hurried and aggressive manner. Hart turned his radar on and within seconds it beeped a warning. Despite the big car trailer that the Mazda towed, it was speeding. Switching his engine on, Hart let the Mazda race past. He was about to pull out in pursuit when he jolted. The car on the trailer was the white Nissan!

Thinking quickly, Officer Hart turned to his companions. "You two stay here – I'm going after this one."

"We'll come," they both spoke eagerly.

"No, I got this," he hissed. "They'll be wrapping it up soon and I want you to get anybody we missed on the way in."

"You sure?" they were disappointed.

"I shouldn't be long," Hart nodded. "Hurry up."

The minute his colleagues had stepped out of the car and closed their doors, Officer Hart accelerated forwards in pursuit. The Mazda was already some distance ahead but he closed the gap slowly and then tailed it, following cautiously and hoping that his unmarked patrol car wouldn't stand out. He shadowed the Mazda back into the city and through several suburbs until it turned into a small street. Staying well behind, Hart watched the wagon roll down the street and come to a stop, before proceeding to reverse its big trailer vigorously up the driveway of a small unit.

He had lost! He had lost against the Silvia! He had let Markus down! But how had it happened?? He had been ahead. He had been winning! Through his rage and frustration, Andy dimly realised that he was now outside his home. Turning in his seat he rudely backed the trailer up the drive. Almost jack knifing, he cranked the steering wheel furiously and managed to straighten it out, but he was too far left, and the wide trailer scraped down the side of his letter box. Angrily, he accelerated backwards faster and then kicked the brakes and the wagon skidded to a stop.

Scowling furiously, he got out and went to the trailer. Lowering the ramps, he let the first one drop the last foot onto the concrete of the driveway, drawing sadistic pleasure from the loud metallic clang. Going to the second ramp, he freed it and was about to lower it when his eyes were drawn to a dark, tinted Holden, which drove sullenly past his property.

Andy froze and a cold shock hit him in the guts. There was no doubt in his mind that the telltale sedan was a police car. They had found him. Unmoving, his eyes followed the car as it continued on down the street and disappeared. He remembered having seen the same one outside the raceway. It must have followed him from there. But why? What did they know? Did it have to do with Markus? Was it the tyre theft or the chase on his drive to get the roll cage? Why had they left again? Would they come back? What should he do? What could he do? Run? Hide? Where?

Andy looked around him. He lived here. This was his property. He couldn't just leave it, and if he ran they would surely find him anyway, eventually... For many moments he stood completely still, but then his expression turned grim. Let them come. He stepped back and dropped the ramp. The loud crash reverberated defiantly around the neighbourhood.

Cam had woken early that day and couldn't get back to sleep. Taz had of course promised to help him, but to drown their sorrows over the bad luck on the track, they had shared a few too many drinks and he had no idea when Taz might show up. He was known for sleeping late. Not wanting to waste the better part of his Sunday morning waiting for him, Cam had decided to get straight on with it and now found himself in his garage, glowering down at the power plant of the Trueno.

This was his prized engine. He had thrown a lot of money and effort into it. Even though it was now broken, he couldn't just scrap it. He needed to retrieve what he could from it, but most of all he needed to know what had happened. He was still puzzling over the sound he had heard, that agonised noise an engine might make just prior to seizing when it is starved of oil. But there had been plenty of oil. In fact he had done an oil change just days before. So what would explain that harsh grating sound?

Cam applied himself resolutely. It didn't take long for him to drain the fluids, disconnect the electrics and plumbing, and free the engine. Applying the hoist, he swung it out onto the stand. He immediately started to dismantle it and his mood became increasingly gloomy. What would he find? Would it be repairable?

Working on, he removed the head in one piece and exposed the cylinders. This was the moment of truth. He adjusted the leadlight to a better angle and directed it down into the cylinders. The light revealed deep burrs gouged into the cylinder walls. With a sickly taste in the back of his throat, Cam slid his fingers down inside a cylinder, then pulled them away and rubbed them together experimentally. They felt gritty. He held them up against the light in dismay. Silvery particles sparkled at him, metal filings from the engine, but mixed in with them was something else – finely ground granules of a black substance.

"What the..?" Cam blinked. Puzzled, he inspected the particles on his finger more closely. It was definitely not a metal. Confused, he made his way around the car to the metal tray, which still held the oil he had drained from the engine. Dipping his hand into the dark liquid, he ran his fingers over the bottom and felt the same grittiness. The granules were all through the oil. Where had they come from?

Wiping his hands on a rag, he went back with a heavy tread, unscrewed the oil cap again, and ran a clean finger around the mouth of the opening. Immediately his fears were confirmed when it came away covered in traces of the sparkly, finely ground substance. Cam stood stunned and glared at the devilish glitter on his fingers for many moments. "Oh you..!" It came out in a hiss. His hands were shaking. He ran back to the house and snatched up the phone.

Andy woke up early with a blazing headache and an awful taste in his mouth. He groaned loudly. He was lying on his stomach and his face hurt immensely. Raising his head, he reached up and touched his cheek. Pain stabbed through him. Groaning again, he pushed himself upright and looked down at himself. Still fully clothed, he was lying on top of his blanket. Even his shoes were still on his feet. What had happened last night?

He remembered coming home from the raceway and seeing the unmarked police car stalking him. He remembered taking the Mazda and trailer back to Angela's. He also remembered returning home again and feeling claustrophobic at being cooped up inside with the idea that the police might be watching him. He remembered leaving the house and going into town. He remembered drinking beer, a lot of beer and then shooting spirits. But the events after that were a big blank. How had he got home? It hurt to think and he gave up. Struggling off the bed, he forced himself to stand and stumbled to the bathroom.

The mirror immediately explained his sore face. It was battered and bruised, his lip swollen, and he had a black eye. He had obviously got into a fight. Had he won? If he did then his opponent must surely look worse. Andy grinned lopsidedly but it hurt more, which sobered him. He reached up and touched his cheek carefully. He looked almost as bad as he had the night after Markus died. How long had it been since he had last seen his friend? Was it really only a week? It felt like ages. He shook his head, but caught himself as his headache became more poignant. He stared at his reflection. For the first time in years Andy truly looked at himself. His unkempt, dishevelled hair and pale unshaven skin peppered in black stubble. But it was his sunken, haunted eyes that really frightened him.

"Do I really want to live like this?" he asked his mirror image. Turning away, he opened the shower door and was just about to turn the water on and give it time to warm up, when he saw the mess in the aluminium tray. "Oh, no way," he gagged and shook his head in disgust. He couldn't remember being sick. It really was time to change. With a sigh, he pulled out the cleaning products from the cupboard. He scrubbed until the shower was sparkling and then turned his attention to the rest of the house. In the lounge, he drew the curtains back and was greeted by the golden sunlight. Andy had kept them shut for so long that he had forgotten how pleasant it was to have warm light filtering through. He opened the windows to let fresh air in and then, with newfound vigour, fell upon his self-appointed task.

While he cleaned, he reflected upon his life, the things that had happened and those he had done lately and wasn't proud of. Several hours later the house was gleaming and he finally took his shower. When he stepped on the drain grate it squeaked loudly, metal rubbing against metal and he was suddenly reminded of the last, painful shrieks of the Toyota.

The enormity of his betrayal hit him and for the first time he felt remorse. He wondered if and how he could make amends and still protect his identity. Perhaps there was something he could do to help put things somewhat right. There was really only one option open to him, he concluded. Pondering some more, he couldn't deny that it felt appropriate. Why not, it was only money and he could always make more, after all.

"Hey," Taz answered the phone. "I was just about to come over." He sounded still half-asleep.

"Taz, you know why the engine died?" Cam blurted, but didn't wait for a reply. "Some prick chucked something into the oil."

"What, like sand?" Taz asked incredulously.

"Yeah, maybe," Cam replied and Taz could tell that he wasn't joking.

"Who would've done that?"

"Don't know," Cam admitted. "But it must've been somebody at the drifts. Probably did it when we were at the battle brief, that's the only time we weren't near the car."

"We need to find out who it was, then I'm gonna pour sand down their bloody throat and see how they like it."

"Yeah," Cam murmured. "You think maybe it was Leon?"

Taz was silent for a moment. "I can't see him doing that. He's a good guy and besides, he was with us at the briefing."

"Yeah, true... But who else could it have been?"

"What about that guy with the Cefiro," Taz mused. "None of the others like him... And didn't you even say you saw him looking at ya weird?"

"Yeah, that's possible," Cam remembered the shifty look in the other driver's eye. "Do you remember if he came late?"

"I don't," Taz admitted. "Damn, I should've just stayed with the car... What will you do?"

"Not sure, but that motor is only good for the dump now, so I'd like to find out who did it," Cam muttered and frowned. "Who is that now?!" He had heard somebody at the front door. "Is that you, Joey?" he called out, but there was no reply.

His flatmate usually worked on Sundays and shouldn't be home yet. Cam cocked his head to listen. It sounded as though someone was pushing mail through the slot in his front door.

"It's probably just the postman."

"There's no post on Sundays." Taz pointed out.

"Good point, it better not be more junk mail. I purposely put a sticker up." Cam's temper flared, finding a target for his frustration. "Hold up, I'm gonna give them a rark-up." Before Taz could say another word, he put the handset down and ran to the door. He wrenched it open and bowled outside. Looking up and down the street, he searched for a sign of the junk-mailer. But as far as he could see the street was empty. Uncertain if he had misheard, Cam checked the street one last time and walked back inside. Fuming, he slammed the front door behind him and then saw the letter lying on the floor. He stooped to pick it up. It was very thick. He ripped it open and his mouth gaped when the contents fluttered out.

The floor at his feet was littered with bank notes, a lot of bank notes. Cam crouched down and picked one up. It was a $100 bill. He examined it closely and rubbed it between his fingers. It was the real thing. He picked up another and scrutinised it, before he ran his eyes over the many that remained. They were all $100 notes.

"Far out...!" Turning the envelope over in his hands, he noticed that something was scrawled on the back. 'Sorry about the Trueno.' Cam was stunned. He walked back to the lounge, holding the money in disbelief. Together with the envelope, he laid it on the coffee table and sat down on the couch. Slowly he reached out, picked up the stack of notes and counted them out on the table. He leant back again. There was easily enough to replace the engine in his Toyota.

"Cam?!" a muffled voice called his name and he looked up. "I'm hanging up in a minute."

He had forgotten his friend. He ran over and scooped the phone up. "Hey."

"What took you? You didn't kill them did you?"
"Dude," Cam paused. "You won't believe this."

Officer Hart had been waiting for over an hour and he was getting bored. He was supposed to be on traffic duty again, but instead here he was staking out and trying to catch the young punk that had so far evaded him. The house was dark and all the curtains drawn, when suddenly they were whisked back and he could see somebody work busily to clean up. Sometime later the garage door opened and Hart straightened up in his seat. The white Nissan pulled out onto the street.

Officer Hart trailed in the unmarked Ford, which he had swapped for the Holden. He kept well back to give his prey plenty of room. Ten minutes later the Nissan turned down a narrow street and pulled over. Hart swung into the driveway of a nearby house and watched the driver run up the path to a small townhouse. The driver slipped, what appeared to be an envelope, through the postal slot in the front door and quickly returned to his car and drove off. Hart noted the street number of the townhouse and followed him.

The Nissan turned in the direction of the hills and soon they were heading up a steep road. Officer Hart puzzled over their destination. He did not want another high speed chase and he considered pulling the Nissan over and ending it, but he refrained and continued to trail stealthily at a distance. There was the possibility that the driver was meeting somebody. Perhaps he could catch more criminals in the act. If he was going to work on a Sunday, he might as well make it worth his while, Hart thought grimly.

At top of the hill the road levelled out with a grassy incline on their right, sloping away steeply down the hillside and offering a panoramic view of the city. But Hart kept his eyes on the car in front of him. Where was he going? Well ahead, the Nissan finally pulled off the road and into the car-park of a deserted lookout, where it came to a stop. Trying not to draw attention to himself, Hart drove on and saw the driver get out. What was he doing?

Officer Hart rounded the next corner and the Nissan slipped out of sight. Should he apprehend him now, or was somebody else going to meet him? He continued for another fifty metres before he made his decision. It was time to end it. Turning around, he spotted the driver leaning on the sheep fence around the edge of the lookout. Turned away from him, he appeared to be gazing down the hillside. Officer Hart stopped beside the Nissan. The driver had not turned around. Hart picked up his baton and opened the door. His leather boots crunched on gravel as he walked over to the driver, who continued to look down the hillside. He came to a stop a couple of metres behind him, baton in-hand and ready.

"Morning, son," his voice was low and insulting and he tapped the baton into his palm. The driver made no sign of having heard him. "I'm talking to you," Hart's eyes narrowed and he was about to take another step forward when the driver responded.

"What do you want?"

"I've come to take your car for a start," Officer Hart paused and smirked. "I know you swapped the registration plates with another."

"If you want it," the driver pulled a set of keys from his pocket and removed one from the ring. "Take it." He threw it over his shoulder and it clinked on the ground between them. "Now leave me alone."

"I'll decide when to leave you alone," Hart sneered. "Now what's your name and address?"

"You know that already, you've been following me right?"

Officer Hart's fist clenched tightly around his baton. This was not going the way he had intended. "If you fail to give your full name and address I have the power to arrest you and take you down to the station."

The driver hesitated, but then he turned around and Hart's eyes opened wide. "What happened to you?"

"Got into a fight, I guess," the driver shrugged. "Can't really remember..."

"I see." Officer Hart produced his notepad.

"My name is Andrew Reed," Andy said quietly, also giving his address. "Now if you don't mind, I'd like to be alone."

Hart said nothing. He looked past Andy and his eyes fell upon the big burnt patch of grass some distance down the slope. "You knew him?"

"Best friend," Andy spoke quietly and stared at the ground.

"A bloody stupid friend – racing around these hills, endangering himself and others. It's punks like you and him that give other young drivers a bad name."

"You're right, it's not worth it." Andy nodded slowly. "I realise that now." He looked up again and met Hart's gaze. "But you might want to think about that yourself before you chase somebody at 150km/h..."

"I'm the police. I can do what I want," Hart replied curtly.

"So if you wanted to catch me – why'd you let me go?" Andy challenged him. "You could've called ahead."

"I knew I'd see you again," Hart smiled thinly.

"You like to take the law into your own hands – don't you?" Andy shook his head. "It's cops like you that give the others a bad name."

"Shut your face," Hart raised his baton aggressively. "And pick up your key." Andy hesitated, but then bent down slowly and picked it out of the gravel. Straightening up, he extended it to Hart who ripped it from his hand. "COMMS, this is CHW2C, requesting next available tow-truck," Officer Hart held the radio to his mouth.

"This is COMMS, ten-two," the radio crackled.

"What's the ETA?"

"Twenty minutes."

"Your car will be gone soon," Hart lowered the radio again. "I'll make sure they crush it for you." He was disappointed at Andy's lack of response. "Now what was in the package?"

"What package?"

"Don't play dumb," Hart flared. "You pushed it through the door before."

"Oh, that was money."

"Money? For drugs or stolen parts?"

"No," Andy shook his head. "I wanted to make it up to him, you know."

"Explain yourself."

"Um, I raced against him yesterday, but, well I sabotaged his engine..."

"And today you feel bad?" Hart looked at him searchingly.

"Yeah."

"How much money?"

"Quite a bit – easily enough for a new engine."

"I don't believe you. It just doesn't add up."

"Guess I finally realised I was the bad guy..." Andy replied quietly. "And I'm sick of it." He turned away, back to the fence and sloping hillside.

Standing behind him, Officer Hart turned the key over in his fingers. Many thoughts ran through his head. He remembered the many fines he'd handed out and people he had apprehended, sometimes even innocent people. His eyes were again drawn to the black, charred spot on the slope. He stared at it for a long time and then his gaze shortened to Andy's hunched shoulders. His best friend had burnt to death on that very spot. The immensity of it suddenly struck him. Hart didn't even have any close friends. Slowly he lifted the radio back to his mouth. "COMMS, this is CHW2C again."

"This is COMMS, go ahead."

"Cancel my request – the tow-truck is no longer needed."

"Affirmative."

Andy turned slowly from the fence as Officer Hart finished the call.

"Go get your car properly warranted and registered on its original plates," Hart held out the key, but Andy hesitated. "Take it," Hart insisted and dropped it into his hand. "But don't let us catch you driving it until you have, and when you do – stick to the limit."

Officer Hart walked back to his car and drove away. Andy stared after him for a full minute, before his gaze turned to the Cefiro. He was thankful he still had her. I will make you fully legal, he promised himself and, taking a deep breath, turned back to the slope. The wreckage had been removed, but the charred and blackened spot stood out like a bomb crater. He thought of his friend, the good times and the bad. He remembered Markus scolding him after he crashed the 180SX at the drifts. He remembered his words: 'Yeah man, mint while it lasted.'

"Yeah, it was mint while it lasted," Andy's voice was hardly audible. "But it should've lasted a whole lot longer…" He took another deep breath, letting it out in a drawn out sigh. "I know it's my fault." His lips were trembling. "I'm so sorry. I wish I could undo it." He shook his head and was silent again. "I miss you."

Around him, the grass was rustling as a cool breeze whispered up the slope. It played on his face and ruffled his hair. Fidgeting, he stooped to pick up a fallen leaf and when he straightened his focus turned to the huge pine tree, which still stood tall and dignified in the middle of the incline. It had saved his life. He had been given a second chance and it was time to make something of it.

As he continued to stand there, an engine rumble intruded on his thoughts and for the first time Andy experienced resentment towards the sound. The vehicle approached quickly and went past on the road behind him, but then its engine note eased and Andy heard it slow and turn around.

The car retraced its run and pulled into the car-park, stopping a few metres behind him. Although he loathed the intrusion, Andy reluctantly turned to the new arrival. A candy-red car stood beside his Cefiro and a tall, attractive girl climbed out.

"Hey," she came towards him. "I saw the Cefiro," she explained. "That was you drifting at the comp yesterday, right? Andy, isn't it?" Still a few steps away, the girl stopped and stared at him. "Wow, are you okay? You look like you didn't just fall down the stairs." Andy recognised her then. She was the one who had helped tow the Holden back onto solid ground, the night of the diesel burnouts.

"I could be better," he admitted and the girl laughed.

"Well maybe we can work on that..."

"We? What about your boyfriend?" he asked. She looked at him squarely and raised an eyebrow.

"What boyfriend?"

On Sunday the weather could not have been better. At Lorna's suggestion they had made their way out to Brighton Beach. As he lay back on his towel, eating his ice-cream, and enjoying the warm sunshine and the company of his friends, Leon had to agree, it was the perfect way to unwind. Even Simon had come out with his new girlfriend.

"So are you guys ready to hit the water?" Byron peeled off his t-shirt and stood up.

"Let's go," the three girls piped up.

"Give us a minute," Simon shook his head, busy with his ice-cream.

"Look at our drift pros, they can't even eat properly," Byron accused. He had of course finished his before they even got to the beach.

"Some things I like to take my time with," Simon winked and squeezed the girl beside him.

"Yeah well, don't take too long – last one in the water buys the first round," Byron raced away and the girls took up his challenge.

"Whatever," Simon called after them.

"So you like Olivia?" Leon inquired when they were alone.

"She's cool," Simon replied distractedly as he watched Byron reach the water and immediately turn to splash the girls. "Yeah, I like her – a lot," he smiled at Olivia's antics. "Owe you one."

"No way," Leon shook his head and had to laugh as the three of them ganged up on Byron. "You've been helping me heaps and besides, Olivia was all Lorna and Alisa's doing... Though I'm sure you winning the second comp in a row helped – few girls can resist a hero."

"Yeah, that's me," Simon also laughed. "So what about you then, will you keep drifting or let those talents go to waste?"

"We'll see, we'll see. Right now I think Byron could do with some help," Leon rose to his feet. "And you heard what he said: last one in buys the first round!" He bolted for the water and Simon tore after him.

SHIFTLIGHT

When Cam and his mates discover a disused road just out of town, it doesn't take them long to hook up a night of car madness. But a hyped up crowd of street racers, smoking up the tarmac in their wild rides is bound to lead to trouble…

"I have read this book three times and am starting to read it a fourth. This is by far the best book I have read and perfect for a car enthusiast like myself."

"It flowed at a perfect pace, with a perfect mix of romance, humour and action."

Available on

Just Us

DAVID JUBERMANN

Tyler's parents are in jail. He lives with his grandma on the rough side of town. He dreams of Āio – the place of peace. When fate throws him together with Natalie, a girl from a wealthy family, the two connect instantly and make plans to run away together. But tragedy strikes and their lives will never be the same. Can the pair make it to Āio or will they be forced to give in to those who are desperate to tear them apart?

Just Us tells a remarkable story about growing up, about escaping hardship, about running away and about love and friendship...

Available on

David Jubermann was born in Germany in 1982 and immigrated with his family to New Zealand in 1990.

In 2006 he published his first book, Shiftlight. The story was prompted by his personal experiences and those of his friends.

Apart from writing, David has a keen interest in travelling, technology and motor sports.

Find out more about David by visiting his website.

www.DAVIDJUBERMANN.com

And join him on Facebook

www.FACEBOOK.com/DAVIDJUBERMANN